The Fledging of Hawkwings

Katherine A Smith

Book Two of the Northnest Saga

Available from author Katherine A Smith

The Northnest Saga

Hawkwind's Tale
Hawkwind's Tale (illustrated editions)
The Fledging of Hawkwings

The Dragonic Voyages

Dragons to Loose
Dragonic Freedom
Dragonic Pride
Dragons to Keep

Children's Books

Otter Twin Magic
Otter Sea Magic*

*Forthcoming

The Fledging of Hawkwings

Katherine A Smith

Book Two of the Northnest Saga

Kasmith
Art & Books

Kasmith Art and Books
Fort Bragg, CA

For everyone who has to grow up.

The Hawk Line

Chapter 1
The Urge to Fly

Jessika Hawkwings whirled and smashed first one and then her second truncheon towards her enemy's face, but he was too quick, bringing up his heavy staff with strong arms and absorbing the impact of her strikes. She kept turning, letting the strength slip from her attacks as soon as she saw that he would block them. She stepped past him at an angle, pivoting, using the rapid rotation of her body to fuel the power of her next strikes, and angled them low, towards his legs, bending her knees, adding the force of gravity to her strikes and dropping down to thwack solidly into his right shin. She turned her pivot and descent into a shoulder roll, getting out of range of retaliatory staff strikes and coming back to her feet behind him.

"Ow," her enemy objected. "Alright, I yield. You've broken my knee."

"Well, I would have," she agreed, "if you hadn't been wearing those guards."

Rikah Hawkdare bent down and rubbed his leg inside the padded wooden shin guards.

"I still felt it," he complained. "You're just too quick."

Jessika forced herself not to smile much at the compliment. "If you'd gotten even one strike in, or if you'd managed to keep you defense perfect until I ran out of energy, you would have whacked me first."

"I don't think you ever run out of energy."

She patted herself on the chest. "Lots of running up and down stairs makes for a strong heart."

"Yeah, and steady all day work in the fields doesn't do that as much."

She walked up to him and chucked him on the biceps with her knuckles. "But it gives you all these big muscles."

"Yeah, I'm a draft horse and you're a little speedy racing horse."

Rikah went to put his staff on the pair of hooks in the wall meant for holding it. The griffins had built this sparring room for the human children of the Aerie a few years ago, when they'd started to complain about not having a place to sharpen their fighting skills for the day they retook the kingdom they'd been born in. The room was big enough for running about during a fight, but not so big it couldn't be given a little heating in winter. Like nearly all the structures in the Aerie, it was built of stacked and mortared stones and had no windows, but there were air holes for ventilation and magical lights to keep the room as bright as day.

Jessika didn't leave her truncheons behind; she'd taken to carrying them with her nearly everywhere she went. The griffins had very little metal, so a sword was too much to ask for. Initially she'd trained with a staff, but as she'd grown up she'd been more inclined to fight swiftly and agilely. A big staff was too heavy for her, and once she tried using two smaller sticks instead, she'd given the staff to Rikah—and dragooned him into being her sparring partner most of the time.

Kassandra Hawksky wouldn't touch any weapon these days, and pre-ferred avoiding fights altogether. Karolan Hawkrain carried only a short knife, but he had burgeoning magical abilities, and Jessika assumed that he would learn to use those for any fighting that had to be done. His teacher, Thornfire, didn't use his magic offensively very much—at least not that Jessika has seen—but Thornfire was a griffin, and had a wicked hooked bill and sharp claws and talons, which were what he usually relied upon in a fight.

"I want a bath," Jessika commented. "You should get one, too. You smell like the draft horse you resemble."

"Like you know what a horse smells like," Rikah teased back. "Let's go."

The sparring room adjoined the set of caves and buildings used by the Hawk Line in South-scree Aerie. A few twisting stairs and hallways brought the two young Hawks to their quarters where they grabbed fresh clothes and towels. They then made their way down a good number more stairways and naturally inclined cave floors to a small room deep below the ones the feath-ered members of the Hawk Line used.

Griffins rarely bathed in water: usually only in summer, out in the riv-ers and waterfalls around the slopes of the mountain where they made their home. The rest of the time they took dust baths and fastidiously cleaned each other's feathers by preening. Soap was unheard of, but they did put into their big communal dust baths certain crushed herbs that helped prevent feather mites and other unwelcome parasites. Jessika wouldn't say that griffins had a bad smell, but they always had a definite scent of *griffin* about them. It was nowhere near as bad as unwashed human, however.

This cave had been discovered and developed after the children had come to South-scree to stay, some ten years ago. Although water could be heated on a fire or by a griffin mage, that took the energy and attention of a mage or the consumption of more wood than anyone wanted to use up above the tree line. This little cave had been carved out by an underground spring and the water was warm. There hadn't been much water there to begin with, but a magical artifact called the Moonstone had been installed in the room, and what had been a pool that wouldn't reach even Karolan's knees was now deep enough to walk into up to Rikah's waist.

Starbright had given the midwinter gift of using some earth magic to shape the rock into seats around where the water bubbled up, so Rikah and Jessika could strip off and comfortably sink into water up to their necks. A basket at the side of the room held soap traded for at a human village and Jessika tossed a piece to Rikah. They scrubbed up, the dirty water being carried out a rough, natural hole at one side of the chamber, although they had needed to brick it smaller once the potential pool volume had been increased. Clean, they both leaned back against the shaped stone, letting the mild heat of the water soak into them.

"We should move the Sunstone down here and heat up the water," Rikah murmured.

"We need it up there to keep us warm in winter. You know that," Jessika grunted back.

"We could move it down here for the summer."

Jessika didn't reply. Sure, they could, but who wanted to carry a big rock up and down all those staircases twice a year to just make the water a bit warmer during the warm season?

"Wings, how long are we going to keep practicing fighting—and waiting?" Rikah said into the silence.

"I don't know," she whispered back. "I'm scared, I guess, and I don't know how to start."

"We should talk to Mother about it?"

Mother: the Hawkmother, real name of Hawkwind, of course was not their real mother. Their mothers, fathers, siblings, and everyone else had died when Northnest had been conquered, as far as they knew. Rikah, Jessika, Karolan, and Kassandra were only alive because Hawkwind had managed to escape with them. The conquerors of Northnest had held power for over ten years now, unless something had happened to unseat them, but even if it had it was unlikely word would have reached the griffin Aeries.

"I suppose that's it," she said mainly to herself. "We don't know what's going on down there now. None of us have been back to Northnest. We'll need to go scout it out."

"Go there?" Rikah echoed, sounding incredulous.

"Of course go there," Jessika retorted. "How are we going to take back our kingdom without going there? Do you think we can just tell all the griffins of South-scree to go attack everyone in Northnest who looks threatening?"

"No, of course not, that's not what I meant," Rikah countered. "I guess I'm scared, too. I don't want to go there."

"It's our home. We have to go take it back."

"You want to be Queen of Northnest."

Jessika crossed her arms. "Not necessarily. I mean, yeah, maybe, if everything works out, and the people want me."

She turned, pushing herself out of the water and staring to dry off. In the glow of a basket of magic stones hanging from the ceiling, she knew Rikah would be able to clearly see the tattoo on her back, of golden wings. He was probably staring at it. None of the other three human children had it: only she. It was a tattoo given to everyone born to the royal family of Northnest. Jessika had been the child princess, third born, never likely to become the Queen, but the rest of her family was dead now. Hawkwind had rescued her only by chance, when she'd grabbed the only live children remaining in the nursery.

Jessika was sixteen years old now, a year older than all the other children. Griffins considered fifteen years old to be when an individual became an adult. Perhaps it was time for Jessika to do what it seemed she'd been intending to do ever since she realized that her home country was taken and her family dead: retake it.

She pulled on her clothing, all of which she'd sewn herself. Griffins didn't wear clothing, but they did make a little cloth, and when they worked leather they used sharpened bone needles and twine. Based on that example and what few human clothes she'd had access to, Jessika had set herself to making all of them new clothing. Over the years she'd gotten quite skilled at it.

Dressed now, she turned to look at Rikah.

"I will talk to Mother about it," she said. "It's time to start planning some reconnaissance."

Jessika found Hawkmother in the nursery. She also found the six chicks of the Line there, and was fighting for her life within a moment of them noticing her.

"Day, Night, Dawn," Hawkmother scolded. "Get off Wings; you know better. And you, Dusk, you could damage your new quills besides."

The two biggest and oldest, Hawkday and Hawknight, were eight years old now, fully fledged, and had reached the size of young unicorns, although their anatomy and physiology made them considerably lighter. The others were incrementally smaller down to the youngest, Hawknoon, who would still misstep and flop on her face for every dozen attempted steps. She was thereby considerably slower than her brothers and sisters, and not quite as responsible for nearly smothering Jessika. Almost as troubling as the near-smothering was the near-deafening, as the six chicks squeaked, chortled, chirped, and squealed their pleasure at seeing their two-legged big sister.

"You'd think I never visit the nursery, the way they act," Jessika managed to grunt out from the bottom of the griffin pile.

Day and Night had backed off at their mother's chastising, but that still left four enthusiastic shrieking chicks atop her. Then the chicks tumbled away, batted off by the practiced paws of Thornsoft, a charcoal gray adult male who often hung around the Hawk nursery—and whom Jessika suspected was the sire of at least two of the chicks, but griffins didn't talk about which males had sired which chicks. That was one of the peculiarities of griffin society, and Jessika respected that, so she'd never brought it up.

Thornsoft rumbled authoritatively at the chicks, and they all paused to look his way, except for little Hawknoon, who tumbled into one of her siblings before realizing what was going on and following suit. Thornsoft rocked back onto his hind legs and lifted his hands, beginning to gesture sternly.

Thornsoft had been born in Snow-in-lee, an ancient griffin settlement that had in recent times been in control of the talis: monstrous finned serpents with the ability to hypnotize almost any griffin. The talis had been keeping a captive population of griffins there for sacrificing over two old magical artifacts—the Sunstone and Moonstone: the latter of which was now down in the humans' bathing pool—to keep them powered, to keep Snow-in-lee's natural spring hot and flowing as a constant mineral bath for the cold-sensitive talis.

It had been a practice of the talis to mutilate the vocal chords of all new-born griffins among their captive population. As such, Thornsoft was mute, but the Snow-in-lee griffins had developed their own sign language for communication. It seemed the talis weren't bright enough to realize it. When the Snow-in-lee griffins had been freed and distributed to the wild griffin Aeries, they'd brought their sign language with them, and all the chicks since then learned it as a second language.

Now, unable to speak aloud, Thornsoft delivered a gestural scolding augmented by body posture, feather positioning, and the warbles and chirps he could still produce from some avian organ deep in his chest. Jessika, too, knew the sign language and could understand him perfectly.

"Hawkwings is smaller than you and does not have fur or feathers or claws or talons," he was saying. "You must not damage her."

"We know, Thornsoft, but we were excited to see her," Hawknight replied aloud.

The adult male shook his head. "You must learn to be gentle with your greetings and contain your excitement. Hawkwings, are you hurt?"

"No, I'm fine, but I was almost suffocated, and deafened."

She gave the chicks just a bit of a glare. Their happiness at seeing her was something she adored, but they were getting bigger and stronger, and while she might once have been able to hold them in her arms as babies, she couldn't even lift Night or Day anymore, and Dawn was getting pretty heavy, too.

"You are lucky you did not injure her," Thornsoft gestured.

"I love to see you all," she went on, turning her glare into a smile, "but please remember that I am weak and thin-skinned, and you are all getting so big and mighty."

That pleased especially Night and Day, and they puffed out their feathers. Jessika chuckled.

"We'll be more careful," Dawn, ever the diplomat, said.

"See that you do," Thornsoft concluded imperiously. Then he grinned and invited, "you can jump on me anytime."

The chicks needed no second invitation, and the grey griffin vanished under a pile of white, downy fledglings and half-grown juveniles. Jessika moved past them, towards where Hawkmother, Hawkswift, and Hawkjoy were huddled up for a preening chat. Hawkmother reached out to preen a bit of Jessika's damp hair in greeting, and Jessika returned it by stretching forward to scratch around the big griffin's neck. The greetings were quickly repeated with Swift and Joy.

The three female griffins were the only adult members of the Hawk Line. Thornsoft and another adult male called Thornwing were frequent visitors and particular friends, but they owed their deepest allegiance to the Thorn Line: the Line that they were official members of. Hawkmother, formerly called Hawkwind, was the matriarch, or Linemother, and thereby the highest rank and leader of the Line. Hawkswift was older, but not the breeding female of the Line—as Hawkwind was—so she was second rank, the only elder the Line had. Joy was Swift's daughter, a full adult now having passed her fifteenth year, but neither the matriarch nor an elder, so simply a regular member of the Line who did a lot of the heavy lifting when it came to food providing, cleaning up, and fledgling herding.

"How was your practice?" Hawkmother enquired politely.

"Very good," Jessika said. "I beat Dare again."

The three female griffins chortled.

"I would say 'naturally,' but since human males are bigger than the females, I suppose congratulations are in order instead?" Swift gestured.

Like Thornsoft, both Swift and Joy had been captives in Snow-in-lee, and were mute. Everyone in the Hawk line had adapted so well to making sure to pay attention visually to each other's hands that Swift's contribution to the conversation went as smoothly as though she'd spoken aloud.

"I guess so," Jessika shrugged. "It wasn't that difficult, really. Mother, I have a serious topic to discuss. I feel I am ready to begin investigating what can be done about Northnest."

Hawkmother's lazy attitude vanished, her head and neck straightening up, her wings rising slightly, and her feathers starting to stand on end. She angled her head a bit to fix Jessika with one big, round eye.

"I'm sixteen years old. By your own standards, I'm an adult," Jessika stated, before anyone else could speak. "I'm a full member of this Line now, not a chick anymore."

Thornsoft, apparently curious, came over to fold himself down onto the floor beside the nest of cushions the females were occupying. The six chicks came with him and he idly gathered Hawknoon into his arms for snuggles while the others flopped or sat nearby. Everyone waited for Hawkmother's response.

"I had hoped you might become happy enough here to never feel the need to return to Northnest," she said softly. "But that was a false hope, and I knew it."

"Don't you want to go back?" Jessika asked. "Don't you want to avenge your friends and family? Don't you want to free our kingdom from the invaders?"

Hawkmother's bill dipped downward a little, and Jessika thought she was analyzing her own feelings, so the young lady waited, letting her think. At last, the griffin matriarch looked up.

"I? My place, my home, is here now. My Line is here. My chicks are here," she said. "I still feel sad about what happened. It was horrible. I remember it well, but ten years have passed, Wings. I cannot bring back the dead, and Northnest as we knew it can no longer be resurrected."

"How do you know that?" Jessika retorted. "We don't even know what's going on down there. Maybe the people are rebelling. Maybe they could use our help. Maybe going down there would rally them."

"Maybe," the griffin nodded. "You are correct that we don't know what's happening there. The invasion was brutal. Many people and griffins died in it. It could be that someone organized a resistance and tried to unseat the conquerors. Maybe I was wrong for fleeing with you four instead of seeking out that resistance and joining them."

"No, no, Mother," Jessika soothed immediately. "You were as old then as I am now, or younger, barely an adult, with four baby humans, and you were hurt, and alone. How could you have possibly sought out those who tried to fight back? Who knows where they were or how long it took them to get organized? You did the right thing."

"Thank you for saying that, Hawkchild," she smiled a little, "but I have often questioned my actions. I did what I thought was best. I was afraid of the drakes. I knew I couldn't protect you if they found us. You're alive today only because of the unicorns, and the South-scree griffins, particularly Thornfire. I can't deny, though, that I have secured myself a safe and comfortable place in the world. It wasn't one I initially wanted, but now, I am so happy here."

She took a heavy breath and shook her head slowly. "I cannot bring the dead ones back to life—my sister Hawkcall, the others of my old Line—they are gone. Wings, you must prepare yourself for the possibility that the citizens of Northnest who survived have simply adapted. You humans know how to endure, it seems. Ten years is a long time. Unless the conquerors have continued the killing, the populace may have learned to accept them. Even with your history—" she eyed Jessika meaningfully, for not everyone in the room knew that the girl had been the princess of Northnest "—you might be incapable of leading the people in a civil war.

"The people might just want to go on with their lives, even if they aren't completely happy or there's a little minor suffering, because going to war means true death and destruction. Even if you win such a war, the price would be many people dying and losing their homes and loved ones. The people will remember the conquering of Northnest and the long recovery after. Now that their lives have finally returned to something close to normal, they won't want to go back and have another war like that."

Jessika couldn't help but hang her head a little. Hawkmother's logic made sense, and it had deflated her enthusiasm.

"But I always knew you'd want to go back," the griffin went on, and Jessika snapped her head back up. "I think you should. You'll never be satisfied unless you do, and it's possible you're right. The attack of the drakes and wizards was vicious. If those people are in charge now, the country could still be suffering. Maybe there is a resistance, or maybe not. Even if the country is happy now," she paused, and Jessika sensed the words might be difficult for her, "you're a human, not a griffin."

"You want us to leave?" Jessika blurted.

"No. I love you all," Hawkmother said simply. "But it is selfish of me to want to keep you here, even if you can endure and think of it as your home. You might be happier in human society. You might want a mate someday. Dare and Rain are here, but you should have more options than that, and I promised that you four would not raise more humans here, so if you ever want chicks of your own, you'll have to go live somewhere else. You should go to Northnest, all four of you if you can get Sky to go, and see what the situation is, and learn about human society. If you decide what's needed is a war to unseat the invaders and take back the country, well, we'll talk about that when it's time. So yes, you have my blessing. You should go."

Jessika stared. "That's a lot to think about."

"Don't worry about the distant future. Let's just plan your trip for now." Hawkmother's eyes shifted up and to Jessika's right. "Dare, you want to go, too?"

Jessika turned. She hadn't noticed Rikah follow her in, but of course he would have. If Hawkmother hadn't set such a somber mood with her tone of voice and Thornsoft hadn't recently scolded them, the six chicks probably would have swarmed him, too. At any rate, Hawknoon was dozing now against Thornsoft's keel, and Hawksun didn't look too far from a nap, either.

"I suppose I will go," Rikah mumbled. "Who will take care of my crops while I'm gone?"

"Not much care is needed until harvest time, right? I'm sure Thorndawn can keep an eye on them," Hawkmother suggested.

"Do you think Rain will go with us?" Jessika asked Rikah.

Rikah shrugged. "I'll talk to him. Maybe if Thornfire would be willing to join us, then he could make him come."

Thornfire was Karo's master—his magic teacher. As a mage, Thornfire had recognized the magical potential in Karo not long after they'd met. Since then, the old male griffin had been guiding Karo through exploring and controlling his abilities.

"I don't know if Fire would feel up to another adventure," Thornsoft gestured. "His years have been weighing on him more and more."

"He would make a good leader," Jessika said. "He has a lot of experience and wisdom."

"Not when it comes to human cities, though," Hawkmother countered. "I don't suppose any griffins should go into the cities, or be seen by Northnest people. I wouldn't expect that any other griffins of Northnest survived the invasion, or would be living there anymore. They would be noticed at once as out of place."

"But there might be drakes," Rikah blurted. "It could be really dangerous."

"You'll have to be careful," Hawkmother nodded.

"What about Sky?" Jessika winced. "Do you think she even cares?"

Rikah shook his head. "She's weird now. I hardly ever see her. The last time was just after the snows melted, when I went down to check out my field. I glimpsed her in the shadow of the trees. She waved. She wouldn't come when I called out to her; she just disappeared again."

"You talk to Rain. I'll try to find Sky," Jessika suggested.

Hawkjoy trilled and attracted everyone's attention, and then to everyone's surprise, gestured, "I'd like to go with you, to investigate Northnest, and I'll help you find Sky."

The shift in both Hawkmother's and Swift's feathers conveyed that neither were ecstatic about her request.

"I'm an adult," Joy went on immediately, "just like Wings. In fact, I'm even older. If she can go, why can't I? Is it because you're afraid I'll die, but you might need me to be the next Mother?"

Hawkmother's face showed her chagrin. "I don't want you to have be Hawkmother if you don't want to, but," she grimaced, "your blood would be most welcome in the Hawk Line. Never minding your blood, never minding how much you contribute to our home and health, we don't want you hurt or killed, because we love you."

"I know that," Joy sighed, "but I want to go. My sisters and brothers need help, and who else is better to go than another Hawksib? When there is need, who has the duty to be first to step up?"

Jessika spoke again; she would delight in having Joy along. "As you say, any griffins who go shouldn't be going into the cities shouldn't be seen by other humans. Joy and Thornfire—if he'll come—would be keeping the camp safe, protecting us when we retreat back from the villages and cities," she pointed out. "Other than the dangers of the forest, she shouldn't be at risk."

Both Hawkmother and Swift flattened their crown feathers, but Joy fluffed hers with eagerness.

"Believe me, I don't want to die, either," she said. "Haven't I always been careful?"

"Unexpected things can happen," Swift gestured half-heartedly.

"We'll be careful, very careful," Wings urged. "Thornfire can protect us, if he'll come."

"You should have some others," Hawkmother grumbled.

"We'll go," Night shouted, jumping to his feet. Beside him, Day roused only a little, the set of her feathers indicating that she did not agree with

Night's enthusiasm.

"No," Hawkmother said immediately, and firmly. "You're not adults yet; you stay."

Night whined, but Thornsoft preened his cheek feathers in sympathy. "I think I'll be staying, too," he gestured. "I've had enough adventures, and with Hawkjoy gone I'll need to make some extra hunts to help feed you bottomless pits."

"I'll ask Thornspike," Rikah said. "She'd love to go."

"Anything to annoy Thornmother," Thornsoft contributed with a wry tilt to his head.

Wings clapped her hands together with an idea. "If Thornfire and Rain both come, maybe Starbright will come, too."

Joy had gotten to her feet, nodding with excitement. "I'll ask her."

Thornsoft made a chuckling sound deep in his chest. "Poor Fire," he gestured, "surrounded by young females."

"I could ask Waterleap," Rikah mentioned. "He hangs out with Thornspike and me sometimes. He might want to come; I think he's been bored."

Hawkmother nodded. "The Water Line has somehow produced far more males than females in the last thirty years or so, and they're doing nothing but getting in each other's way trying to do all the duties of the males at once. I can see why he'd be getting itchy wings."

"I'll ask him," Rikah repeated.

After that, they all stared around at each other for a few moments. It suddenly felt settled, and Jessika got a chill along her back and arms.

"You're going away?" Hawkdawn asked from her position between Thornsoft and Swift's main cushion.

Jessika knelt down and scratched the pale gray fur under the fledgling's chin. The little one would have normally trilled at that, but it didn't seem like the bribe of a bit of scratching was going to distract her.

"Not yet. Don't worry, we'll only be away for a little while," she half-lied; a venture such as this might take most of the summer.

When Jessika looked up, she saw that Hawkmother had her bill clenched, suggesting she was angry, but worry swam in her eyes.

"Go recruit your help," she acquiesced. "Be sure you tell me before you leave."

Jessika noticed she glared in particular at Rikah, who had scampered off on his own without telling anyone at times in the past. His cheeks colored a bit and Jessika almost laughed at him.

"We will," she promised.

Hawkjoy leapt over the group in an athletic display, to join Jessika and Rikah, twitching her wings and grinning. Together, the three Hawksibs trotted out of the room.

Chapter 2
Leaving the Nest

Jessika and Joy were gliding down towards the forest, or rather, Joy was gliding and Jessika was riding her. Joy was coming into her full size and weight. She was older now than Hawkwind had been when the latter first came to South-scree and became the matriarch of the new Line by having her first chicks. Plus, Joy had been involved in the whole escape from Snow-in-lee and the fighting that came after while she was still an adolescent, when Jessika had been only six years old. That should have given the girl some perspective on Joy's perspective, she figured, but it was a bit too twisty for her brain at the moment.

They landed at the edge of the forest, making a several minute walk into a less than a minute's flight.

"When was the last time you saw Sky?" Joy gestured.

Jessika thought about it. "After the spring thaw, she left South-scree and went into the forest."

"She's so unlike you now."

"She is. Something changed her, and she won't really talk about it. At this point, I don't even know if she cares about Northnest, but I hope she still cares about us."

They walked in among the trees, casting about with sight and sound for any sign of movement. It only took a few minutes for Kassandra to find them. She stepped out from among the shadows and Joy spotted her immediately, warning Jessika with a soft click of her tongue.

"Kassie?" Jessika called.

The girl approached, and Jessika's eyes widened although she tried to prevent it. Kassandra was wreathed in leaves and spring flowers from head to foot: only her hands, feet, and face exposed. The leaves were mostly the fuzzy kind, like sage only larger, and of the same soft gray-green. The flowers were dainty, yellow and purple. Smaller leaves wove through her long black hair, holding it back from her face better than any braiding. She was barefoot, but her feet looked hard and thick like bark, with the texture of it continuing up her lower legs to where it vanished under her leaf clothing.

"Jessika," she responded. "You shouldn't come looking for me anymore. You need to get used to not having me around. I don't think I'll come back next winter."

"You'll freeze out here," Jessika responded.

"No, there's a safe place, I think," Kassandra said dreamily, eyes focusing off into the distance, as if thinking.

"That's not what I came here for. Kassie, I'm going back to Northnest. Rikah is coming, and maybe Karo, too, I hope. Joy and some other griffins will also come. I'm going to find out what's going on there, and see if I'm needed, or if anything needs to be done, and to learn why we were attacked, and all that."

Kassandra was still looking off, a little crease between her brows, as if slightly puzzled.

"Do you want to come?" Jessika persisted. "We'd like you to come. We'd like you to come back to South-scree, too, and stop wearing plants, and be with us again, like before." She expelled a breath. "What's happened to you, Kassie?"

"I chose a path," she answered immediately, implacably. "It's nothing for you to worry about. You should really just let me be. I've found my place. I chose it, freely." Her gaze shifted finally, and she smiled at Jessika. "I'm happy. I can't go back to South-scree or Northnest. I can't live that way anymore."

"But why not? Do you dislike us that much?" Jessika asked.

"It's not about dislike. I like you all fine, and I think the griffins are wonderful. I wish you all peace and happiness."

Her tone seemed sincere, and her gentle smile never faded.

"I don't understand," Jessika confessed.

The smile faltered. "I know, and you never will," she said.

Jessika made a helpless gesture. "Why? Why did you choose this path, whatever it is?"

The crease came back to Kassandra's eyebrows. "It felt right. There was nothing else for me, you know? You have your destiny, your Northnest. Karo has his magic. Rikah has his farming and crafting—he'll be a fine man one day. But me, I had nothing."

"You can make whatever you want of your life," Jessika insisted.

"And I did," she said, lifting her palms.

Joy glanced at Jessika with a sort of head tilt and shoulder role combination. Jessika shared her confusion.

"But, it's so, uh," she shrugged helplessly, "strange."

Kassandra actually smiled broadly. "Strange is good. Look, Jessa, I'm happy you're going to Northnest. I'm happy you're going to pursue your destiny. I can't say I'll go with you every step of the way, but I might be around, maybe when you need me."

"You're really sure you won't come with us?"

She nodded. "I'm sure. Are you angry with me?"

There was nothing to be done then. Jessika let the tension drain from her posture. "I guess not. It's your choice, and if you've chosen something else, I can't be angry with you. I just sort of always thought the four of us would be together, so maybe I'm a little sad."

"You don't need me. What use was I ever?"

"Being useful isn't the point. You're my Hawksister, and you have been useful."

Kassandra smiled. "That's kind of you to say, but I've been more useful to others than to you."

Jessika grunted. "You would know that the best, I guess. I don't know what you've been doing these past summers in the forest."

Kassandra held a finger up to her lips. "It's a secret."

"Well, it's a little discouraging, but I'm not really surprised," Jessika told Joy as they walked back towards the Hawk Line nursery.

"Perhaps Rikah will have had more luck than we did," Joy gestured back one handed.

Single-handed Snow-in-lee griffin sign language was a bit tricky to understand, but Jessika got it by context. They turned in through the nursery doorway and looked upon the scene before them.

Thornfire stood by the cushions that Hawkmother and Swift still occupied, engaging the two females in conversation. Dawn was sitting beside him, watching his face, her pert little wings tucked in tight with concentration. His apprentice Karo was standing against the nearest wall, arms folded, looking sullen, which he was so skilled at doing.

Thornsoft and Rikah were under assault by Day, Night, and Dusk, the latter of whom was focusing on Rikah and currently had him pinned to the ground while he lifted his pin-feathered wings and crowed in victory. Thornsoft was doing slightly better, but Day and Night were coordinating their attacks, and Jessika could see that his defenses would not last much longer.

Starbright and Thornspike were sitting together a ways off and chatting about something intermittently funny—probably the males. Starbright was cradling a sleepy Hawknoon while Thornspike pretended the chicks didn't exist. Waterleap was in limbo, looking between the two females and Rikah's imminent demise under the merciless claws of Hawkdusk, and not seeming to be able to decide which course of action would be more profitable.

Joy chuckled a little, deep in her chest.

"Ah," croaked Rikah, "salvation. Hawkwings, save me."

"It is too late for you, Hawkbrother," Jessika replied, with a dramatic hand pressed to her heart. "I dare not face the fury of a beast such as that which has slain you."

That was all that was needed for Dusk to spot her and launch himself off of Rikah towards his new target with a baby roar of challenge.

There was just enough time for Joy to jump in the way and gesture, "I'll protect you."

"My hero," Jessika grinned as Dusk careened into Joy, and Joy carefully buffered his arrival with her wings so as not to hurt him or damage his emerging feathers.

As that new battle raged on and Rikah caught his breath, Jessika edged over to Starbright and Thornspike. Starbright was Thornfire's former apprentice—now a mage in her own right—a bit older than Joy and a striking golden color in appearance. Thornspike was a young griffin Jessika didn't know extremely well. She was counter-shaded black and white except for white wing bars and a totally white head. Her eyes were red like a goshawk. She was unusually lean, with a blunter head than normally seen among the South-scree griffins, and much longer and pointier wings. Both lady griffins had been born in South-scree.

"You're going to come with us?" Jessika said as she approached, automatically using a hand gesture for greeting at the same time.

"I'm totally coming," Thornspike stated flatly.

"I think so, if I'm not needed here," Starbright said.

Day and
Night
at play

Joy left Dusk in a panting pile and came up to them, too. "I'm going," she gestured.

"Hawksky wouldn't join us, though," Jessika reported.

"She's different now," Starbright said. "It's all right."

Rikah wandered over, rubbing various bruised bits of his anatomy, and Waterleap followed. Before either could open their mouths, Hawkmother called across the room.

"If the scouting meeting is starting, do bring it over here."

Thornsoft leapt over to take the sleeping Hawknoon out of the way, leaving Day and Night rolling about the floor and deafening everyone in the room with griffin fledgling shriek-giggles.

"Day, Night, enough," Hawkmother ordered, and the two chicks desisted, running off instead to leap with wild abandon into a defenseless pile of pillows where Hawksun had been napping through the whole thing.

Thornsoft carried Hawknoon over to the pile, too, and within moments all four chicks were asleep, leaving Dusk stretched out on the floor, still panting, and Hawkdawn sitting studiously by Thornfire. The others, led by Jessika, joined the gathering by Hawkmother.

"You have your scouting party then?" the matriarch asked.

"Myself, Dare, Joy, Thornspike, Waterleap," Jessika recited. "Starbright, you'll come?"

"I'd like to," she said.

Thornfire hid the slightest sigh. "Did you ask Starmother if she could spare you?"

"Not yet," the golden griffin admitted, flattening her feathers a little.

"It should have been the first thing you did; now go do it," the old mage ordered.

"Yes, Master," Starbright replied automatically and turned to dash for the door.

"What about you, Thornfire?" Hawkmother asked.

He stretched a little, making his wing joints pop. "It seems the Hawk Line will again rope me into its business and force me off on an adventure," he griped.

"Excuse me?" Hawkmother countered. "It was you who roped me into your adventure to find Thornwing, not the other way around."

He drummed his claws on the floor. "Technicality."

"So Rain, you'll come, too?" Jessika called.

Karolan Hawkrain sloped over to the group, brushing his shaggy blonde hair away from his eyes. "Yeah, I guess."

"You don't have to come," Rikah said pointedly.

"I'll come," Karo repeated. "You'll probably need my magic."

Without turning his head, Thornfire said, "your attitude is the worst in front of others. There's no need for your arrogant pose, Hawkrain. Everyone knows you're a mage, and values you."

Karo looked ashamed and angry, folded his arms again and said nothing.

"Well, a cheerful group," Swift gestured with a forced smile.

They'd repaired to a different room, one without the intermittently explosive energy of chicks bouncing off the walls. Thornsoft, Thornwing, and Hawkswift were watching over the chicks now, leaving Hawkmother free to join the conference. Just as she was finishing a drawing of Northnest as she remembered it, Starbright came fluttering in through the doorway.

"Starmother said I could go," the young mage announced.

Thornfire raised his brows a bit, as though he hadn't expected it.

"Great news," Jessika said, and others murmured their approval, too.

"I was still learning the geography of the country when the attack came, and it's been many years," Hawkmother warned. "Plus, since the invasion, things could have changed, but this is approximately what things were like."

Jessika leaned over the table, examining the inked lines. "Well, I don't remember anything," she said, "so this is better than nothing."

"You shouldn't go straight to the capital," Hawkmother instructed.

"I agree," Thornfire nodded firmly.

"And you mustn't tell anyone exactly why you're there, that you lived in Northnest before the invasion, that you're coming back with the idea of rebellion in mind—none of that," the matriarch went on.

"But there's no way for these three to pretend they're residents," Thornfire said. "They won't look or behave or speak like residents, and won't have the knowledge residents would have."

Hawkmother reached out to touch a large dot she'd made. "This is a trade city, or was, at least. Traders from other countries were granted passage along these two roads to enter Northnest and come as far as this city. There, they could sell their wares and buy Northnest products."

Her voice dropped a little. "Feathyrs were assigned to guard these roads and the trade city, in case of foreigners causing trouble and to render assistance if there were accidents. Before the invasion happened, it was looking like I was going to get placed at a station along the southern road for my first assignment as a full Feathyr."

Hawkjoy, sitting beside her, leaned over and preened her neck feathers in sympathy.

"So we could go into that city and not look out of place?" Rikah asked.

"I doubt there are griffins there anymore," Hawkmother said with a sigh, "but you three humans could probably do it, provided trade is still allowed with other countries and it's still done there."

"It sounds like a good place to start," Thornfire agreed.

"The two countries that abutted Northnest were Weldom and Lackland. Beyond them there were more, but I can't remember any of their names. I also don't really know what the countries were like, how the people dressed or acted, so I don't know how to instruct you to act." Her visage darkened. "I also don't know from which country came the invasion. Northnest may be a part of one of those countries now."

"So maybe there's no trade there anymore," Jessika worried.

"We won't know until we take a look," Thornfire said. "It's probably still a big city. People will be less suspicious in a larger city, rather than a town where everyone knows each other. Let's go there."

"Burdened with riders and baggage, it may take you a week to fly there," Hawkmother said.

The griffins looked around at each other.

"Five of us, three humans," Thornspike muttered, "but one old male and one scrawny young male." She looked at Hawkjoy and Starbright. "Looks like we'll be the main beasts of burden, ladies."

Waterleap slicked his feathers with discomfort and Thornfire narrowed his eyes at his Linemate, "watch your tone, Spike."

Thornspike subsided but didn't look sorry.

"I'll carry Wings," Joy volunteered immediately.

"I'll carry Hawkrain," Starbright said.

"Sure, I'll carry Hawkdare," Spike grumped.

"I can carry any other baggage," Waterleap said softly.

The young male bore an initial resemblance in color to Thornspike, mainly black above and mainly white below, but his shoulders and wing coverts, top and bottom, were all slate grey and his head was black. He also had rather lovely blue-grey eyes, and his throat and bill were grey. In build he reflected the most standard buteo-type of South-scree. Thornfire nodded to him.

"We'll depend on you for that then, Waterleap," the mage said. "Being so ancient and old and almost dead, I'll just focus on trying to keep up."

Several people chuckled or snorted in amusement. Thornspike just looked sullen.

"We'll have to pack our best clothes, and blankets for sleeping," Rikah started saying. "I guess we'll be camping out every night."

"Money would be useful, but we haven't any," Hawkmother rued. "It would have allowed you to buy supplies for yourselves once you get to the city. Oh, I know. Take something you can trade for money."

"Like what?" Jessika shrugged. "What do people trade?"

"It should be something light and small," the griffin mused, and then shrugged. "Or I suppose you could try trading whatever you kill for food."

"I have some wooden animals I carved," Rikah mentioned. "I could bring a few."

Hawkmother nodded. "That might have to do."

"We could get real clothes there," Jessika was thinking aloud, "and real shoes, and new knives."

"Our clothes and shoes are fine," Karo interjected.

"But not to blend in with other humans in a city," Rikah argued. "Jessika makes great things for us, but I don't know if they'll look normal around, you know, normal humans. I'll bring some carvings; they're small. Maybe I can trade them and get us money."

"Pack lightly," Thornfire cautioned. "Waterleap will have to fly with everything you add to your pack. Hawkmother, is there anything else of use you can tell us?"

The matriarch shook her head, humanlike. "I wish I knew someone likely to still be alive down there, whom I could send you to, but I don't. I wish I could go with you, but it's more important I stay here."

Jessika didn't quite see how that was true, but then she didn't fully understand griffin politics and society. If Hawkmother said she had to stay, perhaps there really was a good reason. Or maybe she was actually just scared of going back and facing the memories when it was so much easier to convince herself she was needed here. Jessika frowned as something else occurred to her, and she did some mental math. The youngest Hawkchick, Hawknoon, had been born a year ago. It could be that Hawkmother was planning another chick, or was even already pregnant, although she hadn't announced anything.

Jessika tried to tell herself to just accept that Hawkmother wasn't Hawkwind anymore. She had her place, like she'd said, and there would be no more adventuring for her.

It took them two days to gather all the supplies they wanted, properly balance a pack for Waterleap to fly with, and get suitable riding harnesses for Hawkjoy, Starbright, and Thornspike. As they made their final preparations the morning of the third day, Jessika stood in the cold dawn sunlight and shivered with more than just the chill. Hawkjoy came up beside her and nudged her encouragingly.

"All will be well," the griffin signed.

Jessika shrugged. "I hope so. I have no idea what we'll discover. I can imagine all kinds of things, and there's probably lots more I can't imagine, and I don't know what I'll do when I discover whatever the truth is."

"You don't have to worry about any of that until we actually learn something," Hawkjoy replied, giving a little chuckle from deep in her chest.

"I guess not, but it's hard not to keep thinking about it."

Rikah and Thornspike joined them, all suited up for departure. Rikah also looked nervous, but Thornspike seemed eagerly aggressive.

"This is great," she hissed appreciatively. "I get to leave the Aerie, try new winds, hunt new prey."

"Yeah, great," Rikah agreed ruefully.

Hawkjoy clucked a scolding. "It is great, Dare."

He ducked his head a little, rubbing the back of his neck, and submitting before the older female. Griffin she might be, and human he might be, but they had grown up in the same Line, and they both knew their relative ranks. "Yeah, I guess," he nodded instead.

Jessika Hawkwings

"We're ready here," Thornfire announced, striding over with Starbright and Waterleap in tow. "Humans get on."

Karo came over obediently from where he'd been leaning against a boulder and got on Starbright, who gave him a cheery smile. Hawkjoy knelt a little for Jessika, who heaved herself up on the big female's back. The riding harness was designed to interfere as little as possible with flight. Griffin flight muscles were all on the chest, the same as birds, but the wings still needed freedom of movement. Because of that, the riding harness was more towards the hindquarters, and riders always focused on being as small of a package as possible, but still often got in the way of the axillaries and innermost secondaries. As the human children had gotten bigger, carrying them had become more difficult. The griffins would tire quickly even with the best winds in their favor.

Jessika glanced with concern at Thornspike. Unlike the other griffins, her wings were shaped for speed, not lift, and Rikah was the biggest and heaviest. Thornspike made no comment as he climbed up. Jessika figured she was probably stubborn enough to fly herself into the ground before she mentioned being tired.

"You will all follow my lead," Thornfire emphasized. "We'll fly for a while today and test the winds, but we aren't going to fly to exhaustion. There is, after all, no time limit on this quest. We may be away from South-scree for weeks, and certain stages of the exploration may require a slower, more methodical approach. For now, we're headed towards that trade city. We'll make camp this afternoon at the best site we can locate. Any questions or information I should know?"

A few folks gave the gesture for negative or shook their head. Thornfire drew breath to speak again, but then caught himself, his gaze going off behind his gathered group, and Jessika turned to see what he was looking at.

Hawkmother had emerged soundlessly from the path behind them. Hawkknight, Hawkday, and Hawkdawn came trotting up behind her, making far more noise than should have been possible for their size.

"We came to see you off," Night announced in his best I'm-an-adult-now voice.

Hawkmother gave a little smile. "Be careful out there. We'll be waiting for your safe return."

Dawn scampered forward and exchanged one last feather nibble with

Hawkjoy. Day was sitting attentively beside Hawkmother, seeming to be watching and memorizing her every move.

"We'll be fine," Hawkjoy gestured. "I'll take good care of Wings, Dare, and Rain."

Embraces and farewells had already been exchanged before they'd come out for departure, and Hawkmother simply walked in her hind feet and sat, apparently planning to watch until they were out of sight.

"Let's be going then," Thornfire said. "Be well until our return, Hawkmother."

"And you," she replied. "May the winds fill your wings."

Thornfire gave a nod, turned, and ran a few paces before launching off, into the air. Thornspike gave a similar nod, and followed her elder, taking twice as many wing beats to reach his altitude.

"Take care, be well, we'll be back soon," Starbright waved, and then she, too, labored into the air.

Waterleap followed without delay, leaving only Hawkjoy and Jessika.

"Good luck, Jessika," Hawkmother whispered. "I hope you will find your peace with whatever you discover."

"Me, too," she said. "Thank you, Mother. Ready when you are, Joy."

Hawkjoy gently nudged Dawn back towards Hawkmother, and gestured her farewell. Then, she turned and took a running start before snapping out her wings and flapping rapidly to get airborne. Jessika hunched down low, riding out the lurching and jerking until Hawkjoy got herself up high enough to open her wings wide and firm and catch a steady wind.

Jessika stole one last look over her shoulder. South-scree was receding rapidly behind them, but she could still make out Hawkmother and the three chicks, standing and watching them go. The young woman turned her face away, back towards the direction they were flying, and tried to shield her eyes with an arm to deflect the wind while still keeping her gaze on the horizon, so as not to get air sick. The cold wind drew only a few more tears from her eyes than it usually did.

Thornfire called an early camp and Waterleap volunteered to hunt once the packs were off him. No one objected and the little male vanished into the forest without a sound.

"We could go farther; I'm not tired yet," Thornspike announced.

"I am," Thornfire grunted back.

"Fine, I'll go hunt, too," the slender female retorted, and without waiting for comment sent dust, dead leaves, and anything else that wasn't weighted down swirling around the clearing as she powered into the air. Rikah and Jessika had to duck to avoid getting hit by her wings. Joy chuckled, but Thornfire sniffed in disapproval.

"Uppity chick," the ruffled mage grumbled.

Starbright went about returning everything Thornspike had disrupted to order while Rikah went back to laying the fire and Thornfire preened twigs out of his feathers. Between them they set up camp and got the fire going by the time Waterleap returned with a bled deer.

"I ate," he said softly. "This one's for all of you."

"Thank you, Waterleap," Thornfire told him.

Rikah cut steaks from one haunch for the humans, and then Hawkjoy, Starbright, and Thornfire split the rest three ways. Jessika sat by the fire and watched Rikah cook. He'd always been the best at it of the four human children, perhaps because he was always the one that did it. He'd learned to season what he cooked with herbs he grew himself, and had apparently brought a little sack of such spices with him.

"No reason we have to have our food plain," he remarked. "Little bits of dried plants hardly weigh anything."

Across the fire from them, Karo was staring intently at the flames. Jessika raised her eyebrows when she saw him doing something with his fingers to suddenly swirl the flames into a little column.

"That won't help with the cooking, Rain," Rikah commented dryly.

"Hawkrain," Thornfire said simply, and Karo dropped his hands, letting the fire return to its normal fire-shape.

"Whatever. There's nothing for me to do," he complained.

"Give Starbright a massage," Jessika suggested. "She flew you all this way."

Hawkjoy made an entirely un-big-huge-predator-like chirp and Jessika glanced at her.

"An excellent idea," the griffin gestured with a gaping grin.

Jessika grinned back. "I got myself into that one," she said, getting up to join her Linesister in a spot further from the fire. "How do you feel? Anything hurt?"

"I feel great," Hawkjoy replied. "The exercise feels good after a long winter of not doing much."

Jessika went to work: having a fair bit of experience giving griffin massages, she knew some of the best spots to work her fingers into. Griffins could and did give each other massages, since their paws were more like cats', with retractable claws, than birds', and they did have thumbs, but human hands were more agile and flexible still. It was one of the few ways, Jessika thought, that humans surpassed griffins, and part of her loved showing off and being in demand for massaging and scratching difficult to reach places.

To his credit, Karo got up and offered Starbright a massage, too, which she cheerfully accepted. In the midst of the massage, just as Hawkjoy was getting cross-eyed with bliss, Thornspike came winging in, making slightly less of a windstorm than upon her departure, but still nearly scattering the fire into the surrounding vegetation.

"Spike, more consideration on take off and landing at camp," Thornfire scolded.

"Yes, Elder," she responded, as if by rote.

"And where is your contribution to the meal?" he went on.

Thornspike paused. "Uh."

"You ate for yourself and brought nothing back? Hawkjoy, Starbright, and I split a single deer three ways after Hawkdare cut off the humans' portion," Thornfire explained sternly.

"I can hunt again," Waterleap volunteered immediately.

Thornfire hushed him with a gesture of one wing. "We'll be fine for tonight. Tomorrow Spike will bring something back for us."

"Maybe it's too difficult," Jessika suggested. "Her wings are so long and pointy, they're better for speed, not so good for carrying lots of weight."

Jessika hadn't expected the glare Thornspike turned on her then.

"Thornspike's wing shape: sensitive subject," Rikah told the steaks.

"Oh," Jessika realized, "I'm sorry."

Thornspike huffed and paced over to an empty spot, where she curled up and shut her eyes.

"Don't mind her," Hawkjoy gestured. "It's difficult being different."

Jessika had to agree.

Chapter 3
A Detour

Two days later, Jessika spotted a human town in the distance. When they landed she announced her intention.

"I want to go to that village tomorrow. You all saw it, right?" she said.

"That's not our destination," Thornfire replied warily.

"I still want to go. Maybe we can get normal clothes there, so we can walk into the trade city looking like we fit in, and maybe they can give us some information."

Thornfire shook his crest. "There were arguments against that. In small towns there will be more suspicion of newcomers."

"Then I'll just take a look, from the edge of the forest," Jessika revised.

"We'll lose a day of travel when we could be getting closer to the trade city," Thornfire pointed out.

"I just, I really want to go," she insisted.

"Hawkwings."

"I want to go," she repeated. "It's my mission, even if you are the eldest and sort of in charge. Joy, will you take me to the edge of the forest tomorrow, so I can see the town?"

"Of course I will," the griffin answered without delay.

Thornfire growled, but gave up, turning instead to snap at Thornspike, "hunt us something."

"Don't take it out on me," Thornspike spat back, striding away into the undergrowth.

"I'm sure Hawkwings will be careful," Starbright said as the group began setting up camp.

Thornfire didn't respond.

"And it won't hurt us to rest a day," the young mage went on. "We're all a bit sore from flying so much, and we can hunt a little extra to help us recover."

"Shall I go with you, Wings?" Rikah asked as he began unloading Waterleap.

Jessika shrugged. "You could, if you want. I guess I'm not going into the town, so it doesn't really matter. It's just been a long time since I saw other humans."

"So you won't even be accomplishing anything," Thornfire rumbled.

"I don't know what I might accomplish," she admitted, "but it doesn't hurt to go look, and maybe I'll see something important."

The old griffin mage just shrugged his wings and set about clearing rocks and sticks from the overgrown clearing they'd chosen to camp in. Hawkjoy gave Jessika a little nudge and smile, and gestured, "don't mind him," where Thornfire couldn't see her hands.

Jessika shrugged and tried to smile. "His logic makes sense," she gestured back, "but I still just really want to go."

Hawkjoy preened her hair. "Of course. You may have spent most of your life with us griffins, but humans are your people."

Jessika grabbed Joy's forearm. "You're my people," she whispered back. "You're my sister. The Hawk Line is my family."

The griffin didn't try to extricate herself, but she gave the young woman a careful, close look. "Then," she asked one-handed, "why do you want so much to go back to Northnest?"

Jessika bit her lip. Hawkjoy knew about the wing tattoos on her back, but not that it was a sign of her lineage as Northnest royalty. She tried to come up with an explanation—but then thought, perhaps Hawkjoy should know the truth. If they were sisters, family, then she should trust her with the knowledge. Hawkmother and Hawkswift knew, and they had kept the secret. Certainly Hawkjoy would, too. Who would Hawkjoy tell anyway? Jessika tried to get the words out, but some fear stopped her. For so many years she'd kept it to herself, never speaking of it. Some habits were just too hard to break, but Hawkjoy deserved to know. Jessika promised herself she'd tell her soon.

"I just have to see it again, so I can see what I'm missing, so I can learn about things, but my home is in South-scree, with you."

"Tomorrow then, you can begin seeing and learning," Hawkjoy nodded. "I can help you best if you give me another massage."

Jessika smiled knowingly. "Of course, you have all my best interests at heart."

Her Hawksister smiled back. "Always and forever."

As Jessika adjusted Hawkjoy's harness straps the next morning—while everyone else was sleeping in or lazing about—she noticed her Hawksister staring off into space, eyes unfocused, feathers twitching.

"Are you feeling alright?" she asked.

Hawkjoy nodded distractedly.

"Ready to go? I think I'm set."

Hawkjoy nodded again, and gestured. "Let's go."

Jessika got on and Hawkjoy walked off into the undergrowth to find a different clearing to take off in. Once airborne, Jessika gazed around at the morning forest, with sunlight catching the tips of trees and lighting up morning mist as it came over the mountains. Hawkjoy kept low and dove back down into the trees as soon as they drew close to the town.

"We'd better walk from here," Hawkjoy gestured back at Jessika, who nodded her agreement.

Some years ago when Jessika had approached a town with Hawkwind, Joy, Swift, and the other children, rainbow drakes attacked them as soon as they were spotted. A cautious approach was in order. Hawkjoy could travel under the trees more swiftly than Jessika could walk, and morning was not much advanced when they started to glimpse the open fields and distant houses of the town.

Hawkjoy slowed, and Jessika got off. "I'll walk from here, but I don't think I'll come out from under the trees," she said. "You should probably stay hidden back here, just in case."

Hawkjoy nodded her acquiescence, and Jessika began picking her way closer to the town. Despite the early hour, villagers were already stirring. Smoke was drifting up from most of the chimneys, and Jessika spotted a few adults outside the houses: visiting chicken coops or gardens, bringing in pails of milk, or even heading out into the fields to get to work.

She did her best to circle the town, staying hidden among the trees, stomach rumbling at the smells of breakfast—scents that brought back a vague nostalgia but no true memories. The sound of wood being chopped and metal struck on metal reverberated in the town, mixed with the clucks, caws, lows, and bellows of animals.

After a short time, more people emerged from their homes to tend the fields or animals or begin work on other chores. Women carried out baskets of laundry while men sharpened tools or took up sacks and rakes for weeding their young crops. Then the children came out. Older children dutifully or sullenly followed their parents, with older girls often carrying or shepherding babies and toddlers. The children too young to be of much help, but old enough not to get themselves into danger ran off to play, friends from different houses meeting up, with a parent or grandparent occasionally scolding or chasing after to corral a child back into doing some task or other.

A trio of boys made their escape, running towards the forest near where Jessika was hiding, and she snuck away from them in the opposite direction. Behind them, a mother shouted at them not to go too far. Jessika wished she were close enough to hear what the other adults were saying, but she feared leaving the forest and being seen.

Instead, she listened as the three boys started up a boisterous game chasing each other through the underbrush, and adjusted her position whenever she heard them come near while she watched the village. The people looked healthy as far as she could tell, and although their lives were full of hard work, they looked like they had sound houses and plentiful food. Occasionally a burst of laughter would reach her ears.

Jessika caught herself frowning as she watched, and realized she was feeling unhappy that the people were happy. Did she want them to be suffering and discontented? They looked moderately prosperous. Wasn't that a good thing? It was just, if they had been unhappy, they'd be more inclined to reject their rulers, she supposed, but it seemed there would be no angry peasants from this source.

A sudden eruption of childish exuberance shocked her back to her surroundings. While she'd been feeling disgruntled, the three boys had worked their way closer to her again, too close.

"Argh! Get the griffin," a boy shouted, and Jessika had a jolt as she thought for a moment that the children had somehow snuck up on Hawkjoy.

Then one boy came thrashing through the bush, screeching at the top of his voice, arms flapping like wings. The other two boys followed him, brandishing sticks. The pursued boy wheeled about, hands now hooked into clawlike shapes as he crowed rather like a rooster. The other two boys burst out of the shrubbery and yelled.

"Get it, get it, get the griffin," one ordered, pointing at the chased boy.

"Chicken for dinner," cried out the other pursuer.

The boy pretending—apparently—to be a griffin screeched and slashed at the air with his pretend claws. Jessika, out in plain sight now, knew she should hide, but a game that humans hunted griffins bothered her enough that she didn't immediately dive for the trees.

"Hey, who are you?" one of the hunting boys asked as soon as he spotted her.

The other two boys turned her way, too, and then backed cautiously away. The boy who had been being chased was the biggest, with sandy hair and trousers just a bit too short for him. Of the two chasers, one had shaggy black hair and tanned skin, and the other lots of freckles around blue eyes, and blonde hair.

"You don't live in town," the griffin-boy accused. "What are you doing here?"

"Where are you from?" asked the blonde boy.

"I'm not going to hurt you," Jessika told them, refusing to answer their questions. "What were you doing? You play at hunting griffins?"

"Yeah," the griffin-boy said frankly.

"Of course," said the black haired boy, "griffins are bad."

"They're evil," the blonde one chimed in. "But they taste like chicken."

"You've eaten griffin?" Jessika demanded, appalled.

"Well, no," the blonde admitted, "but they're like a big chicken. Everyone says they must taste like chicken." He looked to his companions to confirm and they nodded vigorously.

"Have you ever seen one?" she asked.

"Drawings," the black haired boy shrugged.

"So no one in your village has ever killed one?" she pressed.

"Well, no, but we would if we could," the boy who'd been the griffin said firmly. "Wouldn't you? Griffins are the enemies of our country."

"What?" Jessika stuttered, starting to get truly angry. "No, the Feathyrs defended Northnest. The invaders killed them. They tried to protect us from the rainbow drakes."

The boys looked between themselves. "What are you talking about?" the black haired one asked, utter puzzlement on his face. "The rainbow drakes protect us from the griffins."

"N-no," Jessika argued. "How can you say that? The drakes came with the wizards and took over the country, took it over from the true rulers."

"Oh," the blonde boy grunted, scratching his head, "I guess I heard something about that. It happened a long time ago, but those rulers were bad."

"Bad?" Jessika retorted: fists clenched.

"Yeah, but the rulers now are good, and the drakes protect us," the black haired boy repeated.

All three boys nodded in agreement, looking a little scared at Jessika's anger.

"No, no," she sputtered. "Who told you that?"

"Everyone knows that," the griffin-boy winced. "Why don't you? Are, are you a bad person?"

"No," she declared, making them flinch away from her. "I, I," she didn't know what to say. She couldn't tell them she was the princess. What could she say? "I was there," she said instead. "You're too young to have been alive then, but I was there in the castle when the invaders came, when the drakes came. They killed everyone. I barely escaped. I was probably about your age. How would you feel if a bunch of scary monsters came to your village and started killing everyone and you had to run away?"

They nodded eagerly. "The griffins would come kill everyone if the drakes didn't keep them away," the black haired one, who seemed to be the most assertive, said fervently.

"No, no," Jessika refuted, running her fingers into her hair and gripping her scalp in frustration. "It's the other way around. Griffins are good."

The boys just stared at her with equal parts bewilderment and fear.

"Griffins are good," she repeated, trying not to shout at them. How could these boys have been convinced that the drakes were the heroes and the griffins the villains?

"I heard my mom call," the griffin-boy blurted suddenly.

"We need to go," said the blonde one, jumping on the excuse.

The black haired boy didn't seem quite as frightened, but as a group the three of them bolted, throwing glances nervously over their shoulders as they ran for the village. Jessika growled in aggravation, and turned to go herself. If the boys reported that they'd met some strange young woman in the woods who had been on the side of the evil griffins, their parents might make a search, if the story wasn't dismissed as childhood fancy.

Jessika fought her way back through the undergrowth to where she'd left Hawkjoy earlier that morning, swatting the innocent foliage out of her path with unnecessary violence.

She found Hawkjoy sitting in a patch of sunlight in a little clearing, the light bringing out subtle patterns in her pale grey coloration. The griffin was in the midst of leisurely preening, stropping her long primaries through her bill.

"Are you done?" Joy gestured at once, and went on without waiting for an answer. "Good, let's go back."

Jessika raised her eyebrows a little in surprise. Hawkjoy wasn't usually so blunt, but the young woman went along, getting on her as soon as she finished her last feather and sat up. Hawkjoy didn't delay getting into the air, and didn't ask anything about what Jessika had seen, although Jessika wished she could talk about it with her.

On the way back, the big female griffin kept shivering her skin and twitching, and she flew swiftly, as if truly eager to be back. Jessika hadn't thought Hawkjoy was dismayed at the trip; in fact she'd encouraged Jessika to do it the previous evening. Once they landed, Jessika slid off her back, and was going to ask what was wrong, but before she could, she heard another voice complain.

"Me, why is it always me?" Thornfire growled. "What kind of bad luck is it that I end up on long journeys with young females that awake?"

Hawkjoy's head whipped around to glare at him. "I know exactly what's going on, so you don't have to explain anything," she gestured vigorously. "My mother Swift explained everything to me, and I don't want you."

Jessika's jaw dropped. That was it? She should have guessed it. It wasn't that unexpected, after all. Jessika covered her mouth as a shocked Thornfire backed up a step, endangering his tail feathers with proximity to the campfire, and smothered her laughter. Well, that explained her distracted attitude and focus on returning to camp. Hawkjoy had awakened and could think of only one thing. The implications of the event tumbled through Jessika's thoughts and her laughter faded.

"Well," Thornfire tried to bluster, "that's at least, um, decisive. I'm too old for it anyway these days."

But with Hawkjoy's words, everyone else had swung their eyes towards the other griffin male with the group, and then averted them out of courtesy; a matriarch's choice was a private thing. Waterleap was the only male available if Hawkjoy was rejecting the elderly Thornfire—and he didn't seem too surprised.

Joy awakening meant Hawkwind had gone back to sleep, and Joy was the new Hawkmother. It was a natural process; younger females succeeded older ones. Joy must have recognized that she was in heat: for the first time in her life being able to think of little else besides males and mating.

Jessika caught herself blushing. She sat down by the fire, took some food, and focused intently on it. She heard the sound of movement, humans and griffins walking around and the sound of footsteps moving away and greenery being pushed through.

"Well, there goes yet another day of progress," Thornfire rumbled. "Hawkwings, what did you find out today?"

Jessika looked up. Hawkjoy and Waterleap were gone. Rikah and Karo sat together in awkward silence and Starbright and Thornspike were preening each other amid griffin chuckles.

"I'm glad that hasn't happened to me," Starbright chortled.

"Me, too, thank the skies," Thornspike huffed back. "And it never will. I'm never going to be Thornmother."

"You can't really refuse, you know, if it happens," Starbright murmured.

"It will never happen," she declared. "As for you, you'd better expect it; you're a mage. Female mages always become Mothers."

Starbright snorted. "The new Starmother is young, hardly older than I am. Even if I do get a turn, it won't be for years."

"Don't be too sure," Thornfire grumbled. "It's always a little unpredictable. Some matriarchs only stay matriarchs for a year, just long enough to have a chick, and then it moves to someone else. Hawkwings, did you hear me?"

Jessika pulled her attention back to the old male griffin, while Starbright and Thornspike went on encouraging each other in not wanting to be matriarchs.

"I guess, uhm," she muttered as she recalled what had been so upsetting before the revelation of Hawkjoy's awakening. "I watched the town for a while. Everyone seems pretty happy and healthy," she fumbled. "It looked like a good town, prosperous, you know?"

"So that doesn't tell us much," Thornfire shrugged.

"But then I ran into some kids playing in the trees," she went on, feeling

the anger of it again, but trying to keep her voice from carrying to the two female griffins. "They were convinced that griffins were bad. They thought the rainbow drakes were good. They were playing a game where one of them pretended to be a griffin and the other two were hunting him. They thought my parents were bad rulers and the invaders were good," she raised her palms in frustration, "or something like that."

Thornfire tilted his head. "That sounds like a puzzling shift, but perhaps the outlying villages were not aware of all that went on at the capital? They may have been fed false information to keep them from contesting the new rulers of the country."

"That's what it must be," Jessika agreed helplessly.

"You couldn't talk to any adults, I suppose," he mused.

"I didn't even mean to talk to the kids, but they sort of snuck up on me in the woods."

"We'll get more accurate information at the trade city, I'll bet," Rikah contributed. "Those kids probably didn't know anything. They just made up a stupid game."

"They really thought griffins were bad. They talked about eating griffins, even: compared them to chickens. But they said they'd never seen any and no one in the village had ever killed any."

The mage made a sound of disgust. "Chickens? It is relieving that they've never seen any," Thornfire said, "though it is possible they have heard of rogue griffins, who do tend to be violent and aggressive, but even rogues probably stay away from humans."

"They thought the Feathyrs were bad, too," Jessika protested.

Thornfire was silent for a few moments, staring fixedly at the ground and thinking hard, it seemed. At last, he looked up and spoke slowly. "All we know about Northnest we learned from Hawkwind and you children. All of you were quite young when you escaped."

Jessika's jaw dropped as she realized what he was implying.

"Those were just some stupid brats," Rikah interjected heatedly. "They just made that stuff up. They don't know anything of what's really going on. We'll find out the truth. We know our parents were good people. I know my mom and dad were. We all feel like that about the people who raised us: Hawkwind, too. Maybe there were some bad humans and griffins in

Northnest, who caused trouble sometimes, or something, like in any group of people, but it was a good country. The invaders with their drakes were the bad ones. We were at peace until they came."

Jessika watched as Rikah snatched up a small branch and began breaking it into bits, throwing each fragment furiously into the fire. Thornfire nodded once but didn't speak.

"There could have been something bad going on, in some way," Jessika murmured. "Nobody is completely good, after all. We all have bad moments, every now and then, but I want to believe that my parents were doing the best they could for Northnest, trying to take care of the people, and that the griffins were good."

"Not all griffins are good, Hawkwings," Thornfire admitted. "That's why there are rogues, because we of the Aeries have to exile the ones who refuse to live peacefully in our society, although not very often."

"Maybe," she agreed, "but I have to find out the whole truth of this, of what's going on."

"Young one, you will never know the whole truth of anything," Thornfire sighed, "but yes, learn what you can. Tomorrow, hopefully, we will continue on our journey to the trade city. You will learn more there, as Hawkdare says."

When Jessika awoke the next day, after a night of uneasy dreams, she saw Waterleap and Hawkjoy—should she call her Hawkmother now?—had returned to camp. Rikah was already cooking breakfast; it seemed someone had hunted. Starbright and Thornspike were huddled at one edge of the camp, picking over a pile of red-stained bones. Thornfire was preening blood out of his feathers.

"Get up, everyone," he ordered. "We're going to fly today."

Karo groaned, but obeyed, sitting up on his bedroll and squinting at the light. Waterleap sat up, blinking, looking dazed. Hawkjoy rumbled as if supremely content and rolled over, tucking her head under her other wing. Jessika found herself smiling, and stumbled on weary legs over to her Hawksister. She sank her fingers into the thick fur-feathers of her neck ruff and scratched insistently. Hawkjoy groaned again and pulled her head out from under her wing to crack an eye open at Jessika.

"Good morning, Hawkmother," she whispered.

Hawkjoy's eye widened alarmingly and she snuck a hand out to gesture, "am I? I guess I am. Then Hawkmother—Hawkwind?"

"Hawkwind isn't anymore. Now she's just one of the Line elders," Jessika said.

"She could be elected Eldest," Hawkjoy suggested.

"Maybe, but she's probably still too young for that."

Hawkjoy nodded. Jessika grinned and lowered her voice some more.

"Did you have fun with Waterleap?" she asked breathlessly, a little embarrassed that her face was blushing.

Hawkjoy's cheek and crest feathers rose, indicating a broad grin as she gaped her bill to mimic human smiles. She gestured, close to her chest so no one else would see, "I think I'm going to like being Hawkmother. I don't think I'd ever felt so good."

Jessika's face got even hotter. "So, you both knew how? Like, what to do?"

"My mother explained things to me, and though Waterleap said he'd never had the opportunity before, he still knew the theory. We figured it out, and practiced until we got really good at it."

Jessika thought her skin might burst into flame if it got any hotter. "I'm happy for you," she said. "I'm glad that's what was going on and not that you were getting sick or something. I was worried for a bit there."

"I'll be fine now," Hawkjoy assured her. "At least for a while."

"I said, get up," Thornfire ordered again.

"Yes, yes," Hawkjoy gestured up over her shoulder where he could see it if he was watching. "Show some respect to a matriarch."

Jessika stood, and blurted out laughter as Thornfire reacted, feathers twitching as though someone had poked him in the butt.

"I, I am still an elder," he stuttered, "and the leader of this mission."

Hawkjoy pushed smoothly to her feet, refolding her wings. She somehow looked stronger, bigger, and sleeker than she had yesterday. "Your pardon, Elder," she bowed gracefully.

Thornfire's crest feathers flicked and then flattened. "Granted," he said begrudgingly.

Jessika laughed again and he gave her a glare, but then softened, shaking his head with a little smile of his own.

"Congratulations, Hawkjoy," he told her. "Have a chick and I'll even call you Hawkmother."

"Deal," she gestured back at once. "Now, we were about to get going?"

"The humans need to eat," Rikah insisted from the campfire. "We can wait a few more moments."

Jessika took the hint, going to fetch her seared piece of meat and juggling it between her hands while trying to take bites of it without burning her mouth. As soon as she, Rikah, and Karo were finished, they packed up the last of the baggage and prepared to lift off.

That was when Kassandra came walking quietly out of the trees, and everyone went as still as though she'd pulled their attention to her like wolves to the rising moon. No one moved as she paced up to Hawkjoy, hands cupped in front of her chest. She stopped and extended one hand. Jessika could see from her vantage that it held a white flower with several pointy petals and a golden center.

"We call it the misty starflower," Kassandra said, as though Hawkjoy had asked. "Congratulations, Hawksister, Hawkmother."

Jessika's throat choked with something that could have been happiness or could have been sadness, but she didn't know which: perhaps both. Hawkjoy lifted a hand to gesture her thanks, and then accepted the flower. She carefully reached out to preen a bit of Kassandra's black hair, cautious of the leaves and flowers the girl wore like clothing, and Kassandra showed no fear, just smiled up at her with her face glowing. Looking for a moment like the girl Jessika remembered, Kassie leaned in and scratched around Hawkjoy's neck ruff in return.

She didn't retreat into the forest after that, though. She walked instead over to Waterleap and extended her other hand to him. By stretching up a bit, Jessika could see that she had another misty starflower for the male griffin. He opened a hand to accept it, but looked down with confusion.

"Thank you, Hawksky, but I didn't do anyth—I mean, I'm just like I was, I didn't have a, ah," he waved a hand weakly towards Hawkjoy.

Kassandra's smile somehow didn't change, but equal measures of hurt and amusement crept into her eyes.

"Thank you," Waterleap assured her, perhaps noticing her reaction to his words. "Thank you. I've never had such a kind gift."

Kassandra smiled a little more, and then turned and trotted like a doe back into the forest. The spell she'd cast over everyone lingered a few moments longer. Then Hawkjoy placed her flower carefully into a little pouch on her harness. Waterleap followed suit.

"That was sweet of her," Hawkjoy gestured.

"I wonder why she gave one to Waterleap, too," Jessika mused.

"The males here in the Aeries are rather overlooked, aren't they? And they come to expect to be treated like that," Hawkjoy commented. "When I was a chick, my mother and father both were beloved and important, but in the Aeries, the males may not even know which chicks are theirs and all the excitement is about females awakening and becoming new matriarchs and adding chicks to their own Lines. I don't think Waterleap was expecting anyone to mark his first mating with so much as a word, much less a gift."

Hawkjoy followed as the griffins lifted one by one into the air, and Jessika could no longer see her hands to continue the conversation, but she'd certainly been given something to think about.

Chapter 4
The Trade City

It was three camps later that the group arrived within aerial sight of the trade city. It wasn't easy to miss. The city itself was larger than anything Jessika could remember ever seeing. At its center was a mound of slate-roofed, multi-storey buildings with a large garden in the middle of them. Surrounding that were wooden buildings no more than two stories high with small yards or corrals. Forming the next ring were rows and rows of densely packed tents, which were encircled by a high wall of stone. Beyond that were fields and pastures with farmhouses interspersed among them.

Three developed roads led into the city along with several other smaller roads that served the farms or ran off into the forest to the north. To the south of the city the forest became lighter and shorter, giving way to grasslands and scrub brush. A river ran north to south, paralleling the main road that went deeper into Northnest, entering the city, and exiting to the south in the form of a few smaller streams that vanished off into the grassland.

Thornfire brought the group to a hill that was high enough to overlook the city from a distance, and not so close that they'd be spotted. It was late afternoon when they landed, and they set about making camp among the trees.

"We may be here for a while, so let's make a solid camp," the mage instructed.

"I'll hunt," Thornspike volunteered and turned to go.

"Do not go near the city, Spike," Thornfire admonished as the slender griffin vanished into the underbrush.

"I guess I should wait to go down there until tomorrow," Jessika mused to Hawkjoy and Rikah as she picked a sheltered spot for her bedroll.

"Yeah, we'll go in the morning. I'll bring my carvings and see if I can trade some for money or proper clothes, so we'll blend in," Rikah said.

"And I suppose all griffins will need to stay here," Starbright contributed, having apparently overheard.

"Definitely," Thornfire agreed. "All griffins will remain undetected. We don't know if there are drakes down there."

Hawkjoy shivered. "I remember fighting drakes, that one time, when we were all little."

Jessika patted her shoulder. "Me, too. I think we both still have the scars."

They finished setting up their sleeping spots and campfire, and watched the city as the sky darkened, eating the meat provided by Thornspike. The city remained bright as lamps or candles were lit near windows. Rikah and Karo came to sit with Jessika on the rim of the hill while the griffins did their evening preening.

"We used to live in a place like that," Rikah observed quietly.

"Can either of you remember much?" Jessika wondered.

"I remember my father," Rikah said. "I remember him swinging his hammer, and the sound of metal hitting metal, and the smell of it, and the heat off the forge, hotter than any summer's day."

"I remember my mother," Jessika murmured. "I remember her smile. It was so kind. I remember her long blonde hair. I remember her leaning down to take my hand, or pet my face. And I remember my dad's thick brown beard. I used to like to pull on it when he held me."

"I can remember my mom, too, a little," Rikah added, voice getting a trifle thick. "I used to run up to her and hug her legs, and put my face into her apron. She always smelled like bread."

Jessika nodded, staring out at the city. She expected Karo to contribute a memory next, but he stayed silent. Karolan had never talked much about his life in Northnest. Unlike with Rikah and Kassandra, Jessika didn't know much about his past, because he was so silent on the subject.

"What do you remember from Northnest, Karo?" Rikah asked, and Jessika was glad he'd said it so she didn't have to.

"Not much," the younger boy grunted.

"You don't talk about it, I know," Rikah replied, "but you can, if you want to."

The apprentice mage picked up a stone and pitched it into the darkness. "I didn't live there very long. I came there from Lackland with my uncle, so I don't remember much."

Jessika was surprised. "I didn't know you came from Lackland."

"Well, it doesn't matter, does it?" Karo retorted. "We were all homeless after the invasion."

"You lived with your uncle? What about your parents?" Jessika asked.

"They were dead, weren't they," he said, not a question.

"Back in Lackland?"

"Yeah." He turned his head to glare at her, as if telling her to stop asking. Jessika took the hint.

"So we all lost everyone," Rikah soothed, "everyone but Hawkwind."

"Everyone but Hawkwind," Jessika echoed softly.

For a few minutes they sat in silence, just looking at the trade city.

"You really think you'll accomplish anything?" Karo grumbled eventually.

"I don't know," Jessika replied, assuming the question was for her. "Maybe if you help, Karo."

He just scoffed.

"Don't you care about our country?" Rikah asked.

"I don't know. It's not really my country, is it," again not a question.

"Then what are you going to do? Where do you want to live? What do you want out of life?" the older boy continued to press.

Karo toyed with another stone, bouncing it between his hands. "I want to be strong."

"Strong?" Rikah echoed.

"I want to be able to do everything Thornfire can do, and more."

"As a mage?" Jessika confirmed.

"Yeah."

"What for?" Rikah asked.

"I don't know, all right?" Karo reacted. "I just want to be able to. I'm going to bed."

He got up and strode back to the camp, leaving Rikah and Jessika alone. Rikah chuckled.

"Karo is, um, I'm not sure what he is," he said.

"I think he's trying to figure things out, just like us," Jessika suggested.

"I guess so." Rikah bumped his shoulder against hers. "Well, don't worry. Even if Karo won't come into the city, I'll go with you. I'll help you do whatever you want to do."

"Thanks, Dare," she said. "I appreciate that. I'm nervous. I don't want to go alone."

"I'm nervous, too. We can be nervous together."

Jessika smiled. "That sounds good."

The next morning saw Jessika and Rikah, with Karo trailing behind, walking down to one of the main roads to go into the city. They'd at first thought of taking a lesser road, but after a conference with the griffins, decided it would look suspicious. Strangers to the city would arrive by a main trade road. They weren't the only ones on the road. Horseback riders, carts, and even carriages passed them as they walked along one edge of the road. It didn't seem like many people came on foot.

Karo caught up as they approached the gate through which the road entered the city. Jessika stared up at the high wall; the griffins had nothing like this. Of course, walls meant little to creatures that could fly. She could vaguely remember being always surrounded by walls as a child; it somehow felt familiar and comforting.

There were two guards at the gate, which was wide open. The guards stopped and questioned most of the travelers as they reached the gate, but as Jessika and her young companions approached, the nearest guard just gave them a nod and waved them past.

They stepped into another world. The tents started immediately after the gate and were crammed in wall to wall. They came in a dizzying array of sun-faded colors, and the goods below them and people thronging the streets added so much to the cacophony of colors that Jessika stopped and reached out a hand in the hope of finding something to steady herself on.

She didn't touch anything, but Rikah grabbed her arm and pulled her out of the way of the crowds, into a corner formed by a tent wall and the stone city wall next to the gate. The three young people huddled there, disoriented by the rush and bustle. People were talking among themselves and haggling with the shopkeepers in the tents. Near and far, hawkers were shouting about their goods, trying to attract customers. Horses, goats, and other unseen animals bellowed their fear or objections, adding to the clamor, and Jessika had to resist putting her hands over her ears.

She looked away from the rippling agitation of the city as. The movement of the people seemed chaotic. They pushed this way and that, each person on their own trajectory, dodging others and adjusting their paths to get wherever they were going. Tent flaps shivered and belled in random breezes. Animals ridden, led, or driven by handlers added more variables to the interactions of the people.

The multitude of clothing styles and colors was mesmerizing, too. Jessika had usually only had natural fabrics to work with while making clothes, living with the griffins. One time she'd tried dyeing some fabric with flower petals, but it hadn't really done much. Almost none of these people were wearing plain fabric; they all had some color about them even if it was dull, and a good number of them had clothing that was almost blinding with bright reds, blues, oranges, and greens. A lot of them mixed colors in their outfits, too.

Then there were the scents. Animal sweat and dung were chief among them, and those were natural smells that weren't too startling, but there was a mess of mingling food scents, something sharp and acrid, flowery scents, and other smells that Jessika couldn't identify. Together, it made her nose burn and her eyes water a little. It even seemed she could taste them on her tongue.

"This is crazy," she managed to say to Rikah and Karo.

Karo had backed up against the wall and was staring out, as if in a trance. Rikah had sweat beading up on his brow. He glanced nervously out at the crowds and stayed close to Jessika.

"I didn't think it would be this intense," Rikah commented.

"We have to get through it," Jessika said.

"Where are we going? What are we doing?"

"You brought your carvings, right? We're going to try to trade them for clothing? Let's look for a clothing shop."

"Yeah, yeah, I did."

Jessika seized both of their wrists. "All right then, let's hold onto each other and stay close."

She turned around—dragging the boys along—and almost ran right into a brightly patterned shirtfront.

"Oh, pardon me," said a voice cheerful enough to match the clothing of its owner, "I just couldn't help overhearing you. It sounds like you're new in town."

Jessika looked up at a tall, thin man with fluffy grey hair and a sunburned nose. He smiled widely, showing discolored teeth.

"Allow me to show you around," the man went on. "I know all the best places to buy clothing, and all the shopkeepers, too. I'll help you get a good trade. After that, I can guide you to food or lodging, all well within your budget—"

"Hey," interrupted the gruff voice of the burly guard at the gate. "Move along Skinny Jin. Find someone else to swindle and rob."

The thin man's grin melted faster than candle wax in a flame, to be replaced with a grimace of anger, which in turn was rapidly swapped for a simpering smile.

"Me? Swindle? Rob? Just being a good citizen, sir, just trying to help newcomers," he wheedled, already retreating into the crowd. "Can't imagine what the problem with that is, sir. Meant no harm, no harm, but I'll be going then."

He slipped away like an eel into riverweed, and Jessika turned a puzzled gaze onto the guard.

"You'll find those in the city that'll take advantage of newcomers," the guard grunted, "and you three look pretty green. Are you in from a farm somewhere? First time here?"

Jessika managed a nod, "yes, sir."

He wiped some sweat off his cheek. "It's not my place to be guide and guardian to everyone that comes through the gate, but I can give you some quick directions. What are you looking for?"

"We need clothing," Jessika said nervously, not really wanting his attention drawn to it, but unable to turn away help from what seemed a safe sector.

"Buying with Northborn coin?"

"Northborn?" Rikah echoed.

"This country, lad." He waved vaguely. "Northborn."

"You mean Northnest," Jessika asserted.

The guard eyed her. "No, little lady," he said slowly. "It's Northborn now. I don't know where you're from thinking it's safe to call it, uh, call it what you called it, but it's Northborn."

Jessika clenched her jaw, but didn't argue. Meanwhile, Rikah had dug into his pack and pulled out one of his carvings, unwrapping it from the protective scrap cloth he had around it. He held it up for the guard to see. Jessika noticed it looked like a roaring ice-lion, and it was one of his better pieces. Spending every winter trapped in caves under several feet of snow and ice, carving up bits of wood was bound to make him skilled at it.

"We have carvings, more like this one," Rikah explained.

The guard raised his eyebrows. "Not bad, and I see a lot of goods come through here. Yeah, you can probably trade that for something. Finding a plain clothing maker who will trade for carvings, though, might be a bit of a challenge. There are shops that specialize in a variety of luxury goods that would stock fancy clothes and trinkets like this, but I don't get the impression you're looking for fancy clothes, and you would waste all your stock on a few deluxe bits of cloth."

"Can we just sell them straight for coins?" Rikah asked.

"Well," he scratched his neck, "vendors are supposed to have a license from the Trade Board. There are roaming vendors, but they aren't exactly legal. You'd probably be overlooked by the trade guards if you're just selling a few things one time, but you've got to worry about thieves and being taken advantage of, so I wouldn't recommend it."

The guard glanced over his shoulder and took a step closer. "Say, that's a handsome ice-lion, but do you happen to have anything that a little girl who loves horses might particularly like?"

That gave everyone pause, but Rikah dug in his pack after a moment, replacing the lion, and brought out a different piece. He held it up for the guard to look at. It was a sturdy but beautifully carved unicorn. There weren't any bits so delicate that they were likely to break off. Even the horn and ears were reinforced by the unicorn's artfully curving forelock.

"Ah," the guard sighed, "ah, that looks like just the thing."

He reached into a belt pouch and opened his hand to show an assortment of coins.

"Let me give you an idea what things are worth. There are four different Northborn coin types. These copper bits are the cheapest. Ten equal one of these square bronze ones. Ten of those equal a silver piece. Ten silvers equal a gold. You can find a basic meal for four coppers. A sturdy set of new simple clothing for one person shouldn't be more than two bronze coins. You can find cheaper if you buy used. A room in an inexpensive inn—but no so cheap that you wake up infested with bedbugs and fleas—will be three or four bronze coins, maybe five if meals are included. Don't let them try to triple it because there are three of you, unless you're taking three separate rooms. You got all that?"

Jessika's head was spinning a little from all the numbers and calculations, but she nodded. The guard continued, speaking directly to Rikah.

"Now, a nice, detailed wood carving like this, smooth and lacquered the way you've done it, could get you anywhere from several bronze coins to a silver and change. A bigger one will fetch more. Don't you accept less than that, hear me?"

"Yes, sir," Rikah said.

The guard's voice got a little hoarse and he shifted his weight awkwardly. "My little girl's birthday is coming up next month and I haven't yet gotten anything for her. She's old enough now not to break her toys with rough play, and she doesn't have anything nearly this fine. This unicorn here is a gift for a young lady, and she'll be that soon enough. If you're willing to part with something so beautiful, would you accept eight bronze for it?"

Rikah's jaw dropped, "yes, that would be great, thank y—"

The guard scoffed and raised his hands. "No, no, no, boy, don't accept the first offer. Haggle me up to at least a whole silver."

"Oh, ah," Rikah looked taken aback. "I, uh, no, I want a silver for it."

"Not like that," the guard sighed. "Like this. I appreciate the offer sir, but considering the time I put in on this piece, I can't let it go for less than a silver and two bronze. Say that."

Rikah repeated it back.

"And use some facial expression to show that you're flattered I want it, and feel bad that you have to decline my offer. I'll show you, and you try again."

Rikah obeyed, and the two men took a couple more minutes for practicing.

"Now, I say," the guard went on, "a silver and two bronze is a bit out of my price range, but I could do nine bronze—and now don't you accept that right away." He shook his finger at Rikah. "You have to go back and forth on this haggling thing a few times; at least that's how it's done here. When I saw your carving I had already decided I'd pay you around a whole silver for it, maybe a bit above if you were stubborn about coming down to a silver, and maybe you'd be letting me have a deal on it for a bit below a silver. I already established to you that I really want it by telling you about my daughter, so you can push me up a bit to a higher price and I'll tell you when you've gone too high. You have to act reluctant to let it go at all and emphasize how much it's worth to you, how much time you spent, how it's your favorite."

"Couldn't somebody pretend it's really bad work and try to convince me

I should sell it low?" Rikah asked.

"Of course. That's why you need to know what carvings like this usually sell for, and not go below that. Besides, if someone's telling you it's bad work but they still want it, well then it must be worth something, for them to be trying to buy it from you at all. Alright, now you try to haggle me up to a whole silver."

This haggling business was something griffins didn't do. For the most part, goods were held communally within the Line, and distributed as the administrators of the Line saw fit, based on requests from Linemembers. Over the whole Aerie, the Council distributed goods and raw materials. Some griffins did make finished goods that they traded and sold—there were even a few shop fronts—but haggling wasn't the custom.

At last, Rikah and the guard arrived on the price of a whole silver, and Rikah wrapped the unicorn carving back up and handed it over. The guard patted it fondly and stowed it carefully in a pouch.

"Thank you, young man," he said. "I'll give you eight bronze and twenty coppers, if that's alright with you. It will be much easier to spend than a whole silver, and less likely you'll lose it or have it all stolen. Now, there are three of you, so you each take some, so if one of you gets pick-pocketed, you won't lose it all."

"Pick-pocketed?" Jessika echoed.

The guard stared at her. "Where are you all from?" he asked, exasperated. "Having your pockets picked means someone you don't know sneaks up to you and secretly takes things out of your pockets without you realizing. Then, when you go to take out your money you find that it's gone. In this crowded marketplace it's easy for pickpockets to work, because everyone is so close together, and it's hard for the guards to catch them. You have to be careful to keep your stuff safe. Understand?"

The three of them nodded.

"Now here are your coins, young man," the guard said, counting out the money.

Rikah handed part to Karo and part to Jessika.

"Thank you, sir," he said fervently.

"Yes, really, thank you," Jessika agreed.

"You all be careful out there," he urged.

"Hey, Henrik," shouted the other guard from the opposite side of the gate. "Are you going to do your job today?"

"Coming, Standrey," he yelled back. "Now, if you walk to the east side of the city, you'll find the best prices on basic goods." He gave the three of them one last wave and walked back to his position.

"You have to help out every wet newbie from the farms, don't you?" the other guard chuckled.

"No, just getting my girl her birthday present," Henrik replied.

"Shopping while on the job, and from unlicensed roaming vendors? I'll have to report you, y'know."

"Yeah? And I'll report when you came to your shift drunk last week. How about that?"

The other guard, Standrey apparently, slapped a hand to his chest dramatically, while waving through a pair of horse riders. "You wouldn't."

"Sure would."

"Let's go," Jessika nudged the others. "That guy was really kind."

"I wonder why people haggle here?" Rikah said. "It doesn't really make sense to me."

"Me, either, but let's find a clothes shop. Go east, he said."

Together, the three of them fought through the crowds, trying not to be too dazzled by all the scents, sounds, and sights, until they reached an area with thinner crowds and plainer colors. The shops featured more barrels, crates, and sacks and fewer shiny, sparkling displays. They slowed their steps and looked more closely at the storefronts. At last, Rikah nodded at a big brown-dyed tent with shelves full of clothes and a few garments hanging on racks.

"Doesn't that look about right?" he suggested.

"Sure, let's go," Jessika declared before she could get too nervous to go in. "Remember, two bronze coins for a set."

She towed Karo and Rikah forward by their wrists. There were only a couple other people browsing under the tent, and within moments of entering, a sturdy-looking woman with grey hair bound back in a tail greeted them.

"Anything I can help you all with?" she invited.

"We all need sets of clothes," Jessika said, "just basic and well-made."

The woman smiled. "You're in the right place for that. We've nothing fancy, but for a good set of work clothes, I can fix you up proper. You certainly have interesting sets on at the moment."

"I made them," Jessika confessed, "but they're not really right."

"Well, they're just fine for starters," the woman soothed. "I've never seen cloth quite like this before, in fact. How fascinating. Now, let's start over here. Franklen," she called over her shoulder. "Come help these young gents."

A man whom Jessika guessed was her husband came sprightly hobbling from a back room of the tent. He adjusted his cap and scuttled over to the group, gave them a grin, and promptly guided Rikah and Karo off to the other side of the tent.

"Are you looking for skirts or trousers, dearie?" the woman asked Jessika.

"I'd like to blend in, just look like an average traveler, but trousers I guess. They're more practical for running and riding."

"Do you know your sizes?" The woman had gone right over to a shelf of trousers.

"Ah, no," she admitted.

"No worries, I've a good eye." The shopkeeper looked her over for a moment, and then nodded. "Try these. Do you need under-things?"

"No," Jessika assured her quickly.

One thing she had done was paid the healer-midwife Maryann, whom Rikah had met in a mountain village years ago, to acquire some proper under-garments for her, since they'd been so tricky to invent on her own. She'd been extremely careful about darning them at the first signs of wear, and so far they were still lasting her.

"And try this tunic," the shopkeeper went on. "It's a style common among all the nearest countries. The dressing room is over there. Come on out when you've got them on so I can see the fit."

Jessika did as bid, and as soon as she put them on she could tell the difference between her awkward attempts at garment construction and that made by the professionals, although the shirt was a bit baggy in some places. She emerged and the lady shopkeeper immediately nodded her head as if it were just as she'd suspected. She shoved a different tunic into Jessika's arms.

"This style is more common in Northborn, but it will flatter and fit you better, if you don't mind?"

Jessika took it dutifully and swapped. It did indeed fit better, and when she emerged again, the woman clasped her hands in victory.

"Lovely, lovely, a perfect fit," she said. "Come here to the mirror."

She led Jessika over to an object she hadn't seen since she was a child. Of course she'd seen her reflection in water, but it was different to see it in a vertical standing mirror. This one was only metal burnished to a highly reflective surface, but it was enough to make Jessika stand and stare at herself. She put her hand to her throat. Did she really have such serious, heavy brows, and such tight, pinched lips? Was her hair really that ragged and messy? She put her hand to her head, trying to stroke back her hair.

"You don't like them?" the shopkeeper asked, sounding worried.

Jessika shook her head in immediate denial. The clothes fit her well. She just hadn't realized that she looked like an adult now. She could see the line of her shape, and though she was lean and slender still, she'd gotten so tall. She was only a little above average for a female, she thought, but she was so much bigger than the last time she'd looked in a mirror and seen a little girl in a lacy dress.

"No, no, I like them," she told the anxiously hovering woman. "I do. They're perfect. I haven't had anything this nice in years."

"Not for summer festivals, or your coming of age celebration?"

"No, not where I live." Jessika brushed a hand gently down the tunic, and then tried to comb at her hair again with her fingers. "I guess I'm sort of grubby," she excused herself.

"I know a place you can get a trim, not too expensive," the woman offered.

"Um, yeah, I guess," Jessika nodded. "So, ah, I'd like these. How much?" She hoped she could remember the haggling rules.

"Let's wait until your—brothers?—are ready. Anything else I can get for you? The barber is fairly close. See that street? Take it down a few minutes walk. You'll see the sign on the left. It's a real wooden shop, not very big, called the Pretty Pony."

Jessika thanked the woman and went over to watch Rikah and Karo picking out their trousers and tunics. When they were done, Jessika was able to let Rikah do the haggling for all of them, which relieved her. They bundled up their old clothes into a sack and Karo hefted it on his back.

"If you ever have some extra yards of that strange cloth," the woman said as she saw them to the edge of the tent, "I'd give you a good price to get my hands on it."

"Thanks," Jessika told her. "I'll remember that."

"You folks have a lovely day then."

"Where now?" Karo asked, tugging at the hem of his new shirt.

"Um," Jessika prevaricated. "Do you want to get your hair cut, like properly?"

"Our hair cut?" Rikah echoed.

"Yeah. We always just hack it off with a knife, but we'd look more like we belong if our hair looked like people here."

"How much will it cost?" Rikah wondered, probably doing calculations in his head.

"Let's go find out."

Jessika grabbed their wrists again and towed them off in the direction the shopkeeper had described. It didn't take long to find the shop, and they came to a stop in front of it. The sign was decorated with a painting of a white horse head with a flowing mane.

"The Pretty Pony?" Karo asked with a dubiously raised eyebrow.

"That shopkeeper said it would be cheap. I'm getting my hair cut," Jessika declared.

"You want to look like a princess," Karo went on, under his breath.

Rikah elbowed him, though not very hard. "I'm hungry. We'll go get something to eat and come back."

"You should get your hair cut, too. You look messy," Jessika said.

Karo just rolled his eyes, but Rikah ran a hand self-consciously over his ragged head.

"Come on, Dare, let's get some food," Karo declared, and began striding away.

"We'll come back, and I'll bring you some," Rikah offered weakly, as he turned to follow the smaller boy.

Alone in the trade city, Jessika turned to the door of the shop and paused. Was she supposed to knock, or just walk right in? After a moment of hesitation, she settled for opening the door a crack and knocking on the frame. She stuck her head through the gap. The room at the front of the shop took up the whole width of the building. There were two stools to one side in front of a pair of mirrors—real mirrors made of glass. A few small tables accompanied the stools, and shelves lined the wall opposite the mirrors.

"Um, hello? Excuse me?" she called.

"Oh, be right there," a feminine voice called from some place in the back. "Do come in."

Jessika pushed the door the rest of the way open as a tall, elegantly slender woman emerged from a doorway in the back, drying her hands on a towel as she came.

"We don't often have custom this early in the day," the woman smiled, and Jessika was struck by how beautiful she was.

The woman wore a long pale blue dress with a white apron, and had a long black braid of hair thicker than Jessika's wrist. Her only jewelry was a necklace of grey beads that seemed to shimmer with faint rainbow colors. Her face was narrow with a rather sharp chin, and even sharper cheekbones, under a high forehead. Her eyes crinkled around the edges when she smiled, and her black brows arched like griffin wings. Her brown eyes glimmered, framed with long black lashes, and her skin was even richer and darker in color than Rikah's. Jessika couldn't remember ever seeing anyone so lovely--not that she'd seen many.

"Come in, come in," she chided. "What can I do for you?"

"I, uh," Jessika stuttered, fingers going up to fumble at her own roughly shorn hair.

The woman laughed, not unkindly, and patted the side of Jessika's head. "I can see. Someone's been trimming your hair with a knife, have they? There's enough here to work with; I can clean you up. Is that what you'd like?"

Jessika nodded, feeling painfully awkward, like something was sucking her confidence right out of her chest. Why was this so hard? This returning to humans, to the world she'd come from, was yanking all of her composure out of her, the way griffins pulled guts from their prey. She fumbled in her pocket for the rest of her coins.

"I," she choked, "I don't know. Is this enough?"

The woman tsked, "oh, now, come now." She put her other hand on the other side of Jessika's head and encouraged her to look up. "It's enough," she said firmly. "Whatever you have, you have enough, even if it's just one copper. First time in the city?"

Jessika bit her lip, suddenly feeling a lump in her throat.

"Rather overwhelming, isn't it?"

Jessika nodded.

"Here, can you hold this towel for me? It's just a bit wet with water. Sit there and I'll take care of one thing in the back and be out in a couple minutes. All right?"

Jessika clutched limply at the towel as the woman gave her a gentle pat and turned to go. She got to the stool the woman had indicated and managed to sit on it. Then she held the towel up to her mouth and swallowed a sob. The towel smelled clean, and vaguely like flowers. Some tears dripped and she let them, dabbing them up with the towel, until she could take deep breaths and get herself back under control. Just about the time she'd managed that, the woman returned, still smiling, and carrying a little wooden tray which she set down on a nearby table.

"I'll need that towel now, thank you," she said.

Jessika handed it over and the woman wrapped it snugly around Jessika's neck and shoulders.

"This will keep the bits of cut hair from falling down your collar and making you itchy," she explained. "My name's Delma. What's yours?"

Jessika started to give her name, and then caught herself. Was it still possible the people would remember there had been a child princess called Jessika?

"Hawkwings," she said.

"What a colorful name. I like it. It's a pleasure to meet you."

"And you," Jessika replied.

"So who's been cutting your hair for you?"

"Just me," she admitted.

"By yourself?" Delma was examining her head from every angle. "What sort of soap do you use on it?"

The four humans could remember from their early childhood being bathed with some kind of soap. Jessika in particular still had a memory of being in a tub of water and playing with soap bubbles, but she hadn't known how to make soap. Only since meeting Maryann had she been able to get the kind of simple soap that peasants used. It couldn't make soap bubbles, but it did help clean off skin oils and dirt.

"Just simple soap made by common people," Jessika answered. "Nothing special."

"That seems to be good enough. Your hair is pretty clean, but let me wash it with something special first, and then I'll trim it nice and even."

Delma took Jessika over to a sink with a chair that leaned back where she could have just her hair washed. Having someone else touch and wash her hair was a feeling she could hardly remember. Griffins could retract their claws, and did have thumbs, but their hands still were a little clumsy when it came to washing hair. As soon as the four children had gone to live with them, the boys and girls started washing each other or washing themselves without help. Jessika had taken over all her own hygiene long ago.

Delma's massaging fingers created sensations that tingled and rebounded and brought relaxation. The soap smelled of guava: a scent Jessika hadn't known she'd nearly forgotten. There were no guava trees in the griffins' mountains; the fruit came from much farther south, but she'd eaten it as a child. She suddenly recalled a garden with white benches and red flowers in green shrubbery, and a pink dress that she'd gotten dirty. She could almost taste the fruit and feel the juices running down her chin.

She sat up for Delma to dry her hair with several towels until it was nearly fluffy and then retook her seat on the stool in front of the mirror.

"So where are you in from?" Delma asked cheerfully.

"A little village in the mountains," she answered, figuring that was a mostly true and safe answer.

"I'm from a country south of Weldom. This place felt strange when I came here, too."

"Why did you come up here?"

Delma began carefully trimming Jessika's hair with a pair of scissors, holding some of it out of the way with little metal clips while she cut other parts. The soft, shimmery sound of the scissors was somehow soothing.

"There was some trouble in my country and many people were leaving," she explained. "We had a drought and the crops were dying. Then people started fighting over the remaining food. With my parents, we did what many people were doing; we went north, towards the water. Weldom wasn't accepting refugees, so we had to keep going, either into Lackland or North—well, at the time it was Northnest. Lackland was having some troubles, too, but we didn't know that we'd be coming into Northnest on the eve of a war."

"Were there signs? Was everything destroyed?" Jessika asked.

"I didn't see many signs. Somehow the conquerors had gone straight to the capital, but people were confused. I suppose up in the mountains you didn't know what was going on either."

"I was too young to remember much," Jessika said. "This is the first time I've been allowed to come to the trade city, and I'm wondering what the whole story is."

Delma gave a little sigh. "I'm not sure anyone knows the whole story, and I didn't live here for long before it all changed, but it seems now like it's peaceful enough. I married a Northborn man and my mother was granted permission to stay as well. My father passed away, sadly. The journey north was just so difficult. He sacrificed so much for my mother and me."

"Oh, I'm sorry to hear that. My father passed away, too."

"It is difficult to lose a parent," Delma agreed. "I'm almost finished here. It will look much tidier than before."

"So who changed the name to Northborn? And who is in charge now?" Jessika asked.

"The name change happened after the griffin revolt was put down. The king decided on the name change, and he's still in power. He seems a good king, if a bit, well, firm."

Jessika had almost jumped up, but managed to restrain herself. "The king is alive? And the griffins revolted? I never heard about that."

In the mirror, she could see that Delma had furrowed her brow a little. "They say the griffins did manage to kill the rest of the royal family, but the king survived. Luckily the mages and rainbow drakes arrived in time to save him."

"What?" Jessika uttered. "But, but the drakes attacked Northnest. They killed the royal family. The griffins were trying to protect them."

"There were some rumors like that at first, but people don't talk about it anymore," Delma nodded, still somber. "The king himself issued a proclamation. He said the griffins rebelled and tried to drive the humans from the kingdom, but his spies heard of the plot and he called for help. Only something else that could fly and fight, like drakes, was able to defeat the griffins."

"But, but," Jessika stumbled over her words. "That, that's not what happened."

Delma looked at her with sympathy. "There were lots of stories. Talking about anything other than the official story is discouraged, so you might want to be careful. We may never know the whole truth, but the country is peaceful now, I guess you'd say. There, finished. What do you think?"

Jessika first craned her neck up at Delma. "You'd say?"

"The drakes scare people, although they aren't around all the time. The mages scare people, too, and the peace-keepers are sometimes more violent than peaceful. But, how do you like your hair?"

Jessika swung around to look in the mirror. She felt her mouth open a little. In the new clothes, with her rough haircut all evened out and cleaned with something fancy that made it silky and smooth, she looked like a different person.

"I," she swallowed, mouth dry, "I look good, like I used to, like before." She touched her hair. "I look like a," she didn't finish. She didn't dare use the word 'princess.'

"Are your clothes new, too?" Delma asked, smiling again.

"I just got them. The shopkeeper said I should come here. She didn't tell me her name, but her husband—I think—was Franklen."

"Oh, Sherise," Delma clasped her hands. "She's a friend of mine. I'll have to thank her for sending such a lovely young lady to me. It's my joy to help people look their best."

"You did great. I could never cut hair this well," Jessika told her.

Delma pulled up a stool and sat facing her. She reached out and took one of her hands. "Listen, you're new in town, and you've heard a lot of different rumors. It's really a good idea if you don't talk about them."

Jessika gestured helplessly. "Yeah, the guard at the gate said the same thing, but Delma, I need to know."

Delma shook her head. "No, you don't need to know. Just live your life. Keep your head down and be good, and all will be well."

"But," Jessika grimaced, "I, no, it won't all be well. Don't you wish you knew everything that happened back in your country?"

"What would be the point?" Delma replied.

She sagged with frustration, holding back most of what she didn't think she should say, not knowing how to convince Delma.

"No one can ever know all of history," the woman told her gently.

"Where would I start if I wanted to, though?"

Delma's face was somber. "Really, you shouldn't go asking questions and digging into this. The peace-keepers will hear about it and come to discourage you. They don't like people causing dissention."

"You don't mind living with people who try to stop you from talking about things?"

Delma's brows lowered. "Well, it's not like we need to talk about the past, is it? It doesn't change the present."

"I guess not," Jessika agreed, "but if you found out that someone did something evil in the past, and now they're the ones in charge, wouldn't that change how you feel about being ruled by them?"

"I suppose it would," she allowed, "but if they aren't doing evil things now, it would be a lot of trouble to get rid of them. It could mean war."

Jessika looked away. That was basically the same thing Hawkwind had said. Was her need to find out what had happened and what was going on now really futile?

"Look, Hawkwings, I don't know everything," Delma said. "I just know what I've observed. My life here is better than I've ever had, so of course I don't want it to get worse, either from the peace-keepers or a war. You're right that evil people shouldn't be in charge, but sometimes we can't stop it, and sometimes we can't know who is really in charge or if they're evil or not. All we can do is try to live our lives."

Jessika nodded. Delma's words did make perfect sense, especially for someone without any power to change anything or ability to see the whole of the situation she was in.

A sudden heat rushed into Jessika's chest, and with it a fluttery butterfly feeling in her belly. Delma was one of her people, one of the citizens of her country that she was supposed to take care of. It wasn't Delma's purpose to do all the things Jessika was suggesting need be done—it was Jessika's purpose. That's why she was there.

"If there's something wrong," she murmured almost without conscious control, "I'll find it, and I'll make it right, so you can keep your good life, and make it better."

Delma looked puzzled, but tried a smile after a moment. "That's kind of you, but, be careful, Hawkwings."

"Yes, but, sometimes you have to do things, and you can't do them if you're always thinking about being careful."

Delma didn't seem very happy to hear that. "Well, you come back and see me anytime you need another haircut, alright?"

"I will. What do I owe you?"

Delma stood and put her stool away. "My usual fee is a bronze, but a few coppers would cover my basic expenses, and don't worry about it if it's beyond you right now."

"No, I can," she dug in her pocket. "I have six coppers."

Delma found another smile somewhere as she accepted them. "Thank you, dear, and please, do be careful."

Jessika smiled back at her. "I'll be as careful as I can be."

There was a knock on the door, and she turned to see Rikah and Karo standing outside. Rikah held up something that looked like it might be food in one hand.

"I need to go," she told Delma.

"Of course, thanks for coming by."

Now, Jessika didn't feel that good anymore. Somehow she'd soured Delma's sunny cheer, and fractured her own confidence, even as she'd realized her birth-duty.

"Thank you," she tried, slightly pleading, as she retreated towards the door. "I love my hair now."

Delma gave her a little smile again. "You're welcome."

Jessika turned and left, telling herself she wasn't running away.

Chapter 5
Quetal of Grace

The three of them had found a shady corner against one wall to cluster while Rikah shared out the snacks he'd bought.

"These are too sweet," Karo griped.

Jessika had swallowed down the sticky treat of mashed fruit in a bread-like shell, and sat now, back against the wall, knees pulled up, staring down at the dirt as though it had personally wronged her.

"What's wrong with you?" Karo went on, nudging her with his knee.

"Your hair looks really good," Rikah commented, mouth half-full of pastry. "We should all get our hair cut."

"I need to find out the truth," Jessika declared. "Where can we go, whom can I ask, to find out what happened when Northnest was invaded, and how things are being managed now, and who's managing everything?"

The two young men looked between each other.

"I don't know," Rikah said. "Should we ask whoever is in charge?"

"Do you think they'll tell us the truth?" Jessika countered, and she told them about what Delma had said.

"Then, would some historian know?" Karo suggested.

"Maybe," Jessika nodded, "but how do we find that person? Delma wouldn't really tell me where to go looking for answers."

"Answers? I have answers, all the answers you'll ever need," cajoled a voice from behind them.

Rikah and Karo rounded on the owner of the voice and Jessika looked up. Fluffy grey hair and a sunburned nose topped the thin body of the man who had accosted them at the gate a while ago.

"That guard called you Skinny Jin, right?" Rikah identified. "What do you want?"

"It's not what I want," the man simpered, "it's what you want and how I can help you. I hear you're looking for answers? Pray, tell me your questions; I'll tell you the answers."

"That guard must have chased you off for a reason," Rikah said, eyes narrowing. "I don't think we want your help."

The man giggled—a distasteful sound. "What other help do you have to turn to?"

"You'll try to cheat us," Karo accused.

"How unfair of you to judge me before you even know me," he scowled. "Tell you what: I'll answer your first question for free. No strings, no cheating, no fee. You don't even have to ask me additional questions. I'll just answer your one question to the best of my ability and be on my way. Once you've verified my honesty by investigating the answer yourself, I trust you'll come seek me out with further questions, and then we can negotiate a fair fee. How does that sound?"

Rikah looked dubiously back down at Jessika where she still sat. Skinny Jin was mostly right: what other help did they have?

"Very well," she said slowly, trying to pick her words with care. "Where can I find this city's most knowledgeable historian?"

Skinny Jin blinked with what seemed to be surprise. "A curious question," he mused. "What sort of history are you interested in?"

"That of the last twenty years," Jessika clarified.

The man put his hands together, drumming his fingertips lightly against each other, and regarded her seriously. "You seek dangerous knowledge."

"Do I?" she pressed back.

"I'm not sure there are any in this city with all the information you seek," he said.

"I didn't ask for someone who knows everything, just the most knowledgeable," Jessika insisted.

"So you did, so you did, young lady." The thin man smiled, but it looked a shade nasty. "One wonders why you wish to know such things."

"It's none of your business," Rikah put in. "You're just going to give us an answer so we can see how good your answers are, before we bring more questions to you. Remember?"

"A sharp young man," Skinny Jin smiled more widely. His eyes darted about and he licked his lips with what seemed a bloodless tongue. "Such knowledge as you seek can get you in trouble if you advertise that you know it, deeper trouble if you discuss it too widely. I will advise you to be cautious little newcomers, but if you wish to know, it is Quetal of Grace you must seek out."

"I asked you where I can find that person," Jessika reminded him.

"So you did, so you did," he whispered, looking somewhere between angry and scared. "Go to the fortunetellers' district and look for the sign. Do not speak of how you know. Do not give my name. Do you understand?"

"Alright," Jessika agreed. "Thank you."

"You thank me now," he sneered. "Keep your mouths shut, or you'll not thank me from the inside of a kill-pot."

Without another word, the man swept away, only casting one look over his shoulder at them before his fuzzy gray head vanished into the crowd.

"That guy's sort of messed up," Karo commented. "Are we going to follow his advice?"

"It's all we have to go on," Jessika shrugged.

"He could be sending us into a trap or something," Karo went on.

Jessika pushed to her feet, brushing off her clothes. "Nothing ventured, nothing gained," she declared. "That's what Thornwing always says."

"Thornwing spent a number of years imprisoned by the talis," Karo reminded her sharply, "after one of his ventures."

"Which led to the liberation of the Snow-in-lee griffins," Jessika countered. "Let's go."

They had to ask three people for directions until they found the fortunetellers' district, and afternoon was wearing on. It turned out to be a narrow alley on the edge of the area of wooden buildings, and was the gaudiest area they'd yet seen. Most of the buildings had been painted with wild colors and some had colorful awnings or banners out front, too. Paper lanterns hung from any available protrusion, fighting for space with wind chimes of metal, wood, pottery, and—was that actual bone?

Each building had carved or painted signs on the front or hanging with the lanterns and wind chimes. Jessika led the group down the alley, reading each sign as she went, and silently thanking Hawkwind for teaching her Northnest writing along with griffin writing. Near the end of the alley was the sign she was looking for.

"Quetal of Grace," Rikah read aloud. "This must be the place."

The building was narrow, painted plum purple, with faded blue banners and a pair of yellow lanterns hanging out front.

"He sent us to a fortuneteller?" Karo scoffed. "We want the past, not the future."

"Let's go in." Jessika led the way.

The door stood open, propped by what looked like a stone carved into the shape of a human skull. Just inside, shelves and narrow tables crowded both sidewalls, each jammed full of trinkets and statuettes, pendants, bracelets, crystals, and scrolls. The back of the entry room was curtained behind another table. Within moments of their entry, the midnight blue curtains flew open and a person—presumably the shopkeeper—emerged with a flourish to face them.

"Welcome, welcome," the personage greeted earnestly, hands clasped.

Jessika paused, taking a moment to assess, as she found she couldn't quite identify the shopkeeper's sex right away, but decided it must be a female, based on the long hair and lack of any sign of facial hair.

The shopkeeper was fairly young and not particularly tall, and wore a few layers of overlapping colorful clothing, although none of it looked like anything fancy: no silk or satin or anything like that. Jessika could spot trousers under a split skirt, with a long shirt and patterned robe over everything, festooned with multiple heavy necklaces. Below a faded green, misshapen knit cap, her hair spilled out in long black sheets, immaculately straight and clean. Her face was friendly, but not effusive.

"What can I do for you?" the shopkeeper asked. "Amulet or advice?"

"Ah, we were looking for Quetal of Grace," Jessika said.

"And you've found her," the woman nodded. "Now what?"

Jessika took a breath to brace herself. Meanwhile, Rikah had turned aside, looking at a row of carved wooden animals on one of the shelves. Jessika rather wished he'd stayed focused on their task at hand.

"I heard you know about the past," Jessika began.

"Quetal of Grace knows everything," the shopkeeper smiled.

Jessika gestured weakly at the shop in general. "I don't really mean fortunetelling. I'm looking for someone who can tell me what really happened when Northnest was invaded, and what the situation is now. Who's in charge, and why?"

The shopkeeper's smile faded with every word, but didn't disappear entirely. She opened her mouth to talk, but Jessika beat her to it.

"I know, I know they're dangerous questions. Everyone keeps telling me that," she said.

The shopkeeper shut her mouth, took a breath, and spoke. "I'd say the answers are more dangerous than the questions."

"But you know them, and they haven't hurt you," Karo pointed out.

"I wonder whom you've been talking with, that they sent you to me. I don't advertise for anything other than protective amulets and fortunetelling. I don't think I can help you. Are you interested in a guardian animal totem?" she asked towards Rikah.

The young man turned. "Ah, no, sorry, not really. I was just seeing what animals you have, and comparing them to my carving."

"Ah, you carve as well? My supplier is a fellow out of Lackland. He comes up here a couple times a year."

"You don't have any griffins," Rikah said.

Quetal's brows lowered. "I'd not be so bold as to sell griffin statues."

"Are you sure?" Rikah pulled his pack off and extracted one of his rag bundles. He unwrapped it and set its contents on the sales table.

It was a carving of Thornwing; Jessika recognized him at once without any fur and feather coloration. Rikah's skill was so great that he'd captured Thornwing's exact proportions and personality. Quetal of Quetal's rapidly indrawn breath at the figure's emergence was audible. She picked up one of the scraps of rag and used it between her fingers and the wood to gently rotate the carving on the tabletop. With her other hand she drew out a small hand lens, and bent forward to examine the details of the face.

"It looks real," she murmured. "How can you create such a thing?"

She gazed up at Rikah from her half-crouched position with wonder radiating from her eyes.

"And how do you dare?" she went on breathlessly.

"Trade secret," Rikah demurred. "You can have it, if you'll help us."

"Have it? Even hiding this in my home would be dangerous. I'd never dare show it to anyone."

"But you could see it, every day."

Her expression of amazement soured. "This is bribery."

"No," Rikah denied, "just due payment for information that is difficult to come by, and something to remember us by, to remember the time you helped some young people who really needed your help."

"Please," Jessika tried. "Please tell us. I need to know."

Quetal of Grace eyed her dubiously. "Why?"

"I want to know what happened."

She shook her head. "That's not an answer. What are the consequences if you don't find out this information?"

Jessika lifted a hand helplessly. What were the consequences? Well, she supposed there weren't any really, except that nothing would change, but she wracked her brain.

"Wrongs might go unrighted," she said finally. "The truth may never be known. Evil people might remain in power. I," she pressed a hand to her chest, and caught herself. "I might never know if," she didn't know how to finish.

Quetal had watched her every move, and seemed to be shrewdly reading her emotions. She eyed the intricate griffin statue again, taking in the perfection of every feather and contour of every muscle.

"Who are you?" the woman asked.

"Hawkwings," Jessika said. "Hawkdare, Hawkrain," she introduced.

Quetal's eyes narrowed. "A partial truth: interesting."

Jessika's breath caught.

"But my name is a partial truth as well," the shopkeeper confessed.

"We used to live in Northnest," Jessika admitted, "before the invasion."

"You must have been quite young."

"Yes."

"Now you're coming back. You seek to regain some kind of honor," she murmured, eyes narrowing. "You want revenge."

Jessika gulped a little, and looked between her Linebrothers. "It won't hurt to just talk, right? They're just words."

"And you're going to keep asking for this information until you get it, aren't you? You are willing to trade a masterwork that could have brought you several gold—if it were sellable in the current market. You're going to get yourself in deep trouble." She made a sound somewhere between a sigh and a growl. "You are risky people to have in my shop," Quetal went on.

For several long moments she stared down at the griffin statue, as if it were telling her what she should do. At last she sighed, wincing away like she might from seeing a farm animal killed.

"Very well," she whispered. "I'll accept your bribe. Pick that up for me and come into the back."

The shopkeeper stepped through the curtain and held it open. Jessika followed before she could stop and be indecisive or jump with happiness. Rikah bundled the carving back into its cushioning rags, and he and Karo followed her. They found themselves in a room draped with more of the dark blue fabric the curtains were made from. A round table sat in the middle, draped with the ubiquitous fabric and surrounded by a half dozen wooden stools and one upholstered chair. A lantern hung from the center of the room.

"Sit," Quetal ordered, and they obeyed.

Rikah set the carving down for her, opening the rags so the lantern light cast strong shadows on it that made it look almost alive. The woman sat opposite them in the chair and steepled her fingers under her chin.

"Listen to me," she began softly. "What happened to Northnest years ago was a tragedy. Many lives were lost and the government was destroyed. There were few survivors and most of them fled, disappearing into the general populace and hiding their identities."

"I heard a rumor the king is still alive," Jessika whispered intently at her.

"That appears to be true. I have seen him, although from a distance," Quetal confirmed.

That news hit Jessika like a heavy weight and sunk deep into her belly, both cold and hot at the same time. She couldn't decide yet how to feel about it.

"Then why is he working with the invaders?" she demanded.

"That is where the confusion begins," Quetal nodded. "The official story is that the griffin Feathyrs were plotting to destroy the royal family, and expel all humans from as much of Northnest as possible, and retake the territory for themselves."

"But that doesn't make any sense, and it's not true," Jessika objected.

"Keep your voice down," Quetal admonished her. "Supposedly, the royal family's spies learned of the plot and the king secretly called for help. The wizards and drakes arrived and put down the revolt, killing or capturing all the Feathyrs, but only the king managed to survive."

"All the other royals were killed?" Jessika asked.

"I witnessed the burial. The caskets were all closed, but there was one for every member of the family, except the king," Quetal explained, eyes narrowed suspiciously. "Of course that means nothing, as I can detect you've guessed."

"You said some Feathyrs were captured," Rikah prompted. "What happened to them?"

Quetal shrugged. "I do not know. There have been no griffins in Northnest—or rather, Northborn—since then. By now I assume any captives have been killed."

"Are there still drakes?" Karo asked.

"For some years after the, hm, event, drakes were common. There were garrisons of them all about the country, but they were gradually removed as the populace settled down and showed fewer signs of discontent."

"So there was rebellion at first?" Jessika jumped on the hint.

"Some places had to be pacified," Quetal nodded. "People had to be convinced to accept the official story."

"But what's the real story then? We know the Feathyrs weren't planning anything like that," Jessika said.

"The real story," Quetal of Grace breathed, now sitting back. Her eyes went slowly between each of them, lingering on their faces as if examining something there. "You're playing a foolish game. You are all going to get into trouble, and by telling you things, I am getting myself into it, too, when I decided to get out of it a long time ago."

"We won't tell anyone about you," Jessika promised.

Her eyes went out of focus. "That's irrelevant. It is too late. It is already beginning."

Jessika glanced at her companions, who both shrugged in confusion. "What do you mean?" she asked.

Quetal closed her eyes. "I can see things. That's why I'm a fortuneteller."

"Are you a mage?" Karo asked.

She shook her head. "It's not the same thing," she said quickly. "Besides, there are no mages in Northnest, Northborn. That's why there was no one to stop the wizards when they brought in their rainbow drakes. Didn't you know that?"

"Um," Jessika mumbled.

"I saw it coming, and could do nothing to stop it," Quetal grimaced, opening her eyes again. "It is always that way." She leaned forward intently. "I was advisor to the royal family, even young as I was. My parents saw to it that my gifts were put to use and gave me to serve. I knew something was coming and I tried to foresee enough to stop the invasion, but I couldn't do it. I was too young still. I had not yet developed the skill to control my talents. Even now, I cannot see everything."

She reached out and grabbed Jessika's hands. "Listen to me. Listen quickly. They are already on their way. I will see you out the back in just a moment, and then you must vanish wherever you can."

Jessika nodded without really understanding, disconcerted by how hard Quetal of Grace was gripping her fingers. Her gaze bored viciously into Jessika's eyes.

"You will go to the capital. You will find a woman called Chika. She will show you the secret ways into the palace. If you want to know all, that is how you will do it, but listen, girl. If you do this, you will suffer and bring suffering to others. I cannot tell how much or how far it will spread."

Quetal's eyes went out of focus again.

"You wish to know if your father yet lives," she whispered. "You will learn, but not without price."

The shopkeeper's eyes came back into focus and she stared at Jessika again, shaking her head as if to clear it.

"The real story," she went on, "the wizards came here. They wanted something they could only get here, and they found it. That much I know. What it is exactly, you will have to discover for yourself. When I try to see it, I see only darkness and torchlight."

Quetal gripped Jessika's hands so hard she nearly gasped with the pain. The shopkeeper's expression was fierce, and Jessika tried to recoil.

"You," Quetal breathed. "You must go now. Hurry."

She let go, and Jessika surged to her feet. Quetal of Grace's arm shot out, pointing the way to the back of the shop.

"Thank you," Jessika tried to say, but Quetal was already shaking her head, standing up and stumbling towards her storefront.

"Come on," Rikah urged, leading the way through a gap in the curtains.

The building didn't have a large footprint. As they passed through the curtain, they saw only a tiny kitchen with a basin, small stove, a table pressed into one corner, and another stool. In another corner a ladder led up through a trapdoor in the ceiling, to the second floor. A narrow door opposite the curtains opened onto a tight brick-laid pathway between the rows of buildings

Quetal
of Grace

just large enough for a person to pass through.

It was dark back there, hidden among the shadows of the tall, crowded buildings and not much illuminated by the late afternoon sun. Rikah was still leading and was first out the door, but he went only a few steps before rebounding off of something in his path.

"Stay where you are," a gruff voice ordered.

Jessika and then Karo ran into Rikah's back, knocking him again into the massive man standing in their way. They backed off, trying to turn and go back into the shop, but Karo exclaimed in surprise and stopped short.

"We just want a word," a second voice said.

They were surrounded. They couldn't go back; a pair of large men in formal-looking grey uniforms had blocked the path behind them into Quetal's shop, and the one in front of Rikah took up the whole walkway forward.

"We haven't done anything wrong," Rikah declared. "Let us pass."

"Calm down, young sir," the first man barked. "You'll just come with us for a chat, so we can all understand everything."

He reached for Rikah's arm, and Rikah snatched it out of his grasp, but the man was not to be deterred so easily; he grabbed again, catching Rikah's wrist and giving it what seemed to be a simple sort of twist, and then Rikah's knees were buckling as he cried out in pain and tried to wriggle away.

"Cooperate with us and everything will be easier," the man growled.

Jessika looked frantically around at the big, burly men closing in on them, trying to think of a way out.

"Wings, get away," Rikah cried as the man's grip forced him towards the ground.

Jessika sent a swift glance at Karo. The young mage had turned around to face the two men behind him and raised his hands, although he didn't seem to be making any kind of magical effect that she could see.

Get away? How was she supposed to do that? And how could she leave her Linebrothers?

"Go," Rikah demanded again.

The man holding him had reached down to grab his other arm now, starting to get him back to his feet but in firm custody.

"Just stay calm, miss," Rikah's captor grunted. "I'm not hurting him."

The twisting of Rikah's face said differently. Behind her, she saw that the two men facing Karo were not attacking, but neither was Karo doing anything other than glaring at them—but then Jessika saw his hands move.

"Climb up the wall to the roofs," he gestured, using Snow-in-lee griffin sign language. "I'll drop down and boost you up."

Jessika looked at the wall. It was indeed rough, with many protrusions and gaps between boards. She could probably climb it. It would mean leaving Rikah, but maybe she could come back and save him somehow. Would Karo be able to follow, or would they grab him? Rikah's captor had him on his feet now, held quite securely. He looked straight at her eyes.

"Do it," he choked out.

Jessika bit her lip. "Alright, now, Rain," she shouted.

Karo yelled out, and a piercingly bright flash lit the whole scene, but the two men he faced took the most of it right in the eyes. Then Karo whirled, dropping down to one knee, hands open and ready to receive Jessika's foot. She planted it there, bobbed once, and then vaulted upwards. Karo grunted as he shoved up, giving her a couple feet of extra distance.

Jessika scrabbled at the wall as she heard below her the sounds of Karo being subdued. Desperately she reached for higher handholds, searching blindly for footholds as she did. She made it up another few feet, and was just thinking she might be out of reach, when she felt someone grab her ankle and yank.

There was no way she could hold on with just fingers and toes against that. Jessika came off the wall, shouting with panic as she fell, but hard arms caught her and pulled her against a solid chest. She thrashed, kicking back with her heels, jabbing back with her elbows, and slamming her head back futilely against the man's collarbones.

"Little wench," he growled as some of her strikes left bruises.

"Damn fools," one of the other men scolded. "You'll have it worse for all this resisting."

Amid her struggles, she saw that Karo and Rikah both had their hands bound behind them now. One of the men was restraining both of them. The third man approached Jessika and her would-be captor.

"Don't make me hurt you, little lady," he said, looking almost reluctant.

"Let us go," Jessika shrieked at him. "We didn't do anything."

His hand snapped out, faster than she could dodge and caught one of her wrists. Then he caught the other with his other hand. She tried to wriggle her slender wrists out of the grip of his big hands, but now he twisted just a bit, and somehow that was all it took; sharp warning pains shot up Jessika's arms: her body telling her that her bones weren't supposed to twist that way, that they'd break if it went on.

"No," she cried. "Ow, stop."

"You stop, and be good," the man said in reply.

The man holding her set her down, and the twisting of her wrists drove her down to her knees, tears starting to bud from the pain.

"That's a good girl."

Arms still twisted, he got her bound like her Linebrothers, and then forced her back to her feet. The three of them were marched down the narrow path until a cross path led them back to fortuneteller's alley. There waited two more men in the same grey uniforms. With them was Quetal of Grace, bound up just like Jessika and the others. Before Jessika could say anything, a sharp look and a faint shake of Quetal's head stopped her.

"What happened to you, Derot?" laughed one of the men holding Quetal.

"Shut it, Vert," the man Jessika had thrashed with feet and elbows spat back.

"Did the children hit you?" he chortled. "Can't handle a few little babies?"

"I said, shut it."

The five men brought the group together and began marching them off down the alley. They walked long enough for the sun to begin to sink, passing through the area of wooden buildings and deeper into the city, where the wood gave way to stone. At last they approached the monstrous edifice of central buildings.

Their five guards took them around the border of the conglomeration of structures to one particular set of stairs that went up through an archway. Stone statues of snarling drakes guarded the stairs on plinths on each side. By glancing around, Jessika reassured herself that there weren't any real drakes hiding in the shadows. Without a word, the four prisoners were marched up and through the doorway at the top.

The doorway opened onto a hallway watched over by a pair of guards dressed in grey uniforms with black trim. Their captors didn't hesitate, leading them right down the hall, which shortly opened into a room staffed by yet more officers. Jessika wondered just what all these people were—perhaps these were the so-called peace-keepers? Their captors paused at a wide desk where a stern woman whose grey uniform had a lot of black on it was sitting.

"Dissension and conspiracy towards disruptive behavior," the man who had initially grabbed Rikah said without preamble.

"Interrogation and reeducation recommended?" the woman queried in a bored, nasally voice.

"To be determined after review, I suppose."

"Detention rooms seventeen and eighteen," the woman said, scribbling notes into a book. "Submit your reports for review and stand by for further questioning and reassignment."

"Aye, ma'am."

Their captors urged them off in a different direction, through a few doorways and halls until they reached a long corridor with a couple dozen doors leading off it. They were prodded down the hall to a pair of doors: the two men to one door, the two women to the other.

"Please, sirs," Jessika said as the doors were being unlocked. "Will you tell us what's going on, why we're here? We haven't done anything wrong."

"Dissenters require correction," one of the men grunted. "You'll be here until it's decided how much correction you need."

"We have things to do," Rikah said. "We can't just sit here. We need to get going."

"You'll sit here for as long as we say," another guard declared.

"How long will that be?" Jessika asked.

"However long it is. It's not our decision. The higher-ups will decide. Now get in."

"But—" Jessika didn't get to finish.

The guards pushed them, physically, into the open doors. Rikah turned about and tried to push back and a guard shoved him.

"Behave and I'll unbind your hands," the guard scolded. "Otherwise you can sit with them like that."

"Do as they say," Quetal of Grace murmured, the first thing she'd said since they were captured.

Rikah glared and scowled, but complied.

"That's a good young sir," the guard said as he removed the bindings.

Another push, gentler this time, sent Rikah into the room with Karo. Jessika had one last glimpse of their faces before the guards nudged her and Quetal into the other room. The door was shut and locked behind them. Jessika rubbed her sore wrists and looked around the little stone cubby of a room. She and Quetal had it to themselves.

There was a hole in the floor in one corner—from which the privy stench was coming—and a bench along each wall. Beside the door was a basin full of water, with a spout above it. Opposite the wall with the door were several slots near the roof, for air circulation, she supposed. Light trickled in the slots, but there was no other light source.

Quetal went to a bench and sat, putting her head in her hands. "I should have turned you away, but I hoped they wouldn't come in time. Who sent you to me? Whoever it was betrayed us both."

"A guy called Skinny Jin," Jessika answered.

Quetal lifted her head with an expression of disbelief. "You should have paid him more."

"He didn't ask for payment."

Quetal just stared at her. "He gave you something for free, and you didn't question it?"

"Uh." Jessika didn't know how to respond. Hearing Quetal say that, it did sound stupid, but it hadn't seemed stupid at the time. Jessika took a seat opposite her. "So what do we do now?"

She spread her hands. "We wait. The peace-keepers will decide what to do with us, just as they said. They'll probably question all of us individually and decide how dangerous to the peace each of us is."

"Then they're going to punish us somehow?"

"Possibly. They might just detain us for a while to try to teach us a lesson not to talk about things they don't like. They might also lecture us and we'll have to admit we were wrong and agree verbally with their version of events."

"But they aren't true," Jessika protested. "We know what happened. We were there."

"Yes, but they don't care, and they won't let us go until they make us into liars just like them. The only way out of this is to speak words that aren't true." She shook her head a little. "I don't like it either. I've had to do it in the past, but you can sort of forgive yourself for it if you think of it as saying things to trick them, instead of thinking of it like lying or giving in."

Jessika had a sudden fear and looked around nervously. "Do you think they're listening to us now?"

Quetal sat up a little and looked around, too. "I don't think so," she said, but she didn't sound certain. "That sounds like a lot of effort. They'll get to hear us when they question us, and they don't really care what we say; they'll punish us however they like, regardless."

"Oh."

For a few minutes they sat in silence, staring at the floor. Jessika was trying hard not to get too panicked. They couldn't stay here. Thornfire and Hawkjoy and the others would worry when they didn't come back. What if they were kept here for weeks, or longer?

"How do we escape?" Jessika asked in a whisper.

Quetal slowly looked up at her. "Escape? We can't."

"I have to get out. There are people waiting for me. They'll wonder where I am."

"They'll just have to wait. I have a business to run, but there's nothing I can do, either. My neighbors will keep an eye on my shop, but I'll just have to accept the lost sales. It'll be easier if you accept what you can't change."

Jessika bit her lip. What would Thornfire do when they didn't come back? Surely the griffins wouldn't come looking for them—that would endanger them, too. They couldn't even send Kassandra, not with the way she—dressed wasn't the right word, but—the way plants grew out of her skin now. Was there any way to contact Thornfire? Jessika couldn't think of anything.

"It's nightfall," Quetal announced, getting up to take a drink from the basin of water. "I'm going to sleep."

She returned to her bench and lay down.

"Good night," Jessika murmured weakly.

With nothing else to do, she lay down, too, and closed her eyes. Eventually, she fell into a restless sleep.

A hatch opened on the bottom of the door and a tray was pushed into the room. The noise woke Jessika from her fitful sleep. Her back hurt, and her shoulders and hips and head, from lying on the hard bench. She was cold, too. By the time she managed to sit up, groaning, the hatch had been shut.

Quetal of Grace was stirring, and once she opened her eyes, Jessika caught her attention.

"Food, it looks like," she said.

"I guess we should split it," Quetal grunted. "Starving won't accomplish anything."

There were two bowls of some kind of thick, soupy grain and an apple apiece. Breakfast, it seemed.

"Take a little bite of the apple with each spoonful of porridge," Quetal advised. "It'll make it taste better."

Jessika followed her advice. The porridge was indeed tasteless and gummy, but the sweetness of the apple made it palatable. As they were part way finished with the food, Jessika pricked her ears at the muffled sound of raised voices. Quetal arched her eyebrows at it, too.

"Sounds like they're starting with your," she tilted her head enquiringly, "brothers?"

"Yes," Jessika confirmed.

Quetal shrugged. "They don't look anything like you, especially that Hawkdare. Adopted brothers?"

"Yes," she admitted reluctantly. "We grew up together, in the same family, so we're as good as siblings."

"After the invasion of Northnest, I'm assuming."

Jessika buttoned her mouth. Quetal was too good at getting information out of her. She'd have to learn better.

"How did you escape?" the fortune teller went on.

"I can't talk about it," Jessika said.

Quetal shrugged again. "You had better keep all that information to yourself, and you'd better hope your brothers are doing the same. If the three of you give different stories to the peace-keepers, they'll know you're lying."

"What should I say?"

"Stick to pleading for mercy," Quetal said. "Emphasize how silly and ignorant you are. Tell them you're young, never been in a city before, and didn't know better, but don't give them any details. If they start pressing you for them, cry and say you're scared and sorry. The only details you can give are things you did in the city yesterday."

She gestured with her spoon. "Don't talk about where you come from or why you wanted to know about the past. Talk about how overwhelming the city was. Talk about the things you saw that confused you. Talk about how scary Skinny Jin was, if you want. I know the man only vaguely. He's always getting in trouble for theft or scams. He must have turned you in as a chance to score some points with the guards."

She sat back and tossed her spoon into her empty bowl. "That's the best I can advise. I hope your brothers keep their mouths shut, or are smart enough to play stupid."

Jessika swallowed down a big mouthful of apple and porridge. "I hope so, too."

"We can practice. I'll pretend to be the interrogator, and you pretend to be silly and scared."

She looked up hopefully. "Really? We can do that?"

"Sure. Finish your food and we'll get to it. Then you'll be all ready when they come to fetch you."

So Jessika practiced, and waited, and practiced some more, but the summons to tell her story and play-act a silly-scared girl did not come. The morning progressed into afternoon and then evening. Eventually, out of sheer boredom, she got up and did some exercising, only to realize afterwards that she'd gotten herself all sweaty and there was hardly any way to clean up, and no clean clothes to change into either.

After that, she and Quetal shared songs they knew with each other. Quetal knew a lot more than Jessika did, so one woman taught the other and they sang until their voices started to get hoarse. Interspersed with that, they spent long hours staring at the floor or ceiling or walls. Quetal did not ask her more questions about her past, although she sensed from the sidelong glances that the fortune teller might want to.

Around dusk another tray of food was shoved into the room, and Jessika hopped up and ran to the door.

"Please, how long are you keeping us here? There are people waiting for me," she called out.

There was no response, and though she kept trying for another minute to get some answers, no one deigned to reply. Frustrated, she snatched up the tray and brought it to Quetal's bench. She put it down between them and they each picked up a bowl. Dinner was apparently stew: there were chunks of vegetables, mostly potatoes and other roots Jessika couldn't identify, mixed with beans and just the faintest hint of shreds of meat. It had gotten cold, but was surprisingly filling and not entirely bland. There was even a hard lump of bread for each of them to dip into it. After eating, they used the bowls to scoop out water from the basin for drinking.

The daylight was fading as Jessika sat back on her bench, seething with annoyance, but at least not hungry. She rubbed her face and couldn't restrain a growl.

"Maybe tomorrow," Quetal said quietly.

Jessika ran her fingers into her hair; it was getting grubby. Despite the food she felt light-headed. "No," she groaned. "How are we just supposed to sit and wait? Even if I didn't have people missing me and things I want to do, how do we keep from going raving mad in here?"

"They keep you for a while so you'll do anything to get out," Quetal offered. "It's part of their breaking process. I've never heard of them using physical abuse to make their prisoners submit, but keeping you penned up works on your mind without leaving evidence of damage on your body."

Jessika ran her hands back down her face and covered her eyes with her palms. "This must be how Hawkjoy felt, all her life trapped in Snow-in-lee, but then maybe if you're born into it, it feels normal," she muttered.

Quetal didn't respond at once, but then she asked. "Who's Hawkjoy?"

Jessika caught her breath. Oops. "From a legend," she said quickly.

"That's not true," Quetal whispered back, "but never mind. Keep your secrets. I'm going to sleep."

Jessika heard the little rustle of clothing as Quetal lay down. Jessika wished then as hard as she could that she had some magic, or some way of communicating over long distances. Her eyes popped open. Karo had magic. She had no way to communicate with him, but Karolan was an apprentice mage. If anyone could escape, surely he could. Could that have been the commotion she'd heard this morning? Had it been Karo and Rikah making their escape, going to get help, and not them being taken away for questioning? She really didn't know how much Karo could do; he was so private about his abilities.

She knew Thornfire and Starbright could make fire, light, freeze water—

in general manipulate the elements. Starbright had also done the remarkable feat of reshaping the stone of the pool Jessika and the other used to bathe in. She couldn't remember all the details, as it had happened when she was much younger, but she recalled that Starbright had waded out into the water and placed her hands on the stone. Then, she'd pushed, sculpting the rock as though it were clay: smoothing and squishing it into new shapes. Afterwards, Jessika had gone down to where the griffin had been working and put her own hands on the stone, but it had returned to solid, impenetrable rock. Starbright had just smirked, proudly.

If Karo could do that, he could make holes right through the prison walls. It was always possible that he wasn't advanced enough for that, though. Starbright had been training as a mage for years and years before Karo had even come to South-scree. Maybe he at least had a way of sending a message to Thornfire, although Jessika had never heard of a mage being able to do things like that. Maybe Thornfire could instead sense Karo and where he was?

Mind awash with fluttery wishes for magery, Jessika slept again.

Chapter 6
Interrogation

It was about a week later that the door finally opened, and Jessika rushed eagerly towards it, only to wrench herself aside as several spears poked into the room.

"Stay back and remain calm," a thunderous male voice directed.

Jessika picked herself up from where she'd nearly collided with the wall to avoid getting skewered, and stepped back.

"Fortune teller Quetal of Grace," the man went on. "Come with us."

Jessika stifled a meep of desperation and clasped her hands under her chin. Quetal got up slowly from her bench and gave her a look of sympathy.

"Good luck," she whispered from under the wing of her long, black hair, "if I don't see you again."

The spears parted just enough to let Quetal pass in among them, and then they withdrew, taking the fortune teller with them. The door was shut and locked, and Jessika wanted to scream and hit things in frustration.

Instead, she thumped down onto her bench, staring across at Quetal's. As horribly annoying as it had been to be locked in here together, she came to realize over the next few moments, that being locked in here alone, without Quetal for company, was going to be much worse. Jessika put her head in her hands and tried to find a spot of stillness and hope inside, so that she wouldn't start crying or raging, which wouldn't accomplish anything.

Evening came and a tray of food was pushed into the room again: service for one. Quetal did not return. Whether that meant she'd been freed or placed into a different room, or worse, Jessika couldn't know. Of course she hoped the woman had been released, but couldn't help missing the sounds of her sleeping breath and occasional nocturnal snort. The silent room felt as empty as a sky without griffins, and even though it wouldn't accomplish anything, there in the dark Jessika filled that sky with rain.

Three more days passed. Jessika could never remember being so crawly with the need for a bath. She'd even stripped all her clothes off and bathed with water from the basin, but her brand new clothes were still grimy with sweat and odor. She washed them, too, although she had no soap, and sat shivering in them until they dried. She was passionately grateful that she'd finished her last lady-week shortly before being captured, so didn't have to deal with that mess, but worried what would happen if she were kept so long that she came up on her next one, as she didn't have any of her necessary supplies with her.

She hummed and sang the songs Quetal had taught her. She paced. She spent hours tracing the faint veins of color in the rock walls with her fingertips. She stared off into space, thinking of nothing. She hadn't heard any more commotions that might indicate Rikah and Karo being taken from their cell, if they were even still in it. She tried not to cry. The nights were the longest and darkest she could remember, even though they were lengthening with spring.

As days passed, Jessika's world narrowed to the dull walls of her room. She spent the most time lying on the bench, until it started making her back hurt, and then she would sit up until her bum hurt. Then she would pace. She hummed and murmured snatches of songs almost without realizing she was doing it. She ran her fingertips across the nearest patch of wall over and over, until they started getting sore, which would make her realize what she was doing, and stop for a while. Her mood alternated between weary weeping and silent apathy.

The opening of the slot in the door for food or the fall of fresh water from the spigot would startle her each time they happened. Depending on her current mood, she'd run to the door and call out, desperate for words from another human voice, or she'd remain sitting or lying on the bench, unable to dredge up the energy to go fetch the tray. Eventually, hunger would pinch at her a little and usually inspire her to get up and eat, but there were times she ignored it, and left the tray untouched.

One day she thought she saw a feather falling down through the light from the window slots, and she sprang up with a gasp, rushing over to grab it, but her hand closed on empty air. A little while later, she thought she saw another feather, but again she could find nothing physical of it. She learned to ignore those glimpses of falling feathers when the sunlight streamed in, but a tiny bit of her mind commented that seeing things that weren't there wasn't a good sign.

She slept badly at night, and woke up from nightmares she couldn't remember, heart pounding like she'd been fighting, coated in sweat, panting out of control. Then she would leap up, circle the room with her hands and forearms pressed to the walls, searching for something she couldn't express, until her panting turned to sobs or helpless shouting and she collapsed. After some time of near unconsciousness she'd wake again, understanding that she was still trapped in the cell, recalling how she'd gotten there and that she was waiting to be taken out. In those moments she felt the most normal. She thought about Hawkjoy and Rikah and Karo, and her life in South-scree. She could acknowledge that being stuck in the cell was making her go a little crazy.

Eventually she'd go back to sleep on her bench, or Quetal's, and get somewhat better rest, but within a few hours of waking the next morning, the empty sameness would overcome her again, and she'd sink back into unfeeling. Once the sun began streaming into the cell, she'd sit and watch the feathers falling through the light.

When the door finally opened again, something like another week later, Jessika startled, frightened, and backed into the far corner of her cell, pulse racing. Frantically, she tried to calm herself; this was what she'd been waiting for. It could mean something good—or at least different—was happening. After a few moments, she looked over at the open door like a lost chick hearing wing beats, and began a staggering walk towards it. The spears emerged, and a male voice called out.

"You are called Hawkwings? Come with us."

Jessika tottered closer to the door, not sure if she should believe what was she was seeing and hearing.

"Let's go," the man ordered.

She obeyed, walking slowly into the embrace of the long spears. A half dozen men and women stood in the hallway, holding the shafts of the spears, and as she approached, they retreated and reorganized themselves until they ringed her. They each held a portion of their spear shaft against her waist, keeping her pinned from all angles.

"Wrists," commanded the man in charge.

Jessika looked up, feeling dizzy. She didn't recognize the man as being among the ones who had initially captured her, but he was just as big and bulky as they'd been, and he had a thick grey beard over darkly tanned skin. A heavy war hammer was strapped to his back. He was close enough to touch, holding out his hands, and even though she didn't know him, her throat choked up; she wanted so much to reach out to him, another person. She held out her hands, stretching to put her palms against his huge callused hands. At the touch, she almost sobbed; she'd been so long alone. It didn't matter who he was; he was real and here. With quick and well-practiced movements the man secured her with metal cuffs and pulled his hands out of her grip.

He jerked his head. "This way. You just keep being good and maybe you'll get out of here."

The spear-wielders urged her down the hall, keeping her in their midst, moving at a practiced and steady pace, even the ones walking mostly backwards as they faced her. She went along placidly, without any feeling of wanting to resist, and wondered how they could think she was so dangerous that she needed both manacles and a six-person spear containment formation. They didn't have far to go: stopping at a doorway into another rock-walled room. This one had a heavy wooden table in the center and a few equally heavy chairs, with a storage box of some kind in one corner.

The big man in charge went first in, and the spear-wielders adjusted their positioning again, pushing Jessika into the room with the reverse of the movements they'd used to extract her from her cell. If she hadn't been so beaten down she would probably have admired their training and technique. Someone shut the door, audibly locked it, and the big man gestured to one of the chairs.

"Sit," he said.

Jessika obeyed. The man fetched a length of rope and tied one end to a metal ring embedded into the tabletop near Jessika, and the other end to the cuffs she wore. It was short enough to prevent her from doing much more than standing up. If she suddenly became violent it would stop her from jumping on anyone. Her captor took a seat on one of the other sides of the table and eyed her speculatively.

"We'll be joined by some other folks shortly," he explained. "Let me give you some advice. Just be polite and honest. We understand that people make mistakes and we'll forgive you. We want to help you be a good citizen, so you never have to come back here again."

Jessika nodded warily, feeling her pulse speed up. She felt like a part of her mind was slowly waking. She began to remember details of the time right before she'd been alone in the cell. Quetal had been with her, and then been taken out. Quetal had said to play stupid and ignorant, but now this man was looking at her with what seemed to be sincerity. It was as though she had fallen asleep on one of those sailing ships she'd read about, and all the ropes and sails had come undone. She'd been lost and drifting at sea, but now she was awake again, hungry and thirsty and dizzy, and trying to start lashing the ropes back down where they were supposed to go. Once that was done, maybe she could figure out where she was, and the sails would fill with wind, but she still felt like she was staggering about, dangerously close to falling overboard.

A knock came on the door, and someone slid the lock open. Jessika jumped in her seat, and twisted her neck to see two more people entering. One was a man, thinner and shorter than her big captor, but still much larger than she was. He wore the most formal-looking uniform she'd seen, and his white-blonde hair was cut sharply short. The other person was a woman with curling dark brown hair cut close to her neck. She, too, wore formal-looking clothes although cut more femininely and with a long skirt instead of trousers. She also carried a small sack.

The man sat down opposite Jessika and the woman opposite the big jailer. The woman gave her a slight bitter smile and the blonde man cleared his throat. He nodded to the others.

"Peace-keeper Malkom and Sub-justice Lonika," he introduced smoothly. "I'm Investigator Branwall. And you are?"

"Hawkwings," Jessika whispered, voice cracking with disuse. "Just a girl, nothing special."

"Really," he said: somehow not making it sound like a question, but just like he was bored.

"Where are my brothers?" she asked, unable to stop herself.

"Don't worry about them now," the Investigator replied, leaning in to put his elbows on the table. "You were observed participating in the spread of untruths about our country. Are you aware of how much you hurt your fellow citizens by doing that?"

All those words rushed over her, and she didn't have to feign the bewilderment they caused bouncing around in her ears, but somehow a bit of meaning got through. "I didn't know," Jessika said, trying to put some pleading into her voice, like Quetal had suggested. "We were just talking."

"Talking of that sort doesn't help anyone."

She was trying to gather her scattered sleeping wits and kick them into line. "I was just curious."

Now the woman leaned forward, too. "It's natural to be curious, sweet, but you went to the wrong place for answers. I can't image why you thought a fortune teller could give you the truth. Don't you know that fortune telling is fake?"

There must be a good response to that. She fumbled in the dark with numb hands, trying to find one. "But a man on the street sent us there," Jessika shrugged at last. "We didn't know he was a liar. I guess we were stupid."

A glance passed between the man and woman, and the man sat back again and rested his fingertips against each other. The big jailer, Malkom, was sitting silently and staring at his own folded hands, face blank.

"Well, we can tell you everything you need to know," the woman went on. "All you would have had to do is approach any peace-keeper with your curiosity, and he or she could have answered your questions or sent you to someone here who knew the details you were curious about."

The blonde man tried to spear her with a look. "You don't need to worry about these complicated histories anyway," he lectured. "What importance do they have in your life?"

Jessika shrugged again, and gave in to giving a stupid, submissive answer. "None, I guess. I can see that now, but I was just curious. I'd never been to the city before."

The woman gave her another little smile. "Of course, of course."

"The city is so big," Jessika said, adding a bit of whine to it, starting to feel like more of her brain was working. "I didn't know anything. Then, when the peace-keepers came I was scared, and then when I got locked up here I was even more scared. My family must be so worried when I never came home."

"Poor thing," the woman crooned. "It's unfortunate, but we're so busy we can't talk to everyone right away."

Jessika nodded, sniffing as though near tears. Inside, her heart was hammering away at her sternum, and anger was starting to rise against such an idiotic excuse for keeping her locked up in a room, alone, for weeks. The blonde man across the table was staring at her the way she'd seen griffins focus on the prey animal they'd chosen to try to bring down. Now he leaned forward again, as if ready for the stoop.

"So, you wanted to know our history," he said, voice low and even. "I can tell you. This country was ruled—peacefully—by an alliance of men and griffins for hundreds of years, but due to many complicated factors the griffins decided they no longer wanted to share with us humans. Some people will try to turn the griffins into evil beings, but the simple fact is that, unfortunately, over the years the compounded inbreeding of the griffins caused a great many mental problems for the animals. They were only barely our equals in intelligence to begin with, and they simply devolved to a state of being vicious beasts over the generations."

He spread his hands as Jessika fought to control her facial expression, partly grateful for the long speech, as it gave her more time to get her thoughts in order, and partly disgusted at how he spoke of creatures she knew and loved as equals.

The man went on. "How can we be angry if an ice-lion doesn't understand our words, or a dog we thought was trained fails to cooperate? How can we blame the griffins for what happened? It was a sad, sad, unfortunate event. When the leaders of the griffins began to reject us and become aggressive, and their packs followed their lead, what were we to do? The griffins were supposed to be our protection, but what do you do when your sword turns in your hand and attacks the wielder? Do you see?"

Jessika swallowed down everything she wanted to say, and instead produced, "that would be bad."

"It was very bad," the man agreed. "We needed help. Luckily, our leaders, in their wisdom, managed to call in some allies who also had large, strong, flying creatures as protectors, but these beasts were purely servants, and well controlled. Have you heard of rainbow drakes?"

Jessika nodded. "Yes."

"They are beautiful creatures of every color imaginable. They came at the behest of their masters and saved us, defeating the griffins and putting an end to their madness. It was most unfortunate what had to be done, but it was a mercy to put the mindless beasts out of their suffering."

Jessika had to exert her will not to clench her fists or grit her teeth.

Instead, she hung a weepy expression on her face. "They were suffering?"

The man gave her what he must have thought was an understanding look, and Jessika hoped he couldn't see through her fake expression as well as she could see through his.

"Imagine knowing you were once great, but now having fallen to the level of the crudest animal," he sighed. "Imagine seeing your society crumble around you, and knowing only that you are hungry and impeded by the weak, helpless humans around you."

Jessika felt her throat choke up, but not with the sorrow the Investigator clearly thought he would be inspiring. She wanted to shout and throw things at him.

"So the drakes saved us," he said eventually, when it became clear that Jessika was only going to bite her lip and swallow hard. "They couldn't save all of us. There was much death. The whole royal family except the king died. He was found trying to defend his wife and children, his sword stained with the blood of a dozen crazed griffins, but in the end he could only barely protect himself. Luckily, he was rescued before his wounds took his life."

Jessika throttled down the urge to leap to her feet and scream at him how it had been a griffin—Hawkwind—who had fought off a half dozen drakes to save her and the other children. What had really befallen her father, she didn't know, but she wanted to tell this man of the terror that still visited her in nightmares: of watching the drakes pluck away her playmates, one at a time; of watching the little children hardly older than babes die under those brilliantly colored claws and jaws; of seeing the shock and despair in their eyes; of the combined horror of their deaths, and the relief and guilt that she'd not yet been snatched up.

Then she wished she could show him what she'd seen next: one young griffin leaping to her rescue, facing the drakes, outnumbered, fighting in a whirl of feathers and blood, beating them to a standstill with all the passion and loyalty in her trembling body. Jessika's love and gratitude for Hawkwind thrummed in her chest, surging with every beat of her heart. She closed her eyes, squeezing them hard shut, so she wouldn't glare with naked malevolence at the lying man across the table from her.

"It broke his heart to lose his family like that, yet with the same courage as he defended them, he continues to lead us," the Investigator went on. "A supportive and knowledgeable set of advisors helps him now to lead Northborn."

"Why is it called Northborn now?" Jessika managed to ask without snarling.

"Ah, yes, well, griffins live in nests, don't they, and that doesn't seem appropriate. They all died tragically, and it's best that the event not be dwelled upon. We are all born of this northern country, however, so we can feel united with our new name of Northborn."

Jessika nodded, face pointed at the table, stringy unwashed hair fallen to hide most of her face. "That makes sense," she said, even as she disagreed; the wizards who brought the drakes were not born of the north, and nor were the drakes themselves. "Someone told me that not all the griffins were killed."

"You were misinformed," the Investigator said immediately. "There are no more griffins, unless there are some living somewhere on the other side of the world, and may they have peace and prosperity there."

The woman Sub-justice sat up straighter now. "Which brings us to another question," she interrupted.

Jessika looked up as the woman reached for the sack she'd brought into the room. Jessika tried not to wince as she pulled out Rikah's carving of Thornwing, the one that they'd traded to Quetal for her help. The woman set the carving carefully on the tabletop, beyond the reach of Jessika's bound hands.

"Where did you get this?" the woman asked lightly. "It's quite intricate, even realistic."

Jessika stared, mind racing. If they'd questioned Rikah and Karo and Quetal about it, they might have already gotten three different answers.

"That fortune teller, Quetal of Grace, had it in her shop," she said.

That was only true. It wasn't the whole truth, but the carving had definitely been in her shop at one point.

"And do you know where it came from, before it was in her shop?" the Investigator asked her slowly.

Jessika hesitated.

"It's an easy question," the man said, tracing his lower lip with a finger. "Yes, or no."

"No," Jessika blurted, hoping it was the right answer.

"Then you don't know to whom it should be returned?" the man murmured.

"I, uh, maybe to Quetal?" Jessika hazarded, trying not to wince outwardly; Quetal hadn't wanted it known that she possessed such a statue. "Maybe she knows where it came from? I mean, I don't think it was hers. Maybe she was selling it with all her other statues?"

The Investigator tapped his fingers together. "Funny. She said it belonged to you."

Jessika hoped her frantic breathing wasn't showing too much.

The Investigator pushed calmly to his feet. "Well, it seems that it doesn't belong to anyone then, since no one wants to claim it. We were hoping we might return it to its rightful owner, or even learn the name of its creator. Such a master craftsman would also no doubt be pleased to have it back. I don't suppose you know his or her name?"

Jessika's voice stuck in her throat.

The Investigator shrugged, as if saddened. "Alas, it seems it's been abandoned by all. Well, we have no place here for displaying trinkets like this." He made a lazy gesture. "Malkom, if you would."

The big guardsman stood up. Jessika's eyes widened in horror as the man drew his war hammer from its sheath on his back. He hefted it in two hands, face still impassive. There was a pregnant pause, and Jessika looked over at the Investigator, whose face seemed to draw her eyes irresistibly.

"I," she croaked, "I mean, if no one else wants it."

He shook his head, just a little. "No, Hawkwings," he said, lingering over her name.

Jaw starting to quiver with dread, she slowly stretched her bound hands towards it, but couldn't reach. "Please," she breathed.

The man nodded towards the woman, who promptly spoke, as if reciting a speech learned by rote.

"We understand you were confused, but we have judged that you meant no harm and that you understand now how damaging rumors and falsehoods can be. We judge your case resolved and you shall be released with no further punishment."

"Unless," the blonde Investigator said, with a lifted eyebrow, "you have anything else you wish to tell us?"

The little statue of Thornwing smiled back at her, his wooden face frozen in a moment of eternally elegant happiness. Reluctantly, Jessika withdrew her hands and put them back on her the edge of the table.

"No," she let go.

The Investigator gave her another moment, before turning to nod curtly at Malkom. The guardsman's heavy hammer came falling down, and broke the statue into fragments.

Jessika hardly noticed as the Investigator and Sub-justice left the room. She barely felt it when Peace-keeper Malkom took her wrists and untied the rope, and then unlocked and removed the manacles. The broken pieces of Rikah's masterwork stared up at her, and she couldn't stop looking at them, even as tears ran unheeded down her face.

A small part of her mind wondered why she was crying. Yes, it had taken Rikah weeks to carve that griffin, but he could make another. It was just wood. It wasn't like the guardsman had hit the real Thornwing with a hammer and broken him. So why did it feel like something was broken inside her, too?

It wasn't until Malkom took her arm and tried to get her to her feet that Jessika realized what was going on. She was going to be released. She looked up at her captor.

"Where are my brothers?" she asked.

"They're not here anymore," he said. "You'll have to go find them yourself."

She didn't dare ask after Quetal. She only hoped the fortune teller had gotten off as easily as she had. The big guardsman frowned down at her and then looked to the tabletop.

"Would you like the pieces?" he asked, gruffly, but softly. "All I have to do is dispose of them, but it doesn't matter how. You can take them, hide them, never tell anyone where you got them, or that I gave them to you. You want that?"

Jessika felt like something ripped in her chest and she started sobbing. "Yes, please."

"Hush now, hush," he growled. "You stop that. You hear? You take these and you leave town, and you don't come back. Understand?"

The man picked up the sack the Sub-justice had brought and quickly shoved the pieces back inside it. Jessika took it from him when he held it out to her. The guardsman propelled her towards the door with a hand like a slab

Thornsoft and Hawknoon

of venison on her shoulder.

"You understand about that," he grumbled. "Right sorry, but you know why that happened. You get out of town."

Jessika couldn't speak for the effort of holding back her sobbing, until they reached an exit to the building and she saw the late afternoon sky.

"Th-thank you," she stuttered out.

"Get going. Get out of the city before they close the gates: eastern gate is the closest. You'll have to find a farm nearby. You look harmless enough. Someone will take pity on you: give you a place to sleep tonight, maybe a bit of food. Tomorrow you find your brothers and get on the road home."

Jessika nodded automatically. The street in front of her looked immense and scary, even though she knew there was nothing frightening on it. It was just so big. Despite that, she wanted nothing more than to get out of the city and away. She wanted trees around her. She only hoped Thornfire and the others would be waiting, and Rikah and Karo with them. Without another word to the jailer she stumbled away, towards the darkness of the east.

Jessika heard the door close behind her, but she'd only gone a handful of steps after that before a dark, hooded shape detached itself from the shadows of a building and strode right at her. She barely had the wits to recoil before the man seized her arm with a firm grip. A protestation died unuttered on her tongue when the man spoke.

"Shush, it's all right, it's me, Hawkwings," he hissed.

"Rikah," she breathed.

Then she threw her arms around him, shuddering with the fear of ever being alone again, needing to hug him more than she'd ever merely wanted to hug anyone before. She didn't let go, even when he made some embarrassed protestations, and clung with a grip that was nearly strong enough to hurt.

"I'm out, I'm out," she repeated, jaw chattering as if with cold. "They let you go."

"We got out," Rikah confirmed, apparently giving in and hugging her back. "It's alright now. You're free. We're going to get away from this place, but we need to go."

He looked furtively around, as Jessika forced herself to let go of him even as she wanted to keep holding on, but they didn't seem to be attracting the attention of the few people on the late-day street.

"Let's go," he urged, "eastern gate. I've been coming here every day, hoping they'd let you go. I'll tell you all about how I got out once we're out of the city."

Too overwhelmed to object—if she'd even wanted to—Jessika let Rikah guide her through the streets towards the gate. She gripped his arm with a hand, elbow linked through his. He moved surely and quickly, as if he knew the path well. Within a few minutes, the gate was in sight, and as they passed out, a vaguely familiar guardsman gave the pair of them a nod and what seemed to be a relieved smile. Jessika thought it was probably the man Rikah had traded his unicorn carving to weeks ago. Rikah waved back, and took Jessika out into the fields beyond the walls.

"This way," he urged. "We moved the camp closer to the city, but it's still really safe and secret."

"Can we stop a moment?" Jessika asked, panting. "I'm so tired."

"Here, then."

Rikah pulled her over to a cluster of three trees by the road, and they sat down in the midst of them. Jessika huddled against his side.

"Are you hungry?" He handed her a lump of something wrapped in a corn husk.

Jessika opened it, discovering two thick slices of bread sandwiching a substantial slab of some kind of meat. Her mouth watered and she bit in eagerly.

"You wanted to know how we escaped," Rikah said softly as she ate. "It was Karo that did it, the first night we were there. He asked me to boost him up to the slats in the wall where the air and light comes in. I couldn't hold him up there a long time, so we had to take rests, but he used some kind of magic to melt through one of the slats."

Jessika nodded as she ate. "I thought he might be able to do something like that," she said after she swallowed.

"He could, but it made him tired and weak, and once it was cut through, then we had to figure out how to get ourselves through the gap. I could boost him up, but then I couldn't get up; it was too high. Finally, we used all the clothing we had to make a sort of rope. I boosted Karo up, but then he fell getting down from the gap on the other side. It sounded like he'd fallen pretty hard, but he managed to hold the rope for me, and once I got over I saw that he'd hurt his foot. He couldn't put any weight on it and was in a lot of pain."

Rikah looked at Jessika, grimacing. "We were going to try to get you and Quetal of Grace out, too. We really were, but Karo was having a hard time even staying quiet, he was hurt so badly. He couldn't concentrate to do any more magic, and was worn out besides, so I decided just to try to escape the city, him and me, and then come back for you."

He shook his head. "I had to practically carry him, and the gate I got us to was shut since it was the middle of the night. We huddled by it until dawn, with Karo in pain and me not able to do anything for him. Finally the guards came and opened it and we got out. It took us all day to get to the edge of the forest, Karo hopping on one foot, and me supporting him, and we were both exhausted. I left him hidden and ran to the camp. Thornspike and Joy and I snuck back down to where I'd left him and carried him back to camp."

Jessika had finished the sandwich and got to her feet, ready to keep moving. "So he's fine now? Thornfire fixed his foot?"

Rikah had a helpless gesture. "He couldn't. I didn't know it, either, but magic can't fix broken bones. He said he could see with magic which bones were broken, and line them back up right by pushing with his hands—though he had to compare my healthy foot to Karo's broken one to know what they were supposed to look like—but he couldn't fuse them back together. All he could do was help with the pain and swelling some."

"So Karo can't walk," Jessika summed up.

They started moving again, with Rikah leading the way to the new camp as sunset neared.

"Right. He can't walk, and he's still hurting, so he couldn't come back to get you out, but I came back every day and waited in case they released you. I had to get a disguise, though, since I'd escaped and I'll bet they were looking for me. That's why I've got this robe and hood."

"They wouldn't tell me anything about you," she said.

"What about Quetal?"

"They took her away first, days before they took me out of the cell for questioning. Oh, that's right." She lifted the sack with the all but forgotten pieces of sculpture.

Jessika stopped walking, and Rikah stopped, too. Carefully, she extracted a few pieces of the broken carving.

"I'm really sorry, Rikah," she breathed around the lump in her throat. "When they questioned me, they asked where it had come from, who made it, and I didn't know if you were free or not, or what you or Karo or Quetal might have said. I said I didn't know anything about it, and they broke it. I couldn't stop them. I'm sorry."

Rikah took the pieces she offered him with a sigh. "It's sad, but I knew that any pieces I brought with me on this trip might get lost or broken, although I didn't expect it would be in this way. Don't worry about it, Hawkwings. It wasn't your fault. I'm just glad you made it out in one piece."

He suddenly gripped her shoulder, not hard enough to hurt, but urgently. "They didn't hurt you, did they?"

She shook her head, fighting to keep up a calm, brave front. "Not physically, no, just, they kept me in there so long, all alone once they took Quetal, and I didn't know what would happen to me, what they might do, how long I'd be there. I—I sort of went a little crazy. That was difficult."

Rikah squeezed her shoulder, and the look her gave her made her think he suspected she was more troubled by all that than she was letting on. Jessika managed a tight smile.

"I'm glad to be out. Let's get back to the camp," she said.

Rikah nodded, stowed the fragments of carving into his pack, and they kept walking.

"Where did you get these robes and everything?" she asked. "You said you bought them?"

"I traded some more carvings for money, so I could buy them, but no griffin carvings. I know that's too dangerous now."

"I'm sorry you've had to give up your carvings for all this."

Rikah gave her shoulder another quick pat. "Don't worry about it. I can make more: better ones. Besides, I learned a lot about the city while I was doing it."

"Did you go back to the fortune teller area?"

He shook his head. "No, I didn't think it would be a good idea."

"I hope Quetal is all right. I agree; it's probably too risky to go back and check on her."

They moved as quietly as they could in the fading light up into the edge of the forest. It was difficult to see under the trees, and Rikah produced a glowing stone—no doubt crafted by one of the mages in the party—to guide them. They hiked for several more minutes in silence, up, deeper into the woods.

"I haven't forgotten what she said, you know," Jessika whispered.

Rikah didn't respond for a moment, but Jessika could nearly feel him ruminating.

"Quetal," he murmured at last, as they made their way through the shrubbery.

"Yeah. Chika, in the capital."

"Are we going there?" he asked softly.

Jessika took a deep breath of the night air. "Yeah. We are."

Chapter 6
Reunion

Jessika's arrival at the camp was greeted by cries of happiness and exclamations of relief. Hawkjoy was the first to bound over, pushing between Thornspike and Starbright with no sign of regard for their neatly preened feathers. She nearly bowled Jessika over, trying to greet her with head bumping and hugging while mouthing her filthy hair in place of nibbling crest feathers and uttering sharp chirps of distress and burbles of affection.

"I'm all right, I'm fine," Jessika assured the frantic griffin over and over. "I missed you, too, but I'm back now. I'm safe."

At last, she just wrapped her arms around Hawkjoy's neck and clung, as a way to stop getting buffeted by wings and bill. Hawkjoy hugged her back almost too tightly, repeatedly trilling her relief. It was a couple minutes before they released each other, while everyone else voiced their pleasure at her return.

"We were so worried," Hawkjoy gestured, still intermittently trying to preen Jessika's hair.

As they made their way to the campfire, around which the others were gathered, Thornfire heaved a deep sigh.

"You've saved my life by returning, Hawkwings," the old mage glared. "I don't know if I could have survived Hawkwind's response should I have had to tell her that I lost you."

"I'm sorry to have worried you all," Jessika said. "I wanted to come back, but they wouldn't let me go until today."

Under their urging, Jessika told the tale of her confinement and interrogation. After, Thornfire sat pensive, staring at the fire and lost in thought. Rikah turned the fragments of his Thornwing carving over and over in his hands, until finally placing each piece into the fire. Thornspike had roused her feathers and was flexing her hand talons in and out, as if wishing she could set them into something's—or someone's—hide. Starbright just looked upset over the whole story and Hawkjoy seemed to alternate between Thornspike and Starbright's reactions.

Karo growled from his reclining seat across the fire: "I wish I could go tear down their stupid prison, with them inside it."

"Not all the people there were bad, or not completely bad," Jessika commented.

"Societies are complicated places," Thornfire put in, "and they are difficult to run fairly. Tearing down the prison probably would only make the situation worse."

"How could it make it worse?" Karo retorted.

Thornfire flicked his crest feathers. "You can't anticipate the consequences of such an act. When you're young you think you can just do radical, drastic things and it will somehow solve the underlying problem, but with experience you come to understand that true solutions are much more complicated."

Karo just shrugged and looked away, glowering instead at a nearby rock as though it had done him some malicious harm.

"Quetal of Grace gave us some information," Jessika spoke up. "She said we should go the capital and look for a woman named Chika, that she would show us the secret way into the palace."

"You want to go into the palace?" Thornfire repeated slowly.

"It, I," she stuttered. "My father might still be alive, but for some reason, if he is, he's letting these wizards stay, and making people believe lies about what happened with the Feathyrs."

Thornfire's crest feathers rippled, a signal of a griffin contemplation and acknowledgment. "That may be worth investigating," he allowed.

"And Quetal said that the wizards came here, to Northnest, to find something, and that they found it, but she didn't know what it was," Jessika went on. "That could be important."

Thornfire frowned. "Something that mages want? Something that Northnest had or has?"

"I don't know what it could be, either."

"I can only imagine it's something to allow them to better utilize their power, or make them more powerful," the griffin mage surmised. "But it could be something else, maybe something to do with the drakes, or something that gives them mundane power, or political power."

"Don't you think we should find out what it is?" Jessika pressed.

For a moment he locked gazed with her, and then his wings relaxed and he lowered his roused crest. "Certainly. This is a mission of discovery. Let us go to the capital and learn what we may."

Jessika released her held breath. "Thank you."

"Of course," he gave a little smile. "That will also take us back closer to South-scree. Someone can fly Hawkrain back where he can finish healing in comfort."

"No, I want to help," Karo objected.

"You can't stand," Thornfire scolded, and Hawkjoy seconded the sentiment with a hiss of her own.

"Let's just get to the capital and find a place to camp, and maybe we can see how his foot is then?" Jessika suggested.

"If he stands and walks on a foot that badly broken, I suspect he could cripple himself for life," Thornfire stated flatly. "Is that what you want? To never be able to run or jump again?"

Karo returned his sullen gaze to the rock he'd been glaring at before.

Thornfire sighed. "Apprentices."

Across the fire, Starbright giggled a little.

Thornfire eyed her. "You glared at rocks, too. Want me to tell everyone how many?"

She swallowed her next bubble of laughter. "No, Master."

"That's what I thought."

Thornspike grinned in Thornfire's direction. "How many did you glare at, Elder?"

He lifted his chin, feathers prickling back up, and Jessika worried he was about to smack the insolent female: not hard, but enough to make a point.

"When I glare at rocks, they burst into fire," he rumbled instead. "Same thing happens to uppity Linemembers, only brighter and hotter; feathers are more flammable."

Jessika almost laughed. Thornspike's grin faded and she shuffled her wings, showing her submission with the flattening of her crest, but she winked at Jessika and Rikah as soon as Thornfire transferred his attention off of her.

"Let's rest here tonight, and maybe tomorrow," he said to the group. "Hawkwings can get a good sleep, clean up, and eat well. Then we'll go."

Everyone nodded or otherwise showed their acquiescence. Jessika wished she could bathe right then, but going to find a stream or river in the dark would be difficult and potentially dangerous even with griffins to guard her, and she was worn out enough to sleep deeply even in grubby clothing. Rikah pointed her to a bedroll, and Hawkjoy came over to join her, curling up around her for warmth and providing a forearm for a pillow. After her weeks of nights alone on the hard prison bench, it was as comfortable as her featherbed back home. For the first time in many nights, sleep brought her true rest with Hawkjoy beside her.

They didn't leave for the capital for another day, giving Jessika plenty of time to visit the stream the humans had been using for bathing. Hawkjoy went with her, leading her to a part of the watercourse where a deep pool had naturally formed. Jessika waded into the chilly water, and used soap and a scrap of cloth to scrub herself until her skin was pink and raw, and washed her new clothing, too. Then, Hawkjoy went into the water and bathed like a bird, tossing up so much spray with her vigorous body-dipping and thrashing wings that Jessika was surprised she didn't empty the pool entirely.

They sunbathed on some flat rocks beside the pool after that, stretched out and letting the heat bake away everything but the scent of wet stone and damp griffin. The heat after the cold water was soporific. Hawkjoy slowly and hypnotically preened her feathers, adding the rasp of her bill to the music made by the rustle of trees and trickle of water. Jessika lay on her back, face in the shade, and gazed upwards. The open sky was both glorious and a little scary; she hadn't seen it for so long. The cooling of the breeze on her naked skin and the little sounds around her left fresh impressions on her senses, like new footprints in untouched snow.

"What was it like, Joy, all those years in Snow-in-lee?" Jessika asked eventually, and timidly; she wasn't sure Hawkjoy would want to talk about it.

The griffin raised an eyebrow, but not with displeasure, and left off her preening. "I don't really remember much," she signed. "It was like I wasn't alive. Coming out of that room was my true birth."

"What did you do every day?"

"We slept a lot, and groomed each other, told stories, and played some simple games, but not much else. Our parents taught us to talk with our hands and to read, but we only had so many books. We read them until we had them memorized and then there wasn't any point to it anymore. We contributed to carvings on the walls; generations of griffins had scraped shapes and words into the walls with their claws. We carved them deeper. Like I said, it really wasn't like living."

"I would have gone crazy," Jessika said. "Being imprisoned by the peacekeepers, I thought I was going out of my mind."

"You had a mind to go out of," Joy went on darkly. "I think that's why some of the Snow-in-lee griffins couldn't keep up during the escape, and why more couldn't ever adjust to being free."

"What do you mean?"

Joy nibbled a talon for a moment, forehead feathers puckered in the way that meant her brow was creased.

"We never ran, never even walked more than a dozen steps before you freed us," the griffin explained. "The rooms we were kept in were rather large, bigger than the usual sleeping rooms the Hawk Line has now, but we'd never been physically active, really. As chicks we played, of course, but eventually we got too big to jump and chase without hurting ourselves or our family members. Being asked to walk and run such long distances felt completely unnatural. It was difficult to force myself to keep going."

"It's hard to imagine," Jessika murmured.

"The younger griffins adapted better, more quickly," Joy observed. Her feathers rippled some more as she struggled for words and expression. "Besides that physical limitation, the bigger one was our minds. We sort of knew that there must be more outside of the four walls of our rooms, but we all stopped trying to imagine it after a while; there was just no point. You had to resign yourself to an imprisoned existence. We couldn't spend every moment frustrated and distraught."

Jessika nodded. "That takes energy," she agreed. "I found that out, too. You can be angry for a while, but eventually you just can't sustain it anymore."

"Because we became so content, so accepting that the four walls were our world, even when we got out and got the chance to see what we might have once imagined, it didn't make us excited. Instead, it was frightening and unpredictable. The four walls were what we knew: what was safe."

"You came out willingly," Jessika questioned.

Joy gave her a tight little griffin-smile. "Yes. There must have been some small spark left in us that still wondered, that was still curious. For some of us, that spark grew once we were out, but for others the fear overwhelmed it."

"I remember some of the chicks were really excited," Jessika smiled back at her.

Joy's grin grew. "I was pretty excited, too. Sometimes I think it was only my enthusiasm that kept my mother going. I remember her watching me a lot, letting me lead, and trying new things only after I tried them and showed her."

The griffin sighed with pleasure and lifted her damp wings a bit, spreading the feathers more to help them dry.

"We all had the instinct that our wings were meant to make us fly," she continued, now looking up at the sky Jessika had been lost in a while ago. "As chicks, stuck in those rooms, we all knew it. We all got excited when our feathers came in. We opened our wings. We tried to leap up. We knew what they were for. Our parents looked at us and couldn't hide the sadness in their hearts. They knew. They remembered."

"And then you got to fly," Jessika beamed.

Joy's eyes closed with the memory. She continued gesturing as she leaned her head back, raising her crest and neck feathers, although some still clung wetly to each other. "I remember when I first saw one of our rescuers fly. It was Thornwing. He was hurrying to check our back trail, to watch out for talis."

Jessika saw her muscles clench all down her throat and chest and her wingtips trembled. Joy continued signing, slowly, as if her fingers savored each word.

"I saw him. I saw him in the air. His wings were open wide, stretched. He banked, and soared, with his legs tucked up, his tail spread into a fan. The dawn light was touching him, lighting up his feathers." She trailed off, and then shook her head.

"I can't possibly convey how I felt. Partly, I felt vindicated. I knew. I knew my wings were made for that, and there I was proved right. That was joyful. I also knew, as soon as I saw him flying, that I was going to do that, too. I was going to fly, and that realization made me so ecstatic I could hardly move, hardly think. It terrified me, and made me want to cry out, and laugh, all at the same time."

Jessika found she'd clenched her own fists as she felt perhaps a shadow of what Hawkjoy was talking about, imagining herself in the griffin's place, all those years ago, on the desperate overland march away from Snow-in-lee, when the sun crested over the mountains to chase away the cold bite of moun-

tain air: the first free air she'd ever breathed.

"I was also angry," Joy went on, her gestures smaller, sort of like whispering. "I was angry at the talis: so angry. I was sad: sad that I had lost all those years of my life trapped in a box. And I was grateful: grateful that I had been saved, that I hadn't been one who had come before, who had lived and died knowing only the box, only seeing the sky when the talis finally took them out, to dangle on the hook."

Jessika couldn't take it anymore. She got up and threw her arms around Hawkjoy's neck. Joy immediately encircled her with a wing.

"What I went through was nothing like what you went through," Jessika told her. "I can't believe I ever thought to compare a few weeks in that prison to the years you suffered in Snow-in-lee."

Joy trilled reassuringly at her, and Jessika turned her head so she could see the griffin's hands.

"You suffered, too," Joy said. "You need not pretend or say that it was nothing just because you know someone who has suffered more. If that were the case, there would be only one person in this whole world ever allowed to complain or cry, when we have all endured things worth crying about."

Hawkjoy turned her head to gently nudge Jessika's shoulder, and the young woman petted her crown.

"So cry," the griffin said, "if you need to."

"Alright," she agreed, still feeling a little tight in her throat.

"Otherwise, while you've got your hand there, scratch."

Jessika laughed aloud, the sound blurting from her unexpectedly, like a chick tripping over nothing. Hawkjoy joined her with a chortle.

"Yeah," she giggled, "I can do that."

They left for the capital the next day. It would take several days of flying and camping until they came within human walking range of the city. Jessika was actually worried about having the griffins' camp too close; the capital would surely be more well guarded than the trade city, or so she assumed. There might even be rainbow drakes still living there. They stayed to the wilderness, veering eastward at any sign of human habitation, deeper into the mountains.

When at last they spied the fir-crowded towers of Northnest castle,

Jessika waited like a fox sensing movement in the brush, to observe what her feelings would be of seeing her birthplace again after so many years. Furtive apprehension frolicked with flutters of fear in her chest and belly, but no sensation of warmth or longing joined them. While the griffins whistled and chirped astonishment at each other, Jessika stared blankly.

It was her home, but it did nothing to welcome her.

There was only one bitter, tender sensation within her—her father. Was he alive, as the people of the trade city had said? She couldn't believe it. Hawkwind had always said that everyone in the castle had been killed in the invasion, that she'd seen the rest of Jessika's family dead. Could she be remembering imperfectly? Perhaps in the fury and haste of battle the young griffin had not seen everything she'd thought she'd seen. Maybe she had been mistaken.

Or maybe it was a lie, or an imposter, provided as a way to help keep the people of Northnest placid. So much could be a lie, to prevent the populace from revolting and attempting to reject the invaders. She wouldn't know until she faced the man and saw for herself. Sternly, she lectured her heart about hoping; she still believed her birth family was dead, and hoping otherwise would do her no good.

The griffins coasted downward, following Thornfire to a camping spot he'd apparently picked out. The humans set up camp while the griffins hunted and scouted the area. They ate roasted meat for dinner caught by Thornspike and seasoned by Rikah. Karo was still understandably grumpy about his injury and inability to do much, but otherwise the mood of the party had improved considerably, especially with the capital in sight.

"Tomorrow, you'll go to the castle?" Hawkjoy gestured to her as the griffins preened and the humans finished their meal. "Are you excited? Nervous? Scared?"

"You may have to plan to spend your nights there," Thornfire suggested. "This camp is too far away for you to accomplish anything if you spend hours travelling to and from the city each day."

"I guess we'll be going," Rikah said to her, "since Karo can't come and the griffins obviously can't come."

"I wish you could come," Jessika told Hawkjoy. "We have to go find that woman called Chika, and that means moving among humans. I can only imagine what bringing a griffin into a crowded marketplace would do."

"They used to be there," Karo murmured wistfully. "Griffins used to be all over in the capital. I can remember seeing them, a little bit."

That comment soured the mood for a moment.

Jessika turned to Hawkjoy, reaching up to scratch her neck and head. Hawkjoy purred and closed her eyes, her crest lifting.

Jessika brought her face close to the side of the griffin's head, where her ear was. "I only hope that this visit to the capital will be less problematic than the trade city, but somehow I doubt it," she whispered.

Hawkjoy raised a hand, hidden from the others by Jessika's body. "I know," she signed. "I doubt that, too."

Rikah and Jessika strode towards the front gate of the outermost castle wall. Northnest castle was not an easily accessible one. It had been built wedged among the lower peaks of the mountains. Rock and brick took over where natural stone left off, completing an encircling, thick barrier wall that contained all the castle buildings and some courtyard area.

Approaching the castle, the road ran through progressively more rugged terrain. Further out from the castle was actually where most of the farms, shops, and inns were situated, rather than clustered up against the walls of the castle, but some structures still managed to find a spot to cling, although not many farms. There were some sheep and goat ranches, as plentiful fodder grew along the steep cliffs, and Northnest had long bred animals that could safely navigate and thrive on the challenging terrain.

Any land that hadn't been cleared and wasn't rock was coated by fir trees and other conifers with a thick brush of ferns and hunterberry bushes between the trunks. Even on the rocky cliffs, here and there tenacious little twisted pines managed to grow with their roots wedged into cracks. Beyond the castle, back into the clefts of the mountains, was even deeper, denser, trackless forest. Up there were the unicorn glades, and beyond them the territory held by South-scree. It was into that wilderness that Hawkwind had escaped with Jessika and the others so many years ago.

"How will we find someone who knows Chika?" Jessika murmured to Rikah as they drew nearer to the walls, passing through one of the towns along the way.

"I don't know. Quetal didn't really give us much help, only a name to go on," he replied under his breath.

There weren't many people out on the main road, but those they passed gave the newcomers curious, distrustful looks.

"Let's go in there and ask," Rikah suggested, stopping suddenly and pointing with a jerk of his head.

Jessika followed the gesture. "Where? There? That inn?"

The building was crammed right between two sharp outcrops of stone, made of wood itself, and looked to be about three stories high. Jessika squinted her eyes and examined it, noting the hand carved sign that swung over the door.

"Inn the Middle?" she read.

Rikah grinned at her. "I like the name."

"Fine," she decided brusquely. "We'll start there."

Jessika strode off like she was going to start a fight—or finish one—and Rikah trotted after her. A smiling patron was just leaving as they approached, and the man courteously held the door open for them. Jessika thanked him and walked inside. At once, a heartily plump woman in a mended but clean dress and apron turned and beamed at them.

"Come in, come in, dearies," she caroled. "Welcome to the Middle. Have a seat wherever you like."

There was a wide bar along one wall. Opposite it was a fireplace built into the stone crag that formed one wall of the inn. Between the two were tables of a variety of sizes, with mismatched stools, chairs, and benches jumbled around them. Plentiful lanterns made the room almost as bright as day and cheerfully colored banners and tapestries hung from the ceiling and along the walls.

A hefty man with an excessive black mustache was behind the bar: cleaning cups and glasses with a rag that looked blessedly clean. He looked up from his task long enough to echo the rotund woman's smile—although his face fur hid most of it. There were only a few other patrons working their way through mugs of something or plates or food. Jessika was relieved to note the rich culinary scents that carried no stink of spoilage.

She found the barkeep's smile reassuring, and went to claim a tall stool at the bar. Rikah followed her.

"Not every day we have such fine young ladies and gents in our inn," the mustachioed man greeted them. "What can I get for you?"

Jessika pondered for a moment, while Rikah made his stool squeak by shifting nervously.

"Do you have a specialty?" she asked. "Some kind of food that's only made here?"

"We do," the barkeep nodded. "For two?"

She knew Rikah still had some coins from his most recent sale of a carving, and based on what that guard had told them back in the trade city it should be more than enough for two meals.

"Yes, please," Jessika told him.

He grinned again. "So polite. Not that our customers aren't polite, just less, hmm, formal maybe." He called out. "Nona, two plates of pie in the middle."

"Right up," the woman who seemed to be the main server called back.

"Pie?" Rikah repeated curiously.

"A variation on pot pies," the barkeep explained, going back to cleaning, now moving on to large wooden and pewter mugs. "You'll have to try them and tell us what you think. You've traveled many places and tried many different kinds of food?"

"Not really," Jessika admitted. "We haven't left home that much until lately."

"What brings you to the capital? Business or pleasure?"

Rikah gave her what seemed like it might be a look of warning, but she ignored it. They'd never get anywhere if they didn't ask for help, and the warm, friendly feeling of the inn and its keepers had washed away most of her trepidation.

"Business, I suppose you'd say," she shrugged. "We're looking for someone."

The barkeep gave her a raised eyebrow as the woman, Nona, brought out two shallow bowls, each with a steaming piece of meat and vegetable pie. The scent made Jessika's mouth water.

"Anything to wash that down?" the barkeep asked.

"Ah, we've never really had anything, um, like beer or anything," Rikah apologized.

"I can bring you both some water," innkeeper Nona suggested, as she turned to fetch it. "Boiled, so it won't give you a tummy ache."

"When you're ready for something stronger, you come to me," the barkeep winked. "I can tell young folks like you the best place to start, and give you recommendations based on what you like."

"Thanks," Rikah replied, with such genuine goodwill that Jessika wondered if he was really thinking of taking the man up on it.

"So, looking for someone, eh?" he went on as Nona brought out a pitcher of water. The barkeep set two glasses on the counter and Nona filled them. "I hope no one's in trouble."

"No, no trouble," Jessika assured him. "We're not angry at the person or anything. We were just told they could help us, if they want to. We wouldn't force them or anything, just ask, politely, and maybe too formally."

The barkeep and Nona both chuckled a little. Rikah had snatched up a fork and was already captivated by the flavor of the pie, judging by the expression on his face. At least he wasn't trying to stop her from talking about it, and she silently thanked the pie. So as not to seem too serious, she picked up her own fork and took a bite.

In an instant, she understood what had captivated Rikah so. The crust was flaky yet somehow still moist. The gravy hit her tongue first, just barely below hot enough to burn, and the fatty, herb taste of it awoke sensations and half-remembered memories that transported her consciousness away, into the past. The memories dissolved as she tried to snatch at them, and she felt frustrated, as though she had almost brought back some distant scenes of her youngest childhood.

She bit into a firm but not hard piece of potato—at least, she thought it might be potato. When she got to a piece of meat, it was chewy but not tough, and melted in her mouth without being stringy. Other bits of vegetables seemed perfectly cooked, too. Nothing was so squishy it was soggy, and nothing so hard it was jarring. She recognized carrots and peas—both of which Rikah had mastered the growing of—but others were unfamiliar, or vaguely familiar as though she'd had them before, but not for more than a decade.

Jessika opened her eyes, not realizing she'd closed them, as she swallowed her first bite.

"This is good," she said, voice gone husky. "I've never had anything this good."

Both Nona and the barkeep grinned so widely Jessika feared their eyes might vanish into wrinkles of skin. Beside her, Rikah's hand was trembling. He'd eaten half his pie in a rush, and Jessika thought he might be forcibly restraining himself now, to make the experience of eating it last longer.

"The cook will be delighted to hear it," Nona told her. "You'll have to come back for another piece once you finish your business."

"I'd love to," Jessika said.

"Been to the capital before?" the barkeep asked.

Jessika's answer caught in her throat. "Not for a very long time," she said finally.

"Ah," the barkeep murmured, face going shrewd and nodding, as though he'd understood something deeper from her reply. "Who're you looking for, if I might ask? It might be we know them and could set you a guide."

"That would be very kind," Jessika said. "I only have a single name: Chika."

The reaction from both Nona and the barkeep told her that they knew the name. She seemed to have mildly surprised or concerned them, and they glanced at each other.

"You know her?" Jessika pressed.

"Most know of her, though few know her personally or count her as a friend," the barkeep explained.

"Not because she is not worth having as a friend," Nona quickly put in. "Chika is a sweet and generous woman, but her situation is complicated."

"There are some who dislike her," the barkeep explained, leaving off his mug cleaning to lean forward onto his elbows, "despite that she has done nothing to harm them. It's rather unfair. Most people simply tolerate her and her family." He gestured at Nona and back to himself. "We find nothing but good about them, try to do them a kindness whenever we can."

Jessika looked between the two innkeepers, a little disconcerted. "What's wrong with them?"

"They're a bit different is all," Nona said with a faint smile. "They can tell you about it if they're inclined to."

The barkeep gave a short cough. "Now, we do feel somewhat protective towards them. I wouldn't want to bring anyone to them that might wish them ill."

"No," Jessika assured him. "I don't want anyone to get hurt. I just want to ask them a question, although it might mean asking them to do me a favor, but if they don't want to, that's all right. I'll find another solution to my problem."

The barkeep gave her a smile. "Well, that's all fine and right then. Finish your pie before it gets cold. When you're ready, our Betto can run you over to see Chika."

Chapter 7
The Family

Rikah had long since finished his pie and licked the bowl clean. Jessika was just taking her last bite. It had been so good; she savored it slowly. She followed Rikah's example of cleaning the bowl, but with her finger: not by picking the bowl up and licking the gravy off like a dog. She took a few deep drinks of water, finishing the glass, and relaxed, elbows propped on the bar.

After another minute, Nona came by to collect their dishes. Rikah fished some coins from his pocket.

"Four coppers each," Nona said, "and I'll call Betto to guide you."

She was gone before he could hand over the coins, and a moment later a skinny, blonde, freckle-faced boy a few years younger than them came ricocheting through the tables.

"Going to see Chika? I'm Betto. Let's go," he said in a rush.

As they left their stools, Jessika saw that Rikah had placed one coin on the counter: a bronze. Jessika approved: what they had received and were receiving was worth a little more than Nona had billed them.

Betto, the blonde boy, blundered through the clustered buildings on a level area of land to the east of the castle gate. A sort of crunched together village had sprung up there, with no space between the houses, and some of the structures being a few stories tall. He just careened his way among people, goods, and animals, with his shaggy hair in his face, like a griffin chick who knew the adults around him would tolerate his impoliteness. Jessika and Rikah followed in his wake, trying to dodge around everything he upset with his recklessness.

At last, he stopped at the end of a blind alley where the houses were painfully crammed together and jerked his head.

"Chika and them live there," he said.

Then he held out his hand, palm up. After a moment, Rikah guessed what he was waiting for, placed a copper in his hand, and Betto clenched it and ran off like a wolf were after him.

Jessika and Rikah shared a nervous look at each other, and then turned their gazes onto the house at the end of the alley. It was narrow—only a little wider than Rikah's stretched out arms—and three stories tall. Its neighbors seemed to prop it up, and vice versa, as though the houses were all drunken friends leaving a bar together. For all that, it looked weatherproof, and someone had whitewashed the walls and painted the door and window trim pink, or perhaps red, and it had faded.

Around them, the pair could hear children chattering, an occasional fussing baby, and sounds of adults at work on any number of chores from food preparation to laundry and other cleaning. There was a common water pump in the middle of the alley with a basin under the spout. Laundry lines were strung across the second and third stories of the houses and festooned with drying clothing. Most doorsteps had potted plants—mainly cooking herbs—and more plants grew up among the cracks between the paving stones, but mostly weeds. Everything looked relatively clean and there was no stench; it didn't seem like that terrible of a place to live.

A woman with a pail came out of a house to their left and headed for the waterspout, but stopped short as soon as she saw them. "Can I help you young folks?" she asked.

"We're looking for Chika," Jessika said.

"Now look here," the woman responded crossly, "we like Chika and her kids around here, do you ken? We won't have anyone making sports of them. Off with you."

"We're not here to bother them," Jessika told her. "Someone from the trade city told us Chika might be able to help us, and we wanted to ask her a question. That's all."

The woman didn't look completely convinced. "Chika's had enough trouble in her life."

"We don't want to give her more trouble," Rikah contributed. "It's just that she might be the only one who can help us."

"I take it you've never met Chika before," the woman guessed.

"That's right, ma'am," Rikah nodded.

"Well, you sound like you might be proper enough."

Both of them nodded and repeated, "yes, ma'am."

The woman scowled mightily at them for several heartbeats, and then turned on her toe and walked to the white and pink house at the end of the alley. She gave a soft knock, called that she was coming in, and went right inside, shutting the door behind her. Jessika and Rikah exchanged glances but made no move to follow her.

"I guess we wait," Rikah muttered.

They saw curtains flick in one of the windows, but nothing more from the house for several minutes. A few other people moved through the alley, looking at them curiously, and a couple times they had to explain why they were standing there looking silly.

As they were starting to think they should go knock, a young person came walking past them towards Chika's house. He wore a plain vest over a simple white shirt and enormous billowing pantaloons of a faded blue. On his head he'd perched a puffy brimmed cap that seemed to be failing to contain his profusion of curly auburn hair. His eyes looked unnaturally large and round and were as warm and brown as an embrace.

He smiled a cherubic grin at them as he passed, more full of springtime than any Jessika thought she'd ever seen. Then he paused halfway between them and Chika's house. He pointed.

"Here to see my mom?" he asked cheerfully.

Jessika nodded.

Although the young man was a bit shorter than average, she got the feeling he was around about her age, just from his poise and form. He looked finished, not like skinny Betto who'd obviously gotten his body's length before its girth.

"I bet Maura's in there already, isn't she?" he went on. "Saw you coming and jumped right away to defend my mom? Tall woman from that house, likes to frown a lot?"

Jessika nodded again. "I think so."

He grinned more widely. "You look fine. I'm Kopricariko, but call me Koki, alright?"

"Sure, of course," she agreed, not certain she could reproduce that long name without hearing it a few more times first.

"I'll go in and tell everyone you're fine," the young man smiled again. "Just a second."

He skipped forward and slipped smoothly through the door with practiced agility. Jessika thought she heard a raised voice from inside the house, and then the door was opened again, and the woman who'd stopped them came tromping back out. She gave them a dubious look, apparently forgot to fill her pail, and stalked back to her own house without any water, not quite slamming her door.

The young man in the plentiful pantaloons stuck his head out of Chika's door and waved. "Come on in."

Exchanging another nervous look, Jessika and Rikah approached and entered as Koki held the door open for them.

"Look," he said softly, suddenly bending close, "my mom was hurt pretty bad a long time ago, so she's not beautiful on the outside anymore. So, just don't be too startled, alright?"

Then, before either of them could respond, he gave another of his beaming smiles and trotted towards the back of the house. The house was narrow but deep, with a doorway leading to another room at the center of the back of the front room. They passed a steep stairway on one side and what seemed to be kitchen counters and cabinets on the other. Shelves stuffed with bags, boxes, and boots, and coat racks full of cloaks and jackets occupied every scrap of empty space. They passed through the back doorway into what was clearly a sort of living room.

The back wall had a stove and both sidewalls had chairs and couches squeezed in side by side. More shelves held books, candles, crafting supplies, jars of preserved foods, and half-finished projects. From the ceiling hung more dried foods and bundles of herbs. On the most comfortable couch sat a woman with her lap full of knitting.

Jessika caught her breath and saw why Koki had warned them about Chika's appearance. There were burn scars on half her face, neck, and the back of one of her hands, and scars that looked like they'd come from a knife on exposed skin that didn't have burn scars. Some of the knife scars looked serious enough to kill. She was fully clothed, but Jessika suspected the scarring continued on other parts of her body. The scars made it somewhat hard to tell, but Jessika didn't think she was all that much older than her and Rikah, maybe ten years older at the most.

Despite the scars, the woman gave them a welcoming smile. "Come in, sit, and don't be bothered by how I look. Koki, tea for our guests."

"I'm on it," he obeyed, taking a teakettle and heading for the communal pump.

Jessika and Rikah sat across from Chika, not sure what to say first.

"It's nice to see fresh faces," their hostess offered. "You're new to the capital?"

"We are," Jessika replied, "sort of. We—" she glanced at Rikah, who made no visible objection, "we were born here. Then we left. Now we're back."

"Welcome home."

Koki came back in with the kettle, still with a little smile, and put it on the stove. He crouched down to add some coal to the fire.

"And what brings you to my humble abode? I don't take it that you're here just to gawk at the unusual," Chika went on.

"You are correct," Jessika said softly. "Quetal of Grace gave us your name."

Koki went still in the midst of dropping tea bags into the kettle, then seemed to catch himself and resumed.

"Ah, Quetal, my good friend," Chika sighed, sounding pleased. "How is she? You've seen her recently?"

"A few weeks ago, and she seemed well," Rikah said.

"Her business is doing well, too," Jessika added.

"That makes for good hearing. I'm curious, of course, why she sent you to me—if I might ask your names?"

"Oh, yes, I'm sorry," Jessika blushed with embarrassment. "I'm Hawkwings."

"I'm Hawkdare," Rikah said.

In the ensuing silence, the sound of Koki gently setting the metal lid onto the kettle seemed unnaturally loud.

"Curious names," Chika muttered, sounding less like a gossiping girl and more genuine now.

Jessika and Rikah did not reply.

"So, why are you here, and keep your voices down," Chika cautioned.

Jessika licked her dry lips. "Quetal said you might know a secret way into the castle."

Chika did not respond, verbally or physically, but Koki turned his head to look at them, his ever-present smile replaced by the wary expression of a buck deer that's heard what could be a predator in the brush.

Before anyone could say more, the front door burst open and two more people came jumping into the room.

"Mama, Mama, were back," sang out the smaller one.

"We got everything you sent us for," added the larger one, setting down a basket she'd been carrying on her back. "Oh, we have guests."

The larger person turned out to be a young woman about ten years old, Jessika guessed. She came into the room, a little flushed and sweaty from carrying her load, but still smiling prettily—only she had something strange about her skin on her forehead and cheekbones and on the dorsal side of her arms and hands. She was a green-gray color for starters. Plus, she sort of glimmered in the light as she moved, and Jessika realized the glimmering came from tiny scales, or something similar, like on a fish or lizard. She also had her head artfully swathed in scarves, and Jessika had the sudden thought that the young woman might not have any hair.

The littlest person ran into the living room and jumped up beside Chika to give her a vigorous kiss on the cheek. It was another girl, this one perhaps five or six years old, and she seemed perfectly normal—except that one of her hands looked strange, and Jessika saw that it had either been maimed or she'd been born with a couple fingers missing and the other two fused nearly all the way together. From her shrieking giggles as Chika returned her sloppy kiss, her hand not quite being like normal didn't seem to bother the girl at all.

"I'm Verika," the older girl introduced pleasantly enough, extending her hand to shake, "and yes, I have scales. It's alright."

Jessika and then Rikah shook her hand.

"The little one is Meridan, Meri, we call her," Verika went on. "We're Chika's family, with Koki over there."

"It's nice to meet you all," Jessika said, finding that she really meant it.

Chika smiled broadly at her with her arms full of knitting and cuddling Meri. "You'll stay the night."

It wasn't a question.

Dinner happened in the living room. Rikah, who was much better with food and cooking than Jessika, helped Verika and Chika with preparation while Koki and Meri showed Jessika where the folding trays they used for eating were stored. They set them up in the middle of the living room with edges touching so they sort of formed a table, and placed cloth napkins, pottery dishes, and flatware on each one. Because some of the food was prepared by cooking in a pot on the stove in the living room, there was much dancing about to avoid colliding with each other.

The food was simple stuff, but filling, and afterwards everyone worked together to clear the remains away and wash everything at the basin of the communal water pump, just as the sun set.

"My, that goes much faster with six people instead of four," Chika remarked as they headed back into the house.

The four oldest sat down with another cup of tea while Verika helped Meri practice her reading with a worn storybook. When the little girl came to the end of her patience for it, Verika took over, reading the rest of the story, and by the time she'd finished, Meri was sleeping.

"I'll get her to bed," Verika whispered, picking up the girl and disappearing up the steep staircase with her.

"Thank goodness for my Verika," Chika sighed. "I don't know if I could handle a little girl on my own and get my knitting done. It's our main source of income, though Koki is a speedy courier."

Chika took a deep drink of her tea and held out her empty cup for Koki to refill.

"So, you two want to sneak into the castle," she said conversationally, but not loudly. "I'm curious to know why you'd want to do that. Not much good to be found in there these days."

Jessika winced a little. "Isn't it dangerous to talk about the rulers and everything? In the trade city, I was imprisoned for a while because we asked Quetal about it."

"That's because it was the trade city," Chika said. "Not many foreigners come all the way to the capital; it's discouraged. In the trade city, though, our neighbors from other kingdoms mingle with us, and we can't have them thinking the wrong sorts of things about us, now can we?"

Her rueful expression showed just what she thought about it. Jessika almost laughed.

"No, I suppose not," she agreed.

"So we can speak of things here, but not too loudly," Chika said. "I am of the opinion that our rulers watch the borders with far more attention than they give to things going on right under their noses. As long as you don't walk up and poke them in the eye, you'll be ignored for the most part."

"That's good," Rikah said, sounding relieved.

"Is it? When you're about to break into their house?" Chika retorted. "That sounds like poking them in the eye to me."

"I just want to see the king, and talk to him," Jessika explained, "and discover what really happened when Northnest was conquered, and see if the people are suffering, and if something should be done about it."

Chika sipped her tea. "That's a long list, child."

"And big dreams," Koki added softly from where he was sitting on an arm of a sofa, but it didn't sound like he disapproved.

Jessika looked uncertainly between them. "Do you think it's hopeless, that things should just be left the way they are?"

Chika stared into her cup. "Let me tell you this. When people have suffered and manage to escape the suffering, the last thing they want to do is anything that might bring that suffering back onto them." She made a vague encompassing gesture, mostly at Koki, and then at Verika as she came back down the stairs to the living room. "We have suffered, and escaped it. We're able to live a tolerable life, one that even has some joy in it. Helping you to go poke the dragon in the nose is not something we'd really want to do."

Jessika could see the point. "I understand. I've heard others say that, as well. I have loved ones, too, and I don't want them hurt. So you think it's better to leave things as they are?"

"Things were better before the wizards and the drakes came," Chika murmured darkly. "The country was happier. People were more prosperous. The laws were fairer. Is it worth it to spend blood and lives to try to return us to that? And how could we? The Feathyrs are dead. Who would fight the drakes? We never had magicians to begin with, so who would fight the wizards?"

She suddenly eyed Jessika sharply. "And who are you to think it's your job to poke into it at all?"

Rikah looked slowly to Jessika, and she could hardly move. Part of her wanted to answer. These were her people. She wanted to tell them. She wanted to trust them, but was it the right time? Would they keep her secret?

She swallowed and wet her lips. "You all live here together," she began awkwardly, not sure what she was trying to say, but grasping after it like searching for a stone underwater. "You, Chika, someone's clearly hurt you, and you,

Verika, you look different from most people, and I saw Meridan's hand, and Koki, I suppose there must be something different about you, too. You've come together to make a family because you're all different, and I have this feeling that the current rulers of Northnest—or Northborn—have all hurt you somehow?"

She trailed off, looking around at them with her lower lip caught between her teeth.

Chika gave a slow nod, although Koki and Verika didn't react. "You could say that, child."

"I, um, I don't really know what I should do, only that I can't abandon you. You and others they've hurt, or are hurting even now," she blurted, "and I don't know how to fix it, but I had to come here and try something."

Confusion had seeped into all their faces. Rikah was nervously still and silent, not trying to stop her, and yet obviously worried.

"I," she swallowed.

Body oddly numb and tingling, Jessika stood and turned around, presenting her back to the room. Her senseless fingers fumbled at the ties of her shirt for a moment before she managed to get them loosened. Trying her best to preserve modesty in front of these people she hardly knew, she worked her clothing off her shoulders until it slipped halfway down her back.

Chika's indrawn breath was audible as Jessika exposed the golden wing tattoos on her shoulder blades. Jessika stood with her arms clasping her clothes over her chest, head bowed, starting to tremble with fear of their reaction.

"Dear blessed ancestors," Chika whispered.

Then Jessika heard the creaking of the couch, and hands warm from holding hot tea touched her back, taking the edges of her clothing and tugging it back up.

"Cover that up, won't you, child?" the woman murmured. "Can't have someone spying in the window and seeing you like this."

Her gentle words brought the sting of tears to her eyes, and Jessika found herself biting down hard on sobs, but they still made her body twitch and shake.

"There, there," Chika crooned, turning Jessika with motherly pressure on her shoulders until they faced each other, and Chika drew her into her arms.

"Shh, shh now," the woman went on, stroking her hair and rocking her a little side to side, as though she were a decades older granny, not someone closer in age like a big sister. "So that's the answer, I see now. How you escaped and where you've been is a story for another day. Don't worry. Tomorrow Koki will show you where the tunnel is. Tonight you'll just get some good rest, aye?"

Jessika nodded against her shoulder, ashamed at her tears and flooded with the sensation of being held like a child, by someone like a mother. As wonderful and caring as Hawkwind had always been, she was still a griffin. There had been no one to hold her or Rikah or Kassie or Karo as a human mother would. With Chika's caring hug, memories of other times were resurfacing, from long ago, when she'd been held such. They swept over her and she surrendered to them like a leaf carried away in the wind.

After a trip to the communal latrines and a chilly evening scrub from the waterspout, Koki and Verika led Jessika and Rikah upstairs.

"I have the best room in the house, Hawkdare," Koki was saying, softly so as not to awaken Meridan. "It's all the way at the top. I hope you don't mind sharing; we don't usually have guests."

The second floor of the house was where the women slept. Chika had a bed at the front side of the house, wedged between a wardrobe and a chest of drawers. An open curtain looked like it could be drawn across the room to hide Chika's end of the floor. At the far opposite end, another curtain was hung to section off one corner, where Jessika assumed Meridan was now asleep in her own bed.

"I'll sleep with Mother tonight," Jerika whispered, "since her bed is the biggest, and you can have my bed."

"I don't want to put you out of your bed," Jessika whispered back. "I can do just as well on a couch downstairs."

"It's no hardship, really," Jerika replied, with a small smile. "Until we got this house, I slept with Mother all the time, and then for a while I shared with Meri. I'm used to it. Please, take my bed."

Hesitantly, the scaled girl put her hands on Jessika's upper arm and gave her a little push. Jessika gave in.

"All right. It's very kind of you, really, thank you," she murmured.

Verika's bed was bracketed by more dressers and a wardrobe. A set of bookshelves served as a partial room divider. Verika drew a clean sleeping shift from a drawer and handed it to Jessika; then stepped away to give her privacy to change while the two young men scrambled up a ladder that led to the third floor.

A few minutes later, Chika came up to join Verika in the big bed. They called good night, turning out their lamp, and Jessika heard the sound of the big curtain being drawn across the room. Jessika settled herself in Verika's bed and was just reaching for her own lamp when she heard a creak from the ladder to the third floor. She looked over, expecting Rikah coming down to say good night, but it was Koki, crouched halfway down the ladder with eyes glimmering in the lamplight. His blue pantaloons spilled all the way down to the next rung.

He gave her a little wave along with a shy smile. The room was so narrow that she could have reached out a hand and touched him with ease.

"Thank you for sharing who you really are," he whispered to her. "I know that was hard. I suppose your real name must be Jessika."

She swallowed, nodded.

"It was brave," he went on.

"Thanks," she whispered back.

"I want to share with you who I really am," he said, as his smile faltered.

Apprehensive but curious nonetheless, Jessika nodded again. "All right."

Awkwardly, his hand fumbled at the cloth of his voluminous pantaloons. Looking as though he was steeling himself, he pulled them up to his knees.

Jessika stared, fascinated and surprised. His legs were brown and furry, with a short pelt like a deer's. He had cloven hooves, and hocks like the hind legs of most all four-legged animals, including griffins. She wasn't sure what to say.

"I'm a faun," he explained: face pale. "I lost my family when I was little and now I live with Chika, but my horns are coming in, and I don't know how much longer I can stay in the city. Most people sense there's something different about me, but only Chika, Verika, and Meri know the truth, and you."

He let the pantaloons drop back into place and clasped his hands against his chest. "You think I'm strange?" he asked.

The hint of fear in his voice shook Jessika out of her fascination. "No," she said levelly. "No. I know people much stranger than you. I think you're pretty neat."

She caught herself smiling at him, but didn't try to stop it. After a moment, he smiled back.

"Some say fauns are a magical mistake from hundreds of years ago," he went on.

"You may be magical," Jessika replied at once, "but you're not a mistake."

Koki's smile widened two-fold. "Thanks," he said.

"You're welcome."

For a few moments more they smiled at each other. A twist of eagerness mixed with anxiety grew up in Jessika's belly and into her chest. The sensations warred with each other until eagerness won by a shred, and she shakily extended a hand toward the faun. His eyes widened a trifle, but his smile didn't fade, and after a moment he echoed the gesture. Their fingertips touched and then interlaced as far as their knuckles. His skin was warm and dry.

"Well, good night, princess," he grinned.

She smirked at him, shaking her head. "Don't call me that."

"I won't," he promised. "Just this once."

"All right."

"Good night, Hawkwings."

"Good night, Koki."

She wanted to hold onto his hand, not let him go, but as he stood, she allowed him to draw away. Koki climbed back up the ladder and vanished above. Jessika turned out her lamp, and lay down to sleep.

A breakfast of oatmeal with dried berries was followed by a nervous gathering in the dining-living room.

"Will you actually sneak into the castle today?" Chika enquired, voice soft. "You do know it will be perilous; you're almost certain to be caught. There's no telling what they might do with you then, but, Hawkwings, I truly think you shouldn't go. Perhaps you can send someone in your place?"

She made a vague gesture towards Rikah. He nodded at once.

"I'll go alone, if you want me to, Wings," he offered. "I know you want to see your father—if it is your father—with your own eyes, but maybe I could scout it out for you, and then lead you to the right place."

"It's my duty, no one else's," Jessika replied, trying not to sound defensive or like she thought he couldn't do it. "I'm going."

"You'll at least take Hawkdare with you?" Chika hoped.

Jessika shifted self-consciously. "I'm not sure who should go with me. Once we know where the entrance is, we'll have to talk about it."

She tried to give him a look implying what she meant—she wanted to talk about it with Karo and the griffins, too.

"But I'm not going in there today, except maybe a short distance, to get the idea of what it will be like," she went on.

"As I understand it, these tunnels under the castle were put in place as escape routes in case of emergency," Chika said. "They interlace at the deepest levels under the castle, and then link up with normal use halls, corridors, and rooms. At those points you'll find locked doors stopping your progress."

Koki cleared his throat with a little cough. "Well, you would, but you could also use these." He jangled a few small, slender bits of metal. "If you know how to pick locks?"

Jessika and Rikah exchanged glances, and she answered for them both. "No, we've never done that."

"It takes a little time to learn, but I could teach you," he offered with a shrug.

Chika scowled at him a little. "I don't like thinking of you as a thief, Koki, but you're making me do that."

"I don't steal," he said quickly. "There are just times, like these, when you need to get somewhere that folks don't want you going."

"I guess you'd better teach us," Jessika agreed.

"Great," he smiled. "We can do that first and then I'll show you where the tunnel is—without getting us in trouble," he amended, seeing Chika giving him a warning glare.

"It sounds like you'll have a full day," the woman grunted. "Just be careful, dear hearts. You'll come back to stay the night again?"

"I'm not sure," Jessika said, glancing at Rikah.

"It might depend on how late it gets," he agreed.

"Well, you're welcome here any time," Chika promised.

"Thank you. Next time we come, we'll see if we can bring you all dinner," Jessika added.

"That would be lovely, but not required," Chika smiled. "We have plenty to share. Now you had best get going. You're wasting daylight."

They said their farewells and Koki led them out into the streets.

Koki took them first through back ways and alleys to someone's locked gate. There, he pulled out his ring of metal bits.

"So," he began, "these are called picks, or lock-picks. With them, you can open just about any lock."

"But," Jessika pointed out, "do you know whose gate this is?"

"No, but it's fine. We won't go through the gate," he emphasized. "We'll just practice opening the lock, and when we're done, we'll lock it again and go away. As long as we don't trespass, it's alright."

Jessika puzzled over that for a moment. It almost made sense. Once Koki had demonstrated and explained how to select which pick or picks to use, how to insert it, and fiddle around inside until it opened, he offered Jessika and Rikah the opportunity to try, and talked them through it. Jessika didn't find it a quick skill to pick up. Even with Koki's hands on hers, guiding her, it wasn't easy to feel for the levers he spoke of, and it took several attempts and more than several minutes before she triumphantly opened her first lock.

Rikah picked it up much faster, and Jessika wondered if it was because of his experience carving wood, moving a blade carefully through the alternating bands of hard and soft wood in a carving. Koki also showed them how to oil the hinges, explaining that sometimes they might squeak and alert someone he didn't want alerted.

After they'd both mastered the first lock, Koki took them to another, this one a padlock, and they began again, using a different pick. Rikah had it popping open after only a few tries, and volunteered to fetch some food—as by then it was getting on towards noon—while Koki continued trying to teach Jessika.

"Do you feel here?" he asked, pushing on her fingers, clearly trying to get her to detect some difference in how the lock pick felt prodding at a certain spot.

"I don't know," she confessed. "I don't know what I'm supposed to be feeling for."

He was patient, even when Jessika thought she would have thrown up her hands in frustration long ago, had she been her own teacher. Koki didn't linger over her failures. He simply told her what she was doing wrong, and how to correct it. The only problem was that she couldn't seem to understand what she was feeling with the tips of the picks, and couldn't visualize what the inside of the lock looked like or what the pieces Koki referred to were doing.

"I can feel you lifting a few of the levers every now and then, but you have to lift them all, and then push the bolt back," he explained.

"I'm sorry. I don't even know what those are," she said.

So he showed her again and again, firmly guiding her hands, helping her to open it over and over, giving less help each time. Her confidence grew, but her hands seemed colder without his around them. Puzzling over why that was provided yet another distraction, which made her fumble, and led Koki to return to hands-on guidance—but she did make an effort not to fumble on purpose. Finally, as Rikah returned with a trio of stuffed rolls, she popped the lock open by herself. Grinning and relieved, she wiped sweaty strands of hair off her forehead.

"Excellent," Koki praised with a smile.

Jessika unconsciously decided not to analyze why his smile and his hands both made her feel so warm.

"I think I'll just call you to open all the locks I find, Dare," she rued, accepting one of the rolls with her cleanest hand.

"Hopefully, there won't be many locked doors down there," Koki said, "but if you practice some more, you'll get good at it. Let's move away from here while we eat; better not to spend more time around people's locks than you have to."

They found a sunny corner between two buildings and leaned against the walls.

"Were you really a thief?" Jessika asked Koki before she bit into her roll.

Koki winced only a little. "Not really," he murmured. "Sometimes you just need to get places, for reasons. I never stole anything, much."

Rikah smiled, and Jessika resisted the urge to do the same. After all, taking things you had no right to really wasn't polite.

"It'll be getting late," Koki went on. "We should probably leave off the picking and go to the tunnel now. I can let you borrow my picks for a while; I shouldn't need them. Just bring them back when you can."

Even though Rikah was the better lock picker, Koki handed them to Jessika, who stowed them in her pack.

"I'll be sure they get back to you," she promised.

Koki nodded shortly. "Alright then, this way."

Jessika followed Koki through the maze of buildings and streets, stony protrusions and open areas too steep to perch even the most persistent house on, until they descended a rocky pass choked with gravel and pebbles between a series of upthrust crags. One hand on each wall of rock for balance, they picked their way downward until tenacious, twisted pines and firs closed off the sky over their heads. The spurs of granite gradually diminished until they walked in true forest, although the ground was still steep and rough.

Koki skipped ahead, the little metal lantern he'd clipped to his belt bobbing on his hip, pausing from time to time to wait for them. They would inevitably come upon him crouched down at the side of the game trail, watching a slug make its way across the leaf litter or examining a cluster of mushrooms growing from a rotted log. Then he'd spring up, eyes twinkling, and lead them on.

The path described an arc from the village Chika lived in, around the side of the castle and one of the small mountains it perched on, to the far side where the land sloped up to the rock wall. Koki didn't take them to the base of the wall, though. He led them into the underbrush for several more yards, among densely growing trees, and then dropped down over a cluster of roots into a tiny hollow hidden by overhanging ferns.

He was crouching to one side of a small pool of water that had collected at the bottom as Jessika and Rikah hopped down beside him.

He pointed. "There."

Below the roots they'd just clambered over was an opening large enough for a griffin. The roots encircled it like a doorway, except for the threshold. The floor consisted of chunks of jagged rock through which a bit of a stream trickled. Everything was coated in shaggy moss, dark green near the water. The tunnel was black, without the slightest hint of light. Cool, clean air thick with the scent of earth and wet rock breathed from the opening.

"You want to go in?" Koki asked, not sounding much interested in the idea himself.

Rikah and Jessika exchanged a glance.

"I suppose we should take a look," Rikah winced. "We don't have any proper supplies to make it a real attempt, though."

"Is the tunnel this big all the way?" Jessika asked.

"I think so, unless there have been cave-ins," Koki answered. "It had to be big enough for griffins to escape through, after all."

"It's barely big enough," Jessika critiqued automatically.

Koki chuckled. "How would you—?" he started, and then broke off.

"I think we can find this place again," Rikah said firmly, and a trifle too loudly. "But let's take a peak inside just to be sure it doesn't dead end right away or anything."

Koki held out the little lantern. "Be my guest."

While Rikah got the wick trimmed and lit, Jessika turned to crouch by Koki.

"So how do you know about this tunnel? Does the whole city know?" she asked.

"I don't think many folks know," he replied. "It's possible not even the castle people know anymore, since they're, you know, different castle people from who used to live here."

"Maybe different," she murmured.

"Yeah," he allowed, "maybe different. At least some of them are different, but maybe some the same." He didn't sound convinced.

"Ready," Rikah announced.

Jessika was so eager to enter the cave she failed to realize that Koki hadn't really answered her question.

Chapter 8
The Tunnels

"So," Rikah whispered, "do you think this is the same tunnel that—?"

"No," Jessika replied at once.

"You mean you remember which tunnel we used?"

"No, but this one comes out in the wrong direction. I don't think Hawkwind circled the castle with us, and I really don't remember that hollow with the pool."

"That could have changed, though," Rikah pointed out, "as the forest grew and changed, but I don't remember it either."

"It's possible this one connects to that one somewhere," Jessika shrugged.

The tunnel remained level, and the jagged rocks underfoot gradually smoothed back into a floor clearly made by the hands of humans. For a while they had walked trying to keep their feet out of the stream of water among the rocks, but the water had dried up after some dozen or two yards, as the walls and ceiling of dirt and stones were replaced with actual bricks and mortar.

They came to the first fork in the tunnel and paused. Looking down each path, they saw only more tunnel stretching out before them.

"The walls seem solid," Rikah commented, slapping one lightly. "I think we'll be safe exploring down here."

"We could get lost," Jessika said.

"Maybe we'll need to draw a map as we go, and keep track of our turns."

"That's a good idea."

They gazed about for a few more moments.

"Do you think we should bring the griffins down here?" Jessika mused.

Rikah seemed to think about that. "Well, we can't bring Karo; his foot is all messed up. We'll probably want them to fly us down here and back each time we explore. They might as well come in with us."

"I guess we could do two teams then," she agreed. "Me and Joy, you and Thornspike, I guess?"

"Makes sense, as long as they're willing, and Thornfire or Starbright can make light stones for us."

"We'll have to pack some food."

"We can dry meat over the fire."

"Sounds delicious," Jessika smirked.

"We don't have much money left, but we could buy a little food. We'd have more but I lost a couple bronze coins in Chika's couch."

Her smirk turned into a smile. "On purpose," she confirmed.

"On purpose." He smiled back.

They turned to go back and she reached out to briefly comb her fingers through a bit of his hair. Growing up with griffins, who preened each other as greetings, farewells, and at any excuse for a sign of affection or appreciation, the humans had translated the gesture to combing at each other's hair or through the neck fur-feathers of their winged friends and family with their fingers. Somehow as they'd gotten older, the gesture had become a bit embarrassing and awkward with each other. Jessika assumed it was because they were adults now and any touch could be construed as courtship behavior.

Rikah, however, returned the gesture with no sign of anything other than brotherly affection. Jessika, Rikah, Karolan, and Kassandra had grown up as a family after the fall of Northnest, even though they'd been born to different human parents, but they all knew they had separate bloodlines and could be potential mates for each other: well, except Kassandra, who seemed to have gone and fused with a plant or something, and spent all her time with the unicorns.

"You're doing some heavy thinking there," Rikah remarked, jolting her from her thoughts.

"I guess so," she agreed.

"We're almost out," he said, pointing ahead. "Watch your step; it's getting rough again."

They emerged to find Koki sitting where they'd left him: gazing steadily down at the little pool, with his cap pulled low over his eyes. He looked up as they came out slipping and balancing on the rocks.

"How does it look?" he asked tonelessly.

"It seems to be in good repair," Rikah said. "No cave-ins or anything, so far as we went."

Koki accepted the lantern back and blew out the flame.

"So, you're really going to go in there," the faun mumbled, not a question, and stood up. "Anything else you need?"

"No, I suppose not," Jessika replied, a little put off by his sudden stoicism.

Koki nodded, hands on hips, not looking at her or Rikah. "Just bring me the picks back when you're done with them if, y'know, you survive going in there."

Jessika bit her lip. "You really think it's that dangerous?"

Now he eyed her, all his usual mirth gone from his face. "Yes," he stated.

She didn't know what to say.

"Don't go," Koki ordered.

"I, I have to," she stuttered.

"No, you don't," he retorted.

The three of them just stared at each other for several heartbeats: Jessika taken aback and a little scared, Koki looking caught between anger and fear, and Rikah just seeming several measures of uncertain.

Suddenly, Koki moved, striding forward with the hems of his pantaloons dragging through the pool. He seized Jessika's hand and lifted it, pressing the back of it to his cheek, his palm against hers. Eyes on the ground, head bowed, he held it there for a long breath. Jessika was too startled to move, but she felt her own cheeks heat with a blush, even as she felt Koki's cheek burn under her hand. Looking down at his bowed head, she thought she saw two peaks in his cap, near his forehead, and wondered if they were from the points of the horns he'd mentioned were growing in.

"Don't die," Koki said, voice rough. "My family died in there."

As graceful as a deer, he fled, dropping Jessika's hand and bolting for the forest with his legs propelling him rapidly up over the lip of the hollow, vanishing before either of them could call him back.

Jessika blushed hotter as Rikah turned to stare at her.

"What was that about?" he asked, bemused. "Like, because you're the princess, some kind of obeisance?"

Jessika had the hand Koki had held clasped in her other hand, cheeks still overly warm.

"I guess it could have been, but it, I," she swallowed, "I think, it sort of felt like that was courting behavior."

Rikah nearly recoiled with shock. "So he," he blurted, "he wants you for his mate? Or wants to, uh, mate," now Rikah was blushing, "with you?"

"Um, not exactly," Jessika managed. "Courtship is different with humans," she went on, stopping since Koki wasn't human. He'd been mostly raised by and among humans, so was he behaving like a faun or a human?

"I guess it sort of means that he," she puzzled out, "I guess he likes me, um, romantically."

Rikah's head snapped around. "And do you like him?"

"Um." Her face was burning again. "I'm not sure, but, maybe."

Rikah didn't say anything for a while. Then finally he began pulling himself up out of the hollow.

"Come on," he called. "Let's get back to camp before dark. It's a long ways."

Jessika went to follow him, but before she did, she pressed the back of the hand that had been against Koki's cheek against hers. She closed her eyes, and tingled with a sensation she could not explain.

Rikah spoke about the tunnel under the castle at the camp that evening. Jessika found herself feeling oddly solemn. Hawkjoy immediately volunteered to go with her into the tunnel, prompting Thornfire to raise his crest with concern.

"Hawkjoy, presumptive Hawkmother," he rumbled, "if this adventure is as risky as implications suggest, you are unwise to put yourself in jeopardy this way."

"We could even run into rainbow drakes or something," Rikah pointed out.

"We're going to be cautious," Jessika contributed. "This is no good if any of us get hurt or killed."

"I suggest you return to South-scree, and perhaps send Hawkswift in your place," Thornfire said.

Jessika cringed a little. "That actually might not be that bad of an idea."

Hawkjoy shook her head. "You both described the tunnel as being narrow, barely big enough for a griffin. My mother is considerably larger than I am, as she is much older. I will be able to maneuver through the tunnels better than she would be able to. Everything will be fine."

Her decisive, sharp gestures made her tone of voice clear, but Thornfire was still glowering.

"I don't like this," he said. "It might even be a better idea for Hawkwings and Hawkdare to go alone."

"But what if they do encounter a drake, Master?" Karo pointed out from his reclining position by the fire.

"I doubt there will be drakes down in a tunnel under the castle," the griffin mage scoffed.

"There could be other things, even if not drakes, that a weak little human can't handle," Karo went on. "Even like a group of other humans."

"Griffins and humans shouldn't fight each other," Jessika put in. "Not even humans should fight each other, or griffins fight each other, but for us to fight each other is wrong, so wrong."

From birth she'd been taught that griffins were her allies. Northnest had been founded upon that alliance. Of course now everything was changed in her former country, but her convictions remained.

"I agree," Thornfire said, "but it may be that other humans, other griffins, too, won't feel that way. They won't see friends and allies where we do." He twitched his wings and lowered his crest in surrender. "Perhaps having a griffin along will be useful in the tunnels," he allowed, "but I still don't think Hawkjoy should go."

"I'll go," Thornspike volunteered. "I want to go."

Thornfire now eyed her, too. "You're also an important member of your Line, Spike. Your blood will be refreshing when you're Linemother."

"I don't want to be Linemother," she spat back.

"Watch your tone," he scolded.

"I'll go, Master," Starbright said softly, "if you need me to."

"You're valuable, too," Thornfire refused. His eyes flicked at Waterleap.

Thornspike mantled a little. "So, what, only males get to go do dangerous things and explore new places, because their blood is expendable? That's unfair to everyone."

"I hope it won't be that dangerous," Jessika interjected before Thornfire could give the retort that the prickling of his feathers indicated was coming. "Sure it'll be scary and we'll have to be careful, but I think we need stealth, not a direct assault. I just want to get in and see if I can find my father, and if he is alive, find out what's going on, see if he's being influenced or something, or if he really is in control of the country and has just changed his personality, or what."

She stared directly at Thornfire. "I don't want to fight anyone or anything. Perhaps you can give us some magic tools or items that will help keep us safe."

The griffin mage ground his bill, making everyone wince at the sound. "I suppose I could come up with something."

"And I want my sister with me, if she is willing to come," Jessika went on, placing a hand on Hawkjoy's stretched out forearm. "There is no one else I would rather have at my side, and there are other females in the Hawk Line now that could take over as Linemother, if necessary."

"But South-scree will lose the blood of the Snow-in-lee Hawks if Hawkjoy does not produce at least one chick," Thornfire argued.

Jessika didn't raise her own voice to match him. "South-scree never had it before, and can do without it if it must. Hawkjoy's worth is in more than just her blood, as is true for all griffins. I think South-scree has benefitted and will continue to benefit greatly from both Hawkwind's reintroduced bloodline and from all the other griffins now in residence who came from Snow-in-lee. Thornsoft and others have all contributed to strengthening our Lines in the past ten years."

Thornfire actually looked a little chastised.

"I'll be careful, and I will go," Hawkjoy signed. "I am Hawkmother, and though you are an elder, you are not of my Line, respected Mage Thornfire. I will decide my path, but do not worry. South-scree will have chicks of my blood."

"I see you are determined to go," he grunted, as though the words were pulled from him unwillingly.

"Yes," Hawkjoy gestured gently.

Thornfire glared, fidgeted, and sighed, but finally surrendered.

"I will make you some contact stones, and Starbright will make you some light stones," he grumbled.

"Thank you, Thornfire," Jessika told him sincerely.

He glared, but nodded. Hawkjoy preened a bit of Jessika's hair, and she patted the griffin's arm.

"Tomorrow then," she said, "we'll make our first foray."

After dinner, Jessika lay resting but awake while the three mages worked on what Thornfire had promised, muttering to each other and palming half a dozen smooth stones. Her mind wandered among thinking about her father, Koki, and the tunnel labyrinth. None of the thinking was productive, but it was difficult to stop, and she didn't figure that talking about it with any of her companions would accomplish anything either.

"Here, pay attention," Thornfire summoned finally. "Hawkwings, Hawkdare."

Jessika pulled herself out of her stupor and scooted over to the mage. Rikah joined her, and Joy and Thornspike looked over.

"These are light stones," he explained. "You've all seen them before. Any of us three can renew them whenever they get low." He held out a few others. "These, however, are new to you; they're contact stones."

Thornfire handed one each to Rikah and Jessika. The stones felt and looked perfectly ordinary.

"These are only to be used in an emergency, if you get lost or are in trouble," the mage explained. "Use them too much, and of course they'll need to be recharged. Hold one tight in your hand, until your body heat warms it." He held up two more stones that were slightly different colors.

"Hawkdare, this darker stone is keyed to the one you carry. The lighter one is keyed to Hawkwings'. When you hold your stone tight, mine will heat up to alert me, and I will sense it magically as well. I will be able to detect the general direction your call is coming from. I will also be able to send heat pulses to your stone. I can send them in patterns that will convey different messages."

"How do we talk back?" Rikah asked.

"You can't, unless you're a mage," Thornfire lamented. "Since neither of you are, all we can manage is one way communication, from me, to you."

"It's better than nothing," Jessika declared, pocketing the contact stone.

"Not so fast," Thornfire said. "You have to learn the patterns now, so you'll know what I'm saying when I send you messages."

Jessika drew her stone back out and clenched it in her hand until it got warm. Thornfire held his stone, too: his eyes half shut in concentration, and a few moments later, Jessika felt two distinct, quick pulses.

"That's the code for 'I hear you,'" the mage said. "Next, is 'I'm coming to you.'"

Jessika and Rikah memorized the patterns, which were all relatively simple, for 'wait, can't help now,' and 'stay where you are.'

"The other weakness of these stones is that I won't know if it's actually you using the stone. Anyone could pick it up, hold it tight, and make me think you're trying to talk to me. Only a mage will be able to detect anything special about the stone, though. To anyone else, it will look like nothing more than an ordinary rock and they won't have any undue interest in it, unless you tell them what it is."

"Alright, I think we understand," Jessika nodded with a quick glance at Rikah to confirm.

Thornfire gave them a serious look. "If you get in trouble down there, under the castle, and call to me, it had better be for a good reason, because it will mean more griffins putting themselves at risk for you if we come try to save you."

Jessika met his expression as bravely as she could.

"I wish we could talk back," Rikah sighed.

"I get enough back talk from impudent Linemembers," Thornfire smirked, hooking his thumb towards Thornspike.

Both Jessika and Rikah grunted a laugh, but Rikah muttered, "That's not what I meant."

"I know," the griffin mage soothed, setting a warm and furry griffin paw on the crown of each of their heads. "Just be careful down there."

"We will," Jessika promised again.

"Get some rest then. You should probably leave early."

She nodded, turning away to see Joy lifting a wing, inviting her to snuggle under it. She couldn't help but smile, a little nervously, and dragged her mat and blanket over to the she-griffin's side.

Jessika, Joy, Rikah, and Thornspike left at dawn, their packs full of dried meat, some parchment and charcoal sticks for map-making, their magic stones, water skins, and a few other essentials. Jessica slipped her two truncheons into their special straps on her pack. Unlike their forays into cities, she figured this was an appropriate time to bring them along.

The group took the risk of flying down closer to the castle, since it was quicker than hiking, skimming just over the tips of the trees, close enough that the griffins occasionally brushed one with a wing. They found a narrow clearing to drop down through and made the rest of the way on foot. Coming from a different direction, it took a little time to find the hollow with the entrance.

"We'll barely fit through there," Thornspike remarked, lowering her head over the edge of the hollow and twisting it about with avian mobility. "And we'll get filthy."

"You'll live," Rikah told her.

"If you say so," she deadpanned back.

"Let's go." Jessika dropped down first and drew out her light stone.

Hawkjoy followed her inside without a flinch. Rikah and Thornspike came after them. The big bodies of the griffins blocked out nearly all the light from the entrance, so only the light stones lit up the walls and floor. They walked in silence as far as the first forking of the tunnel, where Rikah and Jessika had gotten to yesterday.

Rikah squeezed past Joy when she stopped. Jessika was pulling out her parchment.

"We're separating?" Rikah confirmed.

"Left or right?" she replied, nodding.

"Hmm, left, I guess," he shrugged.

"I have Koki's lock picks. If you run into a locked door, I don't know what you'll do."

"Try a different way, I suppose," he grunted, getting out his own parchment. "I don't expect this will be the only fork in the tunnel."

"I've decided that Joy and I will stay to the right, always taking the right hand path, for starters. When we've exhausted those tunnels we'll go back to the most recent branching, and the take the left, then stay right again, and so on."

"I see your strategy," Rikah said. "We'll do the same then, but bearing left except for locked doors."

They sketched out the first fork and then met gazes.

"We won't be able to tell day and night down here," Rikah mused. "We have some water and food, but."

"I was thinking, when the water is half gone, we go back," Jessika suggested.

"As good a plan as any."

Thornspike
and Rikah

"Let's go then," Thornspike urged from behind Joy.

Rikah grinned. "At least someone is eager."

"Right, let's go," Jessika agreed. "Joy, to the right."

"See you later," Rikah muttering, his grin fading.

"Be careful."

The pairs parted, and Jessika led Joy into the unexplored tunnel. The walls were stone and brick, with an occasional tree root poking out or a bit of fallen masonry on the floor. They stepped carefully through shallow puddles of water and sections slick with mud. After some minutes they reached another fork. Jessika pulled out her map to make note, but the tunnel to the right did not inspire confidence.

"Looks broken," Joy commented by hand.

"It certainly does," Jessika agreed by the same method.

Now that they were alone she found she wanted to keep quiet, as if to avoid notice, and the Snow-in-lee sign language was ideal for that, as long as they kept their hands in the light. The tunnel in question was half-caved in with rock and dirt. Joy wouldn't fit through.

"Stay here," Jessika gestured. "I'll take a look."

Joy caught her shoulder. "You shouldn't go alone. Let's just skip this tunnel. Nothing's going to be down there."

"There could be something," she said. "I have to check."

"What if you don't come back?"

"I'll come back. At the first sign of any danger, I'll retreat."

Joy's expression showed her dismay.

"I'll be extra careful, really," Jessika promised, laying her hands on Joy's chest.

Before the griffin could protest further, the human turned and trotted into the tunnel, stepping around the first pile of earth and moving deeper, light stone held out. It meant leaving Joy behind in darkness, since she didn't have a stone, but the griffin wouldn't be going anywhere, and had excellent hearing besides. Jessika bit her lip and tried not to think that Joy would be frightened, standing in the dark, waiting for her to come back.

Tree roots had penetrated the tunnel walls in several places, so Jessika thought this tunnel must be near the surface, but then it took a steep turn down, and she had to slow her aggressive advance to avoid slipping. The floor was as steep as a stairway, but without steps, and she put out her hands to the grimy walls for balance.

The incline continued for more than a few minutes, and she noted the air getting warmer. Was it supposed to do that? The steep grade began to level out as the tunnel got narrower and started making sharp turns left and right, as though it had to go around big rocks. Gradually, brick vanished from the walls, to be replaced with actual bedrock stone, so it appeared the tunnel had been carved out of the rock, not dug out of dirt and cleaned up with masonry.

A true cave-in where the ceiling had fallen in nearly blocked off the path after another turn, but Jessika squeezed by it and was able to go a little further, until a solid pile of boulders ended the journey. She put down her light stone and got out her map to mark it, and only then, with the light stone on the floor and her charcoal stick poised over the parchment and casting a shadow on it, did she notice another source of light.

Jessika looked up, searching, and finally climbed a bit up the rock pile to peer between boulders until she found a gap where faint light was seeping through. Light had to mean people, didn't it? Excited, she pulled herself up, trying not to slip, and looked through the gap—hoping to see a room beyond with friendly-looking people, or at least a hallway lit with lanterns.

Instead, she saw empty space. As near as she could tell, she was looking out into a rather large room or cave, but from her angle, with the blockage of boulders, she could see nothing but a distant rock wall. Frustrated, she turned her ear to the crack instead. Frowning, shutting her eyes, she thought she heard the far off sounds of movement, of people walking on dirt and gravel, and some kind of clanking or crunching, but nothing more. It could even have been her imagination.

There was no way she was going to be able to shift the weighty boulders that blocked her way. She couldn't even remove a few stones to make the light hole bigger; everything was wedged in too tightly. Jessika slid back down the pile and fetched her parchment, making notes of what she'd observed, and then, with one last look at the blockage, she turned to retrace her steps back to Joy.

"Finally," the griffin signed when Jessika came into view. "I was starting to worry."

Briefly, Jessika shared what she'd seen as they began to move off down the left hand path.

"At least there's some sign that there's something down here," Joy commented, "even if we can't get to it yet. It was good that you went and explored it."

Jessika agreed, and hoped the next tunnel would lead them down and give them access to the area she'd seen, but it wasn't to be. The tunnel forked again, they went to the right, and to the right again at yet another fork. That tunnel didn't lead down at all, but to a series of rooms without doors, which might have been storerooms, except that they were empty now of everything but a few disintegrating wooden crates and burlap sacks.

They retraced their steps to the most recent fork, and went left. That tunnel went up a set of stairs. At the top, they encountered their first door. It was still large enough for Joy to pass through, but solidly constructed of wood, and firmly locked. From the accumulated detritus around its edges, Jessika thought it probably hadn't been opened in many years.

"Can you hold this?" Jessika asked, handing Joy the light stone. "I hope I can pick the lock."

She drew out Koki's picks and examined the keyhole.

"I'm not very good at this," she rued. "It could take a while, and the lock looks old; it could be rusted shut."

Jessika knelt in front of the door and went to work. Joy adjusted the angle of the light whenever she needed it, and long past when her fingers had gotten achy, she got the rewarding clicks and clunks of the lock opening.

"Did it," she whispered. "Now I hope there's no one on the other side of this door."

Joy pushed forward and put her head to the doorjamb, listening, and then shook her head. She gestured Jessika out of the way, and took a hold of the iron ring that functioned as a door pull. Setting her feet, she leaned back against the weight of the door. Bits of accumulated dirt and grime began falling out of the gaps between door and frame as the griffin pulled, and the hinges groaned.

Jessika winced at the sound, but there was no sign of notice from the other side of the door. As soon as the door was cracked open, Jessika put her face to the opening. A gust of cool, dry air greeted her, and not a hint of light.

"Another hallway," she gestured to Joy. "Keep pulling."

Joy had to open the door all the way for it to admit her girth. When at last it stood wide open, Jessika moved cautiously into the other side. The tunnel continued straight away.

"This might have been a secret exit, I don't know," she murmured. "Let's keep going."

The hallway turned into more upward stairs, and then the scent of people and a wash of light brought girl and griffin to a halt.

"Stay here," Jessika signed.

Joy flattened her crest, but didn't protest.

Jessika continued edging up the stairs, hiding her light stone now. The scent of people grew stronger, and ranker, until it included all the odors of filthy bodies, rotting food, and neglected privies. Now sounds reached her ears: slight moans and groans, rough breathing, and the infrequent rustle of straw bedding.

With silent steps, Jessika crept closer, until a turn in the tunnel brought into view another door blocking the way. There was a window in it, covered by a metal grate. She snuck up to it and cautiously took a peek through. She saw a hallway lit by a few scattered lanterns. On either side were floor-to-ceiling metal bars, and behind them she spotted a few miserable humans huddled on pallets or in corners.

She looked hard at the people, wondering if she might recognize anyone, didn't, and figured that was to be expected; she could hardly remember her own mother's face, much less anyone else's. Still silently, she turned and left the way she'd come, back to the big door she'd picked.

"Shut it, please," she gestured to Joy. "We're not going that way until we've exhausted all other options. It leads to some kind of prison."

Joy shut the door, but not far enough to latch and engage the picked lock, and they went back to the next unexplored left-branching hallway. This time they walked long enough to take a small break for food and water, until they came to not a fork, but an intersection. Two tunnels led off from theirs at right angles and their continued straight.

"I knew there would be a lot of tunnels, but this could start getting complicated," Jessika remarked.

She mapped out the new development.

"We'll go to the right again."

The right tunnel led them up to another locked door. The gap at its threshold showed no light beyond, and neither of them could hear anything. The door was wood again, but not as heavy as the previous one she'd picked. There was no window in it. Jessika knelt down to pick the lock, and this door swung open easily, although it was narrower than was comfortable for Joy.

Jessika entered first and slowly into the room's darkness, feeling an uneasy chill as she did so. The air was cool, and carried a stale, gnawed scent, like wet campfires. She held out her light stone to reveal a room a few yards wide, and just in time; she almost toppled forward into a pit in the floor. Then she saw what was in the pit, and took a hasty step back, unable to stifle a gasp. Joy squeezed through the door beside her, just her forequarters, stopping as abruptly as Jessika had.

Together they stared down at the illuminated pit. There was no telling how deep it was, but the top layer of its contents was about Jessika's height down from the walkway that ran all the way around it. It was a good thing Jessika had seen plenty of animal remains before, or she might have been more deeply disturbed. Clumps of fur, broken feathers, empty skin, and stained bone poked up out of the morass. There were no flies, and no putrescence.

"This is old," Jessika gestured. "It's so dry in here that it didn't really rot, just desiccated."

They stared for another few moments at the irreverent tumble of corpses.

"I see feathers, big ones," Joy signed beside her. "These are griffin remains?"

Jessika knelt and then lay down on the dusty floor. She lowered her hand into the pit, holding the light stone. There were indeed numerous ragged feathers, and as she moved the stone it gleamed on a hooked bill and empty eye sockets: a griffin skull. There were other remains, however, that did not look like griffins, such as sections of crumbling scaled skin and some things that might have been horns or antlers, or frighteningly large teeth. She even glimpsed a skull that looked almost human, except that the jawbone was too heavy and the incisors too long.

She shivered, at the same time reminding herself both that the dead could not harm her, and that these poor beings were past suffering. She wondered how many there were. The pit was so large that they couldn't see everything, unless Jessika carried her light stone around the whole perimeter. She got up and dusted off her clothes.

"What are these remains doing down here?" Joy asked her.

"I don't know, but there are griffins in there. I'm pretty sure the Feathyrs didn't treat their dead like this, like trash."

"There are other creatures, too."

"Yeah, and I don't know why any of them would be down here, all mixed up like this."

Joy pointed with her bill at the far wall. "I think I see another door."

Jessika hugged her arms, still feeling chilled by the room. "I'm not sure I want to know what's on the other side of this. The door we came through is too small for griffins, really, so they must have come through that one. I wonder," she winced, "if they came in already dead or not, and who put them in here."

She went nevertheless to the next door. It was locked and she set about picking it. She succeeded with gratifying speed, but when she gave it a push, it wouldn't budge. She checked around the frame, but nothing seemed particularly tight. It was a large door but it didn't look like it should have been that heavy. Joy finally managed to contort herself enough to make it through the first door, although she lost a covert feather against a rough edge, which Jessika pocketed. The griffin came over to help, but she couldn't shift it either.

"It could be barred on the other side," Jessika shrugged. "We'll just have to go another way."

They backtracked—Joy squeezing herself through the pit-room door again—to the previous intersection, and took the next tunnel, the one that continued straight from the tunnel they'd initially come by. They paused along the way for another bite of food and sip of water, and Jessika started thinking maybe they should begin heading back. Then she decided they'd just go see what this tunnel led to, and if it wasn't anything useful they'd turn around, and come back tomorrow to explore some more.

The dampness of the underground gradually vanished as they walked. The walls and floors both became smoother and cleaner, although there was some sand and grit still underfoot. They also started finding lanterns bolted to the walls at regular intervals, although all of them were cold and dark, with rusty metal fonts and sometimes broken chimneys.

Then they found a door. It was not a door that blocked their way, but a door along the left side of the passage. It had a barred window, and through it came faint, indirect light. Jessika looked through it, seeing quite a clutter of boxy shapes in the room, but couldn't discern much detail. She saw the source of the light: it came through the barred window of another door leading out of the room.

She shared a glance with Joy.

"It looks like we're getting close to people," she gestured. "Someone keeps a light lit in the hallway or room beyond this one."

"We should be quiet," Joy advised. "You want to search this room?"

"I do."

Joy nodded, the angle of her feathers showing her growing anxiety. Jessika knelt to work on the lock, only to discover that the door was unlocked, but both the handle and lock looked rusty. She reached for the handle and bit her lip.

"I'm afraid of it squeaking," she explained, going to Koki's bag of lock picks to find the little bottle of oil he'd included in it.

She applied some oil to the hinges like he'd shown her, and carefully swung the door open, hiding her light stone as she did. The hinges made only a slight squeak, and Jessika moved into the room. She slowly put out a hand to touch the nearest box-like object, and after a few moments of examining it by touch in the low light, she identified it.

"It's a cage," she gestured to Joy.

She went to the next object, and the next.

"They are all cages," she said by hand. "It's a room full of cages, small ones and big ones."

"None large enough for griffins," Joy contributed.

"So then, for other animals," Jessika surmised.

She squinted closely at a few different ones. Some had perches like a bird might use. Others were strung with ropes as though the occupant might have been a climber. A few large ones had ramps going to a second level. Most had food and water bowls, and bedding or even a sleeping box. Some still had dried droppings in the bottoms of them. Faint unwashed animal scents came from the dirtiest cages, but even those scents were old, years old.

"These haven't been used in a long time," she concluded. "Whatever lived in them—"

"Is probably in that pit room now," Joy gestured darkly.

"You think so?"

The idea had occurred to her, too. Had the animals in here been pets, kept for food, or for some other purpose? There were no bodies in any of the cages, so they hadn't been abandoned to starve to death at least. Still, the empty cages took on a menacing air in the dim room, and Jessika tried not to imagine the ghosts of their former residents still clinging to the bars.

She walked resolutely to the other exit of the room and peered through the window. She saw a hallway leading off in opposite directions. Like the door she'd come in through, this door was along one side of a hallway, not at its terminus. One lantern lit the hallway, several yards away from the door next to a stairway that vanished upward. If they went that way, she thought they'd be likely to encounter people. She wasn't sure if she was ready for that.

Trying not to admit that her hand was trembling, she reached for the door latch and opened it as silently as she could. It wasn't locked either. She moved the door slowly, ready at any moment to stop to oil the hinges if they squeaked, but they stayed mostly silent. She put her head through the doorway, looking left and right. Her heart was pounding.

She saw no one and nothing of note. The hallway looked well maintained, with the cleanest floor she'd seen yet. Jessika stepped out into it. To her left it vanished into darkness, but to the right beckoned the stairs and lantern. Making her steps as quiet and cat-like as she could, she approached the bottom of the steps—eyes up, watching as her advance revealed each stair in turn.

She reached the foot of the stairs, seeing only more stairs above. Her nerve failed her; she was not ready to go up those stairs. Jessika turned to go back, and actually startled as she realized that there was another door beside her, to her right. She'd been so intent on the staircase that she'd not paid any attention to the hallway itself. This door was smoother and shinier than the others she'd seen so far, and the handle was clean and polished by frequent use. There was also stronger light coming from under the bottom edge of the door.

Jessika backed up, heart pounding again, not ready for such a door, either. She forced herself not to run back to the cage room, but she wanted to. Swiftly, she shut the cage room door behind her and turned, seeking Joy's familiar, warm presence. Jessika hid her face against Joy's chest, and the griffin gave her a one-armed hug.

"I'm scared," Jessika gestured. "Let's go back."

Chapter 9
The Skire

Hawkjoy made no mention of Jessika's fear when they emerged from the tunnel exit into the hollow where Rikah and Thornspike were already waiting, and Jessika was grateful. In the late afternoon light, her fear almost seemed a silly thing—unless she thought about the pit room, the cage room, and the final stair and door.

"Good, you're back," Rikah greeted. "We were starting to think we wouldn't reach camp until after dark. Find anything good?"

"Sort of," Jessika hedged. "You?"

"We found a couple other exits to the outside," he replied eagerly. "Maybe even the one Hawkwind used to get us out as kids. The locked doors stopped us from getting anywhere else interesting."

"You can use the picks next time," Jessika offered.

"Sure," he agreed, his enthusiasm deflating a little at her lack of resonance. "Let's get back to camp."

Thornspike needed no further encouragement, and turned to push her way through the underbrush, probably heading back to the clearing they'd landed in. Joy gave Jessika an encouraging nudge and Jessika gave her a quick neck scratch in response. They followed Rikah up out of the hollow and in Thornspike's wake reached the clearing, where the griffins labored into the air with their human passengers. Thornspike in particular struggled; her wing shape didn't give her as much lift as Hawkjoy's did.

Once at the camp, they saw that Starbright and Waterleap had saved them some food and they gathered around the fire. Rikah relayed his discoveries at once, with Thornspike contributing some details as well.

Then they turned to Jessika for her report.

In the warmth and light of the campfire, with distance between her and the castle, her fears had faded somewhat. She pulled out her map and flattened it to the ground: beginning to point out the path she and Joy had taken. Hawkjoy helped describe the rooms, and the others reacted with sympathetic concern.

"And beyond the cage room was a hallway," Jessika was concluding. "It had a lit lantern in it. To the left it was dark, but to the right was a stairwell and another door. I got the feeling that it was an area that was used regularly by people."

"Or at least today," Rikah suggested. "Someone must have lit the lantern for some reason."

"Right," Jessika agreed. She tried to keep her clasped hands from twisting with uneasiness. "So I went up to the foot of the stairs, and didn't see the top landing, and I didn't think I should go up it, or through the door, just yet."

"Hmm," Thornfire rumbled. "Perhaps exploring the occupied areas of the castle should be done at night?"

"At night?" Jessika gulped.

"To avoid encountering as many people," Thornfire nodded.

"That, makes sense," Rikah agreed slowly, looking to Jessika.

"Maybe," she agreed in a small voice.

Thornfire fluffed his feathers. "You will be going back tomorrow for further exploration? This is what you came here for, after all."

"Yes," she confirmed. "Right, of course we'll be going back for more. I just don't want to get caught."

The griffin mage's eyes reflected the flames of the campfire. "Of course. You must certainly not be caught."

Jessika slept that night cushioned between Starbright and Hawkjoy, using their body heat to augment the warmth of her blankets, and using their presence for comfort and a sense of security. Despite that, she found herself waking up over and over again from dreams of approaching the stairs beyond the cage room, or the door.

Time moved slowly in the dreams, each stair being revealed with painful inertia. She saw herself standing in front of the door for ages, unable to move away, expecting it to open at any moment, and fearing getting caught. Or she tried to flee from the sound of approaching footsteps, back to the safety of the cage room, but found her legs weighted down and her attempts at running sluggish.

After each dream she'd awaken, snuggle closer to Hawkjoy, and wish the dreams wouldn't return, but back they would come as soon as she drifted off again. Even there among her friends and family, she felt alone and helpless.

Dawn found her as tired as she'd been when she went to sleep, but she mounted up on Joy with her best smile, and they joined Rikah and Thornspike for another venture down into the tunnels under the castle.

Jessika knew perfectly well where to pick up the exploration. She stood outside the back door of the cage room with Hawkjoy after trekking out to it, and walked past it. The tunnel continued for several yards and took a swing to the right. Then it terminated in front of another door. Rikah had the lock picks today, so if the door was locked, they'd be stopped.

Jessika put out a hand and tried the handle, but it would not turn; the door was locked. With a sigh, she let her hand fall and gestured to Joy that they would go back and try another path. The only remaining option was the fourth tunnel that led from the intersection they'd found yesterday: the one leading off to the left from the tunnel they entered by.

The pair took that way and walked for several minutes, passing one new tunnel branching off to the left, until they came to a dead end. A heavy iron grate aborted the tunnel. Beyond it, pale crystalline light glimmered and danced, and Jessika crept up to the grate with rising curiosity. She saw a circular shaft plunging straight down from high above. Cool, moist air rose up from below and bathed her dry eyes.

Looking up, she could just barely see a circle of daylight. Looking down, she laid her eyes upon a well of dark water a few yards below her tunnel. It was the soft movement of the water that was reflecting bits of dancing light about. Several chains descended from above and vanished into the water, or dangled buckets part way down the shaft.

"This must be the castle's well," she gestured to Hawkjoy.

"It's rather pretty: soothing," Joy said back.

From the level of their tunnel, there was a rim around the shaft, in similar design to the rim they'd seen around the pit in the room of the dead. It looked like it would be possible to walk around the edge of the well, if the grate could be opened. Across from their tunnel Jessika spied another grate. She could only assume it led into a tunnel as well.

A quick search turned up hinges on one side of the grate, and a little lock on the other. She gave the grate a pull, but it resisted. Jessika's excitement sank. Without the lock picks, this way would remain shut as well. They'd have to go back and try that other branching tunnel. Before they left, Jessika made new notes on her map, and took one last look at the shimmering well.

Resigned, they retraced their steps yet again, and took the tunnel that led off to the left from the one that ended at the well. This tunnel ran a long distance, and looked possibly more disused than any other but the one full of cave-ins Jessika had explored the first day. There were loose bricks that had fallen from the wall and ceiling, along with little flows of dirt and mud.

Midway along, the pair paused at a small opening to one side. Jessika poked her head in and discovered that it was only a narrow room not even as wide as her outstretched arms. A cold, dead lantern hung from a hook in the back wall, but she didn't see the room's main feature until she stepped on it. A couple steps into the room her foot came down on wood instead of stone, and Jessika knelt to examine the anomaly.

"It's a trap door," she gestured back to Joy, who couldn't easily fit in the room.

A stout metal ring was affixed to the center of the hatch. Jessika didn't see any locking mechanism, so she set her feet, took a hold of the ring, and pulled. She expected the door would be heavy, but even giving it all her might it wouldn't budge.

"Drat," she huffed aloud, and then signed. "It must be locked from below somehow."

"We're supposed to be going up anyway, not down, right?" Hawkjoy reminded her.

"I guess so, but I'm really curious what could be down there."

"Another time?"

"It'll have to be," she agreed reluctantly, and marked it on her map.

Several more yards along, they passed a widened section of the hallway. Shelves lined the broader portion, and a quick investigation proved the boxes and bags left behind on them to be full of nothing but withered remains and largely unidentifiable fragments. There was a box that held what must have once been new torches. They seemed relatively intact and Jessika thought they might still work.

Just beyond the widened section, they encountered a door in the wall. This door was unlike others they'd seen, as it was larger, solid iron, and employed an uncommon latching mechanism. Jessika put her hand out to touch the wheel that opened and closed the door. She didn't remember much of the escape, but she remembered she'd been taught a little about these kinds of doors. They were the bolt hole doors, which sealed the castle's escape tunnels behind the escapees.

"Hawkmother—err, Hawkwind and I, with the others, escaped through a door like this one," Jessika explained. "She shut it behind us. This must have been one of the escape tunnels."

"Do you think this is the same one you used?" Hawkjoy asked eagerly.

"It could be. I don't remember. Hawkwind just knew where to go, and we went with her." Jessika turned away from the door. "We can keep walking."

"You don't want to try opening this door?"

She looked back at it. Behind it would be the nursery, if it were the door she'd escaped through. Her older brother, the prince, had died in there trying to defend her and the other children. Hawkwind had told her the story a few times; she didn't remember it herself. He'd picked up a crossbow and put a bolt into one of the drakes, creating the distraction that had allowed Hawkwind to act, to fight off the drakes, gather the children, and get them away.

She couldn't remember her brother, except to know that she'd had him in her life for a short while.

"No," she told Joy. "I don't want to try opening it."

"You can't pass by every door, you know."

Hawkjoy's gestures and posture were gentle, not accusatory, but the reminder thunked solidly into Jessika anyway.

"I'm scared to open doors," she confessed. "I have to, to get anywhere further, but I'm scared."

Hawkjoy walked her hind feet in and sat. "This thing you are doing," she began, "I know it is hard, and yet you feel you must do it. You must decide if the risk you run is worth whatever reward you might get from its successful completion."

Jessika stared off at the wall, seeing the griffin skull in the pit room in her memory. All those griffins died, all the Feathyrs, except Hawkwind. Her family died, all except her—or did they? Was her father alive? Did it matter? She hardly remembered him; Hawkwind and Hawkswift, Thornsoft and Thornwing and Thornfire: they were the parents she knew best now. Her father surely thought she was dead, if he did live.

"How can I go through my whole life, and never know?" she whispered helplessly. "I can't get it out of my head. I can't leave it alone."

Hawkjoy touched her with a wing. "I understand, and I want to help you. Well, maybe I can't understand completely, but I imagine how I might feel if I'd heard that my father was still alive. Of course I would want to find him."

"And I would help you," Jessika affirmed.

In the dim light, Joy smiled and nodded. Jessika took a deep breath.

"Alright, I will have to open some doors."

Leaving the storage area and bolt hole door behind, they continued, until their tunnel reached another, making a T junction. Jessika noted it on her map, and led them to the right. A while later they reached another bolt hole door. Jessika walked up to it, and put her hands on the wheel again. At this door, there was no widened storage area, only a small shelf to one side. Whatever had been on it was long gone.

As she looked over the door and the area, she saw something anomalous at the bottom edge of the doorjamb. She bent down to touch it, and found it to be a shred of cloth caught in the door. It wasn't so old as to have crumbled yet. With a yank, she pulled it free, and held it close to the light stone. Colors were not well illuminated by the light stone, but it was pale, maybe light blue, pink, or purple. She rubbed it between her fingers, and then pocketed it.

"I don't think opening these big bolt hole doors is a good idea," Jessika gestured to Joy. "They'll be noisy and noticeable. I think I'll start with regular wooden doors."

"A good choice," Joy agreed, making no comment suggesting the girl was making further excuses.

Jessika led them off again, back to the T junction, and to the left this time. They descended some stairs, and went up some others. Two more tunnels branched off to the left, but Jessika kept hugging the right wall. After some more time, she stopped and covered her light stone, suspecting an alternate light source. Within moments, her eyes adjusted and she could see a delicate light in the distance. It was enough to pick out some details in the brick walls.

"I think it's an exit," she said.

With more confident feet, Jessika strode towards the light, until it became as bright as day. She and Joy passed an open iron door and emerged into the forest through a little cave. Ferns and shrubs surrounded the exit. Jessika stepped past them and gazed around, locating the walls of the castle back behind her through distant trees.

For a few minutes she stood and basked in the forest air.

"Shall we take a break for food and water?" Joy suggested.

"Yes, let's."

Jessika found a mossy seat and broke out the dried meat and water. Joy had eaten heavily only recently and didn't need to eat, but had a few swallows of water. Together they rested their psyches from the anxiety of the dark tunnels.

Refreshed, they headed back in to try some of the other branching paths, but they proved to be sadly mundane after the excitement of wells and trap doors and bolt holes. The pair did discover a few more storage areas, and one caved-in tunnel that was totally blocked, but as they neared the end of their options for exploration, Jessika could only shrug over the monotonous notes on her map.

At last they were down to just one option again, and headed down it, hoping for another dead end so they could get back to camp before dark. Jessika was hurrying perhaps faster than she should have been when the sound of footsteps made her jolt to a halt. She turned part way to gesture to Hawkjoy, and then hid her light stone.

In the total darkness they waited, ears straining. The distant sound of steps on the damp floor came clearly to them, and Jessika began wondering if they should try to retreat and hide in a cross-tunnel. Then a pearly glow appeared in the distance and she heard the familiar subtle sound of feathers rasping against each other as a griffin's wings shifted when it walked.

Tension lifted from her and she uncovered her light stone. It had to be Rikah and Thornspike; their tunnels had intersected. Jessika began moving forward again and purposefully scuffed her feet on the floor to alert them without startling them—she hoped.

"Wings?" Rikah's tentative voice called out.

"Dare? It's us," she replied.

In moments both had rounded the corners keeping them apart, and Hawkjoy chirped with welcome.

"I'm glad it's you," Dare sighed.

"Yeah, but I haven't seen anything alive down here. Have you?"

He shrugged. "No, nothing but a few bugs."

"We're out of tunnels to explore."

"So are we. We've actually been this way before. We were thinking of going to open one of the bolt hole doors, since there's nothing else to open now."

"You opened all the locked doors you found yesterday?"

He nodded. "A couple of empty rooms, and one stairway going up. I followed it. It was too small for Thornspike. It led to a hallway that was actually carpeted. I went a little ways, and then there started to be lanterns, and other doorways off it, and I got worried I'd see someone, and be seen, and I came back."

"Let's walk to the exit," Thornspike interrupted. "We might as well leave now, if we're not going to open one of those iron doors."

"It is getting a little late, I think," Jessika agreed, "but tomorrow we're going to have to get more aggressive about exploring past doors, into inhabited areas. Hawkjoy reminded me that we're never going to get anywhere if we don't."

Thornspike had already turned to lead the way out. Rikah and Jessika followed, side by side, with Hawkjoy bringing up the rear.

"What do we do when someone sees us?" Rikah wondered.

Jessika furrowed her brow in thought. "I don't know. Maybe it will depend on their reaction. Maybe some people won't even take notice."

"But others might ask us why we're there or who we are. I don't suppose we should tell them the truth."

"I don't suppose so, no," Jessika agreed.

"You should try to avoid people," Thornspike commented, as though it were obvious.

"I know, but it could be hard," Rikah replied.

"How so? You're so small. It should be easy," the she-griffin scoffed.

"Except everyone else up there will be about the same size as us," Rikah grumbled back.

"Oh," Thornspike said, as though that hadn't occurred to her.

"If someone does take objection to us," Jessika worried, "we could be in big trouble."

Rikah grimaced in the glow of the light stones. "Yeah, but I don't want to give up and quit."

"No. We'll have to take the risk."

Jessika's sleep was restless again that night, but she tried to minimize her tossing and turning to avoid disturbing Hawkjoy and Starbright on either side of her. She spent drowsy hours staring up at the starlit sky and listening to the slight rustles of night creatures in the forest investigating the remains of the griffins' meals. She drifted in half sleep as dawn approached, and then found herself wide-awake as the first rays of sun broke the night's hold over the mountains.

"Let's go together to one or another of the remaining locked doors, open it with the picks, and then I'll go in," Rikah suggested. "Then you take the picks and go to another."

"I'm pretty sure most of the palace was designed to be large enough for griffins," Jessika said, "but there won't be any griffins there now, so Joy and Thornspike will cause immediate alert."

"I'll go with you as far as is safe," Joy gestured, "but if you need me to stay behind and wait at any point, I can."

"Me, too," Thornspike said shortly.

"Watch yourselves," Thornfire cautioned as he handed back recharged light and contact stones. "Behave confidently. People will be less likely to question you if you act like you belong."

"We'll try that," Jessika said. "Thanks, Elder."

"Come back safe."

"Alright, it's open," Rikah whispered. "Thornspike and I will go this way."

He handed the lock picks to Jessika. She took them, hiding a sigh; she'd wanted to explore the tunnel on the other side of the well, but it was the closest locked door to the area Rikah had been exploring, other than the bolt hole doors, and they'd agreed to leave those for last. There was also the trap door, and the door into the dungeon, but those also seemed less likely to be useful, so they would be left for second-to-last. Then there were also the two hallways Jessika and Rikah had each started exploring and retreated from: third-to-last.

"Be safe," she told her Hawkbrother. "I'll go explore through that other locked door beyond the cage room hallway."

"Right," he nodded, face so tight that he couldn't manage a smile.

"See you this evening at camp," she said firmly.

"Right," he repeated.

Jessika turned to go as Joy and Thornspike gave each other a little part-ing preening. She consulted her map for directions, and led the way, until she stood again in front of the door that terminated the hallway past the back door of the cage room. Her hands were shaking as she knelt and lifted the lock picks. She had to stop to take a few minutes to do some deep breathing to calm down.

"I didn't know this was going to be so scary," she gestured up at Hawkjoy with a rueful smile. "It would be easier to just walk up to the front door and demand to see my father."

"But less effective, I expect," the griffin said back.

"You're probably right. If he is some kind of prisoner, it would just put me in prison with him."

Resolutely, she raised her hands to the lock and set to work. The lock was stiff, but after a few minutes, she got the click she wanted and pulled in the bolt. Tucking the picks back in her pack, she turned the handle and inched the door open. She peered through the crack and saw that it was a big room with a bright spot at the far end where it seemed more than a few lanterns were clustered. Despite the localized light, the rest of the room was shadowy, and nothing moved.

Jessika waited, breath held, for any sign of movement or the slightest sound, but nothing came, and she marshalled her courage to push the door the rest of the way open. Several steps led down from the doorway to the floor of the room. Jessika pocketed her light stone, and tried to make her heart stop beating so fast.

"Let's go," she gestured over her shoulder to Joy.

They descended into a bulbous room as large as a banquet hall. Except for two doorways and a couple sets of shelves crammed with books and boxes and jars and sacks, the room's walls were coated with old black canvas draperies hung on wrought iron poles. Several tables of wood, metal, and stone—some as small as bedside tables and others large enough for an extended family to sit at—occupied the main floor space of the room, all arrayed with storage drawers and some with objects that looked like strange tools on them, but there were only a couple wooden stools. The walls and floor were stone block, the ceiling wood, and the floor had a pair of metal grates in it. It smelled of old rust.

Jessika gestured to Hawkjoy. "Shall we pass through?"

The griffin nodded in reply, and they began walking silently through the room. They were about halfway across when movement from the lit end of the room—where they were headed—made them startle.

"Who's there?" a strong but feminine voice demanded.

Jessika and Hawkjoy backed up a few steps, getting ready to run, as a woman stepped out from where the comparatively bright lamplight had hidden her. As she passed in front of most of the light, Jessika saw that she'd been sitting at a desk where a thick book lay open, as though she'd been reading.

"Don't go," she called out. "Don't be afraid."

The woman approached boldly, although she didn't appear to be armed, and Jessika froze with indecision. She was tall, lean, with grey streaked brown hair pulled up into a bun from which some twisting tendrils had escaped to curl around her neck. She wore a practical, snug-fitting coat and a thick, straight skirt against the underground chill, all in dark brown colors, and knitted fingerless gloves on her long, stick-like hands. As she approached, she lowered a pair of heavy spectacles from her face, letting them dangle on a fine chain against her chest.

"That is, oh my goodness, that's a griffin. You have a griffin," the woman panted, a smile blooming over her face.

"Who are you?" Jessika asked cautiously.

"Goodness me, my manners, gone," she prattled with a wispy wave of her hands, still smiling. "I'm Germaine. Skire Germaine. Welcome to my palace of knowledge."

"I'm Hawkwings. This is Hawkjoy," Jessika introduced warily.

"A pleasure. Well, aren't you a beauty. Just look at you," she gushed, striding closer to Hawkjoy with no sense of fear.

"She can't talk. Her throat was injured when she was a chick," Jessika went on doggedly, but bewildered.

"Injury to the larynx? How sad. Is she gentle?"

"Uh," Jessika traded a look with Joy. "Yeah, I guess."

The woman walked right up to Joy and ran her hands boldly over her fur and feathers. "What lovely coloration, so healthy. She's young, only a couple decades?"

"Uh," Jessika grunted again.

Hawkjoy flinched a little at the uninvited touching, giving Jessika a half amused, half uncomfortable glance.

"Oh, oh my dearie goodness," the woman exclaimed, stepping back with glowing eyes and a gaping, blazing smile, "she's pregnant, isn't she? Aren't you, you beauty?"

Jessika choked on a reply. How could this woman suggest such a thing? How could she know? Had Joy and Waterleap tried for a chick during Joy's first heat? Maybe it had been an accident because they were both inexperienced? From what Jessika knew, chicks usually weren't accidents, but maybe it could happen.

"I don't know. Are you, Joy?" she asked softly.

Hawkjoy made a shouldering rolling duck-of-the-head gesture that Jessika had learned meant she was embarrassed and didn't want to talk about it, but yes.

"You should have gone back to South-scree," Jessika all but scolded. "You shouldn't be running around with me."

Hawkjoy's neck feathers lifted a trifle. "It doesn't bother me yet," she gestured. "We'll be going back soon enough."

"Only a couple months along," the strange woman was going on.

Hawkjoy sidestepped, irritated, as the woman tried to touch her belly.

"Now, now, easy there, beauty," the woman crooned. She paced around Hawkjoy and back to stand in front of Jessika, face still glowing as if with candlelight. "Dear young lady, I don't suppose you'd be willing to part with her? It's been ages since I've even seen a griffin, much less had one come parading right into my lab. I'd be willing to compensate you richly. I've seen so few pregnant griffins."

It took Jessika a few moments to understand what the woman was saying. "You want to buy Hawkjoy?" she retorted. "You can't buy her; she isn't for sale."

"Come now, everyone has their price," the woman said soothingly. "I have great resources at my disposal; I'd give you more than what she's worth. I wouldn't want you to walk away feeling cheated, and after all, it is sort of like two griffins, not one."

Jessika squared her shoulders. "No, you don't understand. She's my sister. She's a person. People aren't bought and sold."

The woman nodded understandingly. "Of course, of course you feel that way, and she seems like a person because she's so clever, but she is just an animal, not like us."

"We're animals, too, we're just smarter than most," Jessika countered, "and griffins are just as smart as humans."

She kept nodding as though she were a marionette on strings. "I've known other people who said the same things, but all my research shows that they are not our equals. Their brains are smaller than ours, in proportion to overall body size, for one. Not to mention behavior: aggression, violence. They are completely promiscuous. Did you know that? Where is her husband who fathered that baby in her? Not here, is he? No, because griffins don't love or feel like humans do."

Hawkjoy hissed.

"Griffins love," Jessika proclaimed back at her. "They are different than us, but they are still people. Let's go, Joy."

This wasn't going right. Jessika hadn't wanted to encounter anyone, much less have someone see Joy, much less have this kind of interaction. She should have checked the room herself before bringing Joy in. She should never have assumed that there was no one behind those bright lights; she should have checked it first.

Now she didn't know what to do except get out, and get away from this bizarre woman. Worse, this could mean trouble for the whole exploration. Now she'd been seen, and if this woman spread the word—Jessika couldn't imagine how far-reaching the consequences could be.

"No, don't go," the woman ordered, and then began babbling, words pouring out like water through a stream in spring. "I will have her. I've only examined one other pregnant griffin—the first one I encountered I didn't know was pregnant until she suddenly gave birth one day—and I won't let go a chance to have another. There is so much more I could learn, so many unanswered questions. My research is incomplete."

Hawkjoy let out another hiss, backing up a few steps. "Yes, let's go," she gestured to Jessika. "This woman is creepy."

Jessika turned carefully as she hurried away, keeping both the woman and Hawkjoy in sight, backing towards the open door to the room. "She might report us," she gestured hurriedly. "What should we do?"

"Where are you going?" the woman demanded, voice nearing a screech. "Come back here."

Jessika slid her hand behind her back to where she could grab the handle of one truncheon; she supposed she'd have to whack the woman on the head, knock her out, and maybe tie her up, so she wouldn't give away their presence immediately. Hawkjoy saw her action, grimaced, but nodded.

"Don't you dare leave with my griffin," the woman screamed. "Altare!"

Her fury made Jessika hesitate for a moment. In that moment, a slithery, wet sound dropped into the room like a splatter of mud, and with a warped glimmer of light a man appeared near the far door. Hawkjoy and Jessika both startled a little, dodging off to one side and ramming into a behemoth of a metal table that shrieked as its legs were pushed over the stone.

"You called, Skire?" the man purred, striding forward with floor-eating steps.

He was not quite as tall as the woman, but just as thin, with a wild bush of black hair and beard to match, making him look as fluffy as a griffin chick. He wore tight red and black garb that flared out around his wrists and ankles. He carried a short stick in one hand that he twirled between his fingers.

The woman's arm shot out, finger pointing imperatively. "I want that," she intoned with an air that fully expected complete obedience.

The man smiled. "As you wish, Skire."

"Joy, run," Jessika ordered.

She ripped out a truncheon and rushed the man at full speed, while Hawkjoy turned to flee. Jessika vaulted a table, pulling her arms back to deliver the strongest two-handed blow she could—but while she was still in the air, a bellow of challenge building in her chest, the man flicked up his slender little stick, pointed it at her and uttered a single guttural word that twisted in his mouth like a worm in a bird's bill.

Jessika's vision vanished as though the room had been painted on a sheet that had been whipped aside, and she was falling into a dark eternity that snatched her consciousness away.

Skire Germain

Chapter 10
Old Man and the Bat-cat

Jessika awoke slowly. Her body ached like she'd fallen down a flight of stone stairs. She lay on her front, chest and hips throbbing, head aching, knees and forehead and chin prickling with twinges of pain where it seemed she'd struck the ground. Cold winds battered her, but for a few moments the rusty scent of Skire Germaine's basement lingered like a bubble of insulating air. Gradually, the winds blew it away, and Jessika's ears popped once and then again.

A weight lifted from her back and she looked up: blood running down her face from where she'd hit her nose and chin. Her truncheon had gone tumbling away several feet and she couldn't reach it. Her hands scraped over rock and pebbles as she struggled to push herself up.

"Mountains," she shivered. "Where am I?"

Hawkjoy wasn't with her.

"How did I get here?" she hissed, sitting up and hugging herself with her arms. "That man: he sent me away, and Joy's still there."

She fought against a futile whine of despair. Whining wouldn't help. Hawkjoy was on her own, and so was she. Jessika checked the sky. It was noon and she was high in mountains that were already frigid. She had minimal survival gear.

Jessika tottered to her feet, checking for injuries: no broken bones. She could walk, and there was no question what she should do. She wouldn't survive a night at this altitude; she had to go down. It didn't matter which direction, as she didn't know where she was anyway. She'd take the easiest path she could find. The further down she went, the warmer it would get. Once she survived the night she'd consider what to do next to find a place she knew, from where she could begin to take steps to find Hawkjoy and the others.

Jessika fetched her fallen truncheon and stowed it, and began walking at her fastest safe pace. She didn't recognize the mountains, but eventually she'd find some kind of civilization and someone she could ask for directions. She nibbled her lips and grimaced. If she was a long way from Northnest and the Aeries it could take days, even weeks, to return.

Of course: the contact stone.

Jessika fished in her pocket and found Thornfire's magic stone unhurt. She held it tight in her hand, and eventually it began to emit a faint trace of heat. The slow response didn't seem like a good thing. Maybe it meant Thornfire was a long way away. She tried to keep walking as she waited for a response, keeping part of her mind on the stone, most on her footing, and as little as possible on Hawkjoy. Worrying about her friend wouldn't help her, and would only hinder Jessika's focus on survival.

Jessika had sighted the first stunted alpine trees when she felt the magic stone begin to pulse. Thornfire had sensed her call and was responding. Now she paused to count the pulses and analyze the pattern, which repeated several times.

He was saying: "we will come to you."

Not being magical herself, she couldn't reply, and since she still had no idea where she was, there was no telling when Thornfire or any of the others would reach her. Jessika put the stone back in her pocket and continued her downward trek. She passed into the stunted trees and then into denser forest, feeling the afternoon air warm as she went.

Under the trees it was harder to gauge the sunlight, so she began looking for a place to spend the night, not wanting to be caught out if darkness fell rapidly. She was thirsty, too, but finding water was secondary to finding shelter for the night; she could search out water the next morning. Again and again she forcibly turned her thoughts away from Hawkjoy and useless hypothesizing of what might be happening to her.

As she wound deeper into the forest, still going downhill, she caught the scent of wood smoke, which brought her up short like a slap in the face. Wood smoke meant people, civilization, and shelter, and maybe even food, but that didn't mean it would be safe. The people could be bandits or rogue griffins— although griffins rarely made fires. Still, it was worth investigating as long as she was careful.

Tracking down the source wasn't the easiest thing, but among the trees there wasn't much wind, so the smoke couldn't have traveled very far. Within several minutes, Jessika was able to pick out the haze of it between the trunks, and a few minutes later she crouched down in the shrubbery to scrutinize the source.

A home was built into a hillside. The smoke emerged from a stone chimney sticking up at an angle out of the hill. There was a crude but sturdy fence encircling the entrance, which had a plank door that stood slightly ajar. Within the fence loafed a pair of goats, and chickens milled about both within and without it, occasionally meandering in and out of a rough wooden coop. A rooster kept watch from one fence post. Wooden storage boxes and large pottery jars stood against the hillside on either side of the door, under a slight overhang of wooden logs topped with earth.

There were two windows, through which burned cheerful lights. Mingled with the smoke, Jessika could smell dinner. It didn't look dangerous, and even though she knew perfectly well that looks could be deceiving, it didn't take her long to make her decision. A night alone in the cold forest would be risky, too. She got up and headed towards the humble house.

As she approached the fence, something screeched from within the house, and Jessika jumped, but then a voice called out.

"Come in, come in; don't mind the shrieking."

The voice sounded male, coarse, and old, but cheerful. Under the attentive eye of the rooster, she cautiously opened the gate, shut it behind her, and approached the door. Another screech, this one more shrill, startled her again.

"That's enough, really," the man's voice scolded. "She's no threat."

There was the sound of scratching and scrabbling over wood and stone, and then the man pushed the door open.

He was of above average height, with a white beard and mustache, and shaggy, patchy white head hair. His face was weathered and wrinkled from sun and smiles. He wore a white and blue patterned robe that he belted at the waist, over practical rough brown pants and shirt, with sandals tied onto his feet.

"Come in," he repeated, beckoning and holding open the door. "Don't be afraid. It'll be dark soon, but this place is safe enough."

Jessika stepped through and into the cleanest, coziest cottage she'd ever been in—not that she'd been in many. The floor was flagstone covered with woven rugs, the walls paneled with wood. A heavy wood table sat to her left, under one of the windows, with a lantern burning brightly atop it. To the right was a kitchen area with a small counter, drying rack, and cupboards and a washbasin. A bit deeper into the house and directly in the middle of the room was the fireplace stove on which dinner was bubbling in a pot.

Beyond the stove was a deeply cushioned reclining chair, surrounded by bookshelves and candle nubs, and a wood framed bed covered in patchwork quilts and knitted blankets. Between the foot of the bed and the chair, a heavy drapery depicting a prancing unicorn covered a two-foot wide section of wall. From the ceiling dangled herbs and pans and baskets and drying laundry on stretched twine. One of the baskets near the stove was swinging vigorously, as though someone had just given it a shove.

"What was that sound?" Jessika found herself asking.

"Just Breeka, a bat-cat," the man answered. "It's a bit noisy, always warns me when company is coming. You'll have to forgive it."

"It?" Jessika echoed as the man turned to the stove to tend the pot.

He poked the swinging basket with the handle of the stirring spoon. "Say hello, nicely," he chided.

A face emerged over the edge and Jessika's eyes widened. If a house cat, a bat, and a human baby had somehow had their faces mixed, it might have looked something like the creature that stared at Jessika now. It had grey fur darker than Hawkjoy's, an upturned leaf-like nose, and green feline eyes with almost human brows and lips, although the upper lip was split in the fashion of cats. Ears somewhere between cat and bat crowned its head. It opened its mouth to reveal a sharp array of teeth.

"What that, strange girl, go away," it spat before diving back down below the edge of the basket. "Ugly face, noisy mouth," it grumbled on.

"I've never seen a, a bat-cat," Jessika managed.

"They aren't common," the man nodded. "If Breeka is male or female, it won't tell me, and I can't tell, and it prefers to go by 'it'. Please don't take any offense to what it says; it's its nature to be mean spirited."

"Of course, no problem," Jessika murmured.

She finally looked away from the basket and at the man. He was smiling kindly at her, stirring spoon poised above the pot.

"I'm Craduticus," the man said, giving a bit of a bow with his head and shoulders. "You can call me Cray."

"I'm Hawkwings," Jessika said. "It's nice to meet you, and thank you for inviting me in."

"Not many hike in the mountains," he mused, turning back to the pot.

"You're wandering around with hardly any supplies and no plan of where to stay the night. However did that happen, I wonder."

"This is your home?" Jessika asked, even though the answer seemed obvious.

"It is."

"Can I barter for food and permission to sleep here tonight?"

"I would be pleased if you did. There are some chores you can help me with in return for food and board."

"No girl, go away," the cat-bat hissed from its basket. "Bad, big mouth, nasty girl."

"Don't mind Breeka, this is normal behavior for it," Cray said again. "It's never violent, won't hurt you, no matter what it says."

"Why do you keep it?" she asked tentatively.

"It can't really take care of itself; it's been injured. You could say I saved its life." He shrugged a little as he stirred the pot. "There are times any voice, even a mean one, makes the house a little less lonely."

The man gestured towards the cupboard, and Jessika went and fetched bowls.

"If you don't mind my asking, why would you live out here if you didn't want to be alone?" she asked.

"I don't mind any question, child, but that is one I prefer not to answer," he replied, softening his words with an apologetic smile. "Perhaps if you tell me why you're out here alone, I will do the same."

His gentle smile turned into a sly grin as Jessika found herself taken aback and fumbling to demure.

"You see? Trust can take time," Cray murmured, now filling the bowls Jessika held for him.

She placed each one on the table, noting that there was plenty of stew for three. She supposed he would normally save it and have it for breakfast, too, like inns she'd heard of where the pot of stew was kept bubbling over the fire for days, with the innkeeper just adding more ingredients to it after serving some of it out.

Under the old man's direction, she placed the three bowls and added big wooden spoons to two of them. He gestured her to the one proper chair while he took a folding stool down from where it was hanging on a peg on the wall and set it up for himself: sitting on it with a creak and a groan.

"Breeka," he muttered, "dinner."

"Nasty girl-thing there," the creature hissed.

"Then you will be hungry if you can't bear to sit and eat beside her." He gave Jessika another little smile. "Please, go ahead. I hope it suits your tongue."

Jessika dipped up a spoonful and sipped. It was lovely: a cream sauce in which floated a great variety of vegetables, including potato, celery, carrot, and some others she couldn't identify, along with a bunch of sliced mushrooms. The heat of it hit her belly and spread out all the way to her fingers and toes.

"This is really good," she said. "I can't remember ever having stew this good. Thank you."

"You're quite welcome," he replied mildly. "I'm glad you like it, but I could have killed you with it."

Jessika dropped her spoon, splashing soup onto the table. "What?"

Cray gave her a soothing smile. "I prepared the food and you didn't wait to watch me start eating first. I could have poisoned it."

She stared down at the food, trying to clean up the splashed soup with her fingers. "I didn't think of that."

"I allowed you to fetch the bowls and spoons, and to place them wherever you wanted on the table, so you can be sure that I did not place poison only into your bowl and then fill it with soup and give it directly to you, but I still could have poisoned the entire pot of soup, and then refrained from eating any."

"I never knew people did things like that," she admitted.

He nodded slowly, beginning to spoon up his own soup. "You've not encountered much treachery in your life, have you?"

"I guess not."

"A rude awakening? For future reference, pay attention when someone else serves you food or drink, and think about if they might have had a chance to put something unhealthy in it." He slurped up soup. "Mm, delicious. I did a good job on this batch."

The bat-cat suddenly scurried down from its basket: dropping to the floor with a thump. It ran across to the table with an odd, shuffling gait and climbed up a scarred table leg to perch on the edge. Jessika tried not to stare, even as it narrowed its green eyes at her. Its grey fur covered all of it except for its forelimbs, which were quite clearly large bat wings. From the wrist joint of each wing sprouted a thumb and a finger. Its hind limbs were short and stubby, and it had a long tail like a cat's, which was currently lashing with agitation.

Breeka lowered its face into its bowl and began slurping and licking up the stew, holding the bowl with its awkward hand-wings. With its face hidden, Jessika felt less uncomfortable about staring, and it was then that she noticed its scars and how one of its hind legs was twisted, like it had been broken and healed poorly. The scars were on its sides and belly, and looked like they'd formed after oddly straight cuts had been stitched closed.

"You have an unusual name, Hawkwings," the old man said.

Jessika pulled her focus off the bat-cat and put it on Cray. "I suppose it is, compared to other's," she said. "I've never heard your name before, either."

"It's a southern name," he said. "You live in the north, I assume, so it would sound strange to you."

"I see," she replied. "You haven't always lived here then."

"In this little cave house? No, indeed, I've been blessed with a most interesting life. There are times I wish it had been less interesting, but we aren't always able to choose where our lives will take us. May I ask where yours is taking you now? Surely you are on you way to somewhere."

Jessika took her time chewing her mouthful of stew before answering. Something about this man made her slightly uneasy. She didn't get the feeling that he would hurt her, but she suspected he was something more than a simple mountain hermit.

"I'm going to meet up with some friends of mine," she said. "And they're on their way to meet me, but I'm not sure how far away they are."

"Ah, you didn't arrange when and where to meet them? I can give you good directions from here to anywhere within a week's walk if you need them."

"We got separated," she admitted.

"Yes," he sighed. "That can complicate matters."

Breeka finished sucking the last of the stew from the bowl and sat up, using its fingers and tongue to try to clean its face. Cray lifted his napkin and brought it towards the bat-cat. Jessika tensed a little, expecting the creature to hiss or slap it away, but it immediately went still, eyes closed, and sat with complete calmness while Cray gently wiped its face. As he finished, it made a low sound, like a chirrup of thanks. Then in a blink it whipped its face at

Jessika and snarled.

"Good soup too good for stupid girl," it spat.

The bat-cat whirled and dropped to the floor, skittered towards the stove, and with a dozen rapid, fluttering flaps, leapt up to snag its basket bed and crawled back inside.

"Don't mind Breeka," Cray repeated softly.

"What happened to it?" Jessika asked timidly.

The man kept his gaze lowered towards his bowl, sipping slowly from his spoon.

"I know you said you saved its life and it was injured, but," she shut her mouth. "I'm sorry, it's none of my business. Please forget I asked."

"I may tell you someday," Cray murmured.

They finished their meal in silence and then Cray directed Jessika to wash the dishes.

"You can clean your face and hands there, if you like, as well," he added. "I do have a stream nearby where I have built a pool for bathing, but that will have to wait for the morning. It's not safe in these woods at night. If you require a chamber pot, you can step outside the front door and turn to your left. There is a covered pot where the house and mountainside make a corner, but you must not go out the gate or step outside the fence. Do you understand?"

"Yes, sir," Jessika assured him.

"Very well," he said.

Cray turned to a carved wooden chest and began pulling blankets out of it.

"You can sleep on that chair tonight. It really is quite comfortable; I myself fall asleep in it regularly." He eyed her little backpack with the two truncheons sticking out of it. "You seem ill equipped for hiking in the mountains. Would you like something to sleep in? I have some long nightshirts and trousers in a chest somewhere: clean and laundered, fear not."

Jessika bit her lip, and then decided to speak the truth. "I would, sir, thank you."

He went to another chest and began digging in it while Jessika finished washing her face, hands, and arms. She felt the desperate need for a bath, but knew it would have to wait. Somehow she could still smell the metallic odor of Skire Germaine's cavernous domain on her skin.

"If you'd like, you can change clothes now and wash what you're wearing. If we hang it above the stove, it will all be dry by morning."

Clean clothes? She took a sniff and nearly gagged: and she thought her skin smelled bad. How could a room leave such a stench on her? Or had it been that man, Altare's, magic?

"Alright, that would be lovely," she told him.

Cray gave her a simple smile as he handed over some nightclothes. "I'll just busy myself making some evening tea over here, and we'll put this blanket over that clothesline so you'll have privacy to change. Ah, and while you're at it, perhaps you'd like a little bucket of water and a clean rag to freshen up with. It won't equal a bath, but it's the best I can offer tonight."

Jessika stood with the clothes held out in her clean hands, keeping them away from the smelly clothes she still wore, while Cray bustled about doing just as he'd said. In a couple minutes she had his little library enclosed with hanging blankets, a candle lit for light, and a small tub and a washcloth sitting ready on the floor.

Her hands hesitated at the ties and buttons for her clothing. She'd never felt embarrassed disrobing around the griffins—after all, they wore no clothes at all—and even bathed with Kassandra, Karo, and Rikah and never felt awkward, but growing up was changing things. Her body was changing, maturing towards its adult form, and Cray was a strange man. She didn't know if she could or should trust him.

The desire to get clean was too strong. As quick as she could—thinking to limit the amount of vulnerable unclothed time—she peeled off her dirty clothes, scrubbed herself as best she could without dripping water over too much of the floor, and wriggled into the nightclothes. They were too big for her, but she rolled up the sleeves and trouser cuffs, and then took her belt and cinched everything around her waist.

Jessika stood, dressed, heart pounding a little. She was fine. Cray hadn't done anything. Now she felt silly for having been afraid.

Taking her pile of dirty clothes and the basin of water, she ducked out under the hanging blankets. As he'd said, Cray had prepared some tea and was sitting back at the table, sipping it while he made notes in what looked to be a journal. He gestured distractedly towards the sink.

"Use that soap I put there to wash your clothes," he directed.

"Thank you, sir," Jessika said.

She began dunking her clothes, working the soap into them. From behind her came the scratching sound of a pen on parchment. The water rapidly turned dark, and she refilled the tub for rinsing. At last she began laying each article over crisscrossing clotheslines above the stove. Breeka watched her with slit green eyes from its basket.

"Are you afraid I'm going to hurt you?" the old man asked, as she was finishing.

Jessika blanched. "Uh," she stuttered.

"Tell the truth," he suggested gently.

"Yes, a little."

"You've decided to trust that I won't?"

"I guess so," she winced.

"It is good that you recognized the possibility of danger, child. It is difficult to judge a situation with a person you've just met. Even someone you've known for a long time can surprise you." He said that last with a sigh that was not quite hidden. "From my perspective, you come armed. I am guessing you know how to use those truncheons?"

"Yes," she said. "I've trained with them a lot."

"I am an old man. Although not completely frail, I am not as strong as I used to be, and I was never a warrior. You could attack me. You might win. You might even come after me while I'm sleeping. If you bludgeoned me unconscious or dead you could take whatever supplies you wanted, what few valuables I have, and be better off for it."

"I would never do that," Jessika protested.

"Calm yourself, child. I believe you would not, but there is always the chance that you are a skilled actress, a bandit who charms her way into making her victims think she is harmless, and then strikes at the most opportune moment."

She scrunched up her brow a bit, thinking on that.

"You can't always trust your own impression of a person," Cray went on. "People can lie with more than just their voices. They can use their behavior and actions to make you think they are something they are not."

"I don't understand, not completely."

"All this time you have been interacting with me, and what you have observed of my actions has made you decide to trust that I won't attack you, but what if I've been pretending? What if everything I have said and done was calculated to make you trust me, so you would lower your defenses? Then what if I wait until you're asleep to act? I could tie you down where you sleep, restrain you, assault you, sell you as a slave or keep you for my own, or just kill you and take your supplies."

Jessika's eyes widened as she began to understand. Fear made sweat break out on her palms.

"Child," Cray crooned. "I'm not going to do any of those things."

"That could be a lie, too. You could be tricking me," she retorted.

He nodded sadly. "Now I have ruined a piece of your innocence, but I had to tell you. Where have you grown up that human treachery has never touched you, never educated you?"

"I," she began, and then buttoned her lips.

He nodded with what seemed an approving grin. "Smart enough to hold onto your secrets. Would you like some tea?" Cray refilled his cup from the teapot. "You can find a cup in the cupboard."

Jessika got one and went to sit down with him. He filled her cup.

"Whatever journey you're on, I want to help you, as much as I am able," he said softly. "I wish you no harm. I hope you will sleep easily. I will trust also that you won't harm me. I understand that you're wary; that's good; you should be. Many people in this world are not to be trusted.

"In most cases, at the best, people will ignore you and not care whether what they do harms you or not. At the worst, they will try to use you, take advantage of you, or take things from you: your security, possessions, health, or your life. Every now and then you'll find someone who really does wish you well, and even more rarely, someone who wants to help you."

"And you want to help me?" she said.

"I think I do."

"Why?"

He stared at her for a moment. "A reasonable question: I have my reasons."

"There's something you're not telling me."

"Yes, lots of things."

Cray poured the last drops into his cup, downed them, and went to put the teapot away.

"I think I'll go to bed now," he said. "You know where the chamber pot is. Feel free to light as many candles by the chair as you wish. Let's leave the blankets hanging up. I'll bank the fire, and the stove will keep the room warm enough all night. I must repeat: do not go outside the fence if you venture out of the house. I cannot stress the nighttime danger enough. Do you need anything else?"

"No, and thank you, Cray. Thank you for your advice, and honesty, and the food, and everything," Jessika replied. "I guess, I feel a little stupid, and lost. I don't mean to be ungrateful."

He smiled at her. "I understand. Don't feel stupid; you are merely learning. Be patient with yourself. I hope you sleep well."

"You, too."

"Blow out the candles out here when you're done."

The old man stepped over to his bed and Jessika turned her back to give him privacy, assuming he would change clothing before getting in bed. She drank her tea slowly, and once the sounds of Cray settling into his bed had faded, she cleaned her cup and went to visit the chamber pot, as unpleasant as that often was.

The night was chilly and the dense trees made it eerily dark. She could look up and see a jagged piece of lighter sky among the treetops, sprinkled with a few stars. There were no sounds of crickets or other nighttime insects. The two goats were curled up together at the end of the fence opposite the chamber pot, apparently deeply asleep. Drowsy clucking came from the chicken coop. The air was still, so there were no rustling leaves or branches. Distantly, she thought she heard the sound of water bubbling over stones: the stream Cray had spoken of.

Jessika found the chamber pot right where Cray had described it. Necessity attended to, she went back to the door of the house, startling only once when an owl called somewhere several trees away. She tried to stare into the empty dark under the trees. What was so dangerous out there? It was just a forest. She'd been in many forests after dark, camped out many times, although always with griffins around her. Griffins made her feel safe—they could fight off and probably eat anything else that lived in the mountains. Predators avoided them.

It was too dark to see anything, but the hair on her arms and neck started to rise. Perhaps it was just the cold air. There was a soft hushing sound, like a heavy breath or wind across rock, but nothing moved that she could see. Jessika turned and went inside, shutting the door as quickly and quietly as she could. She noticed a bar and swung it down across the door. It made her feel a little safer, and she hugged herself with her arms, trying to rationalize away her shivering.

Something had been out there, under the trees that had seemed so empty. She was afraid to turn her back to the door and windows. As she went past the stove she noticed Breeka sitting with its nose and eyes peeking over the edge of the basket, staring fixedly towards the forest.

Jessika paused. "Breeka," she whispered. "Is there something out there?"

The bat-cat didn't look at her, but made a thrumming sound deep in its chest, like a purr and a snarl mixed together. "Ugly girl go to sleep," it hissed. "Bad things stay outside the fence."

Jessika trembled convulsively. She put out the candles except for one by the chair, sat down reclining, cushioned with pillows, and pulled blankets over her. It was almost as comfortable as sleeping at home. She pulled out her magic stone again and clutched it tight in her hand, both wanting to let Thornfire know she was still alive, and for the comfort it would bring her to feel him send pulses of reassurance back.

For several minutes she sat that way, with the hard, smooth rock pressing into her palm almost painfully. Up on the mountain it had taken Thornfire quite a while to answer her call, so she tried to stay awake and waited, and waited. The stone didn't even grow warm except for what it gained from the heat of her body. Eventually she couldn't keep her eyes open any longer. With Breeka and Cray nearby, the door barred, and walls of blankets around her, she eventually felt safe enough to blow out the candle and close her eyes.

The stone remained just a stone, as though Thornfire had never breathed his magic into it. Jessika put it back in her pocket before she could fall asleep and drop it. Maybe the wall of the mountain was blocking the signal, but Thornfire had seemed confident about the stone working anywhere. Why would it stop now? Could they somehow have moved out of range? But he said they would come to her. Uneasiness rolling in her mind like an acorn bumped about by winds, Jessika fell asleep.

Jessika dreamed of Hawkjoy. Her Hawksister was calling for her, needed her, somewhere out in a dense fog, and Jessika wandered, arms outstretched, trying to find her, afraid of running into dark trees that loomed up like pillars as she stumbled about, tripped by roots and rocks. She called back, crying out Hawkjoy's name, but her voice didn't seem to carry. The source of Hawkjoy's keening calls kept moving, making Jessika change direction over and over.

Then something else moved through the fog and Jessika pivoted, putting her back against one of the hard columnar tree trunks. Some four-legged beast with shoulders as tall as Jessika's own was stalking her. She could hear it snuffling, panting, grumbling growls under its breath. Its feet stirred the detritus of the forest floor without concern for alerting its prey, and Jessika knew in the dream that it knew where she was. It was just delaying its attack to let her enjoy her fear of it.

Hawkjoy cried out again, somewhere in the mist, with a shriek of more than need and loneliness. The cry was one of pain, a deep piercing pain that made Jessika shudder and twitch with the need to go to her, to help her, to stop whatever was causing that suffering. She called out, asking Hawkjoy where she was, but nothing answered her. Heavy feet shuffled on the forest floor and Jessika looked ahead of her. There, white eyes opened and saw her. Then the beast leapt.

Jessika jerked awake on the chair in Cray's cottage, heart pounding.

"Shhh," Breeka crooned. "Ugly girl is dreaming. Safe here. Go to sleep."

Jessika closed her eyes again and tried to obey, but didn't fall back into a deep sleep until near dawn.

Chapter 11
The Shadow-beasts

Daylight was flooding the little house when Jessika wormed her way out of the blankets the next morning. She heard the sound of jaunty whistling and smelled dewy forest starting to bake out in the sun. She stood and touched her hanging clothes, found them dry, and got dressed in them. Then she folded up the blankets she'd slept in and pulled down the ones that had been strung up for privacy, and folded those, too, leaving them all on the chair.

The memory of her nightmare was still with her, and she tried to rub her face and head, groaning, to be rid of it, but the images held on, and she couldn't get the sound of Hawkjoy's painful crying out of her head. Was the griffin still a prisoner in that basement? Had she escaped? Had that magician, Altare, sent her to a different mountaintop? The latter would be fine in the griffin's case; Hawkjoy would have no trouble flying herself down off a mountain and finding landmarks she knew to get back to South-scree or Thornfire's group.

But what if she hadn't escaped? What if that strange woman Skire Germaine and the magician still had her? That woman had made Jessika's skin creep. She couldn't imagine what she had wanted with Hawkjoy, and didn't want to think about it.

"There's nothing I can do right now," Jessika whispered to herself. "I have to at least find Thornfire, if I even can." What if the rock had stopped working? What if he were hurt or—? She couldn't finish the thought.

Breeka stuck its face into the open doorway from outside. "Lazy, sleepy, ugly girl is awake," it commented.

"Good morning," Cray called cheerfully from beyond her vision, the whistling pausing for a moment. "Breakfast is on the table: it's all for you."

Jessika looked. Under a hand towel embroidered with blue cornflowers was a small roll of bread, a jar of honey, a pile of cold scrambled eggs, and slices of what she thought was pear.

"Thank you," she called back, "and good morning to you, too."

She took a few minutes to rip the roll in half, and spread each half with honey and slices of pear. The eggs—a delicacy she rarely got a chance to enjoy—she saved for last and savored, even cold. After her meal, she cleaned up the dishes and table and went out to see what Cray and Breeka were doing.

The old man was crouched down with a short knife, carefully carving something into the fence posts around the house. Breeka was lying on the doorstep, soaking up sun like a cat, eyes fixed unblinkingly on Cray, who had resumed whistling.

"Quiet, stupid girl," Breeka hissed an instant before Jessika called out to him. "No talking. Master working."

Jessika bit back what she'd been about to say. A minute later Cray concluded his whistling and stood up, stretching his back with a few cracks and pops.

"One more to go," he told Jessika with a smile, as though she would know what he meant. "Go ahead and get packed up. Breeka can help tell you what to pack. We'll be leaving shortly."

"We?" Jessika echoed.

"Stupid girl no talk," Breeka scolded. "Come, we pack."

The bat-cat scurried back into the house and Jessika, bewildered, followed.

"Here, here," Breeka urged. "This pack, put in the food."

It hopped to the kitchen counter and pawed open a cupboard. Jessika found some fruit, vegetables, bread, and cheese inside. Breeka brought her cloth bags, and she obeyed, packing the food into them.

"Where are we going, Breeka?" she asked as gently as she could.

"Find your friends," the bat-cat sneered. "Ugly girl has friends."

"You and Cray are coming?"

The bat-cat glared at her fiercely, but its voice was soft, almost mournful. "Master go with you, Master get hurt. You get Master hurt."

"No, no, I don't want anything to happen to you or to Cray," Jessika objected.

"Master leaving because of you. Safe here, but Master leaving," Breeka went on.

The cheerful whistling had resumed outside.

Jessika frowned, putting things more slowly into the pack on the floor. Breeka watched her in silence.

"How can I get him to stay?" she asked the bat-cat finally.

"Can't," it said. "Master decided; Master go. No one stops Master when Master wants something."

"I hope no one gets hurt. I'll help you keep him safe," she offered.

Breeka made a soundless snarl. "Stupid girl is stupid."

"Yes," Jessika agreed softly. "Maybe I am. Lately I feel like I don't know anything, and don't understand anything."

Cray came striding through the doorway dusting nonexistent dirt off his hands.

"Are we all ready?" he caroled.

"Cray, why are you coming with me?" Jessika asked.

"My life has gotten too boring lately. I'd like to make a little trip."

He took over filling the pack and she stepped back, fisting her hands for courage. "You're not telling me everything. I don't want to be responsible for you getting hurt. The stuff I'm involved in is not really safe."

Cray straightened up with a bundle of something or other in his arms and winked at her. "I'm old, but not so old that I'll let you be responsible for me getting hurt, little one. I have my reasons for going with you, you're right. You don't need to know what they are yet. Now, I have just a few more things to grab and we'll be ready to go."

Jessika watched as he walked to the back of the room and tossed aside the drape over the middle of the back wall. To her surprise, it revealed another room beyond it. Curious, she crept over and looked through the opening. The room was small and roughly round, with mostly unfinished rock walls, although the floor was planed perfectly smooth. Around the perimeter of the floor were arrayed dozens of partly burned candles, interspersed with rocks and crystals and feathers and dried flowers.

Cray was gathering up various objects from among the mishmash and putting them in another sack. He turned, smiling, with the sack in his arms.

"I'm a mage. This is my workroom," he explained lightly, as though commenting on a pleasant weather forecast. "Pardon me."

Jessika stepped out of the way so he could exit the room, the unicorn curtain slipping from her nerveless fingers.

"A mage?" she gaped.

He prattled on. "I sensed Altare's working yesterday and redirected your path here, to my mountain, and forced the air pressure around you to equalize slowly so it didn't hurt you, instead of letting him drop you into snow on the highest peak some distance from here, which all in all, would probably have finished you off."

"Uh," Jessika managed.

Cray went on packing his bag. "I've sat too long on this mountain, letting him trap me here, letting him continue on with whatever senseless cruelty he's been writhing about in, uncontested. But catching him in the act of murdering an innocent girl," the old man shook his head. "I knew it before. I've known it, ever known it, sitting up here, known that he would go on working his ways, when—oh I might have died doing it—but I might have stopped him, or tried to stop him."

He stood up to swing the pack onto his back, and fetched up a walking stick. It was almost as thick as Jessika's wrist and carved along its length with swirls and symbols and little images of plants and animals. Jessika's mind was whirling as she tried to take in everything he was divulging: rapidly revising what she'd known and assumed about him.

"He was your enemy?" she asked tentatively.

"Oh, no," Cray corrected at once. "He was my apprentice. I taught him everything he knows."

Breeka leapt over and landed on Cray's shoulder, then adjusted itself to even out the balance.

"Every whisper of hate, rune of blood, and working of pain," Cray sighed. "I taught him every one."

He glanced at Jessika, and she got the feeling he was looking to see her reaction to that. She could only give him a shocked stare, but below that she was near to panic: she'd left Hawkjoy with a man like that, and this man before her—he was also like that? He was that man's teacher?

"Why did you do that?" she breathed around the coil of uneasiness in her throat.

"That was what I was," he said with the voice of an old, tired man. "It was all I knew. It was how I'd spent my life, and I thought there was nothing wrong with it. I could do it. It gave me power and status. No one stopped me, so," he shrugged.

"Then, what happened?"

"I changed my mind, or perhaps, my heart."

Breeka warble-purred and rubbed its face against Cray's flyaway white hair. He smiled and reached up to scratch the bat-cat's ears.

"But I couldn't change his," he concluded with a frown.

Jessika stayed silent, but the little worm of fear in her throat melted away, mostly, except for what she feared for Hawkjoy.

"There's another lesson for you," Cray murmured. "Do not leave undone that which you will always regret and never forget. If it's that important to you, that it will always be with you, then better to have done, even if it's hard, even if the price is your life. It is better to face the drake and take what's coming than to always be looking over your shoulder, waiting for the drake to show up and demand its due."

He heaved a deep sigh. "It feels right to be going now, and facing it at last." He smiled at Jessika. "I must thank you for your coming, Hawkwings. Now, let us load up the goats and go."

Cray marched out the door, and Jessika followed. He strapped his packs and bags onto the two goats, with Jessika helping as he directed.

"They aren't really meant to be pack animals, but they'll do fine. I've used them as such before. I hope you'll be kind enough to lead one of them. Here, take Deni's lead; she's gentler. I'll guide Dali; she can be feisty sometimes, can't you darling?"

Jessika took the rope dubiously. She'd never interacted with a goat before, although she'd recognized the animals from distant memories when she was a child. Deni plodded dutifully forward when Jessika gave the lead a slight tug.

"We'll have to share our sleeping accommodations with them, so best get used to the smell," Cray said. "If they reach out and graze the plants around us as we walk, let them. They do that a lot. Well, off we go then."

"What about the chickens?" she called.

"They can forage for themselves. The fence will continue to protect them at night," he replied.

Cray led the way out of the gate with Dali behind him. Breeka had already added itself to the pack on Dali. Feeling as though she'd suddenly been swept away by a river, Jessika followed with Deni.

They hiked on through the day, downhill, among the towering trees. Breeka napped most of the time. Deni and Dali frequently stretched their necks out to grab mouthfuls of the foliage around them as they walked, hardly breaking stride. The going was fairly easy and the day not too cold, but Jessika kept glancing up the path behind. Her neck continually prickled as though something was watching and following, and she thought of the beast in her dream.

Midmorning, she stuck her hand in her pocket and found the magic stone. She'd been afraid to try contacting Thornfire with it again, in case it still didn't work, indicating that it was impossible to reach him for some reason, but she couldn't stop thinking about it, so finally decided to face that chance. As soon as her fingers closed around it and it started warming up, Cray came to a sudden halt.

He held up a hand and stared around at the trees.

"What's wrong?" Jessika whispered.

"We're being tracked," he replied.

The neck prickling intensified and Jessika stepped closer.

"I can taste a spell in the air," he murmured on. "Something is stirring. It's close, near."

His head turned back and forth, eyes casting around, his thin white hair tossed by a breeze. Cray frowned, as if concentrating, and after a few moments, his gaze settled on Jessika.

"It's coming from you," he said. His voice had dropped to a somber tone. "Did Altare touch you, put something on you?"

"No, nothing," Jessika said. Her hand clenched on the stone, and she let out a breath of relief as she felt it start to receive pulses. Thornfire was responding; he wasn't dead or lost or broken.

"What do you have in your pocket?" Cray persisted. "Show me."

"Uh," Jessika winced.

Cray's expression moved closer to an understanding smile. "You have a magical object with you, Hawkwings, I can tell. So come now, show me and tell me about it."

There seemed to be no way out. Jessika pulled out the stone, but didn't relinquish it. "It lets me communicate with my friends, though it didn't work last night."

She could still feel the pulses. Thornfire was repeating that they would come to her.

"Where did you get this?" Cray asked with a raised eyebrow.

"From a friend," she said, biting her cheek.

"One of your friends is a mage? May I see it?"

"You won't take it?" She pulled her hand back a bit.

"I won't take or touch it," he nodded.

Jessika opened her hand flat, letting the little stone sit on her palm. Cray examined it closely without touching it, as he'd promised.

"That is a tidy piece of work," he commented. "So efficient, it employs your body heat to function. How do you use it?"

"I feel pulses," she said. "They come in patterns. Each pattern means something. I can't send patterns, though, only receive."

"So your wizard friend must be holding the other rock that mirrors this one." Cray smiled almost wickedly. "We could give your friend a surprise if I were to start sending pulses back, couldn't we?"

Jessika clenched the stone in her hand and hid it back in her pocket. "We're not going to do that," she said as bravely as she could.

"Of course not," Cray demurred. "I wasn't serious. Thank you for showing me the rock. Now I won't be startled when I sense it working."

He turned back to the trail and they started walking again. Jessika followed, feeling a little uneasy.

"So," she said, after a few minutes, "you were an evil mage once?"

Cray's back stiffened, but he kept walking. "You could say that," he grunted.

Jessika raised her voice. "So when you told me about poisoning other people's food, you've done that?"

She thought he might have sighed. "Hawkwings, the person I was in the past is not one I'm proud of."

"I know, but did you?"

He groaned. "I never killed anyone with it," he said reluctantly. "I did drug food, several times, to render the subject unconscious."

"So you could kill them later?" Jessika challenged, feeling belligerent.

Cray stopped and looked back at her. His face was pained. "Dear child, I don't want to discuss or remember those times. I can understand if you have a morbid curiosity; that's perfectly natural." His voice got softer, and Jessika walked up closer to him, starting to feel bad about pushing him. "I did do cruel and heartless things. There is the blood of many on my hands: some of it is even the blood of innocents. I have been over and over my past actions in my mind. They haunt me in my nightmares. Please don't ask me for details. Will you agree to that?"

Jessika nodded. "All right. I'm sorry."

"Don't worry. I understand your interest and fear. Perhaps, someday, if there is call for it, I will tell you some of it, but not now."

He turned and resumed the hike. Jessika continued to follow.

That evening they reached a little hollow. Cray lowered himself down into it and Jessika followed. The goats managed the climb down agilely. She saw that there was a tiny house hidden in it. The roof was level with the forest floor and now so covered in leaves and moss that it looked natural. Cray levered open a curved door tucked against the wall of the hollow.

"I haven't used this house for a while," he grunted. "It's not as comfortable or secure as the other I've been living in for a long time, but once I renew the spells, we should be safe for the night."

Jessika went into the house after him, ducking to get through the low doorway and leaving Deni outside with Dali. "How long did you live here?"

The little place was about a quarter the size of his other house, and had virtually no furnishings. The walls were lined with thick, cut branches densely aligned, and the floor was only packed earth. The door had a tiny window and likewise the one wall that wasn't branch-lined dirt. There was a dainty fire pit in one corner with a few old cold embers still in it. A battered metal pot sat nearby, next to a clay pitcher.

"A few months, while I worked on my real house, the one you found me in," Cray answered, setting down his pack. Breeka jumped up to a shelf on the wall. "We'll need to fetch water now, before dark. Hawkwings, if you go down the hollow a short ways you'll find a trickle of water coming down the hillside. Will you fill this pitcher? While you're gone, I'll bring in the goats and renew the protective spells."

"I'd be happy to," she said.

"You should also attend to any bodily needs. Once the spells are up, we shouldn't pass through them until dawn, if we can help it. Just make sure to go far from the water source, so as not to contaminate it."

"I understand," she said, picking up the pitcher.

"Don't dawdle. Once the sun is down we must be inside," he warned seriously.

"Got it."

Jessika headed out to find the stream, not wanting to spend any more time outside alone than she had to. Twilight was creeping between the trees, and Jessika fought to keep her balance over the uneven ground while her eyes darted to all sides and up, looking for the stream and watching for danger. She'd never really been afraid of the forest before, but now she felt as helpless as a field mouse, scurrying about, watching for shadows.

The stream was not far, but the trickle was slow, and Jessika had to stand, holding up the pitcher and waiting for it to fill. The forest darkened around her, and she began to hear the sounds of night creatures coming awake. She recognized the raspy squall of the brown and gray owl that lived in the forest around South-scree, and was glad she knew it; if she hadn't, it could have scared her enough to drop the pitcher and run screaming back to Cray. As it was, she still startled helplessly.

The pitcher filled with agonizing slowness, but at last the water reached the top and Jessika made her precarious way back to the little house, trying not to spill any. She set the pitcher down on a flat spot a few feet away from the front door, and climbed out of the hollow to find a place to bury her waste away from the water.

The trees were dark, and mist was moving in. She shivered as she compared it to her nightmare. Quickly, she strode several yards away and found a tree to put her back against. She would be totally vulnerable for a couple minutes, but she couldn't go the whole night without attending to nature's needs. She heard movement through the trees, something walking delicately, and hoped it was a deer. A couple minutes felt like hours. The owl called again, from a new location. The deer—if that was what it was—bounded away as if startled by something.

Something else rustled, something bigger, and Jessika heard a snuffling snort: maybe a boar? Her heart began beating even faster than it had been, and she hurried to finish her business and stand up. The mist was getting thicker, but she could still retrace her path back to the hollow. The sounds of movement through the leaf litter got louder and closer. She wanted to run.

Every instinct demanded she run, and she cast glances around, trying to locate the source of the sounds, but didn't see anything.

A few more steps would bring her to the edge of the hollow. Panting, she made it, and turned to lower herself down. Something dark moved out in the mist—she thought. Maybe it wasn't actually there. She couldn't see any edge to it, but she thought something had moved, something rather large, bigger than her. Hands shaking, she got down to the floor of the hollow and picked up the pitcher where she'd left it.

"Cray, can I come in?" she called, trying to keep her voice from quavering.

"Yes, yes, get inside now," he urged, coming to the little twisted door. "You were gone longer than I'd hoped you'd be. This way."

Jessika ducked in under his arm and went to put the pitcher by the fire pit. The goats were nestled together in the opposite corner. Cray had kindled a fire, and Jessika sat down near it, hungry for its light. She pulled her knees up to her chest and wrapped her arms around them. Cray shut the door and murmured some words.

"Stupid girl scared," Breeka muttered.

"Did you see something out there?" Cray asked, turning at the bat-cat's words.

"I thought maybe I did, but I don't think so," Jessika murmured back. "I think the dark forest just scared me."

"Maybe so," he allowed, kneeling to tend the fire and pour some of the water into the metal pot. "I'll make us some porridge. Perhaps you can arrange a couple of beds with the blankets from our packs."

Jessika moved to comply. It wouldn't be a comfortable night on the dirt floor, but if the fire stayed lit, it would probably be warm enough. Above her head, Breeka leapt to the ledge of the window in the outer wall and peered out. The bat-cat made a gurgling sound.

"Yes, I know," Cray said distractedly. "We'll be safe here until dawn."

Beds finished, Jessika went back to sit by the fire while Cray stirred the pot of porridge.

"What's out there?" she asked in a whisper.

Cray eyed her. "I don't want to frighten you."

"I'm already frightened," she told him.

He sighed. "My former apprentice Altare, whom you had the dubious honor of meeting, wants me dead. He sends his slaves to hunt me, but they can only come out at night."

"Aren't you stronger? Can't you defeat them?" Jessika asked.

He shrugged. "I probably could, but he could always send another, and another, maybe stronger and stronger ones. It would be a waste of my energy when protective spells are easier and keep away the weaker ones, and there's no need for me to go out at night. He just likes to keep me pinned down."

"So they aren't after me?"

Cray raised an eyebrow. "Why would he be after you?"

"He did try to kill me."

Cray stirred the pot slowly. "Yes, he did. Why did he do that, Hawkwings?"

Jessika held her breath, not sure what she should say. She trusted Cray, for the most part, but very few humans knew about the griffins, even fewer knew about Jessika's origin as the princess of Northnest, and Cray admitted he'd once been an evil man.

"Did you do something to anger him?" the mage went on.

"I was in the way," she said softly.

"Ah." The simple sound spoke volumes, as though enlightenment had come to him.

"Does he know you saved me from dying on the mountain? Would he know his spell didn't work?"

"If he was paying attention, he could have noticed," Cray nodded. "Do you think he was distracted at the time?"

Jessika thought of Hawkjoy. If she hadn't been magicked away, too, he would have had an angry griffin on his hands, and that would have been decidedly distracting. "Probably."

Cray was stroking his chin. "He might not know you're alive, but his minions will likely report my movement to another house. If one of them saw you, it might mention you as well. Many such minions are not bright enough to express that kind of complex message, but it could be that he has an intelligent one in his employ."

"So he'll know everything we do?" Jessika asked nervously.

"Not everything, only things they see at night."

"But they'll keep following you. I'll be leading them right onto my friends."

The mage nodded. "I had thought of that. I'm trying to think of a way to keep that from happening."

Cray fished a wooden spoon out of his pack and offered it to Jessika. Then he got out a bowl.

"Take what you want of the porridge," he instructed. "It may not be very tasty, but it's warm and will give you energy."

"Thank you," she said, digging out some spoonfuls into her bowl.

Jessika ate in silence while Cray sat and looked pensive between bites of his own bowl of porridge. She licked the bowl and spoon clean and set them aside to wash in the morning.

"I suppose I'll go to sleep now," she said.

"Yes, go ahead. Breeka will watch the night for us, and alert us if anything happens."

Jessika looked over at the bat-cat still perched on the wide window frame. It twitched an ear but did not otherwise move. Jessika went to one of the piles of blankets and rolled up in it. For some time she lay awake, unable to sleep due to fear of what stalked the night outside, what might have happened to Hawkjoy, and what might happen to Jessika herself due to her company with Cray. Eventually true fatigue took hold of her and dragged her down.

Jessika awoke the next morning with a head muddled by uneasy dreams she couldn't remember, to the smell of Cray cooking porridge again. The hollow outside was lightening with sunrise, the goats were out of the house, and Cray gave her an encouraging grin when he saw her awake.

"All is well," he said. "And tonight's house is a good bit nicer than this one."

"Another house?" she asked.

"When I escaped Northborn, or Northnest, I ran for a few days before the shadow-dogs started chasing me. Then I had to be sure I was safe somewhere with protection spells up for the night." He handed her back her bowl from the previous evening once she sat up.

"Being around other people could bring the dogs down onto them, so I went into the forest. I founded my first house, but it was still too close to a village, so I began working on another house less than a day's hike away from it. I continued the pattern up into these mountains, building houses one day apart, so I would never be caught outside at night, until I found the perfect place for a permanent home, which you found two days ago."

"So," Jessika began, blowing on the hot porridge in her bowl, "how many more houses are there along this path back to the village you started in?"

"There are six more."

"Six more?"

"Of course, I hope your friends will find us before then."

"Yes, but what about the—shadow-dogs, you called them? They'll menace my friends. They can find you wherever you go?"

Cray shrugged. "Probably, but they will come only after me, I hope. If I can return you to your friends, Breeka and I can go our own way, and you'll be safe."

"Unless one of them saw me last night and can tell Altare I'm alive," she recalled from their chat of the previous evening.

"Unless that," he allowed.

"But, go your own way? What do you intend to do? Won't you bring the shadow-dogs onto other people?"

Cray set his bowl down with deliberation. "I intend to go challenge Altare, and defeat him."

Jessika chewed her lip and stared off into space. What if Hawkjoy was still with Altare? She'd need rescuing.

"I want to go with you," she stated.

"Hawkwings, Altare is a dangerous man," Cray said seriously. "What he did to you, warping you away like that, he could do it again, and I probably could not save you next time, not if I am fighting him at the same time."

"I don't want to face Altare," Jessika corrected.

Cray examined her face carefully. "Then what is it that you intend by going with me?"

"There's something else I need to do," she said. "It's important. More important than anything else, and you getting Altare out of my way will help me."

Even if she hadn't loved Hawkjoy as a friend and sister, she knew now that the griffin was pregnant. That made her the new Hawkmother. Jessika knew well enough that the duty of all the Hawk Line would be to protect her and her chicks. There were no other griffin Hawks on this journey, but Rikah

Cray
Breeka
Deni
Dali

and Karo would probably help. Hopefully Thornfire, Starbright, Thornspike, and Waterleap would be willing to help, too. By rescuing a matriarch they would gain favor for their Lines—and hopefully they'd also want to help because they cared about Hawkjoy. She couldn't imagine them doing otherwise.

"Will you tell me what this important thing is?" Cray asked carefully.

"Um."

Jessika didn't know yet if it was safe to reveal the griffins to Cray. He had been an evil man. He was a mage. He came from Northnest. She couldn't ignore the possibility that he had been involved with the attack on her home ten years ago. He had been kind so far, but what would happen if he found out about the griffins, that Jessika was with them, and that she was the only remaining heir to the Northnest royalty?

She looked up at him and regretfully shook her head. "I want to trust you, I think," she said, "but I don't know if I should."

Cray just smiled and nodded back. "That's all right. You may very well be making a wise choice, and only you can make it, so I won't hold it against you. Let's get ready to go. It's quite a walk to the next house."

Jessika did her part to clean up and pack the bags. Then Cray lifted the sleepy Breeka onto his shoulders, they walked out the door, and shut it behind them.

As Cray had promised, the next house was much nicer than the previous one, although nowhere near as homey and permanent as the first one where Jessika had met him. They had been walking through dense forest, where not much sunlight reached the ground, so the tree trunks went up and up with just dead-looking branches sticking off them. There was minimal undergrowth, although plenty of fungi.

The house was built in the middle of a small ring of trees. At first, Jessika just saw it as a huge lump, a dome taller than she was, several paces wide. She followed Cray to one side of it, between two tree trunks, and he levered open a door made of densely woven branches.

"The drawback of this house is that there are no windows, so not much light gets in," Cray was saying.

It was already dim under the trees, and the inside of the house was like a black pit.

"I'll get a fire going," the mage went on. "Unload Dali and Deni, come on in, and put the packs down."

They'd made good time, and had a little while until sundown. Jessika did as instructed while Cray lit a fire in the center of the one big room with magical rapidity.

"This was a semi-permanent home for me," he explained. "I weathered my third winter here. I used hundreds of branches, braced them in between all these tree trunks, and wove them together to form the dome. I layered more branches on top of that, and topped it all off with thick thatching. Before winter, I laid in rows and rows of firewood both inside and outside the walls, along with food, of course."

"How did you get food?" Jessika asked.

"I had a few different sources. For one, I traded some work with the nearest village to get grain and corn. I hunted a few deer and smoked the meat, then kept it cold by packing it in snow until I was ready to eat it. I also managed to put in a little garden not far from here. We should go there. It's been a while, but some of the plants might still be alive and producing something edible. It will also be a good place for Dali and Deni to graze for a bit, since they didn't eat much on the trail today."

Cray laid the sleeping Breeka on his pile of blankets, and the two of them left the house, picking up the leads of the goats as they went. Jessika followed the mage on a short walk to a clearing where it seemed some old giant trees had fallen, making a hole in the canopy to let in sunlight. There was also a stream running through it.

"This spot is the reason I chose to put a house here, and live here a while, but it turned out that I couldn't grow quite enough food. Let's look for anything good before we turn the goats loose on it."

Although Deni and Dali were stretching their necks towards the greenery, Cray and Jessika tied them to branches and began searching through the clearing.

"I haven't harvested here for a while, and some plants certainly won't have survived, but I'm hoping maybe for some root crops," Cray said.

He had to teach Jessika what to look for, but after a few minutes they had managed to locate and dig up two different types of roots, and Cray harvested some greens he said were edible. He even found a handful of ripe strawberries.

Jessika helped him fill a sack he'd brought with as many of the roots as they could locate.

"These will keep for a few days, or longer, and provide a nice change from porridge," he explained. "Well then, let's let the goats ruin everything else."

They stayed to watch while Deni and Dali ransacked the foliage. Jessika took her shoes off and soaked her sore feet in the cold little stream. Cray was sitting against a tree trunk, eyes half closed, maybe meditating. He didn't speak, and Jessika was fine with enjoying the quiet. The sunlight gradually began to fade, and the goats' feeding became less urgent.

"We should go back now," Cray announced. "We'll get ready for the night, fetch water, and cook. I'll lay the protective spells down again."

Jessika went with him back to the house, got a pitcher, and trotted to the stream: determined not to be caught out late again. The stream filled the pitcher rapidly, and she got back before dark. Cray boiled the root vegetables and mashed them with a bit of salt. They ate the leafy greens raw. After that, they split the strawberries three ways with Breeka for dessert.

The goats were bedded down inside. Cray and Jessika spread out their blankets. There was no window for Breeka to watch through, but the bat-cat sat contentedly by the fire, apparently prepared to sit up all night listening for danger. Whatever passed by the house in the night, Jessika neither heard nor saw anything of it. Despite uneasy dreams, she slept through until Breeka nudged her awake in the morning.

Chapter 12
After the Fall

"This next section of the path is rather difficult," Cray was saying as they left the house shortly after dawn. "It's steep and rocky, and more dangerous going downhill than up, in my opinion. Dali and Deni will have the easiest time of it, I'm afraid."

It was midmorning by the time they reached the area Cray was talking about, and Jessika looked upon it with dread. She'd never navigated down such a challenging hillside. The trail twisted back and forth across the steep incline as much as possible, but in other places it went straight down the hill. A few tenacious shrubs grew among the rocks, along with the rare tree or two, but otherwise it was just boulders, rocks, and gravel.

"We must go slowly and carefully," Cray instructed. "You may find that turning so your front is towards the hillside and backing downward is easiest."

"What about the goats? Do we need to hold their leads, can we use them to support us?" Jessika wondered.

"Better not to," Cray said. "Dali and Deni have followed me up and down this hill before. I will trust them to do so again. I'll go first, then the goats. You follow behind them, but not too closely. If you do slip or fall, reach for the hillside, spread out and try to flatten yourself to it. It will give you some scratches and bruises, but it might stop you from falling all the way down. Understand?"

"I think so," she said.

In the past, if there had ever been such a difficult patch of trail, the griffins would just fly her over it. She now bit her lip, thinking that using the griffins as a shortcut had actually hindered her skill development.

"Are you ready?" Cray asked, tightening the straps on the packs the goats carried.

"Yes, let's go."

Cray started down the path, clucking with his tongue to get the goats to follow. Jessika noticed that Breeka was wide-awake now, clinging to Dali's pack with all claws. She wondered if it could use its wings well enough to fly, or at least glide, in case Dali fell; she'd only ever seen it do flapping jumps.

Once Dali and Deni began picking their way down the rocky trail, Jessika started cautiously after them, crouching, turning about, and using her hands as necessary. The rocks and gravel shifted under her feet and she quickly learned to carefully feel for stable toe and hand holds as she went. It was tedious work, but Jessika eventually felt like she'd gotten a good handle on the process. She was about halfway down when the sound of crumbling rock alerted her.

Farther down on the hillside, Cray grunted and started to exclaim. Jessika couldn't see well, but she thought maybe one of his hand or footholds had broken under him. His exclamation turned into a shout of despair as more rock went shifting and tumbling.

"Cray?" Jessika called.

He didn't reply, but it was clear what was happening, and she could do nothing to help him. Leaning out precariously, Jessika got a glimpse of him sliding rapidly down the hillside with falling stones and dirt, surrounded by a growing cloud of dust. She heard him cry out once more, followed by the impact of his body and accompanying landslide hitting the bottom of the hill.

"No, no, no," Jessika moaned under her breath. "Cray, are you all right?" she shouted.

From the bottom of the cliff, she thought she heard him groan in reply.

"Master hurt," Breeka warbled. "I go."

"Breeka, be careful," Jessika urged as the bat-cat spread its wings and tumble-fell downward like a broken winged moth.

Jessika couldn't take the same route; she had to continue working her way slowly down the hillside. The goats as well, kept their steady pace, picking their path methodically. Jessika could tell when she reached the point that Cray had fallen. There were still loose rocks and she had to be careful not to dislodge any more that might fall on her wounded companion. The trail—such as it had been—was nearly gone there, and Jessika and the goats had to take a more circuitous route.

"Cray, are you badly hurt?" Jessika called as she got closer.

"I'm not in the best of shape, but I'll live," he managed to utter.

"At least you can talk," Jessika said under her breath, "and are, you know, alive."

"I'm afraid I may not be able to walk very well," he went on.

That would be a problem. In a few more minutes, Jessika got herself down off the cliff and made her way to the pile of rock and old wizard. Breeka was there, struggling to move a rock that was too big for it, having gotten all the smaller rocks hauled away. Cray was on his back, lower body still buried under some rocks, but not enormous ones. Jessika suspected she wouldn't have much trouble getting them off him. He had a small head wound that had bled a bit, and his hands were scratched and bloody. His clothing had protected him from any other scratching injuries.

As Jessika approached he pushed himself up onto his elbows.

"Let's get this rock off me now," he said. "I didn't have the leverage to do it by myself."

Among the three of them—although Jessika did most of the work—they got the rubble off Cray's legs. Jessika didn't see any obvious deformity, such as with a broken bone, but that didn't mean he hadn't taken some hard blows from the fall.

"Can you stand?" Jessika asked.

"I feel bruised all over," he winced, trying to roll to all fours, "and I'm rather dizzy."

Jessika looked up, checking the sun. It was into afternoon now.

"How far is the next house?" she asked worriedly.

Cray grimaced with pain and dread as he managed to get to his side. "I'll tell you how to get there."

"We all need to get there," Jessika insisted.

She watched Cray try to push up to all fours, wincing even more. "I hit my shoulder, and my knees, and my hand."

He turned one palm up, and Jessika saw where his skin was ripped, the wound crusted with grit and dried blood and his fingertips scraped raw.

"Where did your walking stick go when you fell? I can cut you a new one, two of them," she suggested.

"Give me your arm. I'll try to stand, slowly."

Jessika looped an arm through his and let him pull on her. Cray rose to a shaky crouch, face twisted in pain.

"My ankle hurts," he gasped out.

"Can you lean on one of the goats?"

Deni and Dali had nonchalantly turned to graze on the nearest plants. Cray was gently shaking his head: eyes squeezed shut.

"Oh, Hawkwings, I'm not sure I can continue," he said.

Jessika resisted the urge to shake him. "No, you have to. I'll get you crutches. You need to take me to the next house. It'll get dark soon. I won't be able to find it without you."

Cray sank slowly back down to the ground, sitting sideways on one hip. "I can tell you where it is."

"I'm not leaving you," Jessika all but shouted. "Get up."

She went and fetched the goats, bringing them to stand on either side of where Cray sat.

"Come on, you can lean on them. I'll help you up again," she instructed.

Not waiting for him, she reached down and urged him with gentle but insistent tugging, and he obeyed, struggling half up. Jessika helped him loop his arms over the goats' backs. Just then, Breeka came limping up, dragging Cray's staff.

"Thank you, Breeka," Jessika said. "Here."

She put it across the goats' shoulders, so Cray could lean forward against it with his upper body. The goats shifted and grunted uneasily.

"They've never done this before," the mage warned. "They might not tolerate it for long."

"We have to try. I'll lead them," Jessika said. "Breeka, can you get up?"

The bat-cat flapped up to grab onto Dali's pack as Jessika took hold of the halters both goats wore. Cray groaned as she began to lead them off.

"Not too fast," he gasped out.

Step by agonizingly slow step, the five companions continued as Cray directed for the next few hours. Each time Jessika looked at him, the old mage's face was pinched and bloodless, his eyes glazed and half-shut. His breath was panting, interspersed with moans and grunts, and Jessika felt pain for him just by hearing it.

Sooner than she would have liked, the day's light began to wane.

"We won't make it by dark," Cray mumbled. "Leave me. If you run, you can make it. Take Breeka."

"And where would I go the next day, when you're dead?" Jessika shot back.

"Your friends are coming, right?" he said.

"Without you to put up the protective spells on the house, those things will get me, too," she argued.

"Ah, you may have a point," he admitted.

"What do we do? Can you put up the protective spells without being in a house?"

"I can try. Let's go there, among those trees."

Jessika led them all to the cluster of trees Cray had indicated. There was a little space among them where she helped lower Cray to the ground and then tied the goats' lead lines to some branches. They objected with goatish growls of complaint.

"Cray, tell me what to do," Jessika urged.

The mage was looking around at the trees. "Find some branches, use them to connect the tree trunks to each other, making a sort of circle. I can base spells on that."

Jessika leapt to obey as the light faded, connecting each tree to its neighbor with a length of branch. As soon as she was done, she helped Cray crawl to the trunks, where he quickly chipped some kind of mark into the bark with a knife. When he'd done every trunk, he sat in the center of the rough circle and began muttering strings of words and waving his arms about, making gestures with his hands. It was more than Jessika had ever seen him do, and figured he was depending more on his words and movements than usual, because he didn't have a good physical foundation to put the spells on.

As he was finishing, she began to notice the first furtive movements out in the darkness. They had no light inside the circle, and her eyes had gradually adjusted to the night. Deep back among the trees something moved: just the slightest flicker in the dark. Something was out there. Where she sat, Breeka trembled against her on one side, and Cray panted on the other.

"Breeka," Cray whispered, "climb up."

The bat-cat made a whimper of reluctance.

"Go on," Cray urged.

Breeka left Jessika's side and scampered over to one of the tree trunks. She heard the scrabbling of its claws as it hitched itself up the bark to some perch high above them. The silence stretched out around Cray and Jessika—who had no means of climbing the tall, branchless trunks—as they waited for more signs of company, pressing against each other for the only sense of comfort and security they had. The ancient fear of being hunted stirred deep inside them, and there was nowhere to run to. Jessika had to keep telling herself that the circle of branches with Cray's invisible spells upon them was the best defense there was right then.

There was more movement out in the darkness, slow and languid. She could almost see the shapes of their stalkers as blacker blacks among the lightless black of the forest. Looking up, she could see bits of slightly lighter sky among the leaves and branches, but not a single star or the glow of the moon. Jessika's heartbeat suddenly sounded loud to her, but she still detected the subtle sound of padded feet on the forest floor.

She wanted to speak, to ask Cray if he really thought his defenses would hold, but she was afraid to make any more noise. It might attract the strange creatures out there, and yet she had no doubt that they already knew where their prey was huddling. Time passed and the woods went silent again. Although she strained her eyes, now she couldn't see any shapes of the creatures.

Jessika drifted into a half-sleep, propped against Cray, only to gasp awake sometime later at the sound of more footsteps. She stared around. Cray seemed to be sleeping, and for a panicked moment Jessika thought he might have died of his injuries, but she shook his shoulder just a bit and woke him. Cray sat up, wincing in pain, but didn't speak. He looked off into the dark and tracked a moving beast through the trees. Jessika startled when she caught more movement in her peripheral vision; there was another one.

"They're here," Cray breathed, so silently Jessika could hardly hear him. "All three: there are usually three."

The old man pushed himself up so he was better seated, and Jessika tried to support him, turning around and putting her back to his. She managed to swallow a cry as one of the creatures moved close enough to see. Its body was a big as a griffin, its shoulders nearly as high as Jessika's own. It looked rather canine in shape, but she couldn't see any details, just a shape of blackness with ragged edges.

Another beast crossed behind it, or before it, or through it. This other was a bit smaller and leaner. A few moments later Jessika spotted the third. It was thick and hefty, like a bear. All three shadow-beasts walked with their heads and tails low and swaying. Their feet stirred the detritus of the forest floor just slightly, just enough to make some slight sounds of footsteps. She couldn't see their eyes, but as they approached, she began to hear the sounds of their breaths, like the roar of distant fires.

The slender beast walked up to the edge of the tree circle and stopped. It lowered its nose to the ground, near one of the sticks Jessika had placed and Cray had enchanted. In the same manner it worked its way around the whole circle, while the other two beasts continued to orbit them patiently. After its examination, it trotted back to the other two, as though going to report its findings. The three stood together for a few moments, and then turned their heads as one to look at the prey.

Jessika trembled under their direct attention. While two continued to stare, the third, the big bear-like one, began lumbering towards them. Behind her, Cray straightened to attention.

"It's starting," he whispered. "That one will try to force its way through the circle."

Jessika felt him start to wave his hands and heard him muttering. Meanwhile, the shadow-bear came up to the edge of the circle, between two trees, put its head down like a ram, and started to press against the air. Jessika couldn't take her eyes away, although she could see nothing but the shadow-bear standing there, pushing against the invisible side of the circle. Cray grunted and hissed. The shadow-bear turned slightly, putting a shoulder against the circle.

Something hit the shadow-bear and ripped away some of its substance, as though a breeze had struck a cloud of smoke, but the beast kept pushing. Cray growled and spat and another, stronger breeze hit it, and then another, and another. Each invisible breeze ripped away more of the shadow-bear's essence, and yet not enough.

Jessika wanted to run away. When the shadow-bear lifted a now-emaciated paw and put it across the branch that formed that edge of the circle, she almost bolted.

"Cray," she whined. "It's coming inside."

The mage didn't respond, continuing his stream of mumbled spell-casting, keeping the attacks of wind going. Then he shouted something and the whole circle flashed a deep violet color that Jessika could see, and the shadow-bear's foot was severed from its body. It opened its mouth as though to roar, but only a rolling, rocky rumble came from it.

The shadow-bear reared back and slammed itself against the shield, once, twice, again, and again. Cray was panting and gasping. Jessika looked at him and saw his hands were up, palms out, as though pushing against a wall. The bear-thing plunged through the circle with its good and maimed front paws, and then put its head down low and pushed up, as though levering up a heavy object with its neck and shoulders.

It opened its mouth again, and released that same grating, shaking roar. Jessika began to gather her feet under herself. Cray's arm flashed out and she saw a sharp spark of light hit the bear in the chest, rocking it back and eliciting another cavernous roar.

Then the other two shadow-beasts hit the circle from two other points.

Jessika screamed and tried to scamper backwards as the slender one broke through, wiggling like an eel. Only her awkward attempt at evasion saved her. Instead of hitting her dead on, it plunged past her, clipping her shoulder and knocking her over. Intense cold washed through her: prickling her skin with gooseflesh. The shadow-beast collided with the two goats behind her and they bleated with terror, knocking into each other and tumbling to the ground in a tangle of legs and necks.

The shadow-bear shoved inside, maw gaping. Jessika tried to get to her feet, to run, but her legs didn't seem to be working right; they were shaking too hard. She noticed Cray on his back, the wolf-like shadow-beast pinning him to the ground. Cray was still trying to shout something.

Then the light came.

There were two. They came like falcons diving, like sun breaking over the horizon, like flowers blooming. They were there, among the shadow-beasts, which burst like ripe figs and melted like rotting mushrooms just by being brushed by the light. Jessika shielded her eyes against their brightness, but Cray was on his knees, fallen forward with his forehead and arms to the ground, wailing like something speared and dying.

The two bright lights paced around the circumference of what had been the protective circle. They moved back and forth across the branches with no sign of impediment. Jessika managed to lower her shielding hand and squint a bit, and could resolve what the lights were. Both were bright, swirling white. One was shot through with threads of luminous blue, and the other was laced with silver. Both were four-legged and more graceful than courting herons.

Their manes and tails floated about them as radiant nimbuses, and rapiers of power crowned their heads, one bright as sunlight on snow and the other like heat lightning in clouds heavy with rain.

They were unicorns, two unicorns, but unlike when she'd seen unicorns years ago, Jessika could now barely make them out through their brightness. Cray, however, didn't seem able to look at them at all. Under his obeisant arms, his face was streaked with tears. The unicorns continued pacing slowly around them. The shadow-beasts were more vanquished than icicles in summer, but Jessika wondered why the unicorns had moved to save them, and why they stayed.

"I know you," Cray choked out suddenly. "I know what you are."

The unicorn with essence of blue and sunlight paused for a pace, and his measured words reverberated through Jessika's mind almost painfully. "We see you, Man. We know what you have done."

Cray moaned and jerked himself upright, sitting tall on his knees, head thrown back, eyes still twisted shut. "And I am guilty," he gasped. In one wrench he ripped open the front of his robes, exposing the age-spotted skin of his chest. "Take your vengeance. Do as you will with me. My rotten heart longs for the thrust of your justice."

The blue unicorn, which had resumed its pacing, paused again: head tilted just the slightest bit. The light of his horn shivered like a bird's breast. "Death? You ask for death?" He tossed his head, and the flash of it made Jessika hunch down to the ground. " You ask us to dirty ourselves with you?"

Cray shook his own head. "What I have done cannot be forgiven."

The other unicorn, the one edged in silver like a storm cloud spoke for the first time, and her ringing voice was like an ancient bell hung high in a mountain tower, tolling over all the land. "Silence, arrogant Man. How would your death serve? You have incurred a debt to us that death cannot repay."

She stopped before Cray, and yet was still moving, always moving, moving closer and away, like waves or trees in the wind. Movement nearby on the ground caught Jessika's attention. Limping, Breeka stumped over to stand in front of Cray, between him and the lightning unicorn.

"Master saved my life," little grey Breeka said in a weak voice, yet to speak at all—and moreover to speak to the unicorn—showed more strength than Jessika felt in her whole body.

The pale beast bowed its head with what appeared to be gentleness. "One life saved cannot balance the many taken, all the days of life taken from others, the immortal days taken from ours." She shifted her attention off Breeka and back to Cray. "Would you balance this, Man? Would you repay your debt?"

She continued her pacing around the circle, and Cray slumped, his fervor at imminent death draining from him. His empty, injured hands fell to his lap. "I cannot be forgiven. Nothing can repay what I've done."

The blue unicorn swarmed up before him now, mane crackling and horn blazing like doom. "Silence! Who are you to set the price? Would you repay your debt? Yes or no?"

Cray lifted his head again, pointed towards the glory of light. "If it can be done," he croaked, "yes."

The female unicorn stepped up beside the male, shoulder to shoulder, and they spoke with one voice. "You have said you will repay, now look upon us."

It took him a few tries, but Cray opened his eyes, looking up blindly into the light that must have burned him. Fresh tears streamed down his cheeks, into his beard and hair and open mouth.

"Great Ones," he moaned. "I am sorry. So sorry."

They burst like white fire, lighting up the forest brighter than any day that ever was. "You took his days from him. Now we will have yours: all of yours."

"Anything," Cray agreed at once.

The unicorns' attention shifted to Jessika, and she found herself flattening her body to the ground, much as Cray had, covering her head with her arms and shaking.

"This Woman called Hawkwings, sworn sister of our foal: you will protect her with all your power, all your will, all your skill, knowledge, and wisdom, for all your days, until your death. You will die, if you must, to protect her," the unicorns pronounced.

"As you wish," Cray acknowledged.

The unicorns turned their gaze, hotter than sunlight, back onto the old mage, and Jessika felt able to breathe again.

"It is, of course, your choice," they said. "You may renege on your debt at any time you choose. We merely tell you our price, if you wish to repay. You know what will happen if you do not; you know the consequence. It is your choice. This is how you may balance what you have done to us. As for the others you have wronged, you must find your own way to repayment of those debts."

"I understand," Cray panted.

For another moment he sat, back arched like a bow, eyes blinded in the light. Then the unicorns turned their heads half away.

"You may look away now," the male said.

Cray shuddered, closed his eyes, and crumpled down to the ground, curling into a ball, and wept for a long time, as though he were very young again.

Jessika wasn't sure when the unicorns departed. She recalled the light receding into the trees like the moon in the distance. When she opened her eyes fully the clearing was bathed with starlight and a slender figure was crouching over her.

"Wings?"

Jessika blinked, surprised by what she was seeing. "Sky?"

"They really knocked you out, didn't they? I didn't think it would be that hard on you. Don't worry. I've been keeping watch. Nothing is going to come around here anyway tonight, not after that. Everything can feel where unicorns have recently worked their will."

Jessika struggled to sit up. Cray was prone and unconscious. Breeka was half lying against his shoulders, eyes open and shining and staring at the new arrival.

"Breeka, this is Sky," Jessika introduced. "She's my sister. Sky, this is Breeka, a bat-cat, and Cray's companion. Cray is the man there, whom your unicorn friends scolded."

Kassandra crouched down. She was wearing her usual coating of thick leaves and vines in place of clothing. In the dark, her eyes looked faintly luminescent. "They are angry with him. They have been angry with him for a long time, all of them. I'm not sure why. They haven't told me."

"Sounds like it's between them and him," Jessika grunted. "How did you find me?"

"The unicorns helped me," Sky said, sitting back on her heels.

"Where are Thornfire and the others?"

"They're coming, but unicorns travel faster."

"Faster than flying griffins?" Jessika asked, incredulous.

"Yes."

She blinked. "Uh, all right. Have you seen Joy? Is she with Thornfire?"

"I thought she was with you."

"She was, but we got separated. A mage used his magic to send me to a mountaintop, back that way a few days' walk. He was trying to kill me, but this mage, Cray, felt the magic and intercepted it, so I survived."

"And what happened to Joy?"

Jessika bit her lip, lowering her voice just in case Cray was awake a little. "I don't know. If no one has found her, I don't know where she is. She could have been sent somewhere else, or she could still be trapped back there with the mage, under Northnest castle."

Kassandra nodded. "But if she were just sent somewhere, she would have made her way back to South-scree, or to Thornfire. Griffins don't get lost or killed by being sent to mountaintops."

"That's what I thought, too. She could have gone back to South-scree, I suppose, or maybe she was sent a really long ways away and just hasn't made contact yet. I have the magic stone; she doesn't."

The two sisters sat for a moment in silence, not looking at each other, not wanting to say it. Finally, Kassandra did.

"What if the mage took her prisoner?" the leafy girl whispered.

Jessika shook her head, refusing to think on it. "Joy is strong and brave. She can take care of herself. I'm sure she's fine."

Kassandra's gaze was boring into her forehead, but Jessika couldn't meet it.

"What if she's not? Anyone can be defeated by the right enemy," she said.

Just then Cray grunted and started to stir. Kassandra flinched away a little.

"Maybe you should go?" Jessika wondered. "I mean, you said we'd be safe the rest of the night. You don't have to stay if you don't want to."

Kassandra rose to a half-crouch. "I'd rather fewer people see me than more," she murmured in agreement. "We'll be watching over you the rest of the night. And I'll go back tomorrow and tell Thornfire about everything. He should meet up with you in a few days."

"Thank you, Kassie," Jessika breathed, "and give the unicorns my gratitude, too."

"They know, but I will."

Kassandra melted back into the night as though she'd disintegrated, and Jessika couldn't even hear her footsteps moving away. She went to Cray and helped him roll over. Breeka was making soft distressed sounds.

"Master hurt," the bat-cat whimpered. "Breeka knew Master would get hurt."

"Cray, can you hear me?" Jessika asked.

"I hear you," he croaked. "Just leave me here a bit. Let me rest."

"I'll get you a blanket."

Jessika got up and went to where the goats had been tethered. She hadn't taken more than two steps before she pulled up short, breath caught in her throat and hands clapping over her mouth as she saw what lay before her. She swallowed a sob.

"Oh, Cray, oh, I'm sorry," she choked out.

"What? What is it?" the old mage replied.

"Dali and Deni," she winced. "That skinny monster, it leapt at me, but I sort of dodged, so it ran into them instead. They're, oh I'm so sorry, they're dead, Cray."

She heard his breath leave him in a long, heavy sigh. "It's not your fault, Hawkwings."

"It is," she argued, fighting through tears now. "I went to Northnest. I explored under the castle, trying to get through. That mage sent me away because I was there. Then you saved me—"

"That's right. Stop right there," he interrupted firmly. "I chose to put my life, and Breeka's, and Dali and Deni's lives at risk the moment I intervened. I knew I'd call danger onto myself by doing so. I knew others around me could get hurt. That is not your fault. The shadow-dogs came for me."

"And me, they're coming for me, too," she insisted.

"Maybe, but I chose to leave my home and take Breeka and the goats with me. You didn't make me. It's not your fault, Hawkwings. It's not your fault for dodging either. I'd rather have you alive than them. Now get the packs off of them before all our supplies get bloody."

Jessika had seen dead animals before, plenty of times. Griffins killed as quickly and cleanly as they could, but the butchering always produced blood and offal. It was a little different when the dead animals had been companions, though. She knelt in the near darkness and opened the buckles and straps and dragged the packs away. She petted each goat's head in apology, unable to keep her tears back.

"They may be made of shadow," Cray said softly as she brought the packs over, "but their claws and fangs still cut. The one that pinned me down clawed up my shoulders a bit. I'm lucky the intervention came when it did."

Jessika put a blanket over Cray and wrapped another around herself.

"So," he went on, "you are sister to their foal. How peculiar."

"I don't know what they mean," she countered at once, though that was only partly true. She suspected they meant Kassandra, but Kassandra wasn't their foal. Jessika wasn't sure what she was anymore—she certainly didn't seem fully human—but she definitely wasn't a unicorn foal.

"And they want you protected," Cray concluded.

Jessika clenched her jaw. "So what did you do to them to incur such a debt?"

"Oh," he moaned, seeming more deeply hurt than at the news that Deni and Dali were dead. "Oh, do not ask me for that. I will protect you with all my power, but do not ask me to put into words what I have done. You would be horrified. You'd probably want to kill me, and I'm not sure if I'd try to stop you."

Jessika didn't know how to respond to that, so she said, "we'll be safe here until morning. We're being watched over. You can sleep."

"We should make a fire first, and eat before the meat spoils."

She gasped. "Eat Dali and Deni?"

"Of course. If we don't, the beasts of the forest will, you can be sure. They have been my companions for several years. They have given me their strength and friendship all that time. I believe, if they could speak, they would want to give me the energy of their bodies, now that they do not need them anymore."

Jessika started crying again, quietly. Cray levered himself up off the ground, to sitting.

"It's all right if you don't want to eat any," he said gently. "I'll take care of everything. Why don't you sleep?"

She shook her head, swiping at her wet cheeks. "No, I'll partake of their final gift," she managed. "Wake me when, when," she couldn't finish.

"When it's time?"

"Yeah."

Jessika bundled the blanket around her body and found a spot with a thick cushion of fallen leaves on the far side of the circle from where the goats lay. She closed her eyes and tried not to listen as Cray lit a fire and did what he thought Deni and Dali would have wanted.

Chapter 13
Second Reunion

Morning light filtering through the tree canopy and the smell of roasting meat awakened Jessika. She was surprised to find that Breeka had curled up against her belly and was sleeping soundly. Gently, she eased away from the bat-cat and sat up, trying to stretch out the aches and kinks in her body from sleeping on the hard ground.

"Awake, are we?" Cray said softly. "There's food: quite a lot. Please have some. Then we'll make today's plan."

The old man was on his back, wrapped in a blanket, head pillowed on a pack and another under his knees to prop them up. Jessika moved to sit by the fire and regarded the pile of cooked strips of meat.

"Deni and Dali's final gift?" she breathed sadly. "Thank you."

Jessika picked up a piece and started chewing. Her stomach gurgled immediately and she closed her eyes as saliva flooded her mouth. Thoughts tangled with regret and grief and the heavy inevitableness of death. She ate until her tummy was stretched tight and she feared any more would give her a bellyache.

"We'll take the rest with us," Cray said. "It will keep for a while now that it's cooked. Now we have a lot more to carry, however, and I am not in the best shape."

"I can carry it," Jessika volunteered.

He nodded. "I'm afraid I'll have to depend on you for it. Let me tell you how to find the next house. You can probably get there, come back, get a second load, and get back to the house before dark without too much trouble. I will do my best to just get to the house today."

Jessika listened as Cray described the path, and then helped him pack up the heaviest items. She'd take the bulkier but lighter items on her second trip. Walking through the forest alone felt strange and slightly scary at first, but after a couple hours the freedom and solitude won out, and having her body moving helped banish the dismal thoughts of the morning.

The path was faint, but following Cray's directions she reached first a small clearing with an ancient lightning-blasted tree, and next noticed the path starting to approach a sheer rocky mountainside that jutted up to a height above the tress. Soon enough the path reached it and ran along the base of it, just as Cray had said it would. She was able to drink from any of the several trickling waterfalls that came down the cliff, and step over the narrow streams they made.

Jessika reached the house when the sun was still high in the sky. Her shoulders ached from the heavy load and she was relieved when she could finally put the pack down in the messy remains of a garden gone wild. The house itself was a cave in the side of the cliff. The opening had been bricked up with stones except for a wooden door and a drain at the base of the wall where a stream of water snuck out. The door had been wedged shut with some wooden shims, which Jessika had to first wiggle free before she could open it.

The open door let light into the cave. The floor was packed dirt over rock, except for where the stream wound its way across it. To one side, on a slightly higher shelf of rock was built a wooden frame that was probably the remains of a bed. There was a rough table opposite it. Natural rock ledges held a few pots and other items. On another shelf was obviously a fireplace, but no chimney.

Jessika noticed additional light trickling in from the back of the cave accompanied by the music of falling water. The cave made a slight turn, and she came upon a natural chimney, where water fell down from high above, glittering in a faint beam of sunlight. The water formed a small pool before running away towards the exit near the door. A little bit of moss coated the rocks around it.

Jessika leaned forward over the pool, into the water chimney, and looked up towards the surface, getting a face-full of water and glimpsing a bit of sky among ferns at the top of the shaft. She jerked back, swiping the water out of her eyes, and returned to the front of the cave. Leaving the pack inside, she wedged the door shut again, and turned around to head back to where she'd left Cray.

Traveling unburdened this time, she moved quickly, and encountered Cray partway along the trail, near the clearing with the lightning tree. He was limping his way along with two crutches. Breeka was following him, walking on the ground, instead of riding Cray's shoulders. Cray handed off a few strips of meat to Jessika as she passed and continued his painful progress.

Jessika reached the spot where they'd faced the shadow-beasts the previous night and found the second pack, stuffed to bursting, hidden under some shrubs where Cray had said he'd put it. She glanced around before she left, seeing no sign of the fire pit or the remains of Deni and Dali. She didn't know where Cray had put them.

With the sun westering, all she could do was haul the pack on and turn to retrace her steps yet again. She passed Cray for a second time along the path where it followed the cliff. The afternoon was wearing on when she reached the cave house again, and she spent the rest of the daylight getting the bed ready for Cray, lighting a fire, and scrounging through the wild garden for anything she could recognize as edible, to supplement the meat.

Cray arrived, grey-faced and panting, as the last of the light fell, and Jessika hurried to help him into the house.

"Can't rest yet," he insisted. "I have to set the wards."

Breeka shuffled over to the fireplace and flopped down while Cray managed to sit on the floor just inside the closed door, where he pressed his gnarled hands to the dirt. Leaving him to do whatever he did, Jessika finished up meal preparations. Breeka was already asleep by the time she finished and Cray rose creakily from the floor a moment later.

"It's done. We'll be safe here tonight," he said.

Jessika helped him to sit on a flat rock she'd struggled to wrestle into place between the table and fire. He settled there with a groan.

"Thank you, child," he smiled, wincing. "I see you've made the place quite cozy, and food as well."

Jessika had washed the bowls left on the rock shelves and put what food she'd been able to make into them. She brought Cray another bowl full of water for washing his hands.

"I'm ashamed of my weakness," the mage said once he'd gotten a few mouthfuls of food into him. "I'm getting old. I never would have fallen on that trail a few years ago."

"If the path gave way, it wasn't your fault," Jessika countered. "Anyone would have fallen."

"Perhaps, perhaps not. I slipped, the rocks shifted. It cost us Deni and Dali and now I am injured. I don't think I can make it to the next house in one day."

"Then we'll stay here until you're well again," Jessika suggested. "Speaking

of that, we should bandage your wounds, shouldn't we?"

He waved a hand dismissingly. "By now they've all clotted, not to worry. I also know a trick or two to speed my healing along. I'm too tired now, but in the morning I'll work the spell. Eat up, eat up, we still have so much meat."

They ate in silence for a while, and Breeka roused enough to hop over to the tabletop and take some food, too.

"I'm quite curious about those unicorns, who seemed to know you, Hawkwings," Cray murmured after a while. "Had you met them before?"

"I saw unicorns a couple times, years ago," Jessika admitted. "I don't know if these were the same ones. They looked different."

"In what way?"

"These ones glowed. They were so bright I could hardly see their shape. The ones from years ago looked like any other animal, you know? No glow, I mean."

"Ah, but of course," Cray nodded. "You were a child then. Things change when children grow up. Would you like to know what I saw?"

"Alright."

He took a few moments before answering, chewing thoughtfully. "I knew what they were right away. There's no mistaking their auras, not for a mage. I couldn't look at them; they were too bright, like looking into the sun, or into a hundred suns."

"But they made you look at them."

"Yes, yes, they did. If you were to look into the sun and then see an even brighter shape within it that would be something like what I saw. I could see the shape of their heads, their ears, their horns, and their manes lashing like white fire. More than that, they saw me, they looked into me, saw more of me than I ever could of them, and there was nothing I could hide from them. They know every secret of my soul, as though they walked through it, kicking stones over to reveal the slimy, hidden crawlies below." He swallowed laboriously.

Jessika waited patiently for him to go on, as he took a few more bites and sips of water, not meeting her gaze.

"I feel dirtier than I have for a long time," he muttered at last. "You do things in life for whatever stupid reason, that hurt people, that hurt your-self, that later you realize disgraced yourself." He rephrased, gesturing with his spoon. "At least, some people realize that what they've done has harmed others. Some don't. If you do, and if you believe that hurting others is wrong, then you feel terrible for a while, maybe for a long while, but you can't just go on feeling terrible all the time. You can't survive like that. Eventually, you have to focus on getting through your day instead, and you gradually forget to feel terrible."

Cray sighed, shaking his head. "I've done so much bad, and had gotten pretty good at forgetting how terrible it made me feel, so I could escape it and try to live some kind of a not-bad life. Those unicorns, they made me face it all again. I saw it, as they saw it, saw my former self do what I did, unable to change the past, though I want to so much."

His hand had come to rest, spoon in his half-empty bowl, eyes staring off into the distance. To Jessika, he looked older than anyone she'd ever seen: his face deeply lined, his beard unkempt and straggly, his hair thinning and brittle. Whatever he'd done, he was just a broken old man now, or so she thought of him.

He started eating again. "That was part of their price, to make sure I still remembered, because if you forget too much, you might forget the lessons you learned. As for the rest, it seems I'll be doing all I can to protect you, Hawkwings."

"I didn't ask for that," she said softly. "I suppose that sounds ungrateful, but it wasn't like I wanted them to make you promise something like that. I'm sorry you have to do it."

Cray scraped up the last of his food and set the dishes aside with a grunt. "There's obviously something important about you, important enough for Altare to try to kill you, important enough that you're somehow sibling to a unicorn, and maybe other things, too. Are you going to tell me about it?"

He sat back, folded his bruised arms, and stared at her. Jessika stared back for a moment, and then looked down.

"I can't," she said.

"You won't, you mean," he corrected firmly.

She bit her lip, conflicted.

Cray rose and started gathering the dishes.

"I'll do that," Jessika insisted. "You go rest."

He put the dishes back down, turned without a word, and went to the bed she'd set up. Still silent, he got in, pulled the blanket around himself and closed his eyes. Jessika cleaned up and arranged her own blanket on the flat-test, softest bit of floor she could find. Breeka moved back to its spot by the fire.

"Stupid girl," it scolded in a whisper.

"Yes," Jessika agreed, "yes, I am."

They stayed at the cave house for two more nights. Jessika did what she could to salvage food from the wild garden and mend anything in the packs that had become damaged. Cray showed her how to smoke the remaining goat meat into jerky and she dutifully undertook the task. A few times a day she would take out Thornfire's magic rock and squeeze it until she felt his response. Cray spent most of his time sitting in a shady spot among the flora, meditating, and she observed him growing stronger and healthier hour by hour.

It was the third morning, as they were putting their packs together, that Jessika lunged to her feet when she heard the distinctive contact cry of a grif-fin. As she ran for the door she realized—now was the time. Today, Cray would see the griffins, and they would see him. There was no way to avoid it.

Oh, well.

Jessika encircled her mouth with her hands, tipped back her head, and cried back her human version of a contact call. Immediately, three griffin cries and two human cries answered her. She gave her call again, allowing them to focus on her direction.

"What's all this?" Cray asked, coming out of the house behind her.

She looked over her shoulder, unable to hide her expression of mixed joy and trepidation.

"You said you wanted to know more about me," she said. "Now you will. My friends are about to arrive. Please, don't shoot them with magic or anything."

He raised an eyebrow. "Just what are your friends, that they might inspire a magical attack?"

There was no need for Jessika to answer. Thornspike came banking in first with Rikah riding her. She flared her wings and touched down, tucking her wings in to make space for Starbright with Karo aboard. Since Starbright was bigger and wider-winged than Thornspike, she had to flap a bit more to get down safely. The smallest of them, Thornfire, came down last and with the most grace. He immediately eyed Cray, while Thornspike and Starbright took cautiously defensive positions.

"What's all this?" Thornfire rumbled.

If the tension hadn't been so evident, Jessika would have laughed at his unknowing echoing of Cray.

"This is Craduticus, called Cray," she explained. "He saved my life, and he's been helping me get back to you all."

"So we've heard. Hawksky brought us your message."

Thornfire still didn't look friendly, and neither Starbright nor Thornspike had relaxed.

"So," the griffin went on, "should I extend my thanks?"

"Not necessary," Cray said levelly. "She did not request my help."

The griffin mage gave a curt nod. "Then we are finished here. Hawkrain, you're the lightest, I'll take you. Hawkwings, get on Bright."

Karo started to get down obediently, with Starbright kneeling in deference to his injured foot.

"No, wait," Jessika protested. "Cray promised to protect me, so—"

She broke off when Thornfire's feathers began to rise with threat. "So you want to bring him along? You expect one of us to carry this man?"

"Well," she prevaricated helplessly, looking around, counting griffins, counting humans, and realized the problem. "Where's Waterleap?"

"The question is: where is Hawkjoy?" Thornfire countered, his voice now rising as well. "When Hawksky reported your situation, I sent Waterleap back to South-scree in case she had somehow made her way back there. She was with you. You tell me where she is."

Jessika spread her hands helplessly. "I don't know," she had to confess.

"And unless Waterleap finds her back home and safe, nobody knows," he said. "And this man—he stinks of dark magic."

"It clings, doesn't it?" Cray nodded, trying to smile. "Haven't used it for years."

"It stains, you mean, and it never comes off," Thornfire growled.

"This must be your mage friend," Cray said to Jessika.

"What have you told him?" Thornfire's tone was dangerous.

"Nothing, he just noticed when I used the stone," she said.

"Hawkwings has done a good job of not telling me things, I assure you," Cray said, "despite how many times I've asked her."

"Regardless of what you do or do not want, there are three of us and four humans," Thornfire spoke carefully.

"I did make a promise to a pair of unicorns that I would protect Hawkwings with all my power," Cray said. "It was their price for me to repay a debt I owe them. It seems that the young lady has a conflict with Altare, my former apprentice. He tried to kill her and probably knows I rescued her. He may still be hunting her. If she is to face him in any capacity, my help might be all that could ensure her victory. I expect that is why the unicorns set the price they did. I understand, of course, that you cannot carry my weight." He turned to Jessika. "Where are you going next? I will meet you there as soon as I can."

She looked helplessly at Thornfire. "I don't know. We need to find Hawkjoy."

The griffin angled his head severely. "You carried the stone, not Hawkjoy. She cannot contact me. You say you don't know where she is; nor do we."

"Is she a relation?" Cray offered. "Perhaps a tracking spell?"

"Not a blood relation to anyone here," Thornfire specified immediately. "Nor do we have anything of hers."

"Anything of hers?" Jessika echoed, a little confused.

"Hair, fingernail clippings, anything from her body," Cray explained.

"Oh, I do," she announced. Jessika fetched her pack and dug down deep into it, all the way to the bottom. "She broke a covert when we were exploring and I kept it. Big feathers aren't common, you know? I didn't want a regular person to see it."

She pulled it out. It was only part of a covert feather, but it was almost as long as her palm, and as wide.

"Oh dear," Cray murmured, and then louder, "Hawkjoy is a griffin."

"That's right," Jessika confirmed.

"You were with her when you encountered Altare? When Altare sent you away?"

"Yes."

Cray's face had turned white and bloodless, like when he'd gotten injured. "Altare has her," he croaked.

"What?" Jessika gasped.

"How do you know?" Thornfire demanded.

"I was surprised, even, that he would send away a young woman," Cray said, "as it was his idle hobby to collect any he could get away with while he was my apprentice, but if he was facing both Hawkwings and a griffin, and suspected he might have trouble subduing both, it makes sense. Altare will not have let a chance to capture a griffin get away. I can give you an almost complete guarantee that he has her."

"It was the woman with him who said she wanted Hawkjoy," Jessika mentioned. "He just did what she said."

"A woman?" Cray's face turned even whiter, which Jessika hadn't expected would be possible. The old mage groped for a place to sit. "Please, I know we're not all friendly with each other right now, but I have information you need. I know these people and I know what they do. Hawkwings, can you tell your whole tale?"

The three griffins exchanged dubious glances, but Rikah slid down off of Thornspike and strode over to Jessika and Cray. "Come on, I think we should listen," he said back at the others.

The young man took a seat on the ground and looked up at Thornfire with an expression a bit more belligerent than Jessika had seen from him before. The griffin mage in turn gave him a glare, but then shuffled his feathers and gave up, walking his back feet in to take a seat.

"Very well then, let's have it," Thornfire acquiesced.

"Well," Jessika began, "we were exploring under the castle, like Rikah and Thornspike were, too. We'd agreed to unlock doors, and I picked the most likely looking one and I thought at first the room was empty, so I went in and Joy followed. It was a big round room with tables and shelves and there was a light at one end, and once we came in I realized there was a woman behind the light doing something at a desk. She saw us and came right over, but she didn't seem angry. She was really interested in Hawkjoy, but she wasn't treating her like a person, and she asked me if she could buy Hawkjoy from me, and I tried to explain how she was my sister."

Jessika had to pause for a breath, realizing that she'd been talking faster and faster. Her throat was choking up a bit and her hands were trembling.

"Do you remember her name, Hawkwings? Did you hear it?" Cray pressed gently.

"She called herself Skire, and Altare called her Skire, too, and she had a second name also."

Cray put his hand to his throat, shaking his head a little. "I'm so very sorry, but Hawkjoy is gone. There's nothing you can do."

Jessika's hands and face went cold with shock. Angry eyes turned onto Cray from all sides with exclamations of denial.

"Explain that statement," Thornfire demanded, raising his voice over the others.

Cray took a steadying breath. "Skire is a title used back in the country I came from. It means someone who investigates the world and tries to understand it, analyze it, and discover how it all works. Skire Germaine was young and excited when she joined the army coming to conquer Northnest. She'd been an apprentice in the team developing drake varieties, had investigated drakes and other animals fully, and was extremely excited at the prospect of getting to learn about griffins."

He glanced around at his audience. "This may be difficult for you to hear. After the conquering of Northnest, Skire Germaine was given all the severely injured griffins and mostly-intact dead griffin bodies there were, for investigation purposes. They weren't enough for her, but the captured healthy griffins were pressed into service elsewhere and the commanders refused her pleas to have them, too. She made her corpses and captives last as long as she could, but there was still more she wanted to learn. She demanded to be given any of the slave griffins that got injured or sick and could no longer work, but the slave masters took good care of their workers and she didn't get many."

Thornfire interrupted. "What do you mean when you say investigate?"

Cray's hands twitched nervously. "She examined their bodies, inside and out, and made notes, and drew pictures of, of their body parts, and how they worked," he said.

"Inside and out? How?" Jessika asked, nauseated.

The old mage seemed reluctant to answer, but after a few breaths said, "I'm sorry, Hawkwings, but she would have the griffin rendered unconscious, and then," he swallowed, as though it made him nauseous, too, "and then cut it open. Sometimes she'd try to stitch it back up again afterwards, and let it heal, to keep it alive longer for more procedures, but more often her investigation would result in it eventually dying on the table, never awakening."

Jessika felt her breakfast rise up into her throat. She gagged and fought down the choking nausea. Rikah came over to her and put a comforting hand on her back.

"Who were they?" she coughed out.

"Who were they?" Cray echoed, still gently.

"The griffins, the ones she had, what were their names?" she demanded through angry tears.

"Ah, I'm not sure I ever knew," Cray confessed, "and I don't know if the Skire even recorded their names. We weren't really seeing them as people back then. We decided they were just clever animals that could understand some basic words and parrot them back, even when the evidence that they were our equals was right in front of us. If we had seen them for who they really were, we probably couldn't have done the things to them that we did."

"You, you were with the invaders," Jessika accused, voice rising with pain and anger, "you're one of the ones that conquered Northnest. You killed my family. You destroyed my home. You tortured and murdered my Feathyrs."

Another voice piped up shrilly. "Master saved me."

Jessika turned her head, wiping her face to be able to see. Breeka had hobbled out of the cave house and stood on its hind paws by Cray, foreclaws hooked onto his robes.

"Master saw me and took me away from the evil lady," Breeka went on. It laid its head against Cray's knee. "Master is good."

"I did cruel, unforgiveable things," Cray said, his voice sounding thick with emotion, too, "and you may hate me for them, Hawkwings. I wish I had realized sooner how wrong I was. I can't go back and change them now. I can only try to help from now on."

Jessika turned her face away and tried to get her breathing under control. Rikah put his arm around her, as if to shield her from the others, and if he wept a little, too, she wouldn't tell anyone about it either. The whole group stood in awkward silence for a few moments.

"I can tell you that the Skire would have jumped at the chance to have another griffin," Cray said finally.

"We have to get her back," Jessika declared, even though her voice broke.

"Hawkwings, it's j-just," Cray stuttered, "she probably isn't alive anymore."

Jessika shook her head furiously. "No. No. We have to go get her."

"It's been about a week since the incident? Back then, when she had a bunch of decaying bodies to get through first, the injured griffins were kept for a while, but once she started in on them, they didn't survive for very long. I feel terrible having to tell you these things, about your people. I didn't know any griffins escaped, and that you, Hawkwings, would know them."

That confused her for a moment, until she figured out that he wasn't talking about Hawkwind, but rather assumed that these griffins with her—Thornfire and the others—were Northnest survivors. She didn't see any benefit to correcting him.

Jessika scrubbed her tears off her face and turned around to see that Cray's brow was furrowed, as though thinking hard, and Jessika was regretting blurting out so many hints about her past. She looked up at Thornfire, but he had his bill buttoned, and Starbright and Thornspike were following his lead, eyeing him carefully and remaining silent. Karo was normally reticent anyway, and in this case was also staying silent.

Jessika took a few minutes to think, forcing herself to consider what might be happening with Hawkjoy and the Skire. Quickly enough she was shaking her head with denial.

"No," she announced, looking straight at Thornfire. "Hawkjoy is pregnant."

"What?" he retorted. "How do you know?"

"The Skire knew, somehow, when she looked at Hawkjoy," Jessika explained, glancing at Cray to see his reaction. "And then Hawkjoy admitted it to me."

"Really," Cray murmured, sitting up a bit.

Jessika nodded vigorously. "The Skire said she'd only examined a few pregnant griffins, that her research was incomplete. That was why she particularly wanted Hawkjoy."

Cray took a deep breath. "Then she might well keep her for the duration of the pregnancy. After that, it's difficult to say. You're right, Hawkwings, she might still be alive."

Jessika was distracted from her surge of hope as she saw Thornfire pacing closer to her with menacing measured steps.

"Daughter of Hawk," he rumbled, "because of you the new Mother of the Hawk Line is held captive by cruel and vicious humans who will cut her and her chick to pieces? Do you have any idea what you've done?"

"Uh," Jessika gasped, a little afraid, "I didn't know. Hawkjoy didn't tell me she was pregnant. How could I know?"

He stabbed towards her with his bill and ignored her reply. "Losing any member of any Line would be bad enough, but it is the Hawkmother these vile people hold now. Do you have any idea what the reaction of the South-scree Council will be to this? Hawkwind vowed not to entangle us with your past, and you have broken her vow for her. Unless the Hawkmother is returned undamaged with deepest apologies, this could mean a full attack by the Aeries on Northnest. Can you understand that?"

Jessika had never seen Thornfire like this. His wings were mantled and his neck ruff bristled. She felt afraid of a griffin for the first time. She took a step back, instinctively pulling her arms in against her chest and throat.

"Master," Starbright murmured, disconcerted.

Thornfire jerked towards his former apprentice. "You have no idea either," he snarled.

"She's just a fledgling," Starbright tried, flattening into a submissive posture. "And she couldn't have foreseen this."

"Hawkwings is an adult," he retorted, wings and tail lifting even further. "She asserted that when she insisted on this ridiculous foray. Now she has endangered the new Hawkmother and when I report this it will force the Council to act. A new mother, recently awakened, pregnant, and imprisoned by humans, likely to be slowly tortured and both she and her chick killed? The matriarchs will scream for slaughter of her captors, and they have no idea of the strength of the adversary. These are the people that conquered and destroyed six griffin Lines and their human allies when they took Northnest with drakes and magic."

He paused for breath and deflated slightly. "I," he panted, "I don't know what to do, what we can do, how we can get her back, how we can prevent a war."

Thornfire's feathers began to flatten as he cast about helplessly, as though a solution lay on the ground somewhere near.

"We shall have to get her out without a war," Cray stated boldly. "We must do it by stealth instead of overtly. I agree with you that a direct assault would be a tragedy for both sides."

Thornfire eyed him. "But I will have to report it. I'm the senior member of this mission, and an elder of my Line, I must tell my matriarch everything."

"Perhaps Thornmother will see the wisdom of not informing the Council," Thornspike spoke up. "She is reasonable."

Thornfire glared at the slender-winged female, bill clenched, but at last he growled, "and she has the luxury of discretion when it comes to what she tells the Council."

"And we'll have to tell Hawkwind," Starbright whispered. "She'll be furious."

"Perhaps, perhaps if we act right away, get Hawkjoy back now, we need not report the accident, only its resolution." The griffin mage turned his fierce glare next onto the human mage. "You, old man, you can help us plan a covert assault on this Skire?"

Cray was rubbing his face methodically, thinking. "I think I am your best hope, yes."

"I am going to get my Linesister back," Jessika asserted.

"So I will do everything in my power to protect you on your quest," Cray vowed. He stood, and to Jessika he suddenly looked like a powerful mage instead of just an old wizard. "Now, there are several things that need addressing immediately. Altare's shadow-beasts will come for Hawkwings and me again, every night, but I don't think they know of the rest of you, and they mustn't find out. You should make a secure camp some distance away from us and never be with us between dusk and dawn."

He turned to Hawkwings. "We should make our way closer to Northnest. Three houses from here is a house I lived in for quite some time. I have a workroom there where I can prepare for our covert assault."

"We can carry you there, can't we, Master?" Starbright suggested.

"No," Cray refused before the griffin mage could respond. "The shadow-beasts would report to their master the irregularity of our progress, which would attract more of Altare's attention. We must walk it, as we have been doing. Your kind offer is most generous, but you see the difficulty. I only hope Altare will not detect any hint of this meeting."

"Then shouldn't we get going?" Jessika mentioned. "It's already later than we usually start."

"We should," Cray agreed. "We'll have to move quickly today, but we're both well-rested now."

"We can at least take your packs, right?" Starbright piped up again.

"We don't know where they're going," Thornfire countered.

"Not to worry. We'll be fine," Cray said.

He went back inside to fetch both their packs, and while he was gone Rikah gave Jessika another little squeeze of her shoulders.

"I hope Joy's alright," he whispered.

The night was closing in as Jessika and Cray—with Breeka riding his shoulders—hurried their steps towards his next house.

"Keep going," the wizard panted. "Don't waste energy looking around. I can tell they aren't here yet."

Jessika didn't need to ask whom he meant. She was anticipating the arrival of shadow-beasts at any moment. The sun was down and twilight was fading into true darkness.

"We're almost there," Cray reassured her. "You see that big tree ahead?"

Jessika wouldn't have called it big. It was immense, larger in diameter than any tree she could remember ever seeing, and there were some true giants in the forest around South-scree. This one went straight up, vanishing into the sky above, without limbs. The base of it was gnarled and knobby and twisted like a thick candle with hours of drippings collected around the bottom. That tree was the next house?

Jessika hesitated as she reached it, not seeing any sign of a door.

"This way, this way," Cray urged, limping around to the opposite side of the trunk.

She followed and saw him lifting away a heavy, coarsely woven blanket-door. Behind it was a narrow, crack-like opening through the bark and into the interior of the tree itself.

"Get in, get in," he ordered, and Jessika obeyed.

She had to crouch a little and turn her body slightly, scraping her pack and an elbow against the natural doorframe. Cray followed almost right against her back, with Breeka making chittering yelps of fear. Jessika nearly went down as she stumbled over the uneven dirt floor and took a rapid seat.

Cray grunted a word and soft light bloomed above their heads. A cloudy cluster of quartz crystal was suspended from the ceiling in a tangle of what seemed to be roots. It illuminated the inside of the tree. Perhaps a fire had burned out the core, leaving a room tall enough to stand in and wide enough for a half dozen people to sleep comfortably. The walls slanted upward to the center where the quartz light hung, so around the edges there was no head room, but the middle was plenty big enough for two people and a bat-cat.

Breeka flapped down to the floor and Jessika watched as Cray stumped around the perimeter of the room, touching small engravings on the walls, muttering words. After a minute, he stopped, having made a full circuit, and let his hand fall to his side.

"We're safe now," he said, "but we didn't have time to gather water to-night, and as you can see, this is a primitive house, with no water source."

"There's a little left in my water skin," Jessika offered.

"It will have to do. We can have that and some jerky."

They began unpacking their bags and setting out bedrolls. A couple woven storage baskets tucked along one wall contained additional blankets, and Jessika happily took her share for adding cushion and warmth. A wooden box held a few kitchen items, including a pair of tin cups, bowls, and a few pieces of flatware.

There was no fireplace in the room; Cray explained that was because the smoke would be trapped without a chimney, which the tree-room also lacked. A little cold air snuck through the blanket-door, but the presence of three warm bodies seemed to heat the room up to a tolerable temperature.

The three of them sat around chewing the jerky and sharing the water out between the tin cups. Cray shared with Breeka, who sipped in dainty fashion. They heard nothing from outside, but Jessika's skin prickled with anxiety and her mind had no difficulty in imagining what might be prowling about. That woven door wouldn't stop even a squirrel if it were determined to get in.

"We're safe in here," Cray murmured when Jessika glanced toward the entrance.

"You said if you ever defeated the weak shadow-beasts Altare sends to watch you, that he'd send stronger ones next," Jessika recalled aloud. "The other houses kept them out, but this one—"

The mage spoke across her with a wave of his hand holding a piece of jerky. "Even if he has, the protections on this tree are perhaps the strongest of any of my houses."

"Why is that?"

He gestured upwards. "I asked the tree to participate in their construction."

Jessika swallowed a bit of jerky before she'd fully chewed it and winced. "Really? You can talk to trees?"

"In a way," he nodded. "This tree is ancient. For all I know, it might have stood here since the beginning of the world. It has survived forest fires, land slides, and floods hundreds of times over, and more winters than it has needles. If there is any immortal being in this world, I believe it may be this tree. Live as long as that, and even something without a brain becomes wise and aware."

Cray put out a hand and rested his fingertips lightly on the living wood of the room's wall. "You can talk to it, if you first learn how to listen to what it has to say."

"And what does it say?" Jessika asked curiously.

A light expression of sweet peace came over the mage's face. "It speaks of fawns and squirrels, and their babies, and their babies' babies, and on and on, season after season, all who sheltered below it, or played among its branches. It tells me of birds that pick bits of moss off its bark, and use them to make nests for their eggs. It could share with me the secret of where every single one of the thousands of insects currently burrowing in its body can be found. If I wished for a sip of its lifeblood, it could tell me where a woodpecker has recently made a hole and let its sap flow freely."

"All that is happening to this tree?" Jessika wondered.

"That and more. Down in the soil, creatures of many sorts nibble on its roots in some places, while fungi have made a pact with the tree, seeking out water for it in return for some sugars made up there in its needles and transported all the way down into its root tips. Yet more birds wedge their bills into its cones to steal its seeds for their hungry bellies, but they drop some, and from those they miss sprout this tree's many children."

"And what did you say to the tree to get it to help you with your spells?"

"I'm getting to that," Cray assured her. "Of all things in this world, of all creatures, there is nothing more giving than a tree. Of course, it cannot give all, or it would die, but it provides life to the forest, getting little in return. All those creatures I mentioned, from the fungi to the woodpecker, would have no life, were it not for trees. A tree may not be as exciting as an ice-lion, which runs and leaps and chases prey and plays with its cubs, but the ice-lion would not exist were it not for the tree, which feeds and shelters its prey.

"Because of this," he went on firmly, before Jessika could interrupt again, "it acquires, over time, deep and powerful life energy. It is ponderous: holding a long view beyond anything a mere human could conceptualize. This tree was here long before you or me, and will still be here long after we are both gone.

"So, I meditated here, beneath its heart. It was difficult to get its attention, and I think perhaps it only noticed me the way you might notice a bit of distant, unfamiliar birdsong while striding across a meadow with somewhere important to go. Still, I managed to impress upon it the aspect of the shadow-beasts that hunt me, and hunt among its forest. They are creatures of evil, fueled by hate and death. Although death is a part of life, this death that Altare uses is a part of no cycle. It does not give rise to new beginnings. It is no sacrifice that nurtures the future.

"I sensed the tree's distaste for the shadow-beasts, and offered to let it help me combat them. It assented, so that when I wove my protections, it also inserted a strand of its own life magic. A rope made of twine may indeed be strong, but include a few threads of steel and you make it all the stronger."

Jessika took in his words and rolled them around in her mind, a little bemused by the imagery and passion with which he spoke.

"So this house, this tree, will weather anything Altare can throw at it," Cray said with a hint of glee. "For all his delusions of strength and power, he cannot possibly equal the might of this ancient tree. He is so benighted that even if I tried to explain it to him—as I've done for you—he would not only be incapable of understanding, but even if he did start to grasp the slightest glimmer of this tree's power, he would automatically reject it as impossible, and deny that he could comprehend any of it."

As Cray had spoken, the unease had melted from Jessika's neck and shoulders. Though she was no mage, she could at least imagine what this tree's life magic was like, and knowing it was there gave her a feeling both warm and reverent.

"Don't concern yourself with the shadow-beasts tonight," Cray concluded. He indicated Breeka with his chin. "See? Even Breeka is sleeping. There's no need for it to be on watch while we shelter here."

Jessika nodded, and managed a smile as the wizard put away the last of the jerky and began to fold back his blankets.

"So, don't you want to ask more questions about my griffin friends?" Jessika prodded, feeling soothed enough to be bold.

Cray paused, lifting an eyebrow at her. "Of course, but mages know to be patient. I think I've learned enough about you for one day. I have plenty to think on."

His acquiescent reply almost made Jessika chuckle. "All right then."

"Not to mention that I must think of a way to snatch your Hawkjoy out from under his nose," Cray said seriously.

That sobered Jessika up immediately. "You think she's being hurt, don't you?"

"If not already, then eventually," he confirmed. "Those people, Skire Germaine and Altare, have no kindness for griffins—or for anything else, really. All they will be caring about is what they can get from her, and they will use her up in whatever way necessary to get the most."

Halfway into bed, Cray turned to pierce her with a look. "What could you have possibly been doing sneaking around under the castle?"

"I," Jessika stuttered, feeling more and more foolish about her choice to trespass through the tunnels as more consequences from it piled up. "I had a reason."

He pitied her enough to remove his accusative glare, and got the rest of the way into his blankets. "I'm sure you did. You can't be faulted for making ignorant decisions; it's how a young person learns. I would say you've just had some bad luck that the outcome of your choice could mean the life of a loved one, but you must have had a critical need to go exploring under a castle, as that act is rather more idiotic than the idiotic acts most young persons engage in to learn lessons."

With that scalding speech—although he hadn't raised his voice or filled it with scorn—still hanging in the air, Cray lay down and shut his eyes.

"I'll turn off the crystals in a few minutes, if you'd like to get in bed yourself," he said.

"I'll do that," Jessika whispered, fighting back tears of his scolding on top of her already crushing guilt at getting Hawkjoy into this trouble.

She managed to get into bed, and stifled her weeping in her blankets.

Chapter 14
The Feather and the Pond

A gentle hand on her head woke her the next morning.

"Hawkwings?"

"Yes, I'm awake. Good morning, Cray," she answered, voice still a little muffled under the covers.

"I spoke bluntly last night," he went on, "when I remarked on how you got into your predicament. I was, perhaps, too harsh on you, when you are already feeling so bad about it. I wish to apologize."

She nodded under his hand and then sat up. Dawn light was filtering in through the woven door, and she squinted in it, her eyes feeling gritty and swollen from her spate of weeping.

"But everything you said was true," she shrugged. "Especially that it was an ignorant decision. I know so little about towns and cities and castles. I didn't know how best to go about sneaking in, and I had no one I could really ask."

"No parents or elders? I assume you must live in the wilds somewhere— with your griffin friends?"

"I'm the oldest," she whispered, turning her vulnerable gaze onto him, "of the humans."

Cray's eyebrows lifted with mild surprise. "So, your parents?"

"A griffin is my mother," she went on, even quieter.

"Your human parents," he clarified.

"Dead," she breathed, looking down at her lap, "maybe."

"I see," Cray responded after a moment. "Well, that explains a lot of things." He stood. "We need to get going. The next house is quite a walk, and it's not as secure as this one. Here, chew some jerky as you pack."

They stowed away the extra blankets back into the baskets and prepared their own packs for departure. They stepped out the doorway into sparkling morning light and crisp air. Cray turned with an encouraging smile and led the way to the next house.

They stopped for lunch at a spring Cray knew of. There, they refilled their water skins and drank as much as they could. Jessika found some water-cress, which they ate by the handful. Even Breeka nibbled a bit. In the midst of cramming some more into his mouth, Cray suddenly whipped his head around, gazing all about, as though he'd heard something. The leafy greens dangling down his chin would have given Jessika a laugh, if his expression hadn't been quite so alarmed.

"What is it?" she asked, her own skin prickling with fear.

He chewed and swallowed quickly. "I sensed something."

"Something dangerous?"

"Something that tastes like Altare."

"I thought the shadow-beasts only come out at night," Jessika stated.

"They do," he confirmed, "but if Altare wanted to put some extra effort into it, he could create or summon a slave that could move in sunlight."

"You think he's done that?"

"He's done something," Cray glowered. "He might be scrying us. That's where a mage uses a mirror, crystal, or bowl of water to summon up an image of what's happening at a distance. My shields should be some protection against that, but Altare is strong, probably stronger than he used to be, when I knew him."

"What should we do?" Jessika asked, stepping closer to Cray.

"We should keep moving, and get to the next house."

No sooner said than done, and the trio was off at a fast walk. The loveliness of the forest had been tarnished, but as a few more hours passed, Cray's urgency seemed to diminish, and as afternoon came he turned a smile back onto Jessika.

"I don't sense it anymore," he said. "Perhaps it was just a fantasy of an old man."

They reached the next house before dark, and it was actually a proper house: sort of.

"Used to be a woodshed," Cray explained. "Somewhere under the foliage there you can find the old foundation of the house it once went with. There's a garden, likely gone wild now, where we might find some edibles. I'll go check it out. You might want to call your griffin friends, just to let them know where we are."

Jessika brightened at that, and fished out her contact stone. Within moments it was sending the "we will come to you" pulses back to her. Just as Cray returned from the garden with some roots and greens, Thornfire came circling in for a landing.

The slender male folded his wings primly and gave the woodshed-shelter a look usually reserved for the foulest offal of slaughtered prey animals. Cray just smiled and gave a little bow.

"Last night we slept inside a huge tree," Jessika said, trying to balance the meagerness of the woodshed. "It was really neat."

"I shall assume you mean intriguing, not tidy," Thornfire retorted without so much as the flick of a feather. "Thank you for calling me, to share your location. You have sufficient food and water?"

"We do, thank you," Cray answered, holding up handfuls of roots still covered in aromatic dirt.

Thornfire's look of disgust deepened to the level more often bestowed on imbecilic mage-apprentices.

"It looks much better once cooked," Jessika assured him.

"I found some sage and oregano," Cray shared with a smile. "That will help make a tasty soup."

The human wizard stepped inside the woodshed, whistling.

"What are sage and oregano?" Thornfire enquired softly.

"I'm not really sure," Jessika confessed.

"But you're going to eat what he makes with them?"

She shrugged. "I was intending to, yes. I always do, so far."

"You are certain he means you no harm?"

"I'm really pretty sure," she nodded.

The lay of Thornfire's crest feathers did not indicate confidence in her reply.

"Tomorrow we'll get to the last house, or rather, the first house he ever made," Jessika changed the subject. "He says that from there he thinks he can plan the attack on Altare to get Hawkjoy back."

"He had better," Thornfire growled.

"It was my fault Hawkjoy got left behind," Jessika reminded the griffin.

"It was that man's apprentice that detained her," Thornfire countered. "As the master, he gave his student the skill to do such things, and failed to instill in him a sense of right and wrong."

"Cray has admitted that to me," Jessika said. "He regrets his past and wants to face it, and change things for a better future."

Thornfire looked over at the woodshed, from which strident whistling still emerged. "He had better. If he hurts you or anyone else of us, or leads us into a trap, I," Thornfire grimaced, "I would hesitate to harm a human, a thinking being like us, but I could not allow him to live to continue such evil."

Jessika approached and put a hand on Thornfire's shoulder. "I think Cray is good now. Truly."

The griffin clicked his bill. "I am not certain if people who have done such evil things as this man admits to having done can ever be fully good. I can see the taint in his power signature even still, although yes the majority shows the nurturing and protecting energies of earth, water, and light."

"I think he's being honest, and will continue to do his best," Jessika affirmed.

"I hope, for all our sakes, that you are correct, and that his best is enough."

Thornfire lifted a hand to hug Jessika, and encircled her with his opposite wing. Affectionately, he preened her hair.

"I wish to apologize for becoming so angry with you," he murmured. "I know you did not purposely cause this incident. I am to blame as well, for my actions—also unknowing—contributed to its emergence. I am still distraught, but I know that allowing my feelings to master me will not aid us. Please accept my apology."

Jessika threw her arms as far around Thornfire as she could reach, and snuggled her face into his fur-feathers. Hidden against him, thinking of Hawkjoy, her anguish swelled up inside her, and she muffled a sob with his shoulder.

"I know this must be the hardest on you," the griffin mage went on. "You blame yourself?"

She nodded, unable to speak.

"I know Hawkjoy would never blame you. If you had gone with her to help her find her father, and gotten captured by something, would you have blamed her?"

Jessika sniffed and rubbed her nose on her own sleeve, to avoid leaving anything other than a little tear-water in Thornfire's fur.

"No, at least not at first," she said. "I would be distressed, of course, but I wouldn't blame Joy. I'd still be glad I'd come with her, that I'd helped my sister with something so important to her. But, but," she hiccupped, "if my captors started torturing me, and making me hurt so much, I think I'd get angry at anyone and everyone, including Joy. Even if she rescued me, if I were really hurt, I might never forgive her."

Thornfire met Jessika's gaze with a pained expression. "I hadn't thought of that."

"Do you think she'll hate me forever if we get her out and she's been really hurt?"

The griffin opened his bill, but for a moment nothing came out. "I don't know," he said helplessly. "I can't answer that and I won't make something up to try to console you. All I can say is to try to focus on the present, and what you can do now. Don't waste time worrying about the future, unless it's productive planning. Worrying only makes your mind worse."

"Alright," she agreed.

"Perhaps the best thing you can do is go help with your meal, and make your evening as restorative as possible."

"I'll do that."

Thornfire gave her hair another bit of preening. She reached up and scratched his neck ruff.

"Call me, if it's not too close to dusk, when you reach the final house," he instructed.

"I will," she promised.

Jessika stepped back, and Thornfire forced his aging wings to carry him again into the sky.

The next day, Cray halted the trio several times to cast about for something that might be watching them. Each time he grumbled with frustration and hurried them on after a few minutes of muttering. With all the delays, they reached the final house later than they liked, and scrambled to fetch food and water, attend to the needs of nature, and get themselves inside before darkness came down like a weighty blanket.

"It's too late to call for Thornfire and the others tonight," Jessika said, "but tomorrow, they should come help, right?"

They were finishing their food at an actual table. This final house had been built as a real house some few hours walk from an actual town. It had three rooms and a loft. The big main room included a stove, small kitchen, and a table for dining.

"I'm not sure what they'll want to do," Cray mused. "Do you think Thornfire will be willing to work magic with me? Together we might do more than we could do separately, but I suspect he may have reservations about doing so."

Jessika had to admit that was probably the case.

"I also suspect, however, that he will want to know what I'm doing, and maybe observe," Cray continued. "I have a proper work room here, from which I can create and cast more complex spells. You might as well call your friends in the morning."

"What are you planning to do?"

"Well, first I'll try to scry, although I'm not optimistic. I'll also use that feather you have, to see if I can learn anything about—"

Cray suddenly jerked into stillness, eyes wide and unfocused. Jessika held her breath, waiting to see what was happening. After a few heartbeats, the old wizard relaxed somewhat, but his face was gloomy.

"Something tested my wards," he muttered. "Altare is getting curious about me."

"You know it was him?"

"I think he has an intelligent construct out there, doing the testing for him. It will return and report."

"And then what?"

"Then he will know better how much force will be required to confront me," Cray shrugged.

"You think he will?"

"Either he will come to me, or I will go to him, whichever comes first."

Breeka scooted over from where it had been sitting with its own dinner on the tabletop and tucked itself under Cray's arm. He hugged the little critter and Breeka gave a chirp-whine of unease.

"I think it unlikely that he will move against us tonight," Cray sighed. "Finish your food and get some sleep. There are straw mattresses in the loft that shouldn't be too old and moldy yet. We'll be more comfortable tonight than we have for a while."

Jessika heard Cray getting up at dawn, and picked up her contact stone to begin calling Thornfire.

"I'm summoning the griffins," she called out, still sleep-muddled.

"Excellent," Cray called back as he descended the ladder. "I'll get breakfast and then prepare the first spell. Dawn is when evil things weaken, and a good time to make a first attempt at information gathering."

Jessika levered herself out of bed and put back on her dirty outer clothing. She hadn't had a chance to wash it again for days now, and winced to put herself back into it. Down on the bottom floor she found Cray heating up some grains and water in a pot over the stove.

"Are there any nearby fruit trees that might have anything on them?" Jessika asked.

He shrugged. "The porridge could do with some fruit, but it's unlikely. Too early for apples or anything else, but you can check the trees behind the house. The mumfruit might have something. A few sometimes survive the winter."

Old memories of a furry, grey-skinned fruit with purple and red insides popped into Jessika's mind as she stepped out into the cool morning. Their path had taken them far down the mountain, into warmer weather, and now she didn't even shiver. There was an overgrown path leading around the house, weeds and shrubs festooned with dew. Jessika pushed through it and found a tiny orchard. Some of the trees had new leaves and flowers. In the back of the cluster she found the mumfruit tree: a thick and hardy, squat tree that hadn't leafed out yet. Along it's black-barked limbs Jessika spied a few bulbous grey fruits, and found a long stick on the ground that she could use to knock them down.

As she was bending over to search for the fruits through the long, soaked grass, she suddenly felt a prickling along her neck and shoulders, and jerked upright, staring about her. It had felt like something was watching her. In the forest around her, birds were still wrapping up their dawn chorus. With the exception of their colorful flitting through the trees, she saw nothing moving, but she couldn't shake the feeling that something was out there.

Her instinct told her not to crouch down again for the fruit, that staying on her feet, standing tall was a better strategy. She still couldn't see anything among the trees. For a few more minutes she stood there, waiting and watching while the wet grass soaked her shoes. Gradually, the feeling faded. Trying not to give the impression of a panicking animal, Jessika found the last few fruits she'd knocked down, and went back into the house.

"I thought something was watching me out there," she told Cray immediately.

He gave her a slightly alarmed look. "It's possible. During daylight, and for me not to sense it, if it was not a common predator, but something of Altare's doing, it would be something subtle, which is not a characteristic I commonly assign to him."

"Like what?"

Cray fiddled with his beard. "Well, he could be scrying, but I'd probably detect him if he were targeting me, and I don't see how he could be targeting you without some of your hair or blood or whatnot. His dark creatures must have fled by now. I do still have my usual daytime wards up, which allow things like us to pass through them, but do create some insulative interference. Unless something actually touched them, I might not know it's out there while I'm inside them. Whatever he's been using to track us during the day is probably out again, but it's unusual that you sensed it, as I didn't think you had any magical ability."

"I don't," she replied, "at least, no one has ever said I do."

"A remarkable young woman though you are, no, I do not sense any of that about you." He tapped his fingers against his bearded chin. "Curious."

"I looked, but I didn't see anything, or hear anything other than the birds," Jessika supplied.

Cray's eyebrows jumped up. "Hm, that's a trick I hadn't thought he'd mastered, to look through the eyes of an animal. I wouldn't sense that unless I was specifically looking for it. Odd, though, that you would detect anything threatening."

All she could do was shrug. "It could also have just been my imagination."

Cray gave her a sympathetic smile. "You are under quite a lot of stress, but don't discount your gut. You indeed might have sensed something. Sometimes even non-mages can detect hints of magic at work. Watch over the pot here, and I'll go take a look."

Jessika took the spoon from his fingers, and the magician turned not towards the front door, but to one of the other bottom floor rooms.

"I'll be in my work room for a few minutes," he said as he shut the door behind him.

Jessika gave the porridge a quick stir and then went to the cutting board to peel and slice a few mumfruits. They were juicy and deep purple, and would sweeten the porridge better than honey. By the time she'd transferred the sticky stuff into the pot, Cray was back, dusting off his hands as though after a dirty job.

"Well, whatever was out there, it's not there now," he smiled. "That porridge smells delicious. I adore mumfruit, especially when it's sat on the tree through winter. It gets so sweet."

Together, they ladled out the food, and Breeka came tumbling down from the loft in a controlled fall just as they placed its bowl on the table. Eyes still squinted with sleep: it staggered in the direction of the table. Cray picked it up and placed it on the tabletop, pointed it at its bowl, and Breeka plunged its face in with no delay.

"Yummy," it declared after a few mouthfuls. "Stupid girl makes good food."

Cray chuckled.

"I didn't do much," Jessika protested softly, "but thank you, Breeka."

"Stupid girl," it gurgled, not looking up.

They sat down at the table and were halfway through the meal when Thornfire, Starbright, Thornspike, Rikah, and Karo arrived outside. Jessika picked up her bowl and hurried out the door to greet them. Thornfire was examining the house from a safe distance.

"This appears more like a usual version of human habitation, a sturdier one," the griffin mage remarked.

Starbright stepped forward to greet Jessika with a nibble to her hair and a one-armed hug, which Jessika returned two-armed—after holding out her bowl for Rikah to take.

"I hope Hawkjoy is safe," Starbright whispered.

"Me, too," Jessika replied, trying to keep strain out of her voice.

"This is good, what's in it?" Rikah interrupted.

"That's mine," Jessika teased, snatching the bowl back. "Mumfruit."

Rikah's brow creased. "I'm not sure I remember what that is."

"I do. It's good is what it is. It was one of my favorite things. The flavor reminds me of," she trailed off, somehow wanting to keep those memories of breakfast at a table with a white cloth, with sunlight streaming in, blue crockery and a bowl of mumfruit, with all her family there, to herself. Instead of talking, she took another mouthful.

"They're too sweet," Karo commented sourly. "I never liked them."

"Good, cause I didn't make you any porridge," Jessika sassed back. "So you don't have to eat any."

"We ate," Thornspike contributed. "So we don't need any."

"Thank you, Spike," Thornfire broke in. "What's the plan to retrieve Hawkjoy?"

Cray came to the doorway. "I was just thinking about that. Perhaps first we should ascertain her location? Most likely, I think—if she was subdued—is that she would be kept in that same room where Hawkwings and Hawkjoy encountered the Skire and Altare. That is where the Skire kept her griffins before," he concluded darkly.

"Where? I didn't see any cages or anything," Jessika asked.

"Did you see curtains on the walls?"

"Yes, I think I did."

"Behind those curtains are cells with barred fronts," he explained. "The curtains were ostensibly used to keep the captives calm, but I think more likely it was to keep them from knowing anything that was going on, and to prevent them from seeing each other. That might keep them in a state of despair and docility." He winced. "Of course, there were spells and drugs that did that too them, too."

"There would be shields and wards to protect those cells as well, would there not?" Thornfire asked.

"Somewhat," Cray nodded. "I don't think there were ever any physical barriers, or even barriers to entities, but a barrier to magical communication, yes. If those spells are still in place, attempts to see into the cells might be foiled."

Thornspike made a scoffing sound. "Let us just go and take Hawkjoy back, rip out the bellies of those who stole her, and go home."

"If only it were that easy," Cray sighed. He turned to Jessika. "The way you went in is probably trapped against us now. The alternative is a frontal assault on the castle. With two mages—"

"Three," interrupted Thornfire. "My former apprentice, Starbright, is an accomplished mage as well, and the young human male Karolan is my current apprentice."

"Three and a half then," Cray beamed. "Excellent, yes with three full mages and a skilled assistant, I think we can probably defeat all the traps, but that will take time, and I imagine there will be a watch set night and day for approaching griffins and for active magic, as long as Altare expects retaliation."

"Let us first ascertain—if we can—that Hawkjoy is there and living," Thornfire instructed, "and then we will plan the strike force."

Cray held up a finger. "I know the place, and it's even possible that some of the protective spells remaining there were set by me, unless Altare has been wise enough to replace them. I'd like to try scrying first. The best place for me to do that is in my workroom. Do you think any of you can fit in through the door?"

The griffins all eyed the structure.

Starbright hummed to herself. "I could do it, but I wouldn't like it."

Thornspike snorted. "Likewise."

Thornfire, being male and therefore smaller, gave it a longer look. "Yes, if I must," he grunted.

Cray led the way. Rikah and Jessika followed: Rikah helping Karo hop along on one foot. Breeka looked up, a bit of porridge dripping off its chin, as Thornfire wiggled his way through the door.

"I'm not as young and flexible as I once was," he lamented.

"Big bird," Breeka commented.

"Griffin," the mage said automatically. When he turned his raptorial gaze onto the grey bat-cat, Breeka quailed under the visage of the greater predator, even though the griffin's expression was not particularly fierce at the moment.

"Big griffin," Breeka corrected breathlessly, and a shadow of amusement crept into the griffin mage's face.

Thornfire moved past, worming his way into Cray's workroom.

"I think there's only room for mages in here," the human wizard called out apologetically.

Karo hopped in through the door and closed it after him. Rikah and Jessika retreated.

"I wanted to see," Rikah grumbled.

"Me, too."

Rikah squeezed her shoulders. "This could have happened to me and Thornspike just as easily, if we'd chosen opposite paths. It's not your fault."

"Maybe not, but fault doesn't really matter," she replied. "What matters is that Joy is in trouble."

"Right, yeah, I know," he nodded. "I hope they see something."

They turned to go back outside.

"Big man," Breeka commented. "Ugly."

"Don't mind Breeka," Jessika explained. "It's always like that. Breeka, do you want to come out with us and talk?"

"Breeka waits for Master," it answered, eyes fixed on Rikah.

"Alright."

As she tugged Rikah along, Breeka bent its head back down to the bowl in front of it, licking out the last bits of mumfruit porridge. It appeared it had already cleaned out the other two bowls.

"There's no space in there," Rikah said as they left the house.

Starbright and Thornspike were sitting together, wings slightly open in a patch of sun. Jessika went right away to Starbright and dug her fingers into the griffin's neck ruff. Starbright trilled happily and lifted her feathers so Jessika could get at her skin. Thornspike poked Rikah in the belly with the top curved part of her bill—not the pointy hook.

"You, scratch me," she instructed, "like that."

Rikah complied with a chuckle. The four stayed that way, warmed by the morning sun, until Cray emerged from the house several minutes later. His expression suggested failure.

"Altare has shown some wisdom," the old mage said, interrupting the scratching session. "He's replaced all the wards and shields on the cells with new ones of his own. It seems he is anticipating a meditated assault on the Skire's laboratory. We can't get through with a regular scrying spell."

Karo came hopping out next and Rikah went to help him. Thornfire followed, squirming his way out of the narrow doorway again.

"So what do we do next?" Jessika asked.

"The presence of the renewed wards alone indicate to me that Hawkjoy must be concealed behind them," Cray said. "I think we left no sign that we came to have a look, so Altare shouldn't know we were snooping, but we could use Hawkjoy's feather to try to get through them, except that Altare is more likely to sense it."

"Do you think he could be trying to get his hands on more of us, by drawing us in?" Thornfire asked.

"Absolutely," Cray nodded.

"Then we need to know where she is, if she's really there to rescue, or if his new wards are just a trick to make us think he's holding her there, before we risk such a thing."

Cray spread his hands. "We might also let him know we're coming by doing more intense magical investigations, if he senses them."

"Could we communicate with Hawkjoy?" Jessika broke in, "if we found her?"

"Not visually," Cray said. "There's a chance we could get her to perceive sound. It's not my strongest skill."

He looked at Thornfire, and Thornfire looked at Starbright.

"Bright, can you do it?" the griffin mage asked.

Starbright got to her feet, folding her wings. After a moment, she gave a brief nod. "I can try."

"You have a much better chance than I," he went on. "I've never had the delicate touch on that sort of air magic that you have."

"I'll try," she confirmed.

"We'll have to do it outside then," Cray said. "I can't fit you all in my workroom. Let me gather a few things. If you go that way, you'll find a pond. We can use that."

The griffins and Hawkchildren pushed through the underbrush and came upon the pond Cray had spoken of. It was ringed by bulrushes and reeds; edged with bright slime and clusters of frog eggs. In one spot, a dozen large stones led out from the shore into the center of the pond. Thornfire walked out onto them.

"Excellent, nice and still," he observed. "It will make a good mirror for scrying. Hawkwings, you have the feather?"

Jessika drew it out and stroked it gently between her fingers. It was white tipped with warm grey, like most of Hawkjoy's coverts. Over the past decade, she'd gotten to know Joy's feather colors as well as she knew her own skin and hair colors.

"There's no way we can—I don't know—pull her out here, the way Altare sent me away, if we find her?" Jessika blurted.

A hand fell on her shoulder and she jumped.

"I'm afraid not," Cray said from behind her. "Altare has put shields in the way which prevent it. It's also much easier to take something you have at hand, and send it far away, than it is to get a hold of something far away and pull it to where you are."

"You can't destroy the shields?" Jessika persisted.

Cray accepted the feather from her nervous hands.

"Shields can sometimes be destroyed, yes. You saw how the shadow-beasts broke through my shields the night the unicorns saved us. These shields of Altare's, however, are deeply anchored and cemented with blood and death magic. They're also far away, and distance matters in magic."

He moved out to join Thornfire on the stone jetty into the pond.

"When we assault the laboratory, the shields will have to be broken—if we intend to use magic—but it will be much easier to do that once we are there, and they are directly in front of us. From here, it's just too hard. Think of it like trying to throw a rock over a mountain and kill a bison on the other side. Theoretically, it could be done, but no one has enough strength and accuracy to do it."

Starbright brushed Jessika with a wing. "What do you want to say to Hawkjoy?" she asked. "When—if—contact is made, I will have just a few seconds to try to get a message through."

Jessika bit her lip and thought for a moment. Her throat started to choke up. "We're coming to get you. Don't give up. I love you."

Starbright nodded. "I will do my best."

"Everyone else, wait a few steps back from the pond," Thornfire instructed.

"We won't be able to see anything back here," Karo complained.

Rikah nudged Jessika and then pointed up, at a big tree limb that extended over the water. She took his meaning at once. Jessika heaved herself up the trunk of the associated tree and balanced herself out along the limb, where she lay flat on her belly and looked down at the surface of the pond. Her reflection looked back up at her.

Thornfire noticed and glared her way, turning his head all the way around and up with dizzying avian flexibility.

"She won't be in the way," Cray soothed.

Thornfire said nothing, neither to snipe with the human wizard nor to scold Jessika. She thought she might have detected a hint of compassion in his eyes and the lay of his feathers, but even after so many years among griffins, she wasn't always certain of the expressions she read off them.

"Let's begin," he said instead.

The two male mages muttered among themselves for a few moments, perhaps discussing particulars of the spell, while Starbright waited like a coiled spring for her part. Cray handed the feather to Thornfire, and then sprinkled a bit of something white over the water. He held his hand still over the surface, crouched down and concentrating.

Jessika didn't see any change, but then at some unspoken signal, Thornfire moved the feather to between Cray's outstretched palm and the surface of the pond. A few seconds later, the reflected sky and tree canopy vanished into darkness. It was like black dye had suddenly been dropped onto the water's surface.

Jessika strained her eyes, but for nearly a minute all she could see was solid black. Then slowly, so slowly that she thought her eyes were tricking her a dozen times over, she began to see a lighter shape in the darkness. Even more slowly, a few details appeared. Then she clapped a hand over her mouth to keep herself from calling out.

She saw Hawkjoy's sleeping body. Her sides were moving—she wasn't dead. Her breaths were lethargic, much slower than they should have been. All her flight feathers had been cut off, but Jessika couldn't see any injuries.

On some other unspoken signal, Starbright jerked into movement. Her hand flashed out to hover over Cray's, and the muscles in her arm twitched and bulged. Her talons flexed out slightly and retracted. In the vision, Hawkjoy's head rocked a little, as if in dreaming.

Then Jessika choked back a cry as a crimson flood blotted out the image in the darkness, as though blood had burst in on the window from all sides. The water began to froth and bubble.

Cray cried out something bright and fierce, clenching his hand into a fist, and all color was sucked to the center and banished. The pond returned to reflecting only tree canopy and sky.

Starbright whimpered and clutched her head.

"Bright?" Thornfire demanded. "You're hurt?"

"It was like, he grabbed me, and I had to rip myself away. I got out," she tried to explain, "but his grip was so hard—or abrasive, sharp—that I left some fur behind. I'll be alright."

"He detected Starbright's sending," Cray growled. "It could be that he had a ward that alerted him, and we didn't notice it."

"He didn't get enough of me for a taste," Starbright said, flicking her head. "He won't be able to track me. I think I managed to send the whole message, but I'm not sure how well Hawkjoy heard it. Her brain was sluggish."

"She's probably in a spelled sleep," Cray said. "The Skire knows that drugs can damage the unborn, so she probably had Altare put Hawkjoy under a fatigue cloud. It won't hurt her or her child."

Growls came from all three griffins. Jessika felt like growling, too.

"Well, we know she is in the Skire's laboratory, as expected," Cray said, trying to sound accomplished. "We know where to go."

Starbright retreated off the stone jetty so Cray and Thornfire could also do so. Jessika walked back down the tree limb to the trunk and hopped down to the ground. Thornfire looked around at all of them.

"Let us return to the area of the house and make a plan," he urged. "I want to execute it tomorrow."

"Elder," Rikah protested as they began walking, "Rain's foot is still injured. He won't be able to come with us."

"I want to come," Karo declared, before Thornfire could speak.

"We'll have to leave him behind then," the griffin mage said determinedly. "It's just as well, as there are only three of us griffins. We can't carry more than one human each."

"Just leave me here?" Karo protested.

"Without another griffin, we won't be able to take you anywhere else," Thornfire said.

"I can fly back here and pick him up," Thornspike offered. "Then he could come at least as far as our base camp for the assault."

"And leave an injured human in the forest, alone, without shelter?" the griffin mage scoffed. "He'll be much safer here, in a human structure where there will be warmth and food." Belatedly, Thornfire turned to Cray. "I made the assumption you would permit him to stay here," he said stiffly, "and that it would be safe for him."

"We could lay in some food, water, and wood for the fire," Cray mused, "but might it not be better just to fly him back to wherever your home is?"

"That will delay us some days," Thornfire pointed out.

"We don't know how long or difficult this assault will be," Cray countered. "We haven't even started discussing how many supplies we will need to gather. It could be that we won't be able to move against the castle for a few days."

"I want to leave for the castle tomorrow," Thornfire repeated.

"Elder," Thornspike pushed in, "I can take Hawkrain home, and then come back. I am the fastest flyer here."

Thornfire growled and looked down at the ground, in thought. "If any of us return, there will be questions. When I sent Waterleap home, he will have asked after Hawkjoy, so a few people know she is missing already. If Thornspike arrives with Hawkrain, injured, there will be more questions. Hawkrain will be bombarded with those questions and he can hardly refuse to answer the elders of his Line." The mage shook his head. "No, I must be the one to give the report when it is time. We must not go back yet, any of us. Hawkrain can remain here. Let us plan the assault."

The eight—including Breeka—companions sat together in a meadow not far from the house. Cheerful sunlight streamed down in counterpoint to the serious topic. It glazed the meadow clover in a laquer of bright green and Jessika took a moment to appreciate them; they were so perky she felt bad walking out into the meadow and sitting on them. A lanky variety sent up long stalks with flowers so crimson they almost fluoresced, while pillows of denser clover were studded with pink, and the lowest growing carpet of clover opened humble white petals. Bees and butterflies with pale blue wings visited them all in turn.

Others of the party smiled down on the flowers, too, especially Cray. Meanwhile Karo sulked and seemed impervious to the beauty around him. Breeka mainly clung to Cray, but the others did their best to help build a plan.

"Then we are agreed that the only viable path of attack is to enter the same way Hawkwings and Hawkjoy did," Cray summed up after an hour of discussion.

"It seems we have no choice," Rikah agreed. "All the other ways look to have far more arguments against them."

"But it still won't be easy," Cray said. "Especially having detected our scrying, and knowing now that Hawkwings is with me and approaching, Altare must be anticipating an attack. What we can hope is that he thinks the scrying was done by only me, and he doesn't know about the rest of you."

"I am hopeful that's true," Starbright winced. "I am ashamed I was not subtle enough to escape his notice. I hope he is not sensitive enough to detect that it was not you."

"He does not know me to be skilled with the kind of distance communication you can do," Cray told her, "but we have been apart for several years now, and there are many different skills I have acquired since then."

"Likely that is true for your former apprentice as well," Thornfire warned.

Cray nodded, grey-faced. "Sadly, but inevitably. I also have new allies." He gestured around at the group. "I hope that is not also the case for him."

Several people drew in sharp breaths. No one else had thought of that.

"Altare is fond of power: mainly power over the people around him. I don't think he would tolerate another master, but it's possible he might have companions or servants with magical skill, just none more powerful than him."

"There is no way that we can get in and retrieve Hawkjoy in total silence and invisibility?" Starbright wondered. "Could we avoid confronting him at all?"

"We will try to delay detection for as long as possible, of course," Thornfire answered. "But I think it inevitable that he will eventually notice us, if there are so many shields and wards. Would you agree?"

"There are so many types of detection spells he could be using, it will be nearly impossible to guard against them all," Cray confirmed. "At least we'll have the benefit that holding all those spells will be draining him considerably."

"In situations like this," Rikah commented, "I think it's better to assume that we'll have to face him, rather than hope maybe we won't and neglect considering how to fight him."

Cray gave Rikah an approving glance. "I can tell you his strengths are likely to be in dark and blood magic. He likes bewitchment, deception, and the enslaving of others' wills."

"The strongest counters then, will be light magic." Thornfire looked at Starbright, who raised her crest bravely. "You have skills to keep our vision clear and minds our own."

"I do, Master," she answered. "You may depend upon me."

Thornfire looked back at Cray. "Attacking, how will he be weakest?"

"Physical attack, if we can get to him," the wizard replied, "but he must be occupied and distracted at the time. If you and I can bring the magical assault, another could get into position to strike at an opportune moment."

"He won't have other fighters with him?" Jessika wondered. "What about the shadow-beasts?"

"They will be a problem, but if Starbright is wielding light magic, it will deter them," Cray suggested. "Any human guards with him will probably be at least lightly enslaved. Light magic will weaken their enslavement, but they may still choose to fight for him anyway."

Jessika imagined a dozen shadow-beasts and a dozen human guards protecting Altare, while the three mages tried to occupy his attention.

"I'm sure between Thornfire, Starbright, and Cray," she spoke up, "they can keep his magical attention on them and off of Dare, Thornspike, and me, but if there are ranks of other guards to get through, how can we hope to get close enough to hit him?"

"None of those guards will want to be near him while the magic is flying," Cray said, "and Starbright may have enough ability to break the bonds between Altare and his conjured creations, which would banish them entirely. If he has human guards, they will be a problem, but I am hopeful that the presence of griffins will make them cautious."

A sudden thought struck her. "What if he has rainbow drakes, or any kind of drakes?" she blurted.

"He doesn't know griffins are coming," Cray said.

"Doesn't he?" she countered. "A griffin was with me. What's to stop him from thinking there might be more where she came from?"

Cray's expression turned worried. "You may have a point." He looked around the circle. "We don't know what we'll face."

"If we make it to the tunnel entrance," Rikah said, "we'll face traps and maybe enemies in the tunnels themselves, but how many creatures can he really put down there continually? If we get through the tunnels to the laboratory, we'll be fighting in that room, where again space is limited. He can't bring an army against us."

"But if he has the power and attention, he could summon or conjure enemy after enemy to face us, even as we defeat them, calling more and more," Cray warned.

"That's why you have to keep him busy," Thornspike stated.

"How about this," Jessika said. "What can we bring with us to give us extra help? Thornfire has made light stones and contact stones. Are there other things we can make to give us an edge?"

Thornfire, Starbright, and Cray all tilted their heads in thought.

"Yes, there are a few things," Thornfire said.

"I have a couple ideas," Starbright added.

"Good thinking, Hawkwings," Cray praised. "We can each spend some time this evening making little surprises for the fight."

"We'll also need food, in case it takes us time to get through all the traps in the tunnels," Rikah said. "And water."

"I'll hunt some meat tonight," Thornspike volunteered. "Someone else can dry it on the fire for travel."

"I'll do it," Karo grumbled. "About the only thing I can contribute."

"I'll have you making some tricks and surprises," Thornfire told him. "Not to worry. You'll be busy tonight."

"Altare will know when we spring or disarm his traps?" Starbright wondered.

"If he's checking them remotely," Cray confirmed.

"Then he'll know we're coming," Jessika said.

"We can set illusions behind us, showing them still set," Thornfire suggested. "As long as he's not looking closely, they'll pass."

"I was thinking, what if we get attacked before we even reach the castle?" Rikah spoke up. "What if he sees us coming and sends drakes at us?"

"We'll have to run," Thornfire said. "Then we'll try a different approach another day."

Jessika groaned. "That would be awful. We need to get Joy out of there now, before anything happens to her."

Rikah put a hand on her arm in an attempt to comfort.

"We will do our best," Cray murmured.

Jessika fisted her hands hard until they shook. Her nails would have cut into her palms, if she hadn't bitten them all off in fits of anxiety over the past week.

"We have to go get her," she repeated.

"That's why we'll leave tomorrow morning," Thornfire stated. "We will arrive at dawn, here in this clearing, and fly straight to the castle. We'll use cloaking spells once we get closer, to hide us from sight and magical detection."

"To save time in the morning, Hawkrain could stay with us tonight, in my house. Altare won't detect him unless he's outside the shields after dusk," Cray offered. "It would also give me time to show him the working of the stove, and even how to put the shields down and up."

Karo's face was pale, and Jessika wondered if he feared being all alone in a house in a strange forest for however many days it took for everyone else to rescue Joy, get back to South-scree, and send someone to pick him up.

"I can make the jerky tonight, instead of you," Rikah offered. "I won't have anything else to do since I'm not a mage."

"I can tell you what tricks to make for the fight, and Cray can bring them with him tomorrow morning," Thornfire added.

"I can lay in all the food and water and firewood you'll need," Jessika volunteered.

"I guess it's all worked out and I don't get a choice," Karo groused. "I don't get a choice about anything."

"I can't mend broken bones," Thornfire said gently. "Only your body can do that, and only with time. You're not ready to come with us this time."

"No mage I've ever known has been able to fuse broken bones back together," Cray nodded in agreement. "It's unfortunate, lad, but the best thing you can do for all of us is stay where it's safe and heal."

"I could stay on Thornspike's back the whole time," Karo argued.

"And how would she fight?" Rikah countered.

"Your Linebrother is right," Thornspike said. "I would not be able to fight effectively while trying to keep you safe."

"Fine," Karo spat.

"You can contribute by working yourself into exhaustion tonight, making all the little goodies and surprises your master asks of you," Cray encouraged. "The rest of us won't have the luxury of spending all our energy making items tonight, or we won't be recovered for tomorrow, but you can."

He folded his arms. "I guess so."

"Can anyone else think of anything that should be mentioned?" Cray went on. "We have a lot to get ready, so we shouldn't dawdle here if we don't have to."

Everyone looked around the circle at each other, but no one spoke up.

"I suppose not," Thornfire said, standing. "Let us be on our way then."

Everyone stood, Karo leaning on Rikah.

"Spike, hunt us some food and join us at camp when you're done," Thornfire ordered. "Starbright, Hawkdare, you can go ahead. I'll follow once I've instructed Hawkrain."

"Here, Rain, lean on me," Jessika invited, and Rikah helped transfer him to her.

"There will be shadow-beasts about until the dawn breaks," Cray reminded them all, "so don't come until the sun has actually crested the horizon here."

"Noted," Thornfire confirmed.

Rikah climbed aboard Starbright. "See you tomorrow," he said to those remaining behind.

"See you sometime," Karo corrected, still bitterly.

"It won't be long," Rikah promised.

"Take care, Hawkrain," Starbright called.

The big golden griffin walked to an emptier bit of meadow, spread her wings, and powered her way into the sky with Rikah holding gamely to her harness.

"I'll be off, too," Thornspike said, walking to the spot Starbright had just used. "Winds to your favor, Hawkrain."

The black and white female took off, arrowing away in a different direction than Starbright had, to go hunt. Everyone left walked back to the house, and Jessika fetched a basket and went to pull edible roots to be stored in the house's little root cellar for Karo. She saw Cray and Thornfire sit down with Karo to discuss what magical items they would make and bring.

"None of my affair," she mumbled to herself as she reached into the fragrant, black dirt after the roots. "Much simpler to pull roots and whack the bad guys with a stick."

She also knocked down all the remaining mumfruits she could reach, and added them to her pile. They would keep for the week or so she anticipated it taking for help to come fetch Karo back to South-scree.

"We'll get Joy tomorrow, or the next day, or however long it takes, but soon," she muttered. "Joy can't fly since they cut her feathers, so some of us will walk back with her, but we can send Thornspike on to get us help. It won't take her long to reach South-scree—she's such a fast flyer. Once we have help, she can go pick up Karo; she knows where this house is. It shouldn't be more than a week, probably less."

Jessika delivered her load to the house and checked the supply of firewood. She added to the pile in the wood box at the back of the room. When it was full, she piled more wood outside by the front door. After that, she picked up a pair of buckets on a stick she could balance across her shoulders. The kitchen had a big watertight barrel, which had been empty when they arrived. She'd fill it to the brim to make sure Karo would have enough water for a week—for cooking, drinking, and bathing.

"He should have a cane," she remarked to a passing squirrel. "It'll help him move about when he has to."

After a dozen trips to fill the barrel, she sought out a suitable sturdy stick as the afternoon turned towards evening. On her last trip back to the house, Thornfire was gone and both Cray and Karo were inside. She brought in her stick, triumphantly, and found the two men sitting at the kitchen table, still deep in a discussion of magic.

She almost dropped the stick, however, when she saw a smile on Karo's face. He was describing something requiring a lot of gesturing, and Cray was nodding along, apparently delighted by whatever the younger man was saying. Deciding not to interrupt them, she fetched a knife and began trimming the branch, leaving three blunted offshoots that might work as handles. Only when darkness really started to fall, did she remind Cray to set the wards.

He jumped to his feet. "Oh dear, I totally forgot the time. Not to worry: it's not too late yet. Come, Hawkrain, let me show you how I do this."

Cray helped Hawkrain to his feet and they limped away. Jessika moved to start making some dinner, and noticed Breeka with its chin resting on the edge of its basket, its bat-like ears drooping as it followed Cray's actions with its eyes.

"Are you well, Breeka?" Jessika asked.

"Master has a new friend," the bat-cat whispered.

"My brother Hawkrain is distracting him with talk of magic, but only for today," Jessika said. "Tomorrow we will leave and Hawkrain will stay here by himself."

"Ugly boy," Breeka commented.

"Cray is taking pity on him by showing him how to survive here on his own. Your master is kind and wise."

"Master is good," Breeka said. "Stupid girl knows Master is good."

"That's right, Breeka."

Jessika began cutting up two fat roots the way she'd seen Cray do it last night, then paused, wondering if Karo had any idea how to prepare the roots she'd gathered for him. Rikah was the main cook for the South-scree humans, and had made quite an art of it. Jessika and Karo had always taken more the role of art appreciators.

Cray and Karo came back in, still talking.

"Sorry to interrupt," Jessika called, "but do you know how to cook root vegetables, Rain? That's mostly what you'll have to eat here, plus some grains for porridge, mumfruits, and a little goat jerky."

Cray took over the cooking process, eagerly teaching Karo about cutting and boiling and seasoning. Jessika went instead to make up a bed in the spare room at the back of the cottage, since Karo wouldn't be able to climb the ladder to the loft. She could hear Cray and Karo continuing their chat. She thought maybe she'd never heard Karo talk this much in all his life. Even through dinner, between bites, they kept talking. She wondered if they'd stop even in sleep.

For herself, she spent her thoughts on Hawkjoy. The griffin had been alive this morning. She had to hope she was still alive, and would be healthy and hale when they rescued her tomorrow or in the next few days—depending on how long it took them to reach her. Jessika wasn't sure how far from the capital they were.

After the meal, she put together her pack for the next day. She wasn't carrying much: a water skin, a little food, her truncheons, a spare rag with some grease on it for quieting hinges, and Koki's lock picks. She rubbed the picks briefly between her fingers, thinking of the young faun-man and hoping he was well. Before bed, Jessika managed to get a few words in to offer Karo the crutch she'd made for him, and he thanked her warmly.

"Remember you were going to make some more magic items," she reminded him and Cray, before seeking her bed. All the root pulling, fruit gathering, water hauling, and wood stacking had tired her out.

"I'm going to stay up," Karo told her.

He showed her a small sack of stones and bits of hard wood, all of which could fit comfortably in a human's palm. Cray carried over a little basket with spools of rough twine and more stones, wood, and pieces of something hard and shiny, all with holes drilled through the middle. He set out a little knife beside the sack and basket.

"There are a few different items Thornfire and I had thought to make," Cray explained. "Hawkrain here has the skill to make all but one of them. I'll make a dozen or so of that kind tonight before bed, and Hawkrain will make the rest."

"I might still be sleeping in the morning, when you go—and thank you for making up that bed for me," he said. "Don't bother waking me up. I'd just get in the way of your departure."

"You're sure you'll be safe here, by yourself?" she asked.

Karo gave her a smile. "I'll be alright. Cray says there's a village a few hours walk from here. If things get really bad, I can hobble my way there and ask for help, especially now that you've made me a crutch."

"Stay off that foot," Cray warned. "You'll lame yourself permanently by using it before the bone is mended."

"I will," he promised.

"Well then, I'm going to bed," Jessika told them.

"Bring back Hawkjoy," Karo blurted, reaching out and catching her hand before she could go. "Bring her back safe."

"We will, and she'll be all tucked up in South-scree, waiting for her chick to be born, when Thornspike comes to get you and bring you back there, too, in just a week or less."

"Alright, that's settled then," Karo nodded. "Goodnight."

"Goodnight, Karo, Cray."

"I'll wake you just before dawn," Cray assured her. "Goodnight, Hawkwings."

Jessika went up to the loft, peeled off her now even filthier outer layer of clothes, and got into bed. Below her, the soft sounds of rock against wood and the tying of bits of twine, interspersed with murmured conversation and the whispering of magic words followed her down into sleep.

Her last thought before dreams took over, was that she hoped she could keep her promise to Karo, that Hawkjoy really would be back in South-scree before the week was out.

Cray shook Hawkwings awake when it was still dark. Jessika took her bundle of clothes and followed Cray down the ladder in the silent darkness. Only then did he light a candle. Breeka hopped down from its basket bed onto Cray's shoulder.

"Quickly, some breakfast," Cray whispered.

Jessika went about getting the pot, water, and some grains. She cut up one mumfruit for it while Cray got out three bowls. Once the porridge was cooking she got her clothing on in between stirring sessions. The scenery outside the window was just starting to lighten as they set their bowls on the table and had a somber meal.

"Here, look at this," Cray instructed, voice still low to avoid disturbing Karo. "Most of the magical items we made can only be used by mages, but these three types anyone can use, so I want you to take some."

He showed her three little objects. They didn't look like much. The bits of wood, stone, and shiny material with holes drilled through them had been linked with a simple loop of twine.

"What is this stuff?" Jessika murmured, pointing to the shiny white material.

"Seashell," Cray answered.

She squinted at him. "What's that?"

"I'll tell you more about it later, when we're not in such a rush. How you make these work—break the loop of twine and throw the rest of it. The rock will explode. The wood will burst into a brief, hot fire. The shell will make a bright flash of light. After you break the twine, you have only a couple seconds, so be ready to throw it quickly."

"I understand," she said.

"Here, fill your pockets."

Jessika took several of each item until her pockets bulged. After they finished their food, they washed their dishes and took up the packs they'd prepared the previous evening. Jessika tried not to nibble her lip bloody as she sat, waiting for Cray's announcement that it was safe to exit the house.

Finally, he raised a hand and picked up his staff. Jessika almost tripped over her chair standing up, and let him go first, with Breeka perched on his shoulder. They stepped out into the wet grass and breathed in the damp dawn air. After exiting, Cray turned and murmured a few words.

"I put the wards back up, just in case," he whispered. "Hawkrain knows how to take them down, if he needs to."

The mage pointed off towards the clearing where they'd had their conference yesterday, and led the way among the dark tree trunks. Up, beyond the distant mountains, Jessika could see the sky turning pink, but down in the forest it was still gloomy enough that she feared the shadow-beasts might still be out. She could only have faith in Cray, who could surely sense when they were active and not.

The trio came out into the meadow, and Jessika immediately felt her skin prickle with the same sensation she'd felt before, of being watched. She reached for Cray's sleeve just as he stiffened, too.

"I feel it," he breathed.

The chill in his voice further alarmed her. He backed up a step, almost bumping into her.

"Cray," she whispered.

Breeka hissed. The bat-cat's wide-open eyes gleamed green in the low light as it stared around. The feeling of being watched increased tenfold, and in the distance under the trees, Jessika caught flurries of movement from the corners of her eyes.

"Cray," she said again, this time closer to a whimper.

He put his arms out, as if to shield her.

"Back to the house," he ordered, voice tight.

Jessika turned at once, but the path back looked even darker than before, and cold dread made her hesitate when her instinct a moment ago had been to run. The path seemed to fall away in front of her, like solid land suddenly crumbling down into a plunging pit. Cray collided with her back as she planted her feet. His free hand came down on her shoulder.

"Stay close to me," he commanded. "Something's wrong."

This time she definitely saw movement under the trees. Four-legged beasts of swirling mist were pacing there.

"Shadow-beasts," Jessika babbled. "They shouldn't be out, should they?"

"They've been strengthened to survive sunrise," Cray replied, voice rising with tension. "I sense more than the usual three. This is an attack, a major attack. He's come for us."

Jessika looked all around, heart thudding.

"There's a lot of them," she observed.

"Yes, we're in trouble."

"The others will be here soon. We just have to hold out," she said.

As one, a hum of growling arose from all sides. It vibrated in Jessika's bones until her skin crawled.

"They might stay under the shadow of the trees," Cray murmured.

No sooner had he said it than the first beast took steps out into the open. Under the light it looked as wispy as smoke, but as if that smoke somehow had a skin disease. If they'd been solid beasts of flesh, Jessika imagined they would have had torn, scabby skin and matted fur. They moved strongly enough, though, with perfect balance and poise. Their eyes gleamed like wet pebbles.

A handful of the beasts emerged, circling the old man, young woman, and bat-cat. There was no way Jessika could keep Cray between her and them; they were on all sides. She turned back to back with him and drew out her truncheons. She took a steady stance and watched the beasts on her side of the circle.

After only a few more steps, the beasts stopped, as one, and crouched as if to pounce. They were all of different sizes and slightly different builds. A few that looked cat-like lashed their frothy tails in anticipation. The beasts crept closer with tiny steps. A couple opened their mouths and let slug-like tongues loll freely between white teeth that looked all too solid.

Something barked a roar of command and the crouched beasts jerked into motion. Three or four made abortive leaps and dodged to one side or another, but three others charged their prey, smashing right into Cray and Jessika. Jessika tried to swing her truncheon at one but it was already inside her range.

Burning saliva splattered her face and neck, but the creature didn't try to bite her. Instead, its weight drove her back, shoving her away from Cray and knocking her flat. She lost her grip on one truncheon and it went flying away. The ground was damp earth, not stone, but she still landed hard. The shadow-beast tumbled right over and past her.

A second beast was hard on its heels, though, and Jessika whuffed out all the air in her lungs as it pounced on her back, foiled by her pack. Its growls made her head ring. She was jerked from side to side as the beast bit down on her pack and tried to thrash its head. It soon had the pack half off her, breaking the straps. Snarling in reply, Jessika flailed behind herself with her truncheon, delivering a glancing blow that made the beast release her and hop back, not truly hurt but now cautious. Her pack had been savaged, dropping its contents all over the ground, and Jessika shed it.

When she looked around, she saw Cray had been tossed a good few yards in the opposite direction from her. He was sprawled on the ground in a tangle of patched robes, beard, and staff. Breeka had been thrown even farther, and was trying to sit up, only half-visible in the tall weeds.

"Cray," Jessika called.

The old mage was lunging back up to his feet, leaning on his staff. "Stay down," he ordered.

Jessika felt all her hair try to stand on end and her skin prickled as it sometimes did in winter, when she'd been sliding about on blankets for too long, and then someone else would come walking by and she'd reach a hand out, and a spark would jump between her hand and whoever. This time, the feeling was far stronger, and gave her an ominous sense of dread.

"No," Cray cried, throwing out a hand at her.

Lightning: an actual lightning bolt twisted through the air and struck the ground near Jessika. She flinched back, rolling to the side, dazed by the flash and crack of thunder but unhurt. Through the glare she saw Cray slash his staff around in a circle on the ground, throwing up clods of dirt and plants. The old wizard had actually dug a circle into the ground with that one sweep of his staff; she could only suspect he'd used magic to assist his elderly muscles. Jessika rolled back to her belly and pushed up onto her elbows, preparing to join him.

"Stay down," Cray ordered again, and Jessika remained where she was.

"So," another voice said, a smug, slick voice that she just barely recognized. "My old master thinks he still has a few tricks left in him. This should be pleasant and profitable."

Jessika turned her head to see the same man who had appeared in Skire Germaine's laboratory: Altare. He was wearing dark green this time, but in a similar style to the first time she'd seen him, with the addition of a half cape against the chill morning. His expression was equal parts amused and annoyed. He spread his hands, dangling his short wooden rod from one of them.

Beside him, a particularly thin and agile-looking shadow-beast was purring and pressing itself against his leg like a monstrous house cat. Jessika noted that the grass and flowers around its feet had all died and turned to black sludge, as though the beast were emitting toxins from its skin. A faint haze seemed to rise from its body, as well, like heat waves.

"What's one griffin more or less to you, old man?" he cajoled. "You poor fool, I would have allowed you to remain in your hermit hole for the rest of your natural life if you hadn't gone and done something like this."

"Return that griffin, boy," Cray commanded. "She's not for you or that sick Skire. You've had enough."

"I caught her," he sneered back. "She's mine now. The weak are to be eaten by the strong when the strong choose."

"Others who are strong will challenge you, and one day you will be the weaker, if you continue that attitude," Cray argued. "Will you accept your fate then? Give her back now and perhaps you'll not be eaten for a while longer."

"I will be strong forever," Altare denied. "I suffer you to live, not the other way around. Allow me to prove it." He jabbed a finger out at Cray, who tensed, but no magic flew at him. "You know if you step outside that circle that I'll have you, so watch your pet abomination be torn up while you cower in it like the coward you are."

The young mage made three sharp gestures and a shadow-beast responded from where it had been dully observing on the far side of the circle. It turned its attention to where Breeka was huddled into a ball, trying to avoid notice. The beast's jaws opened, dribbling milky drool.

"No," Jessika grunted.

She still had one truncheon. She pushed herself up to her feet and ran to intercept the trotting shadow-beast. It didn't seem to have expected resistance, and when she lifted her club in both hands and slammed it down on its head with all her strength, it wore an expression of surprise. The thick crack of impact pealed through the clearing, and Jessika grinned with satisfaction.

"What is this?" Altare exclaimed.

The beast staggered, head wobbling, and Jessika reached to snatch up Breeka in her arms. She tried to turn, overbalanced, and almost fell. She could only think of getting back to the house. If she pounded on the door, Karo would wake up. He could take the wards down and let her in. She heard Cray call her name, but she ignored him. The beast she'd struck was still shaking its head as she passed it, trying to run.

"Stop her, my lovely," Altare commanded silkily.

Then something hooked her feet out from under her.

Jessika fell flat forward onto her face, Breeka objecting to the impact vociferously. A panicked glance over her shoulder showed her another shadow-beast closing in—the skinny one that had appeared with Altare. She thought it must have swept out her feet as she ran. One handed, with Breeka clutched close in her other arm, she got herself up to sitting on her knees, ready to lunge to her feet.

The shadow-beast took two paces and leapt.

Its forepaws hit her shoulders, driving her back down and giving her a face full of dirt and weeds. Breeka yowled. Then a full paw of five claws slashed ribbons of fire down her back from right shoulder to left hip, ripping through her clothing and into her skin.

At first, all Jessika could do was gasp in shock, but when the beast repeated the strike with its other talons, making a burning X across her back, slicing deeper than the first swipe because there was now less clothing to help deflect it, a scream of shock and pain blossomed unbidden from her chest.

Another slash followed, and another, each one cutting deeper, until Jessika felt the beast's claws snag on her ribs. She tried to move, to get up, but her arms wouldn't respond right. Her ears were full of the sounds of crashing fire and lightning, which drowned out whatever sounds the beast might have been uttering.

And then: "enough," a voice cried.

The mauling ceased, leaving Jessika writhing and sobbing with a raw throat.

"Hawkwings?" she heard Cray pant.

"Silence, old man," Altare's voice ordered, "or I shall beat you some more." It was his voice that had ordered enough.

The young mage's booted feet appeared before Jessika's face through the grasses. His pet shadow-beast joined him and Jessika saw her blood sizzling on its claws as around them the greenery withered.

"I hesitate to waste a lovely lady like this," he said.

Her back was a field of fire, indistinct yet deeply troubling as her body sent confused messages of peril and alarm.

"Hawkwings?" Altare mused from far above her head.

She heard the sound of fabric being drawn out of other fabric, maybe a handkerchief out of a pocket. From her angle she could see his ankles bend, as though he were about to kneel. Something touched her back, but she couldn't tell anything more than an extra sprinkle of pain, and she sucked in a breath, tasting the salt of her tears. Under her, Breeka was squirming but Jessika couldn't give it any relief.

Altare drew in a breath. "Wings indeed," he exclaimed. "Unfortunately they're rather ruined now, but the evidence remains. Correct age and complexion, and the tattoos: you are Jessika, the missing princess of Northnest. My very goodness."

Jessika could feel blood running down her bare sides, soaking into the clothing still trapped between Breeka and her body. It hurt to breathe.

"I shall have to bring you home with me," Altare purred. "Let me help you up."

"Don't touch her," Cray commanded. "Hawkwings, don't let him touch you."

Altare made a scathing sound. "And leave a lady in distress? I never intended for my little pet to scratch you up, but you did go and get in my way, and gave my other servant quite a smack on the head. You do have spirit. I can admire that."

Jessika sensed him reaching for her shoulders, but Breeka thrashed until it had worked its forequarters free. As Altare's fingers came into view, the bat-cat bit at them and drew blood, so that Altare jerked back.

"Misbegotten vermin," he hissed. "I regret the day I seeded you on your whore mother. Not even the Skire could get much use out of you, before my misdirected master snuck out with you. I'll see you dead yet."

Jessika tightened her arms around Breeka: those muscles seemed to still be working.

"No, Breeka," she whimpered, "stay with me."

"Here," Altare grumbled.

Jessika tried to twist her head up to see him. He was unlacing the half cloak he wore tied at his throat.

"At least let me cover my lady with this."

He lowered the cape down, and it settled over Jessika's lacerated torso. As it landed, so, too, did a light and gentle passivity drift onto her mind. The wounds seemed less painful, the fight less serious, Altare's new knowledge of her identity less worrisome.

"Isn't that better?" he said.

Jessika couldn't reply, even had she wanted to. Words wouldn't form up.

"Ah, yes," he purred. "Oh, that's much better."

Jessika shivered, suddenly feeling far weaker than bleeding could account for. It was although something else was draining from her as well.

"You have beautiful energy, so pure and valiant, but I'll take no more than a taste, for now. Wounded as you are, you can make better use of it than I. Rest easy, my lady," the mage went on. "I'll shortly bring you safe away to the capital. I'll heal your wounds and rest you in a soft bed befitting your rank. Your father still rules Northborn. Surely you must wish to reunite with him. Perhaps that is even why you were sneaking through the cellar, trying to find him? Not to worry, you will see him soon."

Altare's words were pleasant, soothing, and a large portion of Jessika's mind rejoiced at them. Yes, that was all exactly as she wished. Only some other minor shard tried to jerk and tug at that complacent part like a child with a stubborn mule, but was unable to get it to change its mind.

"Hawkwings," a voice called, demanding her attention. Somehow it cut through the lassitude of her thoughts like a slap of icy water in the face. "Hawkwings," he repeated: Cray.

It was hard to lift her head, so hard, but she turned to look over at the old magician. He was on the ground, too, and struggling beneath the pinning paws of four hulking shadow-beasts. Altare made a tsking sound.

"Look away, my lady," the younger man commanded. "This will be no sight for innocent eyes."

Chapter 16
The Phoenix and the Sun

"Hawkwings," Cray repeated, ignoring Altare's approach.

Again, his voice pierced right through the weighty veil of complacency, and she blinked at him with full awareness. Altare was advancing to deal the killing blow. Whether it would be by his own hand or the claws of his servants, she couldn't tell, but Cray seemed completely helpless. The area around him was charred and his hasty circle obliterated. While she had endured the mauling of her foe, Altare and his pets had delivered swift magical defeat to Cray.

"Perhaps I should thank you for returning the last Northnest royal to me," Altare mused, as though he had all the time in the world. "I certainly wouldn't have sent her away had I known who she was. Luckily you helped to remedy the error: a final parting gift for your faithful student."

"No," Jessika managed to croak out, but Altare ignored her, if he had even heard her.

Surely there must be something she could do? Between the wounds and the drugging effect of Altare's cloak, she couldn't move. She could hardly manage to speak. What could she say that would help? Under her, Breeka wiggled furiously in her arms.

"Stupid girl, let me go," the bat-cat hissed.

Letting go was something could do. With a sigh, she relaxed her arms. Breeka went shooting out of them faster than she'd ever seen the creature move. High above in the sky, a tiny flicker of movement caught the very edge of Jessika's vision, but she couldn't twist her neck any farther to give herself a better look.

Breeka streaked straight for Altare. Above, the flicker became a flash of black and white rapidly approaching. The bat-cat, without a yowl of warning or anger, latched itself onto Altare's lower leg and sank its little fangs into his calf—up to the gums. The magician exclaimed and kicked out, but Breeka clung with all four limbs.

Then the flash of black and white struck like a giant from the heavens. Thornspike, as silent as Breeka, stooped on the shadow-beasts pinning Cray, making a spine-wrenching pull out of a steep dive to target them. With fisted hands she struck two of the beasts with murderous precision, audibly cracking their skulls. They broke like wheat under hail. In the next less-than-an-instant, she bound to the two remaining beasts with her hind claws, already angling her wings to take her back into the sky.

The weight of course was too much for her to accomplish such a feat as swooping back up with both of the monsters in her grip. Instead, she yanked them off Cray, flight wobbling and slowing—but still dangerously fast—and dragged them across the clearing with their bodies digging furrows through the grass. The strain on her body must have been immense. She pulled her wings in, crashing into the underbrush and bearing her prey with her, with the clamor of a rock slide impacting a log jam.

Then lightning struck at Altare, who was still dancing about, trying to dislodge Breeka. That was enough for the bat-cat, who promptly released him and dashed for a different bit of undergrowth than that which Thornspike and her prey had demolished. Jessika expected the lightning to have come from Cray, but the old man wasn't on his feet yet.

A raptorial shriek of anger pulled all eyes up. Altare was unhurt, having apparently deflected the lightning, but he retreated a few steps at what faced him from the sky. Jessika managed to twist her head just enough to see. Thornfire was in the air with Starbright. Griffins couldn't hover long unless they had a strong updraft to ride, and the morning was still too cold and calm for that, but the pair was in tight formation circling the clearing.

Starbright was slightly lower and glowing like a small sun. Thornfire, above and ahead of her—Jessika thought maybe pain, the drugged cloak, and a trick of the sun and Starbright's radiance were deceiving her eyes. Thornfire appeared to actually be on fire. Flames, orange and red and flourishing, wreathed his wings and body. A fiery tail streamed behind him and opened into a scarlet fan. Still moving at good speed, the pair wheeled, spiraling downward.

Altare recoiled, rallied, snarled, and made a throwing gesture. Jessika couldn't see what issued from his hand, but then the trees shook as if in a gale, and the two griffin mages were blown away—for a moment. Agilely and in perfect synchrony the pair adjusted their wings and tails, skating right over the wind and resuming their controlled plummet.

Altare shouted, gestured again, and lightning like she'd seen already several times speared upwards, but the griffins didn't flinch. Starbright cried out and emitted a flash of light, which absorbed the lightning entirely. Within range of the ground now, Starbright dropped, landing equidistant from Jessika and Cray. She stretched out her wings, and larger, shimmering versions of them made of light mimicked the movement. Those golden wings spread out over Cray and Jessika.

Jessika felt the compulsion of passivity begin to lessen. Her thoughts started to become her own again, and though she could now move again under her own control, her arms still wouldn't obey her in moving certain directions. The pain of her lacerated back came rushing upon her and she had to hold back her need to cry out so as not to attract attention.

Thornfire wasn't finished. His wings of flame filled the sky now as he dove for Altare. The man was scrambling backwards, mouth working with words Jessika couldn't hear, hands gesturing and pointing with his rod. One of the still-mobile shadow-beasts came leaping obediently at Thornfire, but a slash of one hand made a corresponding hand of flame reach out and incinerate the beast. Hardly bothered, Thornfire landed and faced the human mage.

Now Altare jabbed out his wand and a blue flash burned Jessika's eyes. She didn't see Thornfire's counter, but he was still standing when she looked back. Altare jabbed again, and she had the sense to close her eyes before being blinded again.

Something impacted the ground near her legs, but she couldn't move to get to a safer place. Through her closed eyelids, she saw another flash, and another. A griffin cried in alarm, and she thought it was Starbright. She opened her eyes to look and indeed, another shadow-beast—Altare's special pet—had pounced on the younger mage's back.

It had broken Starbright's focus; the protective glow was patchy and fading. Already, Jessika felt the serenity of Altare's cloak creeping back over her. Another blue flash struck the ground nearby. Starbright would surely be able to defeat the shadow-beast, but while she fought, Cray and Jessika lay unprotected. From his prone position, Cray had wrestled his staff back into his hands. He took careful aim at the shadow-beast and muttered a word.

Some kind of bolt that was just barely visible as a glimmer in the air shot from his staff and impacted the shadow-beast, making it yowl. Starbright pinned it. Jessika's eyes widened as Starbright's hands began to shine. The beast writhed, but with a bursting of light like sun through clouds, the griffin's

magic shattered it with brilliance.

"Well done," Cray croaked.

Starbright turned to him, showing spots on her back where her fur and feathers had been burned black. "Thank—," she began.

Then the next flash of blue light struck him. Unshielded, Cray took the blow across his face.

"Oh," he uttered, sounding surprised.

The old man went limp, and his staff fell into the churned up dirt.

"No," Jessika cried. "Cray!"

Starbright spun about and her protective golden wings spread again to cover both Cray and Jessika. As if he knew what she was doing and wished for artistic symmetry, Thornfire opened out his wings of flame, too. Then he flapped them forward, and the fires crashed down upon Altare with a roar.

Through the inferno, something inky jabbed out, straight at Thornfire, and the griffin grunted, then gasped, but the fires did not relent. Starbright stepped closer, putting a hand on her master's back, and the fires strengthened until they coalesced into a pillar of flame that stood where Altare had been.

After several heartbeats had passed it subsided, leaving a blackened spot on the ground wider than Jessika was tall. Thornfire sank to all fours and the fires died. Starbright's glow faded, but she stepped quickly to her master's side, as he wheezed and almost fell. There was no evidence of injury that Jessika could see, but he staggered like a buck with an ice-lion on its back.

"Bright," he panted, "quickly, help."

His hand went to his chest, and Starbright wasted no time. Jessika watched as the female searched for what Thornfire clutched at and pressed in close to support him.

"Dark dagger," she exclaimed. "Master, I'll blast it out, but I don't have much left."

"Here," called another voice, and Thornspike came stumbling across the clearing.

She had numerous broken feathers and several bleeding wounds, but she limped over to Starbright as fast as she could and put a hand on the larger female's back.

"Take what you need," she said. "I may be exhausted physically, but I have life energy to spare."

"I shall have to," Starbright murmured.

"I'll help as I can," Thornfire coughed out. "You'll need to lead; you're better at this."

Although the trio of griffins hardly moved a muscle, Jessika could faintly sense another battle breaking, as though she were hearing it from the far side of a mountain. Thornspike wilted as the minutes passed until she sat and then slumped towards the ground. Starbright's wing tips trembled and she panted, eyes squeezed shut. Thornfire's breathing became ragged and wheezy.

"It's fighting me," Starbright whispered. "Oh, it is hungry, so hungry."

While the griffins silently struggled, Breeka crept across the clearing to Cray's side. Jessika watched the little critter nuzzle his body, like a kitten trying to suckle at its dead mother. Cray made no response and his face was waxy and slack. Jessika feared that Altare's blue blast had killed him.

"What happened?"

Jessika recognized the voice: Karolan. She struggled to speak, but couldn't force out any words past the numbing effect of Altare's cloak, which had remained behind when the mage was either killed or fled.

"Bad man," Breeka howled, "bad man came. Night beasts came. Hurt everyone. Hurt Master. Master won't move."

"Hawkwings," Karo exclaimed, as if noticing her for the first time. "Where are you hurt?"

She saw him flop down beside her, the cane she'd made for him tumbling into the grass.

"I sensed a fight, or something, something big," Karo went on.

"Help," she grunted. "Cloak."

"Whose is this?"

"Bad," Breeka contributed. "Bad man. Take it off. Throw it away."

"It's—." Karo gasped audibly. "Wings, it's soaked with blood. Your blood?"

She felt him start to lift a corner.

"This is magic," he declared, face screwing up with distaste, "dark, nasty magic." He lifted it more quickly. "Wings," he moaned, "your back, it's, oh, Wings, you're torn up. What happened to you?"

"Cloak," she whimpered again, starting to feel partly freed of the spell of calm. "Get it off."

Karo drew it all the way off and tossed it aside. Jessika took a shaky breath and sobbed.

"It hurts," she wept.

"You're bleeding a lot," Karo whispered. "You're all over blood."

"At least the cloak is off now; I can talk," she went on, trying to steady her breathing and control her crying. "Altare appeared with a bunch of shadow-beasts. Cray fought him, but Altare sent a beast at Breeka and I tried to save it, and got clawed up. Then Altare saw my wings and put his cloak on me, and then I couldn't think or move. The griffins showed up and the fight went on. He might have killed Cray. I think Thornfire beat him, but he hurt Thornfire somehow and now Starbright is trying to heal him."

"Thornfire?" There was silence for a moment. "Yes, there's something wrong. Here."

Jessika felt Karo pressing something down on her back and tucking it tight around under her sides. It hurt, but she bit her cheeks and lips to keep from shouting.

"It's my shirt. I hope it will help with clotting. I need to assist Starbright," Karo babbled.

Jessika heard him stumbling away from her side. She looked back at the three griffins. Karo reached Starbright's side and sat next to her, wrapping his arms around her as much as he could. All three griffins perked up as he joined them.

"Hawkrain, help me," Starbright ordered. "Do you see?"

Jessika closed her eyes; there was nothing she could do; she couldn't even get herself up.

"Wings," a soft voice summoned, and Jessika opened her eyes again.

Hawksky—Kassandra—was kneeling where moments ago Karo had knelt.

"Kassie," Jessika breathed.

"I'm sorry I couldn't help sooner," the younger woman apologized. "I have no skill for war, and the unicorns would not come."

"I know. It's alright," Jessika replied.

"Jessa," she continued, voice even softer, "you're badly hurt."

"I know."

"No, you don't know how badly. I can tell. These wounds are laced with dark magic, death magic. They will not close on their own."

"What?" Jessika's heart thudded. "But, Cray healed himself when he got hurt by shadow-beasts last week."

Kassandra's hand rested on her head. "Stay calm. Getting excited will not help. Yes, Craduticus has the skill to heal such wounds, although not all shadow-beasts create them. I think it was just Altare's primary familiar that could, of these he brought. It will take magic to undo what has been done. I cannot do it; I am no mage. You are losing a lot of blood. I can help only with that until someone can heal you. Here, swallow this."

Kassandra held a flower to Jessika's lips. Its four arching petals were streaked with deep blue and red.

"It has some magic of its own, and will help you replenish," she explained. "Now, swallow it."

Jessika opened her mouth and let Kassie place it on her tongue. She chewed experimentally a few times, but it almost melted away before she swallowed.

Both women startled as Thornfire let out a cry of pain, and Jessika hissed at the pain caused by her involuntary jerk.

"No, I have it," Starbright declared. "I have it, almost."

Thornspike was on the ground now, head still tucked against Starbright's haunch. Thornfire was crumbling to the ground, wings limp. Both were breathing shallowly.

"Can you help?" Jessika asked Kassie.

"I'm not a mage," she repeated.

"Neither is Thornspike."

"My energy is no longer something a mage can touch," Kassie insisted. "I wish I could help them, but there is none to help you, save me. I must stay with you. More help for them will be here shortly."

"Who?" Jessika asked.

Just at that moment the answer came with the crunching of brush, and Rikah tumbled out into the clearing. He was coated with sweat, scratched by branches, and panting. With his hair sticking up every which way and full of leaves, he glanced all around the clearing to assess the situation.

Kassie pointed. "Starbright needs your help."

Rikah stumbled over without objection. As with Karo's arrival, as soon as Rikah laid a hand on Starbright's shoulder, all the others regained a bit of alertness.

"Hawkdare, yes, now I shall have it," Starbright asserted.

"Will Thornfire be alright?" Jessika worried.

"The weapon used upon him is vicious, worse than a starving wolf at mid-winter," Kassie murmured.

"Master," the griffin mage went on, "Master, you must relax the last of your shields. I must be able to reach it where it has burrowed. Please, let me reach in."

Thornfire coughed, as though he were trying to speak but couldn't. He shuddered, and Starbright's feathers lifted with aggression.

"Yes," Starbright whispered. "Yes, I can touch it now. It is mine. I will have it. Just a bit deeper."

Thornfire moaned like a dying beast, but Starbright was growling now, body shaking with energy drain. Thornspike looked nearly comatose, and Karo wasn't far behind, but at last Starbright cried out in victory. Thornfire jerked, convulsed, and lay as still as Cray.

Starbright lifted her hands, rising up on her hind legs, wings outstretched and tail braced on the ground to balance. Between her palms something like a snake of dark smoke writhed, something that made Jessika nauseous to look at. Again, light poured from the griffin's hands, and Starbright shrieked a cry of victory as she created another small sun. Immersed in the burning glory, the dark dagger died, its purpose unfulfilled.

"It is done," Starbright panted, dropping back down to the ground.

Rikah half-lifted, half-dragged Karo a few feet away, and laid him on a bit of less-mucky grass. Thornspike managed to roll away onto her back, all paws in the air and whimpering with what was probably a mix of deepest fatigue and pain from her injuries. Starbright was in a controlled collapse, and came to rest next to Thornfire.

"Master," she breathed, extending a wing over his body. "I didn't know." She wrapped herself around him, much as he had done when she'd been bitten by a talis years ago. "Starkind-mother never told me; you hid it behind your shields all these years." She preened his cheek feathers and seemed to be glowing again. "I never knew. Father. My father."

Rikah and Kassie were the only two fit to stand or care for the others. Karo was simply exhausted, and Rikah first helped him back to the house where he was put to bed with tea and some mumfruit at hand. When asked, Starbright murmured dreamily that she and Thornfire needed no assistance, but Rikah still brought them a water-skin and ordered them to drink, although Thornfire was hardly conscious and almost choked on it. Kassandra declared that the best place for Jessika was where she currently lay, for now, but a water-skin was brought to her, too, and she drank as though parched.

Rikah and Kassie examined Thornspike together. From the fight with the shadow-beasts she'd dragged off into the trees, she had a dozen bites and slashes in her hide, but they had all clotted; she would not have the same problem as Jessika. From the effort of dragging those beasts and the associated impact with the undergrowth and ground, she had several strained joints and bones that were bruised, which wouldn't leave her crippled, but would limit her running and flying for a few months. She groaned deeply whenever she tried to move. Her numerous broken feathers would also take time to regrow.

As for Breeka and Cray: the bat-cat was huddled against the wizard's side with tears that were all too humanlike soaking the fine fur of its cheeks. Cray was unmoving. Jessika assumed he was dead, but then Kassie rose and walked over to the pair. She placed a hand on Cray's chest.

"Breeka, you are called Breeka?" she confirmed.

The bat-cat nodded.

"This man is not dead," she said, and Breeka's flat ears immediately lifted. "But he is not present right now. His body lives, in a dormant state, but magic has sent his spirit elsewhere."

"Master will come back?" Breeka pled.

"I don't know," Kassie told it. "He might. His body will live for a while yet without him. It will swallow if you give it food."

Breeka placed its paws on Cray's shoulder and stared at his slack face. It sniffled.

"Master, come back," the bat-cat begged.

"Let's get a blanket to keep him warm," Kassie suggested.

"I can carry him to the house," Rikah volunteered, coming up beside her. "If that wouldn't hurt him?"

"I think he'd rest better there," Kassie agreed, "if you can lift him."

"I think I can, if you can help get him on my back."

Jessika let herself continue lying still while the pair maneuvered Cray's limp body until Rikah could stand with the man draped over his shoulders. Cray's toes dragged in the grass as Rikah labored to carry him across the clearing and down the path to the house. Breeka hustled along beside them, anxiety in every line of its body.

Kassie returned to Jessika's side.

"What do we do now?" she asked the plant-girl. "How do I get my back fixed?"

"You'll need the help of a mage," Kassie answered, "or a unicorn, but they won't come."

"So, when Karo or Starbright or Thornfire recovers," Jessika prodded.

"I hope so."

She tried to stifle her trembling. "You hope so?"

Kassie held her hand above Jessika's back. "This dark magic; I don't sense it in any of them. I don't know if they have the skill to undo it."

"Then what do I do?"

"I think you need the help of Craduticus."

Jessika widened her eyes. "But he's unconscious. When will he wake up?"

"As I told the bat-cat, I don't know."

"The unicorns won't come for me?"

Kassie shook her head. "I'm sorry. They don't want to enter into this again. They don't like debts on either side."

"What happens if I don't heal?"

Kassie looked at her hands. "I don't know."

Jessika felt the stirring of renewed panic swelling up into her chest, and tried to steady her breathing.

"I can keep giving you the blood flowers," Kassie said.

Tears leaked out and Jessika couldn't stop them. "I can't rescue Hawkjoy now, not until my back is fixed."

Kassie stroked her head and said nothing; there was nothing she could say.

Rikah had to build a litter for carrying Jessika, so she wouldn't have to try to stand. Her back muscles were so lacerated Rikah said he didn't think it would be good for her to do anything that required their use.

"With my shirt here, and Karo's," he described, "your blood has clotted to it, and I think it's slowing the bleeding, but if Sky says the wounds won't heal up, then we'd better be really careful."

Between Kassandra and Rikah they managed to shift her over onto the rough litter with a minimum of gasping and breaking open of the clotting. The pair went to either end of the litter and carried Jessika to the house. They didn't try to get her upstairs. Rikah brought down a straw mattress and they placed it in the spare room where Jessika had made up Karo's bed the previous evening. Across the hall was Cray's workroom.

"I put him in there," Rikah whispered with a jerk of his head. "I thought maybe being in his magic room would help him somehow."

"Once Thornfire is recovered, maybe he can help Cray," Jessika suggested.

"I hope so. Starbright and Thornfire haven't moved since I gave them water. I don't know how badly he's hurt."

"Badly," Kassie contributed. "That dark dagger hurt his soul."

Jessika and Rikah stared at her in shock.

"That's all I know. I don't know what kind of permanent damage it did," she qualified.

"There might be permanent damage?" Rikah clarified.

"Souls are resilient," Kassie said. "Since Starbright caught it and pulled it out before it reached the root that holds his soul to his body, it didn't kill him. We regenerate our soul energy of course; we're always making more. Souls can heal, but they can be scarred just as our flesh can be, and crippled just as our bones can be. Over time, a strong soul can heal away even scars and crippling, but it takes time: years, even decades."

"And what kind of permanent damage might happen?" Rikah pressed.

"All sorts of different kinds," Kassie shrugged. "You won't see the damage with your eyes, but Thornfire will feel it—if there is any," she hurried to say. "There might not be. He might be fine once he wakes up."

No one said anything to that. After a minute, Rikah stood up.

"I'll go check on them. Thornspike is resting out in front of the house there. I think she'll be fine recovering on her own."

He left the room.

"We can't even contact South-scree for help," Jessika remarked. "Not until one of the griffins can fly."

"Maybe Starbright will be able to go soon," Kassie suggested. "Maybe tomorrow or the next day."

"Did you see what happened to Altare, the dark mage? Did Thornfire kill him?"

"I saw," Kassie murmured. "That man was defeated, but fled before death could take him. He is likely seriously injured by burns. He will be long in recovering."

"So he probably won't come back here."

"Unless he has some secret way to restore burned flesh, he will not be mobile for weeks or even months."

"That's something," Jessika sighed, "but the Skire is still free to hurt Hawkjoy."

Kassie petted her head again. "There is nothing you can do about that right now."

Jessika had fallen into an uneasy sleep when bumping and banging awakened her that afternoon. The events of the morning came rushing back and she struggled not to let them plunge her down into depression; she knew that wouldn't help anything.

"What's going on?" she called, not being able to get up and go look for herself.

Rikah came to the doorway of her room, carrying a chair.

"The griffins are coming inside for the night so I'm making room in the front. Starbright and Thornfire are up, but not really awake. Karo is going to put up the wards, just in case, before the sun goes down. I have to bring the front furniture in here."

"I see, that's fine. I wish I could help," she replied.

"You just stay where you are," Rikah smiled. "I've got this. Once they're all settled I'll make some food, but we're not going to be able to get food for the griffins."

"They'd recover faster if we could."

He shrugged. "But we just can't, and none of them are fit enough to hunt. I can try to see if they want any of the jerky I made, but even if they have some, it won't be as much as they really need. Don't worry though, everything will be fine."

Rikah went on carrying pieces of furniture and Jessika could only watch. Shortly after he finished, she heard the griffins struggling in through the front door. A while later, Rikah brought her a bowl of vegetable stew in which he'd soaked some pieces of jerky, almost reconstituting them.

"I'll have to feed you, I suppose," he apologized.

"I don't know what I'll do if I can't get my back healed," Jessika said. "Sky thinks only Cray can do it, and he's knocked out."

"Something will work out," Rikah soothed. "Even if Thornfire, Starbright, and Rain can't help, once one of the griffins is mobile, we'll send to Southscree for help. Maybe one of the other mages can do it. If not them, then we'll send to the other Aeries for help."

"But Sky said it would have to be someone who knows dark magic," Jessika whispered. "I don't think there are any griffins that know it."

"Then someone will have to learn," Rikah replied.

"But dark magic is evil, isn't it?"

Rikah frowned a little in thought. "Thornfire tried to burn a man to death today, and he didn't need dark magic for that."

"But Thornfire isn't evil," Jessika protested.

"No, but you don't need dark magic to do violent things. Thornfire could do evil things, without even having to touch dark magic. Maybe that means that it isn't the type of magic that makes it evil, but what you do with whatever magic you have, dark, light, fire, water, or any other kind. I don't think learning a little dark magic so your back can get healed would be an evil thing."

Rikah fed her some more spoonfuls of soup.

"I would learn it so I could heal you," he said later, "if I could do magic. Karo will learn it for you, if the griffins won't."

Jessika took his hand. "Thank you, Dare. I hope he can learn it without having a teacher who knows it."

The soup gone, Rikah stood. "We'll find a way. Don't worry."

Over the next three days, Rikah continued caring for the six invalids. Karo recovered the fastest, although his foot was of course still broken and limiting his mobility. Breeka stayed with Cray, who remained unresponsive. Thornspike recovered her energy, but her wounds meant her most vigorous activity would be cautious walking for several weeks to come. Thornfire remained curled into a ball most of the time. He wouldn't speak, and reacted only to Starbright. Sleeping or waking, he clutched the pendant he wore around his neck in his hand: the twin of which his younger brother Thornwing wore.

Starbright was the first able to get up and hunt meat for the other griffins, but even she was too weak to fly.

"I had to dazzle it with light magic, so I could have an advantage in catching it," she confessed as Rikah cooked fresh deer meat for the humans. "I never do that, but I just couldn't chase it down without help."

"We know," Jessika assured her from where her pallet had been moved into the main room. "You'll be back to honest hunting in no time."

Starbright put a hand to her own chest. "Perhaps not no time," she murmured. "I spent more of myself than I should have." Her eyes sought out her master-father. "But, I had to."

Jessika gripped the griffin's forearm. "Of course. You saved him. Thornfire would be dead without you."

"My energy will be long in recovering, but not as long as his."

As soon as Karo could get up, he'd gone to Jessika to make his own magical assessment of her injuries.

"This," he'd grunted, hands spread open above her back, "I've never seen anything like this."

"Sky said it's dark magic. Can you fix it?" Jessika had asked.

"Not right away," he winced. "I don't even know how to approach something like this. It's advanced stuff, way beyond what I can do. I'll have to study it."

So each day, morning and evening, Karo would study some more, wiggling his fingers like confused caterpillars at the end of a twig, and muttering like a sleepy owl. After four or five days of it, he'd made no concrete progress.

"All I can do is strengthen the life magic in your back," he reported. "Doing that will keep your tissues healthy even without proper blood flow, and will help hold back the dark magic from getting a deeper hold on you. I should do it every morning and night."

Jessika agreed, and so began a twice-daily ritual for them. Rikah carved an assortment of branches into a back brace, joints bound with twine, and fitted it to Jessika's back to keep her from twisting or flexing too much when he or Kassie helped her with visiting the privy. He also layered more bandages onto her. The flesh might not seal back up on its own, but enough clotted blood in the bandages seemed to keep bleeding in check. He also modified her bedding to make it more comfortable for her to sleep on her belly without tweaking her neck.

Chapter 17
The Apprentice

On a warm day more than a week after the battle, Rikah and Kassie assisted Jessika to a propped up, sitting position outside the front of the house, where she could at least see the sun and watch Thornspike doing some careful stretching. Rikah had stitched the griffin's biggest wounds shortly after the battle, since none of the mages had retained enough energy to cauterize them, but nothing could be done for bone bruises until Thornfire awoke enough to tell them what herbs to gather for poultices.

Jessika settled against the front wall of the cabin with a grimace of pain followed by a smile of delight. Wreathing the house and draping down over the sides like a waterfall was a leafy green plant consisting of hundreds of thin vines coated with three-lobed leaves and dotted with dozens of blood flowers.

"I asked it to grow here," Kassandra explained, fingering a leaf while a vine tendril reached out and wound around her finger. "I fed some of the flowers to Thornspike, too. She lost some blood also."

Karo came out to join them, and the four humans sat together in the dancing mottled sun and shade. It would have been a glorious day for picnics or making daisy-crowns, for listening to distant birdcalls and carving a bit of wood or taking care of a bit of neglected sewing, reading or napping and feeling the Earth grow all around—but none of them could rest easy.

They sat, letting thoughts of despair mire them in gloom, when two griffins suddenly came soaring down into the tiny clearing in front of the house. Thornspike limped out of the way as fast as she could, crest erect in surprise.

"What's going on here?" Thornwing demanded as he landed in a flurry of pinions. "Where is my brother? I saw that big meadow back there, all torn up. Was there a fight? Who's hurt?"

The rust and cinnamon colored male twitched his wings with urgency. Behind him, the other new arrival, Waterleap, peered about, nearly as agitated.

Jessika's jaw dropped open, but Rikah reacted first.

"Thornwing," he cried. "Waterleap. How did you find us?"

"I asked first," the griffin retorted. "Fire called me with his pendant. After the Snow-in-lee debacle, he made them into contact stones. I can't send particular phrases, but he can, and he called me and told me to come to him. I've been searching for days. Luckily, the pendant knows where to go."

He pointed, and Jessika saw that the stone Thornwing wore as a necklace was sticking forward in all defiance of gravity, pointing towards the door of the house.

"Now where is my brother?" the griffin demanded.

"Inside," Jessika, Rikah, and Karo all answered.

Thornwing wasted no time, and Rikah and Kassie hurried to get out of his way. From her position right by the door, Jessika could look in and watch.

"Uncle Thornwing," Starbright exclaimed as soon as the newcome Thornwing squished himself into the room. "You're here."

"I'm here little one," he replied, giving her neck feathers a quick preen. "Are you hurt? What's wrong with him?"

Starbright shivered all over, her crest flattening in misery. "Uncle, there was a fight against a human mage. Everyone got hurt. We did our best. We won, but the human threw a dark dagger at Master Thornfire. I got it out, but barely, and it hurt him."

Starbright's wings shook. "It hurt him deep. I can't heal it, and I can't heal Hawkwings; her back was clawed up by a shadow-beast. And, oh Uncle, Hawkjoy is gone. The human mage has her, and now we can't go get her. And, and, I saw, down deep in him, when I pulled out the dagger," she paused, feathers twitching, "Master Thornfire is my sire, and you, you're my real uncle."

Thornwing's face registered surprise for only a moment, before he preened his niece's neck ruff with true affection. "That's right," he murmured. "Fire didn't want you to know. He didn't want the knowledge out, for several reasons."

He took and released a deep breath. "There will be time later for speaking of that. There is obviously a much bigger story here that I will need to hear all of first," Thornwing meditated. He carefully extended a wing around Starbright in the cramped quarters, and preened her dejected feathers some more. "I am certain you did your very best, and that's all that can be asked of you. We must work with what we have now. My next question: are we safe here?"

"We're safe for now," Starbright nodded. "The human mage escaped, but Master sorely wounded him. He will not be back soon."

"If the dark dagger is out, then Fire is in no current danger, correct?"

"That's right, but he's hurt so deeply."

"Ssh," Thornwing soothed. "We will address it all, one thing at a time."

The male griffin turned his head all the way around to look at Jessika.

"You are injured? I see some strange contrivance on your back," he said.

Jessika nodded, cautious of her impaired muscles. "Like Starbright said, a shadow-beast clawed me up. All the mages, plus Sky, say that dark magic is keeping the cuts from healing. Sky's blood flowers are keeping me from bleeding out, Rain has been strengthening my life energy, and Dare has done a great job wrapping the wounds and making this brace so I can sit up a little."

"A solution will be found for that as well. In time, I am sure you will be healed," Thornwing affirmed.

"But he has Joy," Jessika protested. "We have to go rescue Joy. That mage is called Altare. He and a nasty woman called Skire Germaine trapped her and are going to torture her, and," Jessika's gaze flicked to Waterleap, who was sitting just beyond the front step. "She's pregnant. She has a chick, and Altare and the Skire might torture or kill it, too."

Thornwing sucked in a breath, stiffening all over. "She did awaken then. Hawkmo—Hawkwind wondered. And she has a chick already? And the enemy has her imprisoned?"

"Yes," Rikah answered, "that's all correct, as far as we know."

Waterleap's feathers were slowly bristling. "It's from me," he breathed. "She, we, it's—I have to save her—them."

The young male surged to his feet faster than Jessika could blink, wings mantling and neck ruff rising aggressively.

"Stand down," Thornwing ordered. "This will happen, and you will have your chance, but hold your fury and don't go flying off in a blind rage. You don't even know where she is."

"I know where," Jessika told him. "We were about to leave to go try to rescue her when Altare showed up with shadow-beasts and we fought, and now we're all hurt and can't go anywhere."

Anger and despair warred in her throat and behind her eyes. She swiped at her suddenly wet cheeks.

"It was my fault," she declared through her trembling jaws. "Joy and I were exploring under the castle. The mage caught us. He magicked me away and I didn't know what happened to Joy, but we saw her in a magic vision, trapped in a cell, and he sort of said as much during the fight. Now with my back like this, I can't do anything, and the man who could help us the most lies in that room back there, with his mind knocked out of his body, and we don't know if he'll ever wake up."

Thornwing seemed to take a few moments to digest all that, and then turned and put a hand on his older brother's back. Thornfire hadn't stirred through any of the sudden activity. Only the movement and sound of his breaths showed that he even lived. Starbright backed up, giving Thornwing more space near his brother. The smaller male lay down on his belly and began preening Thornfire's feathers, trilling low and soft in his chest.

"I'll go hunt," Starbright stuttered.

"No, I'll do it," Waterleap declared. "Stay here and tell Thornwing everything that happened, and how to help Elder Thornfire."

Without waiting for a response, Waterleap turned and bolted into the underbrush. The four humans exchanged a raised-eyebrow expression; it was unusual for a younger male to order around an older female—and one who was from a different Line than him and a powerful mage on top of that. Starbright didn't react to the anomaly. She simply stayed with the Thorn brothers, waiting for when she was needed.

Waterleap and Thornwing couldn't fit in the house with the other three griffins; there just wasn't enough space. When Jessika told them of the enchanted fence posts Cray had used to protect his yard at the first house she'd met him at, Starbright and Karo fell into discussion of how to implement the same things here.

That left Thornwing and Thornspike with Thornfire, while Waterleap went off to hunt a second beast—Thornspike having devoured almost the entire first one all by herself. Jessika hoped Thornfire would feel comforted having his Linemembers around him. From her seat on the porch, she watched Starbright driving hefty sticks into the ground while Karo carved something into them.

When Waterleap returned with another beast, Thornspike and Thornwing ripped off bits and fed Thornfire as though he were a chick. Jessika, watching, hoped she was detecting more alertness and energy in the

THORNFIRE AND THORNWING

old mage. He was at least taking the tidbits without hesitation. Rikah came and cut a chunk from the prey animal as well, and went to cook it, before the griffins could gobble it all.

"It's a good thing the griffins can hunt now," he remarked. "We were about to run out of root vegetables for us. I can also make a good broth for Cray out of this."

"Have you noticed any change in him?" Jessika asked.

"Nothing," Rikah replied with a shake of his head. "Nothing good, nothing bad; he just lies there, like he's sleeping."

"I hope he wakes up soon," she murmured. "I wish there were something we could do."

"Maybe Karo and Starbright can talk it over, once they're done with the magic fence posts."

She almost managed a smile at his playful irreverence.

That evening, as Waterleap and Thornspike sat in front of the house with just their heads poking in through the front door, protected by the ward spells the mages had set up, the group had a conference.

"It stands at this," Thornwing was saying. He'd taken leadership of the group, and no one had disputed him. "Waterleap and I are healthy and hale. So is Hawkdare. Hawksky is her usual self, which is to say, perfectly fine, but sort of strange and unpredictable."

Hawksky wasn't in attendance for the meeting. Jessika hadn't seen her since that morning.

Thornwing went on. "Starbright will be fully well again once her magic energy recovers."

"I should be back to normal in a couple more days," the griffin mage confirmed. "I'm well enough for most things now, just not another fight like that."

"Hawkrain is fine, except for his broken foot."

Karo lifted his blonde head. "It still needs some more weeks to heal, I'm afraid. It doesn't hurt anymore, unless I smack it on something, or, y'know, try to walk on it."

"Spike, how are you?"

The black and white female rolled her head in a shrug. "Walking, fine, maybe even trotting, but after trying some wing exercises, I'm still very sore.

I could maybe fly if I had to, but I'm afraid of putting strain on my shoulder joints, and I think I might have cracked a furcula after all." She rubbed her chest where it met her neck.

"Hit the ground at the speed you say you were going, and I'm not surprised," Thornwing remarked, his tone showing her no sympathy.

For once, Thornspike didn't have a snappy comeback. "I had to do it," she murmured instead.

"She did save Cray's life," Jessika pointed out.

Thornwing nodded. "Which brings us to him. He's basically useless right now, requiring a lot of care."

"And my only hope of getting my back fixed," Jessika went on.

"Which brings us to you."

"I'm basically useless, too, and requiring a lot of care," she agreed. "Like Cray, I have no expectation of recovery."

"Unless Cray or Fire recovers."

"What's wrong with him?" she demanded.

The old griffin mage was curled up asleep, as usual, with Starbright's wing stretched over him.

"It's still difficult to say," Thornwing reported. "He won't speak. He looks at me when I talk to him, sometimes, but won't even shake his head for no or yes. His feathers don't even respond right to things. Our feather-language, the way our crests and neck feathers react to our moods and current situation, is instinctive. We learn it as chicks and fledglings by watching our elders, and start doing it as naturally as breathing. That's not even working for him. He just doesn't react."

"Do you think he's getting any better?" Rikah asked.

"A little, he's more alert, and something must be working right, because he grabbed his pendant and sent the pulses to me as soon as he got hurt. He was able to think of me, want me here, and produce the magic to call me, in the right pulse-patterns."

"Is he healthy physically?" Karo asked. "I mean, his body isn't hurt, right? No cuts or broken bones?"

"He can walk," Thornwing confirmed. "I don't see any injuries."

"He didn't get hurt in the fight," Starbright contributed.

Karo suddenly started crawling across the floor on his hands and knees, weaving among griffin limbs, until he sat before Thornfire.

"Hawkrain?" Thornwing questioned.

Karo poked Thornfire's shoulder. "Master, wake up, please," he ordered.

"Hawkrain," Thornwing repeated, voice serious this time.

"Let's find out how he's doing," Karo declared. "Have you asked him? Let's ask him."

Thornfire shifted, slowly bringing his head out from where he'd had it tucked under his wing, like any sleeping bird. He blinked in the light of the lit lantern.

"Master," Karo said again. "How are you?"

Thornfire's head tilted a little, like a leaf afloat on a sluggish stream.

"Do you understand me?" Karo tried.

The old mage's head tipped forward until his bill tip touched the floor. Jessika's chest tightened with pain at seeing Thornfire, so competent, suddenly so aimless. Karo put his hands on Thornfire's cheeks, lifting his head up with a groan of effort and staring straight into his eyes.

"Master," he said. "We need your help. Hawkwings is hurt and the old man Cray is unconscious. You have to come back to us. You can't just sit here and mope or mourn or whatever. You're the leader of this expedition. I know you're hurt, but no one can tell how. We need you to tell us. We need to know how to help you so you can help us. Understand?"

During Karo's speech, Jessika thought she saw Thornfire's gaze slowly focusing. Now his expression definitely showed a change; he was staring at Karo with the intensity he often gave his pupil when Karo had done something hopelessly stupid. From the quirk in Thornwing's feathers, he had noticed it, too.

Then Thornfire opened his bill, as if threatening, but if he'd wanted to hurt Karo he certainly could have moved faster and more aggressively. The skin around the young man's eyes whitened, but he didn't back off. Thornfire rumbled, a deep trill in his chest, the first sound Jessika had heard from him in days, and even though it wasn't a happy sound, it made her grin hard enough to stretch her cheeks to the edge of pain.

Karo ignored the gaping, powerful, sharp-tipped bill and wrapped his arms around his teacher's neck.

"You're going to get better, and I'm going to make you," Karo declared, voice muffled by Thornfire's dry fur. "You've helped me, even when I've been sullen and grumpy, so even if you're sullen and grumpy, I'm going to help you, too, Master. Tomorrow we're going to start taking walks and working on talking and we'll get all frustrated and angry, and you'll get better."

Thornfire clacked his bill together several times and made that rumbling sound again.

"Sounds just like you, to me," Karo teased.

Thornfire shook his head and Karo let go, sitting back, careful of his broken foot.

"That sounds promising," Thornwing muttered. "I think perhaps I should go back to South-scree and report on the situation. Obviously, Spike won't be going for a while, and I don't expect that Fire will be, either. That means establishing a sort of outpost here."

"What are you going to tell Hawkwind?" Jessika wanted to know. "And how are we going to rescue Hawkjoy? She's the new Hawkmother now. We have to go get her."

"You're not going anywhere until your back is healed," Thornwing said.

"Dare knows almost as well as I do where she is."

"Of course I'll go," Rikah cottoned on at once.

"I'll go, too," Waterleap volunteered.

"You'll need a mage," Starbright said. "I suppose I could go."

"Hang on there," Thornwing interrupted. "Fire, Bright, Spike, that old mage Cray, and Hawkwings together barely drove this enemy mage Altare away, and the cost of it was Fire, Hawkwings, and Cray seriously injured, and Spike not much better, with Bright totally depleted of mage energy on top of all that. That was from one encounter, and Altare wasn't even on his home territory."

He stared around at them. "Now you think Hawkdare, Waterleap, and Starbright can face him plus whatever other allies he has with him at the castle, on his turf, plus that person Skire Germaine, and get Hawkjoy out and safely away when we know that her flight feathers have been cut off at the least, and who knows what else has been done to her?"

That gave everyone pause, but Jessika had to speak up. "We have to try. Don't we have to try? How can we just leave her?"

Thornwing glared and ground his beak and flared his crest feathers. "Of course we have to try." He grimaced. "I'm going to have to tell Hawkwind everything. Then we might have to tell the council. Then everyone will get angry."

"They can't go to war against the humans, though," Jessika asserted, wishing she could stand up and gesticulate. "You can't let them, Thornwing. You have to stop them from doing that. Everyone will die. I'm sure Hawkwind will want Altare and Germaine punished and probably dead, but all we can do is sneak in, take whatever personal vengeance is necessary, and sneak Hawkjoy out."

Thornwing was still wincing.

"I mean it," she raised her voice. "I will deal with Northnest when I'm healed. It is my country, and if you attack it, you attack me." She huffed out a breath and revised. "Alright, it's not really like I have any authority over it right now, but it's my responsibility, and I'm going to figure out how to get it back and kick out all the people that messed it up. Let me handle that. You just get Hawkjoy out, alright?"

Thornwing nodded. "I will think over what you've said."

"Alright then," Jessika subsided.

Everyone was silent for a few moments.

"Maybe it's bedtime," Karo mumbled.

"Good idea," Thornwing agreed. "I'll plan to start flying back to Southscree maybe the day after tomorrow, once we've had some time to think and talk a bit more."

No one seemed to disagree. Rikah helped Jessika to her pallet and Karo sat over her for a few minutes renewing his life energy spells on her back. After that, with some whispered good nights, she tried to get to sleep.

Rikah helped her to the privy as usual the next morning, and deposited her with an extra blanket for warmth just outside the front door of the house, in what was becoming her usual spot, afterwards. He went to make the morning meal while the griffins, except for Thornfire, vacated the house to stretch and sun themselves in the chill morning air. Karo came, yawning, to sit by Jessika and do his morning life energy treatment of her back. Jessika plucked a blood flower from the vine that was rapidly covering the house and let it dissolve on her tongue.

Thornwing was looking pensive.

"I have to tell Hawkwind, you know that," he said into the silence. "I will try to convince her not to tell the council. This is, after all, only a real problem for the Hawk Line, although my brother's infirmity does spill over into the Thorn. I hope he will recover soon."

"It does make me nervous to be the only mage going to try to get Hawkjoy back," Starbright murmured. "If we don't tell any other Lines, we can't get any other help."

"The Hawk Line does not have much help to give, either," Jessika pointed out. "The only adults are Joy, Wind, and Swift."

"Perhaps if I focus only on cloaking spells," Starbright suggested, "we can get in and—"

Thornwing interrupted her with a hiss, holding up a hand for silence. Everyone startled and froze. On silent feet, Rikah came slowly to the door, still holding a stirring spoon. Now the griffins were all staring into the forest, and all in the same direction, without consulting about it. Their feathers lifted in an automatic response to fear and threat, attempting to make them look more intimidating than they already were.

Then Jessika, too, heard a little rustle in the distance. Under the trees shadows still lingered—not shadow-beasts, but the normal morning darkness before the sun rose high enough to dispel it. The woods were silent. Even the morning chorus of birds had paused. There was another soft sound, and another, and Jessika became sure that something was out there. Could it be just a curious villager from the town a few hours walk away?

There came a twanging, whooshing sound—several of them—and the griffins recoiled as one: peppered with arrow shafts.

Starbright cried out and Jessika flinched as blinding light flashed under the trees, revealing a dozen archers crouching among the tree trunks, already drawing their next arrows.

Waterleap was stumbling away in retreat, hand clutched to his throat as blood dribbled down his white chest. After her light display, Starbright had lunged towards the house, three arrows protruding from her chest. Thornwing, too, had arrows in his pectorals, but griffins had layers and layers of flight muscles between the outside world and their heart and lungs and other internal organs. Arrows in the chest would impede their flying, but would not be fatal.

It was Waterleap's throat wound that was the most concerning.

Thornspike screamed a battle cry and leapt at the nearest archer, who shrieked with fear and tried to run. She caught him easily, slapping him aside with considerable strength, leaving him bruised to the bone and aching, but not dead like a clawed strike would have done.

Thornwing, too, charged the attackers, sending half of them scattering, but then someone launched a spear from father back. It connected, biting into his chest more violently than the arrows had, and making him stumble sideways to the cover of a large tree trunk.

"Hey!" Rikah shouted. "Stop it, what are you doing? Leave us alone. We're not hurting anything."

The young man advanced down to the house's little clearing, waving his arms for attention. He got it. An arrow sped in and drove into his upper right chest. Rikah staggered, coughing in surprise.

"Rikah!" Karo shouted.

The blonde young man had limped to the doorway. Now his face contorted in anger. He lifted a fist, hand shaking, and then exclaimed a word, making a throwing motion towards the archers. A ball of fire followed his motion, soaring into the underbrush. More men cried out and retreated.

There must have been more archers somewhere. Another volley of arrows sailed in, aimed this time at the house itself, tipped with burning rags. One imbedded itself into the siding a few feet away from Jessika, who couldn't even get up without assistance. Helplessly she watched her companions fighting.

More fire arrows thunked into the house, some landing in the thatched roof. The roof was old and caked with moss, but the burning rags smoldered and almost immediately Jessika smelled smoke.

"No," she cried out, "helpless people are in here."

"Why are you doing this?" Rikah demanded. "Leave us alone."

Another arrow hit him, driving into his thigh, and Rikah fell to the ground, clutching his injuries.

Karo threw another fireball, and now arrows came whizzing toward the doorway where Jessika sat. Karo fled back inside. Thornspike had scared off or swatted a few more archers, but there were more spears somewhere in the back, and one came flying to knock her off her feet where it vibrated straight up like a sapling in a windstorm, sticking out of her side.

"Spike," Thornwing wheezed.

He stumbled over to where Thornspike lay trembling and crouched over her, blood dripping off the end of the spear still stuck in his own chest. Starbright lunged forward and screeched like the eagle she resembled, only the screech shot out like a shock wave and knocked all the hiding humans off their feet—except one.

A slight figure stepped out from behind a nearby tree and took several swift, fluid paces. A couple yards away from the enraged Starbright, it flicked out a hand, dashing a white powder into the mage's face. Starbright recoiled, gasping, and pawed at her eyes. A moment later her front legs collapsed, and she sprawled on the ground, still breathing, but seeming unable to rise.

Karo stepped back out of the doorway as the figure took those same ground-eating strides to stop just out of touching range of Jessika.

"Get out of here," Karo snarled at the invader.

Another flick of the wrist, another puff of white powder, and Karo, too, was swiping at his eyes.

"No," he growled, "I don't know what you're after, but you're not getting it."

Above her, Jessika could hear the crackling of fire taking hold in the thatch. Thornfire might be able to get himself out of the house, but Cray never would, and Breeka hadn't left his side for more than a couple minutes at a time since he'd been struck down. Would it save itself and leave its master to be burned to death?

Karo, already showing signs of discoordination, lunged at the slender figure dressed all in dark grey. Without showing any sign of fear, his target snapped out a hand, palm extended, fingers pulled back, and struck his face with a crack. Karo tumbled over, crying out and clutching his bleeding, broken nose. Moments after hitting the ground, he went still.

Jessika heard the scratch of claws on the floor, and looked over to see Thornfire come to the door, looking dazed. A little dash of white powder later, the griffin was stumbling back, unable to coordinate his feet, tripping to the floor.

"No, what are you doing?" Jessika accused. "The house is burning now, he'll die in there!"

The attacker looked down at her, and Jessika noted feminine features under its close-fitting cap. She had smooth, dark skin and completely dispassionate mahogany eyes.

"It doesn't matter," the woman said. "We're here for you, and now we have you."

Behind the woman, Jessika spotted men with spears closing in around Thornwing and Thornspike. Waterleap had fled behind the house, but if his throat injury was serious, he could already be dead. Rikah was shaking with pain but trying to crawl towards the house now. Jessika hoped maybe the woman attacker would not see him and he'd be able to knock her down and overpower her.

But as if she'd read the thought, she wheeled, kicking out and catching Rikah in the head. He took the blow hard, getting knocked to the side and falling into the dirt, where he lay unmoving. The woman looked back at Jessika and gestured over her shoulder.

"It's unfortunate this was necessary," she said. "Sleep now."

Jessika tried to lunge, or to kick out her feet, but the woman was too nimble, and Jessika too wounded. The last thing she saw before darkness was a burst of white powder, and through it Thornwing trying to fend off four men with long spears.

Jessika thought she might be sick. Bile rose into her throat with the constant, rhythmic rocking of the soft surface below her, and she fought to swallow it down. She opened her eyes to near darkness. A foot away from her face was a wooden wall of some kind, dimly illuminated by greenish light. She flexed her body a little and felt her wrists tied above her head, and her ankles equally restrained.

"Are you awake?"

It was the same dispassionate voice that she'd last heard, that of the slender, agile woman dressed all in dark grey. Jessika tried to turn her head the other way, opposite the wooden wall. The room she was in continued to rock.

"It's best if you lie still. You'll not be harmed," the woman said.

"Did you kill them all?" Jessika rasped through her sore throat.

"The griffins?"

"My family, the griffins and my human brothers, and the other people in the house. Did you burn it to the ground?"

"We did not remain to see who lived or died," her captor informed her. "No one was obviously dead when we left. The hovel was only barely burning. Once we had you, the fates of the others became irrelevant."

Jessika clenched her fists and tried not to rise to the provocative words.

"But you say you had family members there? I was not told of that. It was my understanding that your family members were already accounted for."

Jessika remained silent.

"It doesn't matter. I have completed the first part of my task, as my lord has bidden me. I will complete the rest and be rewarded. My lord made no instruction to improvise based on anything you tell me, only unavoidable necessity."

She again let no reply be her reply.

"I am here to help you," the woman said, and for the first time a bare hint of reproach crept into her voice.

"I did not ask for your so-called help," Jessika responded, trying to make her voice even more expressionless than the other's.

"You should be grateful regardless. I will heal your injuries."

"Leave me be," she ordered. "Let me go."

The woman's voice turned a trifle scornful. "I cannot do that. You may be Northborn's lost princess, but you are not my master. Besides, if I let you go, what would you do? Lie helplessly on the roadside? Your back has been slashed to the bone in places. You cannot even stand on your own."

Jessika couldn't refute that, but nor could she deny her need to be free and back with her companions. They were hurt at the least. Some might be dead. Who would put out the house fire and drag Cray out of his workroom? Who would staunch wounds and sew them up?

"How long was I asleep?" she asked.

"No more than a half an hour," the woman answered. "The sleeping powder is quick-acting, but doesn't last very long."

Perhaps Starbright had awakened soon enough to get Cray out of the house. Maybe Waterleap's throat injury and the spear in Thornspike's side hadn't hit anything so vital that they died in minutes.

"Did you use more powder on the last griffin?" Jessika asked. "I mean the one with the red, rusty coloring, who was trying to defend his friend."

"The guards dealt with him. I did not linger to watch." A tinge of anger crept into her voice now. "Six guards were injured in the altercation, not just your friends. Two of them might not live."

"When people fight, they get hurt," Jessika growled. "You and your guards were the attackers. We didn't attack you; we defended ourselves. You didn't even announce yourself before shooting arrows at us. If any of you got hurt, it's all your own fault."

The woman made no reply for a few moments. "That is an interesting perspective," she said at last. Her voice had again gone as flat as a still pond, and Jessika couldn't tell whether she meant what she said or if she was being facetious.

"Now, I will begin to heal your back," she went on. "You have no choice in the matter and cannot escape, so struggling or trying to interfere will only be a waste of energy. I suggest you lie quietly. The damage is extensive and repairing it will be energetically expensive for me, so it will take several treatments, but we do have several days of travel before we reach the capital. By then, your whole back will have begun to heal naturally."

Jessika's skin shivered. "And what happens then?"

"I do not know. My lord will inform me of my next instructions at that time, and decide what happens to you. Those two things may or may not overlap."

"Is your lord Altare?"

"Of course."

Jessika hid a snarl. "So he survived the battle."

"He is terribly burned. He will be weeks in recovering."

"Good," Jessika spat. "I wish he'd died, but maybe he'll at least have learned a lesson not to go attacking people for no reason."

The woman did not sound like she rose to meet her prisoner's vitriol. "You may ask him when you see him. In fact, I think he will have much to discuss with you regarding that event and others."

Her skin chilled further, but she didn't want to give any indication that the woman's words had filled her with a sense of foreboding.

"So what's your name?" she asked instead.

"I am Vor. I am humbled to be one of my lord's apprentices and servants, unworthy as I am. He takes great pity on me, and has honored me with the task of retrieving and healing Northborn's lost princess since he is unable to do it himself at the moment."

Her voice sharpened. "Now please do hold still so that I may begin your treatment."

Jessika seethed internally, but what could she do? The woman, Vor, was right. Her bonds were firm and secure. She could thrash her body about a bit, but what would that accomplish? She might hurt herself more, and she'd still be stuck in wherever she was. She supposed now that she must be inside a wagon. Unless someone came to crack it open like a nut and lift her away, she was stuck. If her back were healed, however, she'd have a much improved chance of getting herself away, should an opportunity present itself or be made.

"Fine," she subsided.

"Thank you," the woman said. "I will begin now. You may find it uncomfortable, but probably not painful. It seems that the life energy in your tissues is strong and healthy, which will make this a little easier. I will tell you when I'm done."

Jessika tried to relax. She could still feel the cloth—Rikah and Karo's shirts—that had been wrapped around her torso, although the weight of the brace was gone. It didn't seem that Vor needed to remove the cloth. For a handful of heartbeats, she didn't sense or feel anything strange. Then prickling began near her right shoulder, at the edge of the slashed area. The feeling intensified into a rippling, squirming sensation, as though something was wiggling about in her wounds, right down deep into them.

The feeling went on for several minutes. It made her want to scratch and dig at the cuts, and make it stop. She found her functioning muscles tensing and her already queasy stomach roiling in revulsion. She tightened her throat and tried not to utter any sound of disgust. When at last the feeling faded she released her breath in a shuddering sigh.

"I am done for now," Vor said, sounding as weary as though she'd run a mile.

"That felt gross," Jessika told her, "like maggots in my flesh."

"And what is wrong with maggots?"

"What's wrong with maggots?"

"Yes."

Jessika couldn't reply at once, and Vor didn't give her a chance to come up with a reply.

"Maggots, worms, insects and tiny creatures of all kinds, are vital to our survival," Vor said. "What would happen to refuse if they did not exist? Dead bodies would fall to the ground and remain lying there. The waste products of animals and people alike would pile up forever."

Her voice turned scornful.

"You pure-as-rain heroic fools, you call the dark evil. You understand nothing about balance in the world. You think only of light and goodness as the one acceptable solution to everything. You think death is the worst thing you have to fear. You refuse to see the necessity of all balances."

Jessika heard her fussing with some heavy cloth.

"Here, a portion of your back has been cleansed of the dark energy that kept it from mending. It will begin to repair itself now. I have exhausted myself and will rest."

It sounded like Vor got herself into a bed of some kind.

"Thank you for helping with my back," Jessika said.

"It is as I was bid by my lord, but your thanks are noted."

Still bound, there was nothing for Jessika to do but stay where she was. The carriage rocked onward through what she assumed was the forest, perhaps through a village or two, heading to the capital, and all she could do was let it carry her there.

Chapter 18
The Journey

Vor awoke some time later and gave her another treatment. The worm-wriggling sensation was no easier to bear, but Jessika did not complain this time. Vor went immediately back to bed. Jessika's queasy stomach didn't give her any sign of hunger, but hours must have passed, some of which she spent sleeping.

Later that day, when the green light on the wall had started to fade, the carriage came to a halt, and Vor got up from her bed and exited out a door at the back. She heard talking, muffled by the wooden walls. The stationery wagon gradually allowed her nausea to subside, and when she caught a whiff of food cooking, hunger twisted up her insides with a new sort of discomfort.

The door opened again and Vor's footsteps sounded on the floor.

"We are camping for the night," the woman announced. "I will see to it that you have food, water, and a chance to empty your bladder and bowels."

Jessika made a disgusted face at the uncaring wall. Vor didn't do much to pretty up her words.

"I observed you were wearing some sort of contraption on your back that stabilized it. I still have it here. Shall I reattach it so that you may sit up and move about a little?"

Jessika stuffed down a variety of possible responses, and settled on: "yes, please."

"I hope I shall not hurt you," Vor said, voice as colorless as usual.

Jessika did not resist as the woman got the brace situated and strapped back on.

"I will release your hands and feet now. I assure you, I am fully capable of defending myself—especially against someone as injured as you. Although I have orders not to damage you, I also have orders to do whatever is necessary to keep you contained. I hope you will be cooperative. Will you cooperate?"

"Yes," Jessika uttered.

Vor hadn't added any details, like for how long. Jessika silently promised herself that she'd cooperate only until she saw a true chance for escape. Vor was right, for the moment; trying to escape now would not only be unlikely to succeed, she'd probably get hurt in the attempt.

Vor's fingers brushed her knuckles as she untied the top restraint. The bottom one followed, but Jessika noticed that her hands were still bound together, just not bound to the bunk anymore.

"I will help you up."

Used to having to move with extreme care, Jessika allowed Vor to help her swing her legs down from the bunk and attain a sitting position. She leaned back against the wagon wall.

"Well done," Vor said. "I will fetch you food and drink. Please stay here."

Without waiting for a response, the woman exited again. Jessika got a brief glimpse out the door of a twilight forest. She wondered if anyone was alive who might be able to track her down, who might even now be following the wagon. Except for the sleeping powder, Starbright would have been the healthiest, but if others were on the verge of death, she probably would have taken time to help them first. It was what Jessika would have done. What good was there in trying to track down one person and take her back from a troop of armed men if Rikah, Thornwing, Thornspike, and Waterleap all bled to death, or the house burned down and killed Thornfire, Cray, and Breeka, while out trying to find her?

She took the opportunity, while doing some calming breathing exercises, to look around the interior of the wagon. There were two bunks across the center aisle from each other. One of them Jessika had been tied down to, and the other was surely the one Vor had been periodically resting on. Some blankets were crumpled up on it. Besides the bunks, there were cabinets and shelves occupying almost all the other free space. Under the bunks were shoved boxes and a couple barrels and sacks. A window above each bunk looked out on the darkening forest, but there were short curtains that could be pulled closed over them.

She could see none of her possessions, those that she'd carried with her for weeks now. It appeared that Vor hadn't paused to fetch Jessika's backpack. That meant she had no other clothes, no magical contact stone, no supplies for her monthly female cycle, neither of her truncheons, and of course no water skin or food. Also, Koki's lock picks were left behind, too. They might have even been useful, had she retained them. She hoped she'd find a way to honor her promise to get them back to the charming faun someday.

A faint smile surprised her, stretching her lips when she thought of Koki. It was accompanied by a warm sensation radiating out from her gut and chest. The back of her hand tingled, where he'd put it to his own cheek. She recalled how they'd interlaced their fingers a little, that night before bed, in Chika's house. Mostly, she remembered his face and his words. He'd called her brave. What would he think of her now, as an invalid and a captive? Her smile faded.

In a few minutes, Vor returned, breaking Jessika's pondering. She carried a metal bowl in which had been mixed some sort of bland grains, a baked red potato, and pieces of cooked meat. Despite the odd conglomeration Jessika's mouth watered at the sight and smell of it, and she ate hungrily in the dim wagon, after figuring out how to juggle bowl and fork with her hands still tied. Vor exited and returned with a flagon full of water.

"Thank you for the food," Jessika said, trying to be polite.

"My lord has instructed that you be kept in full health on the journey," Vor replied. "I will see to it that you are fed sufficiently. I am sure this fare is plain for you, but we may stop at inns as we approach the capital, and better food will be available."

"This is perfectly adequate," Jessika assured her.

"Thank you for your understanding."

Jessika lowered her bowl and fork for a moment. "I haven't been living like a princess, so you don't need to treat me that way. I'm not accustomed to it."

"You shall have to become so," Vor said with a slightly raised eyebrow. "Once you reach the capital you shall be treated as the princess and eventually the queen, I am given to understand."

"How, uh, what plans does Altare have for me then? He told you what he intends?" Jessika asked with no little concern.

Vor did not reply immediately and Jessika got the sense that maybe the strange woman was choosing her words carefully.

"You are the king's daughter, and thus his heir, his only heir," Vor said at last. "I do not presume to know all that my lord knows or hopes may come to pass, but I can only assume that you will reunited with your father and groomed to take the crown when he is ready to pass it to you. Further details I cannot reveal for I know them not, but my lord is the loyal servant of the king, and will surely have interest in his daughter—as evidenced by this expedition to rescue and return you to your birth home."

"Rescue isn't the right word," Jessika corrected. She stabbed at her potato. "You kidnapped me, stole me, abducted me." A growl entered her rising voice. "You could have asked me to come with you. Instead you hurt and maybe killed the people I love, and snatched me away."

Vor was frowning as though having trouble comprehending what she was saying. Jessika tried another tactic.

"What if a group of armed people came to the castle, shot Altare and everyone full of arrows and spears and knocked you out with some sleeping powder, tossed you in a wagon, and rode off with you? How would you feel?"

Vor's frown was deeper, but she said: "that would never happen. My lord would not be defeated."

"Ha," Jessika almost snarled. "My friend defeated him and sent him running home covered with burns. You can't deny that, can you? Someone else strong enough could defeat him again."

Vor stood. "Are you finished with your meal, Princess?"

"Almost," she growled.

"I will return in a few minutes then."

Vor pivoted on her heel and marched out of the wagon.

"I will give your back another treatment before we both retire for the night," Vor announced. "I will also strengthen the life energy in your damaged tissues, as it seems to be waning."

Jessika was back on her belly on the bunk, tied up again. Vor had helped her to deal with the demands of nature that were a consequence of food and drink, and allowed her to wash her face and hands, before returning her to her prison.

"As you like," Jessika grunted, face turned away to the wagon wall.

She endured the phantom maggot squirming as Vor removed the dark magic from another portion of her back. Following that came a warm, tingling sensation similar to what Karo had been doing for her. She closed her eyes as she heard Vor getting silently into her bunk afterwards.

"We will acquire proper garments for you before we reach the capital," the woman said into the darkness.

"Thank you," Jessika responded. "I hope I can have a bath before putting on new clean clothes. I really need one."

"Yes. I will see to it that you have one. Once the entirety of your back begins healing it will be possible for you to bathe. Before then a sponge bath might be possible at an inn, so you may cleanse the rest of you."

"That would be lovely."

For several minutes the two women lay in silence.

"Do you hate me, Princess? I am only doing as my lord commands," Vor said softly.

"From what I have seen of your lord, he is my enemy. He has done nothing but hurt the people I care for," Jessika replied, trying to be fair. "I distrust anyone who says she works for him. Perhaps he has been only kind to you, and you have never seen the brutal and violent side of him, in which case I suppose I cannot fault you for serving him, if you do not know all that he does. I don't hate you, but I don't like you, either. In time I'm sure I will see if you are another of his victims, or his accomplice in cruelty."

Jessika knew her words were harsh, but she felt the right thing was to be honest. It was always possible Vor would be meaner to her now, or maybe she'd respect her for being truthful, or maybe it would even get her thinking about Altare in a different light.

"I shall think on what you have said," Vor murmured. "Good night, Princess."

She didn't see any point in disputing the title. "Good night, Vor."

Two days passed in much the same way. In the early morning, Vor helped Jessika to the privy, and sat her up for food and drink. As the wagon started moving, the woman gave her back a treatment. At mid-day there was a brief stop and a cold lunch of fruit and a travel bar ration. They stopped at dusk for more food and sleep. Over the course of the day, Vor treated her back five times, each time cleansing an area about half the size of her palm.

On the fourth day, the bumpy wagon suddenly began rolling on smoother road. Jessika heard the sounds of people, animals, and other carts and wagons through the wall. The window across from her showed rooftops. Late in the day, they stopped, and Jessika heard conversation right outside the wagon.

Vor got up from her bunk where she'd been resting and went out. Shortly, she came back in. "We're stopping at an inn for the night," she announced.

From one of the drawers she pulled a long brown cloak.

"You'll wear this for entering the inn," Vor went on. "I have little training as a lady's maid, but I will assist you with washing, help you dress in clean clothes, and comb out your hair as best as I am able. Dinner will be in your room."

"Your help is plentiful," Jessika assured her. "I would have no difficulty with any of that if it weren't for my back."

"I am aware. I will help you stand and put this on."

Jessika submitted, still with the feeling that it was the best course for the moment. Vor led her out of the wagon, which had been parked in a courtyard. A pair of young men was unharnessing the horses. The guards that accompanied the wagon were trickling into the inn's main door, except for the man Jessika had come to think of as the leader. He was big and stocky, with drooping black mustaches and a bald head. His thick leather coat hung on him like a festival tent but when he moved he somehow avoided tripping over it.

Without a word, he gestured toward the inn, and Vor helped Jessika to follow. They didn't pause in the main room. A girl wearing the same colors as the men who'd been taking care of the horses led them wordlessly up the hefty stairs at the back of the room, to a long hallway. She opened a door midway along it and gave a brief curtsy. Vor took Jessika inside, leaving the guard and the servant in the hallway. The room held a bed under a window, a table and chair, some coat hooks on the wall, and a shallow tub of steaming water. On the table waited a towel, a wash rag, and a small bar of soap.

Vor helped Jessika to a seat on the chair and put her shoulder bag on the bed. She began pulling clothing out of the bag, followed by a wooden comb that she dug around in the bottom to locate.

"I have cleansed about half of your injuries now," Vor said, "but I think we shall still have to leave the bandages on. Your wounds were deep, and even the ones I cleansed days ago are still surely not healed. The dressings are not attractive, but they have clotted your wounds shut, and keeping wounds covered ensures the best healing. Let us begin while the water is still hot."

Jessika was able to sit in the tub and wash her own intimate areas while Vor scrubbed at her filthy hair. She'd gone weeks now without washing it. The only caution came in making sure she did not push Jessika's head too far forward, which would pull on her back. Eventually, Jessika rested her elbows on the edge of the tub and her forehead against her palms, for extra support.

The water was grimy by the time they finished, and Vor called for more water to rinse with. The fresh water was cold, but Jessika was too grateful to be clean to have any thought of complaining about it. Vor helped her dry off with the towel, and she stepped into clean clothes for at least her lower body. Her own shoes were largely undamaged so she could go on wearing them. Jessika sat on the bed while Vor combed out her hair and put it back in the leather thong she used to keep it out of her face.

"I will have the tub taken away," Vor announced when she finished. "You may rest here until dinner arrives. Is there anything else you require?"

"No," Jessika said. "Thank you for your help."

"Of course."

Vor helped Jessika to lie down, and left without another word. On her belly, head twisted to the side, Jessika stared up through the window at the blue sky with one eye, and wished for griffins among the clouds.

Vor personally brought Jessika her dinner on a tray. The sound of the door and the scent of spices applied by a practiced hand brought Jessika up out of her dismal half-doze.

"I have your dinner, Princess," Vor said. "I shall help you sit up."

Jessika said nothing, but allowed the woman to do the work of lifting and pushing her about like a doll until she was sitting against the headboard of the bed, propped up by pillows. Vor set the tray on her lap.

There was a bowl of mixed roasted vegetables and chunks of some kind of meat. That was what was sending up the song of savory seasonings. Beside it on a plate was a hunk of brown bread spread with butter, and accompanying that was a round, orange fruit she'd never seen before.

"What's this?" Jessika asked, picking up the unfamiliar food item.

"That is an orange," Vor answered, sounding a trifle surprised.

Jessika eyed her, wondering if the woman she had come to believe had no sense of humor was suddenly trying to make a joke.

"It is orange," Jessika enunciated, "in color. Are you telling me it is called an orange as well?"

Vor blinked for a moment, as if thinking that over herself. "Yes, that is correct."

"Is it called an orange because it is orange?"

Vor's brows knit slightly.

"No one could think of a better name?"

The knitting of her brows became deeper, irritation leaked into her voice like winter air through a gap in the wall-stones. "I am afraid I do not know. Would you like me to try to find out for you?"

"No, nevermind," Jessika subsided. "How do I eat it? Do I bite it like an apple?"

"It requires peeling," Vor said quickly. "May I show you?"

Jessika handed over the fruit and watched between taking bites of the meat and veggie mix.

"See, here, the cook has cut into the peel. That's where you start."

Vor's strong, dark fingers dug into the orange and she began ripping off bits of the peel. The refreshing scent of citrus came to Jessika's nose even over the spices from the rich meat. The aroma tugged at deep memories, bringing back a sensation of time and place without any details. Jessika closed her eyes as the nostalgia washed over her, mentally groping after more information— when, where had she known oranges before? Whom had she been with? How old had she been?

She might as well have been flailing after feathers snatched away in the wind. No images or sounds came to her, only the feeling. When she tried again to grab it and describe it, it dissolved like a sunset. There was no calling it back until it came again of its own whim.

As Jessika opened her eyes, Vor was removing all trace of the peel, and easily split the peeled fruit into halves. She placed the two halves back on Jessika's tray.

"The peel is bitter, although I understand it is sometimes used in cooking or soap making," Vor explained. "I have little knowledge of those arts."

Jessika had put down her fork and reached for the orange. "I've had this before," she mumbled. "I remember, but I can't remember."

Vor didn't say anything, and Jessika picked up an orange half, turned it over in her hands, and pulled off one of the sections. She examined it for a moment, and then put it in her mouth. She bit down.

Memory flooded her mind as the juice flooded her mouth and she almost choked. Eyes closed again, she saw sunlight, blurry grass, a smudge of grey tree trunk and dappled shadow. She smelled spring and citrus. She was opening her mouth wide, sticking out her tongue, making a crude but joking sound, and a woman in a white dress with bronze-brown hair swept across her forehead was holding out a section of orange. The woman was smiling a playful, happy smile. She mimicked the crude sound back. She had some freckles across her nose and cheeks. Her eyes crinkled at the outside corners.

The smiling woman put the orange into Jessika's mouth, and Jessika chewed and swallowed. Her little girl voice rang out.

"Mm, it's good. More, Mommy."

The Jessika sitting in the inn, with a cut up back, being served food by her kidnapper, coughed, clapping both hands to her mouth to stop herself from spraying the orange across the room. Some of the juice had gone down the wrong tube and she hurried to swallow the orange so she could cough with full vigor.

Vor made concerned sounds while Jessika hacked and sucked air. Her back spasmed with pain as the muscles tried to contract to assist. All the physical drama was secondary, however: as insignificant as a rodent to a griffin when there was a deer to eat.

Her mother: she'd seen her mother.

Tears overflowed and she didn't try to stop them. After she'd been taken away from Northnest, once she'd lived with the griffins for a while, she'd forgotten what her mother looked like. Hawkwind had become her new mother, and those old memories had just faded.

"Are you alright?" Vor was saying, repeatedly, and more and more insistently.

"Yes, I'm fine," she managed in reply.

Jessika closed her eyes another few moments as she got her breathing back under control. In her mind she called up the image again, of her mother's face. It was still there; she could see it now anytime she wished.

"Perhaps I should dispose of the orange for you?" Vor remarked.

Jessika's eyes snapped back open. "No, no," she blurted. "No, I like it. I'll eat it. I just accidentally inhaled a bit. I'm fine now."

"As you wish," Vor murmured, but Jessika heard a plentiful measure of doubt in her voice.

She ignored it, and took another piece. This one went down without mishap. Oranges, she decided, might be her favorite fruit.

They left the inn the next morning, early, with Jessika again riding belly-down on the bunk inside the wagon. With the treatments from the previous day, her back was now more than half cleansed of the dark magic taint. The upper part, which Vor had treated first, had started to heal. Although still sore, Jessika could move her arms a bit more now. The returning sense of competence turned her thoughts to escape. The hours of monotony in the wagon gave her plenty of time to ponder.

As far as she knew, no one had come after her. Perhaps they couldn't, either because they were too injured or didn't know where she'd been taken, or both. If she were to get away and try to return to them, it would be up to her. Once they reached the capital and the castle, escape would be much more difficult. If she'd been fully healthy, she figured she would have had a good chance of tricking or sneaking her way free, engineering an opportune moment or taking advantage of one.

As it was, it seemed like her injuries would be fully cleansed just about the same time they reached the capital, and she wouldn't completely heal for another few weeks after that. There would be no crawling through hidden passageways or scaling rooftops until her back muscles were totally healed.

Jessika tried not to seethe too much; it made her body clench and probably did not help with muscle mending. She was tied down again, as before, but she couldn't really blame Vor. She hadn't given the woman any real reassurance that she was content with the situation and wouldn't run away at the first opportunity.

Fine, then. If she couldn't escape yet, and didn't know how to begin planning an escape from the castle, there was no point in getting all agitated. Maybe there was a bright side. Hawkjoy was at the castle. Perhaps—if she must face Altare again—she could find a way to reason with him, or even bargain with him, to get Hawkjoy released. Maybe she'd even have access to Skire Germaine. Maybe, just maybe, there was something she could do for Hawkjoy.

The wagon shuddered onward over mostly smooth roads. Jessika could do nothing but go where it carried her, and wait.

For the next five days they stayed in inns every night. Jessika got baths and soft beds and hot food in the evening, and rode in the wagon strapped down as usual during the daylight hours. When she was in her room in the inn alone, she practiced using her healing back muscles. Arm movement returned, but she was careful not to do anything too quickly, or to try to lift anything heavy. She tried to conceal her progress from Vor, and continued asking for assistance, often with the embellishment of winces of pain.

As they travelled, she noticed the cities becoming bigger and the roads smoother. Finally, over a week since the attack and abduction, they stopped in the biggest city yet, and Vor had an extra announcement when she brought Jessika her dinner.

"Tomorrow we will reach the capital. In the morning I will have a proper gown for you. You will no longer ride in shackles. By the afternoon you will be installed in your own suite of rooms in the palace," Vor explained.

Jessika just looked at her, giving only the smallest of nods.

"Tonight, I will finish the cleansing of your wounds. In the morning, the bandages will have to come off. I will replace them with new, clean ones."

Jessika nodded at that, too.

"I will continue to see to your needs, but I expect that shortly you will be healed well enough that only a common maidservant will be required."

"If that's the case, then I'll be able to take care of myself," Jessika murmured. "I don't need a maidservant."

Vor gave her a glare. "What you need will be decided for you, and you will be grateful, Princess. My lord will see to it that you have everything befitting your rank and status."

Jessika grimaced as though her food were bitter.

Vor said nothing more, and swept out of the room with her back as straight as a fire poker.

Jessika's dreams were unsettled: full of Hawkjoy and Hawkwind and Koki. Hawkjoy was in pain. Hawkwind was angry. Koki was—Jessika blushed to recall. Then she hissed to herself in disgust at her own brain; how could she be having fluffy romantic dreams about a faun she hardly knew when she was a captive, Hawkjoy was probably being cut to bits, and all her other dearest friends might be dead?

Vor was soaking the bandages on Jessika's back with warm water, hoping to loosen any dry clots so the strips of fabric could be removed without ripping at the wounds. The top ones near her shoulders came off relatively easily, and Vor declared that those wounds were well enough healed not to require a replacement bandage. As she worked her way down, however, each removal became more painful, until Vor was blotting at fresh blood and applying pressure while she wrapped new bandages.

"Very good," Vor commented when she was done. "I will help you with your clothing now."

What followed was Jessika biting her tongue to keep her questions in as Vor laced her into a set of undergarments and a heavy, dark green dress that had more buttons and ties than Jessika could ever recall seeing on any piece of clothing in her life. She paid attention, but wondered if she'd ever be able to get herself out of the clothing, much less put it on again. Perhaps she would need a maidservant after all, if she were going to be forced to wear such things.

After that, Vor trimmed her hair even and put it in a much tidier braid than even Jessika—who was skilled at braiding her own hair from many years of practice—could produce. Then, Vor stood back and looked her over.

"Much improved," the woman pronounced. "You will not shame Northborn now."

Jessika bristled and tried to stop herself from snarling. "Yet I am ashamed of myself," she replied acidly.

Vor's eyebrows danced upwards. "You shall have to learn to live with that, perhaps even learn better, and overcome it."

Jessika's insides writhed and she turned her head away.

"My lord Altare will explain all to you," Vor went on. "Then you will understand. In time, you will joyously take your place in the kingdom, just as I have."

As angry as a fledgling whose first kill had been snatched away by an older sibling, Jessika longed to snarl and bite but—was now the time? Would waiting until she was in the castle be too late? Would there be any hope for her there in getting Hawkjoy and making an escape? Was her father really alive and living there? Would she be allowed to see him? What if he were on the side of the invaders, as some of the rumors had said? Would she still be glad to see him?

Maybe she shouldn't go. What might Altare do to her when she was back in his grasp? Her imagination could call up all kinds of unsavory deeds he might try and her stomach turned even as her skin chilled. She looked slowly back at Vor as adrenaline began making her muscles tingle. She was almost healed. Perhaps now she would able to overpower her captor. Vor was a mage, but if Jessika got the first hit in—

The door to the room opened and two of the wagon guards stepped in. If Jessika had been a griffin, her aggressively raised crest would have flattened. She couldn't overcome three, especially with the guards armed as they were with short swords. To try would be stupid.

Vor fetched two more items from the long sack that had contained the dress.

"Your shoes, my lady," she said.

She knelt and held the flat—entirely insubstantial to Jessika's way of thinking—green-embroidered slippers to the floor, so Jessika could shove her feet into them, which she managed to do without growling, although a big part of her wanted to kick Vor in the face.

"Let us go peaceably to the carriage," Vor said next, rising.

She made a gesture to indicate that Jessika should go in front of her. The guards turned first and led the way from the room and down the stairs of the inn. Vor followed at the back.

What greeted them was not the rough, closed in wagon pulled by sturdy plain horses that they had been traveling in before, but an actual carriage with doors on the sides, overlarge wheels, curtained windows, and a pair of matched dappled grey horses to draw it. The inn's stable boy opened the carriage door as he saw the group approach.

The inn was located in the middle of the city, surrounded by buildings and streets. Although she wondered briefly where Chika's house might be from here, if Jessika tried to run, she knew she'd be lost and probably caught, as her dress and shoes would make running difficult; the guards would definitely catch her. Knowing that, she approached the carriage door, but her vision seemed to darken. The empty opening of the door looked like a portal to a cavern: a hollow, aching doom where she would fall and fall until she begged to hit the bottom just to stop the endless plummet.

Her feet faltered and almost tripped on the cobblestones. Her legs stiffened, trying to stop her progress. Her body knew this was just the entryway to

Attare and Vor

something far worse and was trying to stop her. A guard grabbed her elbow.

"You mustn't fall, Princess," he murmured.

She wanted to tell him the carriage would lead to the real fall. He tugged her forward even as her legs became more reluctant. The other guard grabbed her other arm and started urging her on as well. In moments, her resistance began giving them pause, making them actually have to pull to try to get her closer.

"Princess," Vor said from behind. "We must go. There is nothing in the carriage that will hurt you."

Jessika, however, couldn't stop herself from resisting. She dug her heels in, straining back against the pull of the guards, even as the effort made the unhealed parts of her back sparkle with pain.

"No," she panted. "I won't go."

"You will," Vor's voice ordered in her ear.

Now, she knew. She should have made her escape attempts sooner. She should have made them again and again until she died from the trying. If she entered that carriage, it would all be over. There would be no escape.

Even as her mistreated back screamed at her, she yanked her arm from one guard's grip faster than he could tighten up, but the second guard had an extra split-second to brace himself and clench down, and when she tried to jerk her second arm free, she nearly dislocated her own shoulder.

"Hold her," Vor commanded, and the first guard made a lunge.

Jessika sent her bent elbow back at him, connecting solidly with his chin: his combined forward motion and her backwards strike making the hit much more serious than it would have been if he'd been standing still. He stumbled and went to one knee on the cobblestones, clutching his jaw.

The other guard now held her arm with both hands in a bruising grip. Jessika swung herself around him like the moon around the Earth, putting him between her and Vor and the first guard. She tried again to twist her arm out of his grip, but it only hurt her further. In desperation, she set her legs and tried to pull away, inspiring him to pull back on her with equal strength.

Then, she released, letting the man add to her own momentum as she flung herself at him—and drove her knee right up between his legs with all of her push and his pull behind it. He was wearing a light set of leather armor, but not enough to keep a strike like that from hurting. His eyes crossed as he let out a groan and released her arm to clutch his crotch.

Jessika turned and bolted as fast as she could for the open gate to the inn's courtyard. Maybe she could find a place to hide. She had to try. She couldn't get in that carriage of doom.

Behind her, Vor shouted something, and there was suddenly the sensation of a hundred fishhooks catching in the muscles of Jessika's back. A hundred invisible fishing lines arrested her forward momentum. She lost her footing, tried to catch herself, but her feet went out from under her and she crashed forward, striking her knees hard enough on the stones to split the skin through her dress. She thought maybe she'd even split her kneecaps. Tears sprang to her eyes and she choked on a cry of pain.

Her hands came down much more slowly to the gritty road. Vision blurry, she stared at the ground until she saw Vor's grey-booted feet walk up beside her.

"My magic has been in your very flesh, Princess," Vor whispered, "and remains there. You allowed me to put it there without protest. You will not escape this way."

Horror chilled Jessika's breath.

"Guards," Vor's voice called out. "Put her in the carriage."

Trembling, Jessika didn't resist as the two guards—one walking with a tender gait, the other with a spreading bruise on his chin—grabbed her arms again and lifted her up, much less gently than before. The opening to the carriage drew near as they dragged her across the courtyard, her limp feet bumping across the cobblestones.

The stable boy watched, face pale, jaw dangling, as they dumped her onto one of the seats inside. Vor got in after her, and the boy closed the door with weak fingers. Jessika lifted her gaze to find his as the carriage began to move. His blue eyes stared at her out of a face gone shocked and bloodless.

Jessika didn't have the energy to give him any kind of expression in return. Vor pulled the curtains over the windows, and the cavernous carriage bore Jessika away.

Chapter 19
Returning Home

Neither of the women spoke as the carriage bumped its way along the streets towards the castle. Jessika stared fixedly at the woven patterns of the seat cushion across from her while her mind wandered through various emotions. Fear and anger were topmost. Her knees throbbed like a mad smithy was hitting them repeatedly with hammers. She felt a little blood trickling down her shins to stain her slippers, and tried to adjust her dress so it wouldn't soak through the skirt and show.

After an hour or so, she heard the driver call out to the horses to slow and stop. Vor straightened from her meditative slump and peaked out the curtains.

"We have arrived," the woman announced. "You will be escorted to your rooms now, Highness."

Jessika raised her eyes to Vor's in the dimness of the carriage. She didn't try to control her expression to show any emotion in particular. She was too frightened to snarl, and too hopeless to sneer, but she felt her jaw tense with slow-bubbling anger. Whatever she looked like, it was enough to make Vor's eyes widen slightly.

"Send someone to bandage my knees," Jessika ordered. "They're bloody from when you knocked me down."

"I can help to heal them—" Vor began.

"No," Jessika refused. "I'll not have any more of your magic touching my body. I will heal in the normal fashion. I want only assistance in cleaning and wrapping the wounds. See to it."

Vor blinked a few times, straightening her back, but she nodded. "Of course, Princess."

"Let's go."

Jessika stood, but the carriage door opened before she could touch it. A footman was there, folding down a step and extending his hand. Jessika took it, unsteady on her bruised legs, and descended to the pavement. No cobblestones here, the road before the side gate of the castle was closely fitted flagstone.

She held her head high, imperiously, keeping her face blank before the small group that was there to meet the carriage. There was an older woman in plain but finely made garments. Beside her, stood a tall middle-aged man in a tidy sort of unadorned suit. The two guards Jessika had struck were gone, replaced by two new guards in fancier uniforms. There was no sign of Altare.

Vor came out of the carriage behind her. "May I present our long lost Princess Jessika of Northborn," Vor murmured in a voice just loud enough to carry to the whole group.

The woman curtsied deeply. The tall man and the guards bowed.

"Please escort the princess to her rooms," Vor went on softly.

The guards didn't move, but the woman and man in plain clothes stepped up.

"At once, Mistress Vor. This way, please, Your Highness," the woman said, a hint of a friendly smile on her mouth. "I am Amlee, the castellan of the palace, and may I introduce Edgard, our eminently capable steward."

"I'm pleased to meet you," Jessika replied as they began to walk off, motioning for her to accompany them. She took a few steps and felt the scabs on her knees breaking open. With a wince, Jessika extended her arm out slightly from her body. "Your arm, please, good sir," she said to the man. "I am wearied from the long ride."

Where the impulse or words came from, Jessika wasn't quite sure, and she wasn't quite sure they were right, either, but the man responded immediately, stepping to her side and offering his arm for her to hold to. With her knees still screaming pain at her with every step, she found that she needed his support, and leaned rather more heavily on him than she wished to.

"Be at ease, Princess," the woman, Amlee, went on. "You will soon be resting in comfort. A bath is being drawn as we speak, and we are preparing a repast for you, which will be brought to your rooms."

As they reached the doorway Jessika glanced back, but Vor had already vanished somewhere on silent feet. The carriage was pulling away. The guards remained, looking big and intimidating, and Jessika had no thought of challenging them now. She could hardly walk, much less run. Her sense of impending doom had not subsided much, even after meeting such apparently pleasant and normal people as Amlee and Edgard, but another escape attempt would have to wait.

Her two guides led her into the castle she hadn't set foot in for well over a decade. Memories did not return immediately, but a sense of familiarity, that she'd been there before, crept over her. The sensation intensified as they moved deeper, through hallways, and past open doorways that gave tantalizing glimpses of rooms beyond.

The floors were all stone, often covered with woven rugs. Along the walls hung tapestries in some places, but Jessika didn't see any that she remembered from her childhood. Regularly spaced short pillars held candle-lanterns, but hardly any were lit, since all the doors were thrown open and the curtains pulled off the windows, so dim ambient light lit the way well enough. Interspersed with the pillars was the occasional bench or a small table with a dried flower arrangement, candleabra, or sculpture.

After a few turns, they reached the stairs. Jessika came to a sharp halt. Her knees throbbed and she could feel fresh blood inching down from the broken scabs. How was she going to climb flights of stairs? Well, she supposed, it wouldn't kill her. She'd just have to grit her teeth and tough it out; she'd forced her body through painful things before.

"Would you prefer to take the lift, Your Highness?" Amlee asked delicately.

"The lift?" she echoed weakly.

"It's just over here," Amlee continued.

The pair led Jessika to the left around the landing of the stairs, to a closed door that Edgard promptly opened. Inside was something that looked like a human-sized birdcage, or a prison cell. Amlee took Jessika's free arm as Edgard released her other.

"A moment, ladies," the man said in a kind, deep voice.

"Let's step inside, Your Highness," Amlee urged.

Jessika let herself be pulled inside, and Amlee shut the door, but it wasn't dark inside. From the roof hung a thumb-sized glowing crystal fragment.

"Our lord and his helpers make these magical charms that emit light," Amlee explained. "Of course we don't use them except in certain situations. We cannot be demanding all our lord's time in renewing them. In the enclosed lift, the charm is better than a lamp or candle, with the unsteady nature of the mechanism."

It appeared to be the same sort of light stone that Thornfire, Starbright, or Karo regularly made. Apparently, Altare and his apprentices could make them, as well, which wasn't surprising as it had always looked to Jessika like a simple spell.

"Is the lift magical, too?" Jessika asked.

"No, just mechanical," Amlee answered. "It's quite a feat of engineering. Right now, Edgard will be going to a large handle connected to some gears and pulleys in the basement. I'm afraid I can't explain exactly how it works, but it is such that one strong man can pull this lift and passengers or goods all the way up four floors. Shortly, we'll begin moving. You may want to brace yourself, Your Highness."

Jessika frowned at the floor. "I wish you would just call me Jessika."

There was a pause of silence from Amlee. "I'm afraid I can't do that, Princess," she said at last, and Jessika thought she noted a slight shading of sorrow in the woman's voice.

"I understand," she said.

A bell rang.

"Edgard will start pulling now, please hold on."

The lift shuddered and began inching upwards. Jessika took a light hold of the bars that formed the cage of the lift.

"It does not move very quickly. We'll be in here for a couple minutes," Amlee informed.

"I won't need to use this again," Jessika assured her. "Just, right now, I can't really walk well."

"You've had a long journey," Amlee soothed.

"No, I mean yes, I have, but."

Jessika plucked at the skirt of her dress. Before Amlee could stop her or exclaim that it wasn't proper to hike up one's skirts, Jessika pulled the fabric up to above her knees. Even in the dim light of the crystal, the damage was visible. Against Jessika's pale skin the blood tracks showed up black and the bruising a dark grey. She heard Amlee's breath catch.

"What happened?" she asked, voice carefully controlled.

"I," Jessika hesitated, "fell."

She supposed she shouldn't say she was trying to run away after Vor kidnapped her, and Vor used her magic to knock her down.

"Vor is aware. I asked her to send someone to help bandage me," Jessika concluded, dropping her skirts again.

Amlee held a bit tighter to her arm and gave her a small but true smile. "Lean on me as much as you wish, Princess. I've gotten old like old, dried meat gets old: tougher and stiffer the older I get."

"Thank you," Jessika whispered, feeling afraid to let herself trust, but also grateful.

They stood in silence until the lift reached the top. She supposed she could have said more, could have confided some of her situation to Amlee, or even asked for information on the climate of the castle, like how her father and Altare interacted and ruled. That notion made her think about her father for a few moments. He hadn't come to meet her. In her mind he was still nothing more than a fantasy; she couldn't yet believe that he actually still existed.

She tried to eye Amlee without showing that she was doing it. The older woman was an unknown entity. Jessika had no memory of her voice or face from her early childhood years spent in the castle. There was grey showing in Amlee's hair but she didn't look very elderly, no matter what she said about being old and stiff. She looked unbent and only lightly wrinkled. Ten years ago she would have been not much different, and approximately as old as Jessika's own parents, she guessed. Had she been working in the castle then, and Jessika had just never spent much time with her? Or had Altare and the other conquerors brought her with them? Or had she been hired out of the remaining populace after the takeover?

Jessika wasn't ready to ask, but the urge to confide swelled inside her.

At any rate, she didn't get the chance then. The lift swayed to a halt, and Amlee opened the door. They stepped out and a few moments later Edgard came striding up the stairs to the right with only the slightest sheen of sweat on his forehead.

"Thank you," Jessika told him.

He gave her a bow, offered her his arm again, and she accepted it.

"The lift is relatively new," Edgard told her as they moved down the hall. "I'm glad we are able to provide you with its use. If you require it at any time, simply send a maid or a page to get me and I shall be happy to assist."

"Your rooms are just here, Your Highness," Amlee said.

They stopped at an open door and Amlee took over from Edgard in holding Jessika's arm. The man took a step away and bowed again.

"I look forward to serving you, milady," he intoned. "Do not hesitate to call upon me at any hour."

"Thank you," Jessika told him again, "I won't—hesitate, that is."

He gave her a brief smile, turned about and paced off on some other duty. Amlee patted her hand.

"Men aren't allowed in a lady's chambers, of course," Amlee explained.

They stepped forward into the room and Jessika tried not to look too wide-eyed at the furnishings. For someone used to sleeping on a tanned fur sack stuffed with griffin down and sitting on whatever wooden chair Rikah could manage to craft, the suite of rooms was dizzying almost to the point of distress. It wasn't that it looked more homey or comfortable, but it was so finely detailed and designed.

Every piece of furniture was intricately carved and gilded gold or at the least polished to a high shine. The cushions were made of fabric far finer than the griffins could weave in patterned colors Jessika hadn't known there were dyes for. Fabric was expensive in the Aeries because it was so difficult to make—so leather and fur was used much more often—but here long swaths of it were hung over the windows from floor to ceiling. Even the rugs on the floor were colorful and thick, with intricate patterns or even images like tapestries, and Jessika wondered what they were made of.

"This is amazing," she murmured weakly.

"It is your birthright, Princess," Amlee murmured back, "returned to you at last."

The woman's voice was so warm, it sent Jessika into further states of confusion. Surely Altare was evil—he was so cruel she had no doubt of it—but Edgard and Amlee seemed so kind, and the castle was so well cared for, so lovely. She had to remind herself that Hawkjoy was a prisoner down on the lower levels, that Skire Germaine might even now be torturing her.

Jessika forced herself to look around, to try to imagine what this room must have looked like after the invasion. Had anyone died in this room? Had the drakes rampaged through here, destroying the furnishings, splattering human and griffin blood onto the walls and into the cushions? How much had the invaders been forced to replace? Had conquered citizens been forced to craft all this?

Jessika bit her lip, forehead creasing. What was she going to do about it? How could she figure out what was good and what was bad now?

"Would you like to sit, Your Highness?" Amlee asked, sounding concerned.

Jessika allowed her to lead her to some kind of wide sort of chair, almost large enough to be a bed, but with a back and one upholstered arm. Amlee remained standing, and gestured to another open door leading from the room.

"Your bedchamber is this way, and beyond it your bathing chambers," Amlee explained. "This is your sitting room. If you don't like the furnishings, they can be changed to whatever you wish."

Jessika felt a little sick, and swallowed to try to control her nausea.

Amlee hurried back to her side and knelt down on the floor. She took her unresisting hand.

"Princess, are you well?" the woman breathed. "Some water, or tea, wine? I'll have your meal sent up directly."

She made as if to go, but Jessika gripped her hand before she could, and Amlee remained where she was.

"Amlee, I don't understand any of this," she whispered.

"You've not been back," Amlee nodded hesitantly, "since the incident."

"Incident," Jessika uttered breathlessly.

"Where have you been, Highness?" the woman said, so softly Jessika could hardly hear her.

Jessika shook her head. "I'm afraid."

Amlee held her hand a bit tighter, and when Jessika turned to meet her gaze, the woman's eyes held something of comprehension, something of fear of her own, but also wariness.

"Patience," Amlee said. "You'll feel better after some rest and food."

She started to get up again but Jessika didn't let her go.

"Is it drugged?" she asked, voice as quiet as Amlee's had been.

Amlee looked surprised, but not shocked, and didn't reply immediately. "No, I don't think so," she said at last.

"Altare wants me," Jessika explained in a breath.

"Hush," Amlee gasped. "Don't say his name in this castle."

"He's the real ruler here." It was only partly a question.

She could hear Amlee's voice catch in distress. "It's—it's complex, Highness."

"No one can protect me from him." Again, she was hardly asking, yet with a fragment of hope that she cast to Amlee with her eyes.

The older woman seemed to choke a bit, swallow, and then composed her expression. "You are the king's daughter."

Jessika's jaw tensed. Amlee's words held a shading of uncertainty—not that she doubted Jessika was the king's daughter, but that it would protect her. Amlee went to stand up again, and this time Jessika let go of her hand so she could.

"I will return directly, Your Highness, with your repast. Will you be at ease and rest for these few minutes?"

Jessika felt her belly twitch with nerves. What if he came while Amlee was gone, while she was alone?

"Certainly," Jessika said, her mouth dry.

Amlee curtsied and left. Jessika stared around the room at the beautiful, hostile furnishings, and waited.

No one even so much as poked a toe into the room until Amlee returned with a pair of maidservants carrying a tray and a pitcher.

"Princess, would you prefer to dine where you sit, or at your table by the window?" Amlee asked.

Jessika looked over. The table was several steps away. Her knees had started repairing the scabs in the time she'd been sitting still. The thought of ripping them open again if she didn't have to decided for her.

"Here, if it's not too difficult," she said.

"Not difficult at all," Amlee assured her.

Clearly already knowing what to do, the servant carrying the pitcher set it down on the table and stepped out of the room, returning in only a couple moments with a wooden folding table. Jessika only recognized what it was because she'd eaten off of a similar one with Chika—and Koki. A soft tide of warmth filtered through her body and for a little while her knees didn't hurt so badly.

This folding table was ornately carved and polished, just like the furniture. The maid set it up in front of Jessika with efficient, practiced hands, and the other maid set the tray upon in. The first maid retrieved the pitcher while the second stepped back, and Amlee removed the cover from the tray, handing it off to the second maid.

A ceramic plate held a cooked slice of some kind of meat. It rested on a pile of cooked grain mixed with herbs and finely chopped vegetables. Another small plate held a roll of bread. There was a little bowl with butter in it. A second larger bowl contained colorful pieces of fruit. A set of silverware, a white cloth napkin, and a drinking glass accompanied the dishes.

Jessika's stomach, clearly having forgotten its nausea of a few minutes ago, rumbled. Amlee smiled and dismissed the girl holding the lid of the tray with a wave of her hand. The maid holding the pitcher poured faintly pink water into the glass.

"Why is the water pink?" Jessika asked with a nervous glance at Amlee.

"It is rose hip water," she explained. "I made it myself. It's one of my specialties for calming the stomach and refreshing the spirit."

She held out her hand to the remaining maidservant, and the girl passed the pitcher to her and exited. Amlee looked a little embarrassed.

"I have the feeling you might want to eat alone, or might feel uncomfortable with people standing all around you," she said. "It is a custom, however, that royalty have a servant in attendance to see to their every need."

"Ah, is that it," Jessika muttered. "Will you at least sit down with me?"

She gestured at the empty space beside her on the big chair. Amlee hesitated, but after a moment came over to perch on the edge.

"I guess I'll eat?" Jessika shrugged a little.

"Please go ahead."

She dug in, hoping she didn't look like a griffin tearing into an elk. Amlee refilled her glass for her when it got low, but except for that, the food was so good the Jessika almost forgot she was there. She still couldn't identify the meat or some of the vegetables, or the grain, but she was too shy to ask about them.

Once she'd finished, Amlee set the glass and pitcher back on the table, and lifed the empty tray.

"Would you like a second serving, Princess?" she asked.

"No, thank you, but maybe later."

"Whenever you like. I'll return shortly."

Amlee carried away the tray. One of the maidservants came back to retrieve the folding table, and by that time Amlee was back.

"Would you like to bathe now?"

Amlee had said the bath was being drawn, so Jessika figured the water would be getting cold. "I suppose so. I told Vor to send someone to help bandage my knees."

"I'll follow up at once, Your Highness."

Amlee ducked out again, leaving Jessika to again stare around the room. She wondered what she'd be doing, what was planned for her, how soon Altare would come for her, seize her, and take his revenge—or whatever else he had in mind for her. It made a chill run over her skin and then settle in her stomach, wriggling among the good food.

From her spot, she'd gotten plenty of time to visually examine the entire room by the time Amlee returned with another woman, no maid girl, who carried a satchel. Both paused to curtsy, although Amlee's was deeper.

"This is Mistress Jesine," Amlee introduced. "She is the midwife who serves the castle and wealthier citizens, and also helps with any minor illnesses or injuries."

Jesine was a bit taller than Amlee, wearing a solid black gown with painful tidiness. The lines of her face gave her a perpetual frown, although she didn't look so old that she should have had such deep wrinkles. Her brown hair was pulled back into a bun so tight, Jessika thought it should have pulled her face skin taut and smooth.

"Mistress Vor has filled me in on your situation and I am to assume the duty of seeing you well mended, Princess," Jesine said, voice flat.

"Let us move to the bathing chamber," Amlee suggested, going to take Jessika's hand and helping her up.

Jesine followed like an ominous shadow, and Jessika suddenly felt uncomfortable getting naked in front of the two women. Amlee, however, was apparently skilled at preserving modesty, and somehow managed to keep Jessika's most intimate areas obscured either with undergarments or towels through the whole procedure.

She got clean, and got her knees and the bloody parts of her back freshly bandaged. Amlee presented fresh clothing and with the help of the two women she dressed. Amlee carried away the blood-freckled garments, and Jesine stood and looked Jessika over with a sniff.

"So you are our lord's new acquisition," Jesine said, low voiced.

Jessika jerked like she'd been poked with a stick.

"He thinks you're the long-lost princess, does he? Is that tattoo faked?"

Jessika's voice caught for an instant, and then she managed to speak. "No, I've had it forever. I was the third child of the ruling couple before the invasion," she said, voice just as low.

"And you managed to escape the slaughter," Jesine went on, nearly sneering. "How lucky for you."

"I didn't mean to, I mean, I didn't want to die, but I was rescued. I couldn't have escaped on my own. I was just a few years old."

Jesine's expression became positively venomous. "Do you want to know how I escaped?"

That gave Jessika pause, and she tried to think of something diplomatic to say. "Whatever happened to you, it must have been horrible."

"I owe my survival to our lord," Jesine whispered. "I watched my father and brother cut down before my eyes. They were trying to protect us. My sister and I were hiding in a closet. The soldiers raped my mother until she was catatonic and then cut her throat, left her on the kitchen table to die. They set the house on fire after that, so my sister and I had to run out. More soldiers caught us in the street. They were about to give us the same as they'd given my mother, but then some riders arrived: the mages, on their way to the castle."

Jesine's face had gone from hateful to nearly blank.

"Our lord, who was only an apprentice then, commanded the soldiers to stop. He asked his master if he might have us, and his master agreed. There was a cart following, full of other young women. They added us to it, and brought us to the castle."

She paused, her eyes going down and out of focus for a moment. Then she looked back up, her chin higher.

"My mother had been a midwife, and she had been training me. I became the castle midwife. Our lord has been kind and generous. He is a good master." She said this last as if she'd been in an argument over the point and were asserting her position.

Footsteps in the sitting room forestalled any reply Jessika might have made; Amlee was returning. Jesine turned without another word and swept out of the room. The castellan looked only mildly surprised at her rapid exit.

"Are you well, Princess?" she asked softly.

Jessika wasn't sure how to answer.

"Was Jesine improper?" Amlee followed up with.

Jessika went to sit on the wide bench at the foot of the bed. "I think," she began, "she blames me for the invasion, for what happened to her when the enemy soldiers came?"

"Ah," Amlee looked distressed. "She told you of her history?"

"Some of it."

Amlee came and sat beside her on the bench. "War leaves behind many sad stories, but things are better now. The country is stable again."

"Do you think it will stay stable?" Jessika asked.

Amlee hesitated. "That is unknown."

Jessika impulsively took a gamble. "When can I see my father?"

Now Amlee withdrew even further. "I don't know. I believe our lord wishes to see you first."

"When can I see him, then?"

Amlee looked down at her folded hands. "He has kept to himself these past weeks. I'm afraid I can't predict—"

"I'm the princess," Jessika interrupted. "Or am I a prisoner?"

Now she looked stricken.

"Who is the ruler of Northborn, my father or Altare?"

Amlee gave a brief gasp at the name, and stood up. "I cannot answer these questions for you, Your Highness."

"Who can? When will someone tell me what's going on?" Jessika demanded.

"I'm sure our lord will make it a priority to see you," Amlee said. "Is there anything else you need at this time, Princess?"

Amlee was clearly making her escape.

"No," Jessika subsided.

"Should you have need, pull the cord there, and someone will come at once. Good day to you, Your Highness."

Amlee fled.

Jessika growled to herself. Fine, then. She was going to explore the castle, at least the current floor; her knees were well bandaged but she didn't feel up to stairs just yet. It was better than just sitting in her room, and if she was going to make an escape attempt, knowing the floor plan could be essential.

From her door, she headed down the hallway, encountering open doorways at regular intervals that shortened as she went further from the main stairway: the rooms shrinking in size. They were all empty suites and then just single bedrooms, until she encountered what she assumed from the smell was a latrine. After that, the rooms increased in size again, and then she came upon a set of double doors that were thrown wide open into a cavernous room with enormous floor to ceiling windows.

Jessika stepped in and looked around at walls completely covered with shelves of books and rows of scrolls, except for where the windows were. The center of the room was occupied by a dozen different chairs and couches and a half dozen tables ranging in size from tiny ones just a few handspans across to big ones longer and wider than Jessika was tall. Lanterns stood on every table and were mounted between the windows.

"This is a library," she breathed.

The griffins had libraries, too, and some of their books were quite entertaining or informative, but bookmaking was not a common trade and most griffins were more or less indifferent to books unless they needed some information they could get nowhere else. Only a few seemed to be born with a true hunger for reading and writing. Those invariably became historians and recorders. A few even wrote creative fictional tales.

Jessika had read and re-read every book South-scree Aerie had. Although griffins were naturally sleepy in winter, when the Aerie was buried by a dozen feet of snow, and spent a lot of time in slumber, the human citizens of South-scree had found they had tolerance for only so much sleep. Jessika spent a lot of winter reading, and had even tried penning some stories of her own. One winter she'd tried to write down everything she remembered of her years before the invasion.

This library was immense: far greater than South-scree's. She went at once to the nearest shelf and pulled down a book at random. It was something to do with mining. She put it back, walked along, and looked at another. It seemed to be a journal of someone's life, a memoir. She didn't recognize the name at the front.

Time passed without her knowing as she continued glancing into books at random, reading a few pages here, and a few there. Some books were even in a different language she couldn't read. She only looked up when a maidservant came into the room to light the lanterns.

The young woman seemed a little startled to see her, and curtsied without upsetting the pitcher of oil or small satchel she carried. Jessika nodded back, and the maid went to her task, filling the wells of all the lanterns, trimming the wicks, and lighting a portion of the lamps. Before she finished she turned back to Jessika.

"Your pardon, Highness, will this be enough light for you, or shall I light the rest of the lamps?" she asked.

"This is fine," Jessika replied. "May I take some books out of the library to my rooms?"

"Yes, Highness. A record is kept here of any books borrowed, in case they are sought by another." The servant touched a book left open on a small table near the doors.

"Excellent, I will write down what I borrow. Thank you."

She curtsied again and was about to turn to go, when Amlee stuck her head into the room. Her worried expression blinked into a smile.

"There you are, Princess. On your way, Kari."

The maid bobbed another curtsy and exited. "Yes, Mistress."

"Dinner will be served in the small dining room," Amlee announced. "Mistress Vor has invited you to join her."

"Who else will be there?"

"Just the two of you, and the servers, to my knowledge, Princess."

Great. Having to eat while Vor sniped at her sounded wonderful for the digestion.

"When will that be?"

"In just a few minutes, Your Highness."

"Very well, but I'm going to borrow a couple books first."

Jessika went back to the sections she'd identified as being about history and geography. It seemed like, in this situation, having more knowledge about her land would be useful. She pulled down two books she'd left sticking partly out as a reminder that she might want to read more in them. At the open book by the door she stopped to write her name and the titles. She had to pause to examine the writing instrument.

In the Aeries there was an abundance of quill pens—made from molted griffin feathers. This one however had a metal tip, which Jessika wasn't used to, and she blotted the page trying to write the first letter. Amlee politely ignored the sloppy writing, and escorted her swiftly to her room, passing the stairs and lift on the way, at which point Jessika realized the hallways formed a long rectangle with the library at one end and the latrine and nearby tiny rooms at the other.

Jessika dropped off her books for later and followed Amlee back to the stairs.

"Would you like to use the lift again, Princess?"

"I think I can handle stairs going down, but maybe not up."

With the help of the handrail, Jessika made her wincing way down and Amlee continued on, bringing her to a long room with a table of dark grey wood down the center. Several candelabras lit the room brightly. Vor was waiting at the far end. The table was set for three, and Jessika paused.

"Welcome, Princess," Vor called to her. "Do come have a seat."

As two places were set together on one side, and just one on the other, Jessika went down to the single place setting, and took a seat. Vor sat across from her.

"Who else is coming?" Jessika asked.

"She'll be here shortly. I trust you find your accommodations acceptable? Far finer than what you are used to, I expect."

Jessika narrowed her eyes. Her room in South-scree was a cave carved out under the mountainside, which might have sounded primitive to these people who lived in stone and wood houses, but it made Jessika feel cozy and secure. The floor was planed smooth and carpeted with thick furs that kept any chill away. Small holes through the walls kept air flowing and fresh. She had a wooden desk and chair, a set of shelves and baskets for storage, and a lamp. Her bed was made of a leather mattress stuffed with griffin down on top of a thick mat of reeds and rushes. She had more cushions and pillows of leather or fur, all stuffed with down. More furs served as blankets. She'd never encountered a softer, warmer bed.

Compared to her Aerie home, the rooms here seemed stiff and unwelcoming.

"You don't know what I'm used to," was all she said.

Before Vor could reply, the other diner they were waiting for walked into the room. Jessika saw her and stared for a moment, shocked.

It was Skire Germaine.

The Skire stopped, too, staring back, obviously recognizing her, even in completely different garments.

Jessika didn't have her truncheons; bare hands would have to do.

She lunged to her feet, kicking away the chair with a clatter and sped down the length of the table, hands balled into fists. A blanch of fear lit up the Skire's face. Jessika drew one arm back as she reached out with the other to grab the front of the Skire's vest. With a snarl of rage she smashed her fist towards the vile woman's face—and sharp pains like fishhooks in her back jerked her away and off her feet.

Jessika's lower back slammed into the table edge and she collapsed to the floor as Vor released her. Coughing, she struggled up to her hands and knees. Her back throbbed; she'd hit the table right where the worst of the lacerations to her back were still unhealed.

"There will be no such crude behavior here, in this palace," Vor said evenly, as though she hadn't just yanked Jessika off her feet with her magic—again.

"Skire, please come have a seat. I'm sure our princess can behave herself; she just had a momentary lapse. She has had a less than ideal upbringing, and can't be blamed for not knowing how to behave sometimes. Princess, this is Skire Germaine. She is an honorable advisor to be treated with respect."

Jessika reached up to the table to try to get to her feet. There were no servants in the room, so no one else had seen either her attempted attack on the Skire or Vor's retaliation. She wondered what would have happened if there had been witnesses. She ignored Vor's slurs to focus on the Skire.

"You," Jessika growled. "You have Hawkjoy. Take me to her and let us go."

Vor didn't even glance in the Skire's direction.

"My studies are no concern of yours," the Skire said, still looking shaken. "Princesses should not concern themselves with such academic matters."

"You have my sister," Jessika shouted.

"Your sister is in her tomb," Vor said. "I was young, but old enough to remember watching her and the rest of your famiy be put there."

Jessika ignored her again. "I'm not going to sit here and pretend nothing's wrong while you have Hawkjoy trapped down in your nasty room. Take me down there right now."

The Skire raised her eyebrows. "I'll do nothing of the sort. She's a useful subject. I still have more to learn from her. She's just an animal, and I see to it that none of my subjects suffer. Your excessive attachment is ridiculous. I offered you monetary compensation and you refused."

Jessika stalked down the other side of the table towards the Skire, whose face whitened again.

"Princess," Vor said warningly.

Jessika continued to ignore her, and reached to grab the Skire's shoulder. Sharp pain jerked Jessika back a couple feet, but didn't slam her into anything this time.

"How long can you keep that up?" Jessika challenged, wincing.

Vor shot to her feet. "I think this dinner was premature. The princess needs more time to rest after her trying journey."

Jessika snarled silently and made another grab for the Skire, who jerked away and stumbled to stand behind Vor. Suddenly, paralyzing pain shot from Jessika's back down through her legs, pinning her where she stood.

"Edgard," Vor called out.

After a moment, the steward entered from one of the doors at the back of the room, moving as though he'd hurried there from whatever business he'd been attending to. His face immediately reflected concern.

"Our princess is wearied from this tumultuous day. Please have her meal taken to her room, and escort her there as well," Vor instructed.

Edgard flashed a conflicted look at Jessika, but bowed. "Yes, Mistress."

Jessika's face contorted in a combination of rage and grief, and Edgard took her arm with true distress.

"This isn't over," Jessika gritted out.

The pain burst through her body and she almost fell, but she took some small gratification from the sweat beading on Vor's forehead, and the look of effort on her face. It seemed to be taking all Vor's magical strength to keep Jessika immobilized.

"Skire, perhaps you should go as well," Vor said.

"Yes, of course." The Skire exited around the far side of the table and made her escape.

"Your dinner will be sent to you. Please rest and feel better. Good night, Princess," Vor said, and with a sharp turn strode out of the room.

"This way, Your Highness," Edgard urged. "The lift will be made ready for you."

Jessika could barely walk. It seemed Vor was releasing her only slowly, or perhaps she was trying to keep her paralyzed but the spell weakened naturally the further Vor went from her. Once they reached the hallway, there was no telling which direction the Skire had gone. Amlee appeared as if conjured and took her other arm. Jessika didn't miss the complex look the pair shared.

Once in the lift with Amlee, the pain faded further, but left her body aching. She had to lean on Amlee even more than earlier. The woman didn't speak, and Jessika had the sense that she didn't want to get involved any further with whatever was going on between Jessika and Vor, even though it distressed her. Jessika found she couldn't blame her.

Dinner was waiting in her room, but Jessika could hardly eat. Her fear and loneliness for her Hawk family and Starbright and Thornfire and the others hit her harder than it yet had since she'd been kidnapped. Soon enough she was fighting against crying into her soup, and her hand shook so much she could barely hold her spoon. Still, she finished as much as she could, knowing she would need her strength, and then pushed away from the table.

Amlee had stood there the entire time. "Are you well, Princess?"

"Apparently not," she growled, and then regretted it. Amlee had only yet been kind to her. "Sorry. That was rude of me. I don't want to be here. I want to go home. I have," she debated how much to say. "I have enmity with Vor and Skire Germaine, and Altare for that matter."

"I expect the situation is complex, too complex for a humble housekeeper."

So that was Amlee's way of saying she didn't want to be involved. Jessika couldn't blame her; she had no idea how much Amlee stood to lose if she got involved in anything troublesome. "I understand. It is complex."

A measure of tension seemed to drain from the woman. "May I get you anything else, Princess? Would you like another bath, or your bandages changed?"

"Can you help me out of these clothes?" Jessika asked shyly. "I'm not used to them. I don't think I can get all the buttons and ties undone by myself."

Amlee gave her a little smile. "Princess, no lady of rank can get in and out of her formal gowns by herself. Come with me and I'll help you."

Amlee helped her out of the encumbering garments and showed her a selection of nightgowns.

"Are there easier clothes I can handle myself?" Jessika asked as she wriggled into her chosen sleeping shift.

"I can see if I can get you some," Amlee said, though she sounded doubtful.

"And, what can I do during the day?"

"Do?" Amlee echoed.

"Am I supposed to just sit up here and wait for Altare to come find me?"

Amlee wrung her fingers. "I'm afraid I don't have any tasks suited to a princess."

"Where I lived before, I helped out with all kinds of chores. No one treated me as a princess. I'm happy to read in the library, but if there's anything else, it would be nice to have some variety, until," she made a helpless gesture, "whatever happens."

"We haven't had a ruling lady here for so long," Amlee mused, "but surely there are things they would occupy themselves with. I will think on it, and tell you tomorrow."

"Alright," Jessika agreed. "Thank you for all your help today."

"Of course, Princess. It is a pleasure serving you."

Her expression and tone made Jessika think she was sincere, even though it could have been a rote phrase.

"Good night, Amlee."

"Sleep well, Your Highness."

Amlee left, shutting the door of the suite behind her. Jessika went and checked but there was no lock on it, either inside or out. She fetched her two books, turned out the lanterns in the sitting room and retreated to the warm puddle of light from the lamp beside her bed. There she cuddled up on the mattress that wasn't quite as comfy as her own bed back home, and tried to read. Her thoughts kept spinning and she couldn't focus, rereading sentences over and over, but eventually fatigue took over even her anger and grief and muffled her mind. She managed to turn out the lantern before she fell asleep.

Chapter 20
To Rescue Hawkjoy

Jessika woke with a plan in mind the next morning, as though it had hatched all on its own while she slept. She wasn't going to sit and wait for Altare to show up. She'd found the Skire's laboratory from below, and seen the stairs down to it; she would go find it from above, free Hawkjoy, and escape with her.

It was only just after dawn, but she got up, washed, and threw open the wardrobe doors to face the fluffy, shiny garments as though they were an enemy to be conquered. She couldn't run around naked. The clothes she'd bought back in the trade city were long gone, and mostly ruined besides—wherever they were. As she was flipping through the hanging gowns, she heard the main door to her suite open and soft footsteps approach.

"Hello," she called out, to avoid surprising whoever it was.

"Oh, good morning," called a female voice.

A maidservant pushed open the door to the bedroom. Jessika recognized her as the young woman who had been tending the lamps in the library.

"Good morning," Jessika greeted her. "I remember you. Kari?"

"Yes, Princess."

She made a curtsy without using her hands, which were full of cloth. "Mistress Amlee asked that I attend you, and bring you these."

"Easier clothes?" Jessika asked eagerly.

"Yes, Princess. Mistress Amlee had them removed from storage last night and aired. Some may be suitable for Your Highness."

"Thank you," Jessika said, as Kari went and laid her burden on the foot of the bed.

There were several dresses—dresses still, but at least they seemed to be made from far fewer layers, and of sturdier cloth.

"These are garments royal ladies once used for travel, when there were fewer people to impress, so they are more practical," Kari explained.

"Where did they come from?" Jessika asked, suddenly feeling a chill.

"They were in storage here in the palace."

"From how long ago?" she pressed.

Kari bobbed her head in a sort of bow. "I'm afraid I do not know, Your Highness. I can convey your enquiry to Mistress Amlee, if you'd like."

Jessika reached out a hand to touch the nearest dress. "I was wondering if they were my mother's," she confessed.

Some color ran out of Kari's face. "I'm sorry. I do not know."

"Don't worry about it."

She made the little bow-bob again.

"Help me try this one on."

As though grateful to be commanded instead of questioned, Kari hurried to obey, pointing out the much fewer buttons and ties. It meant the dress wasn't quite as perfectly formfitting, but Jessika didn't care. It was also a few inches shorter, so it didn't drag on the ground like the others had, leaving her free to step forward without fearing she was about to step on the hem, trip, and plant her face into the floor.

"Thank you, Kari. This is much better," Jessika told her once she had it on.

"I am pleased to hear you like it, Princess. Shall I arrange your hair? Your breakfast will be here momentarily."

"No, thank you, but breakfast sounds great," Jessika replied.

"I will hurry it along, if I am dismissed?"

"Yes, you can go," she nodded, feeling awkward at being so deferred to.

Kari left.

Jessika brushed out her hair and put it up in a tail, relieved her back had healed enough to allow it. By then, the door was opening again and the scent of a hot breakfast drew her to the sitting room.

"Your meal, Princess," Kari said.

Jessika sat down to eat with a murmur of thanks. Kari hovered behind her, but the other servant departed. Jessika ate quickly: mind too occupied by plans to linger. As soon as she was done, she left Kari to clean up and headed downstairs. Her knees felt much better, making the stairs less of a challenge, and she promptly set about exploring the first floor and looking for more stairs down.

She first discovered three different sitting rooms: one in pastel colors with soft fabrics on the furniture and pastoral landscape paintings on the walls, another with everything upholstered in leather with the heads of animals mounted on the walls, and a third with neutral fabrics and heavy wooden tables. They were located near the front of the building, under the library, and she'd passed them on her way in the previous day. None had a staircase leading down.

Along one side, opposite from where her room was, she discovered a long empty hall. There were benches along the long walls, under broad tapestries. At the far end was a carved wooden throne, elevated by three steps up a dais. On either side of it and slightly back were pairs of stools. Behind the dais were heavy curtains stretching from floor to ceiling. Otherwise the room stood empty and cold. Along one long wall were windows, but the sun wasn't hitting them at this time of day so there was no dispelling of the gloom via light. With a shiver, Jessika left and continued her exploration.

Along the opposite side of the square building, under where Jessika's room was, there were four different rooms for dining: one enormous room that could have held a dozen big tables but currently only hosted one, the smaller dining room from the previous night, and two modest rooms with just a single round table in each that would have sat only five or six people.

Jessika paused in one of the tiny rooms. Both had an air of disuse. The tables were stripped of any covering or place settings and the chairs had apparently been removed for use elsewhere. There was no décor and the curtains were even drawn. Yet, morning light streamed in through the thin drapes, and Jessika went and threw them open. The light splashed a warm honey color over the floor and table.

Jessika went and put her hands in the pool of light on the tabletop and closed her eyes. She thought she remembered this room. She thought she'd sat at this table—or one like it—and had breakfast with her mother, father, and siblings. There was even a vague teasing sensation that her grandparents might have joined her. She couldn't remember their faces or voices, yet she had a sense that they'd been with her and shown her their affection.

There were things to do. Hawkjoy needed rescuing. Jessika took herself away from the breakfast nook and continued her search. The kitchens weren't far away. There were a handful of servants working in them, all of whom were surprised to see her, and Kari rushed up.

"Princess, are you still hungry? What would you like? If you'd pulled the cord in you room, we would have come to you at once."

"No, I'm just exploring," Jessika told her, trying for a smile.

Before Kari could come up with an appropriate response, a tall, thin man pushed forward. He was balding, with short black hair and dark skin the color of orange amber. His long hands and arms had several old burn marks.

"Marklin, the head cook," he introduced himself with a smile that hid his black eyes in wrinkled cheeks. Rather than a bow, he held both hands out. Jessika extended a hand in return and he shook hers with both of his.

"So very pleased to meet you, Princess," he went on. "I wasn't here for the invasion: came after, from Weldom. I'm the best cook you will ever meet."

His warm voice was sincere and straightforward, as though he simply stated fact, not boasting. Jessika wasn't sure how to respond at first.

"Then you must be the one responsible for the delicious food I've been enjoying since I came here," she managed, finishing with a grin.

It was apparently the right thing to say. Cook Marklin's face lit up with a warm blush, his eyes vanishing entirely behind cheeks and furry black brows, showing a generous smile.

"With the help of others," he said. "No one person could accomplish all we do here. You shall continue to enjoy your every meal," he assured her. "Is there anything in particular you'd like to request?"

"I shall think on it," she promised him.

"See that you do," he nodded, still smiling.

Jessika crossed through the kitchen while the servants stared, not obstructing her, and looked outside. The kitchen had two open exits to a wide courtyard with overflowing gardens bisected by a stone path broad enough for a cart, and a well surrounded by basins and clotheslines where two women were hanging up damp white linens. Two other open interior doors in the kitchen showed a pantry and a storage room beyond.

Outside in the courtyard, the stone path turned and ran out of sight through an open archway. There was another door across the far side of the courtyard, beyond the washerwomen and into what looked like another wing of the palace, and a wooden trapdoor angled against the base of one wall to her right.

Jessika glanced over her shoulder to see that Kari had followed her to the door.

"Where do those lead?" she asked, pointing to the two doors.

"The cellar stores wood and coal and root vegetables," the young woman answered readily. "Across the way is the servants quarters, where most of us live."

"Thank you," Jessika murmured, wondering how nosey she should be about stairways going down, or other exits. "So you have to cross the court-yard to work every day, even in bad weather?"

"That's right, but it's little hardship, really. The kitchen is always warm and we dry out quickly."

Jessika looked above and beyond the servants' quarters, which looked like they were only two storeys high. There was another structure in back of them, much taller, with numerous large doors leading out onto balconies. All the doors were shut.

Jessika swallowed, realizing what the building must be, but she asked anyway.

"And what is that tall structure behind them?"

Kari seemed to be swallowing something, too. "That's not in use. The entrances are all closed up. It's structurally unsound. There are always rumors it's going to be torn down, but maybe that's more trouble than it's worth. There's nothing valuable around it that it would crush if it crumbles."

Jessika nodded, but she knew what it was. That was where Northnest's griffin Feathyrs had lived, where Hawkwind had been born and lived, before the invasion.

"Thanks," she said.

"You really lived here," Kari whispered, "before the incident?"

"Yes."

Jessika frowned, trying to figure out what sort of relationship the servants had with Altare. They obviously respected him, and feared him a bit, but it didn't seem like he ruled them with terror or threats. He wasn't trying to keep Jessika isolated from them by tossing her in a cell, or even locking her in her rooms. That freedom was unsettling, and she wondered if that was Altare's objective, to keep her guessing, or maybe even to get her relaxed.

"I'm from the countryside," Kari said. "But I have too many siblings, and my dad died in the fighting. I send my wages from here back to my mom."

"Do you like working here?"

Kari shrugged. "Mostly. It can be a lot of work, but Mistress Amlee and Cook Marklin are both fair in giving out duties. I'm honored that Mistress

Amlee thinks highly enough of me that she asked me to serve you, Princess. My mother will be proud of me, too."

Jessika stifled a wince. "I'm not really that special. I was just born this way, and I haven't been here for a long time, doing my job as princess."

"But you're here now to do your job. You'll be the queen someday," Kari said with certainty.

Another wince threatened and Jessika shoved it down. She definitely wasn't intending to stay, at least not yet. She had to get Hawkjoy and get out. She didn't know what would happen after that.

"Do you know any other ways down or up? I want to explore everything and see what I remember," she told Kari.

"I think," she began, "there used to be more ways around, but old door-ways have been blocked up. At least, it looks that way." Hesitantly, she pointed to the old Feathyr barracks. "Were you thinking of trying to get in there?"

"Not particularly, but maybe. Are there cellars, too?"

"Other than our root cellar? Steward Edgard is in charge of the wine cellar, but only he and a few chosen pages are allowed to go in there. There's a trapdoor down into it from the pantry. Other than that," she rubbed her arms with her palms, "I've never seen any others."

But then the young woman caught Jessika's eyes and gave a short, quick nod.

Jessika felt her brows lift, and then forced them back to normal. "I see." She altered the subject. "I haven't encountered my father's rooms yet. Where does the king live?"

Kari seemed relieved to be on a new topic. "This is the public wing of the palace. It's a little odd you have been roomed here, but there must be a good reason. Most of those who live here as their home—and aren't servants—are in the private wing. Perhaps your permanent rooms aren't ready for you yet."

"That seems likely," Jessika said to get past the oddity. "Will you take me to the private wing?"

Kari glanced over towards where the other kitchen servants were paying avid attention while pretending to be busy with cooking and washing.

"Go on then, Miss Kari," Marklin made a shooing gesture. "See to whatever the princess needs."

Kari curtsied at once. "This way, Your Highness, if you don't mind a short walk?"

"I'd love to get some air," Jessika assured her. "Lead the way."

They walked down the wide path through the kitchen gardens, and Jessika spotted a few plants she knew but most she didn't. They passed out through the arch and turned left. Jessika recognized the courtyard where she had arrived in the carriage, but they passed that, approaching another wide path through another archway, this one with massively thick wooden double doors, which were currently wide open.

It didn't seem to be much shorter than if they'd gone back through the rooms and hallways of the public wing and exited through the courtyard door, but the air was fresher and the light brighter. Kari paused before the heavy wooden doors and pointed away from the palace.

"Those are the inner walls," she explained, "and the entrance through which all traffic to the palace must come. It is guarded day and night."

Jessika saw two guardposts up on the wall, above the square doorway wide enough for two large wagons to pass each other. Human guards manned them, and a pair more guards stood by the opening. From her position inside the walls she could see wood doors wrapped with iron, as thick as her body, standing wide open.

"There are two portcullis inside, one closer to us, and one at the very front, and murder holes in the ceiling," Kari whispered. "There are more doors on the front which aren't as heavy as the inner ones. They get closed at night, but they have a man door in them in case a few people need to get through. You have to have permission to leave the grounds of the castle—at least, the servants do."

Jessika just nodded.

"The private wing is this way," she gestured. "I'm not normally assigned there, but I can show you around."

They left the arrival courtyard and went through the archway onto the path. Jessika's nose was assaulted with the scent of blooming flowers; both sides of the path were devoted to pleasure gardens. Narrow gravel or stone walking paths wound away from the main path among small trees, shrubs, and low flower beds. Back among them, Jessika spotted gazebos covered with climbing vines, benches, tall but unlit lamp posts, and from some distant cor-

Edgard,
Amlee, and
Kari

ner came the music of running water. Birds flickered among the greenery, and two gardeners went about their duties, weeding and pruning.

"This is beautiful," Jessika said.

Kari smiled. "I will convey your compliment to the gardeners. They will be happy to hear their work is appreciated. The main door is this way, Princess."

Jessika followed her down the path until they reached a tall door of dark wood, studded with silver and highly polished. It was shut. She paused as she realized that Altare might not want her snooping around where he presumably lived. That didn't mean she wouldn't go right on and snoop, but putting herself at risk was one thing.

She looked at Kari, who was waiting patiently. Putting Kari, who was only trying to do her duty and send money back to her overburdened mother, at risk was something else. Jessika dredged up a smile that she hoped looked natural.

"Thank you for bringing me here Kari, but now I'd like to be alone to see if I can rediscover any memories from my childhood," she said.

Kari curtsied. "Of course, Your Highness. If there is any other way we can serve you, please don't hesitate."

"I won't, and I won't keep you from your other duties any longer."

Kari curtsied again. "I'm glad I was able to help."

She turned and went back along the path toward the arrival courtyard. Jessika took the handle of the door and pulled it open.

The door hinges rumbled slightly but didn't squeak. Jessika stepped through and closed it behind her. The hallway she stood in was dim, paneled with dark wood. The flooring here was of thick carpet, much softer and richer than in the public wing. A few open doorways along the hall let in only slight light that fell across the floor in pale rectangles, hinting at red and brown patterns in the carpet. Silver lamps mounted to the walls were all dark. It was so silent once the door was shut that it felt like no one lived there.

Trying not to make any noise, Jessika stepped slowly along the hallway. Her feet made hardly any sound. She noticed ornately framed paintings on the walls, separated by drapes of fabric, and paused at the first one. The hall was so dim it was difficult to make out any detail, but it was a painting of the chest and face of a man in rich robes. The next painting was similar, only of a different man.

Jessika peered into the first open doorway she came to and saw a pair of large wardrobes on each side, with a bench under a shuttered window at the back. Across from it was some sort of workroom that looked like it was in regular use, with a broad desk bearing a neat stack of papers and a couple bound books, several cabinets, a wide padded bench, and a cold brazier in the center of the room. The next room had a table and chairs, with cabinets and shelves on the walls; it looked like a small dining room.

The door across from that one was shut. Jessika stood before it, listening, but heard nothing, and no light seeped through the gaps around it. She put hand to handle, and turned it, but it was locked. Wishing for Koki's lockpicks, she had to leave it.

The hall ended just ahead in a central room that held the staircase, much like the public wing, only this staircase was actually smaller. Jessika figured it was because there was no one to impress here, only the royal family and other persons concerned with governing, no visiting dignitaries. On either side of the staircase were small tables with dried flower arrangements in pretty vases and a couple deeply upholstered chairs.

Jessika paused to look up, wondering if her father really did live here. What she'd seen so far gave little impression that anyone resided here, except for the one workroom. One tug inside her urged her to go up the stairs and look for his rooms, but a stronger tug pulled her to Hawkjoy. Her father—if it was he—was seemingly safe and sound, but Hawkjoy was in danger of her life, likewise the unborn life inside her. Her father would have to wait.

She turned to investigate the other rooms on the floor to the left and right of the staircase. Two rooms appeared to be unused sitting rooms of one sort or another, with dead fireplaces and furniture covered in sheets to keep the dust off, all with shutters tightly closed. Beyond them lay a larger room with two hanging chandeliers and hardwood floors. The outside wall had double doors twice Jessika's height and four or five times her armspan, but they were shut tight. She wondered if they let out onto the garden. There was also a massive fireplace at one end of the room, but no furniture except for something large and boxy at the opposite end, covered with another sheet. Jessika went to investigate, pulling up one corner of the sheet. She had to stare at it for a moment, letting old memories congeal.

"This is a piano," she breathed. "It makes music. My mother played it, and my grandfather, too." She looked out at the empty room. "I danced, with my father."

Jessika let the sheet fall back into place and hurried from the ballroom on silent feet, but near the door she slowed to a halt. The shutters here were shut, too, but from this angle just enough light fell on a section of floor for her to notice something. There was a discolored section, darker than the rest.

She crouched down and touched it. The wood was smooth but only because a thick coat of lacquer had been put on it. Under it were scratches, scuffs, and even gouges, and now that she was looking for it, she saw more darkened spots scattered across the floor. There were also some deep grooves crossing the floor, but she couldn't think why they were there. Perhaps the floor had been installed in sections.

Jessika pulled her hand back, wondering if the stains were from blood, from the invasion, and the workmen had been unable to remove them completely. It seemed like they'd tried to repair the scarring of the wood, but if blood had soaked in deeply, it wouldn't have come off. Maybe the grooves were just noticeable because blood had run into them and been too difficult to remove, leaving them darker.

Jessika went to the next room, trying not to feel uneasy. It didn't have to be blood; it could have been from any number of other things, but all that damage to the floor—no dance was that vigorous; it must have come from the invasion. There must have been a lot of fighting in that room. Then she thought about her father living in the home where his parents, wife, and children had been killed, and where their killers now shared living space. It made her belly burn.

She'd reached the back of the building, opposite the entryway. There she slid open a door to the scents of soap and fresh towels: the bathing room. Two round copper tubs, one large and one smaller, dominated the room on an elevated platform. There were curtains hung on circular rods that could surround the tubs, but were currently pulled back. Racks held towels and robes, and shelves held bottles and baskets of what Jessika assumed would be soaps, lotions, and other unguents. There were benches and stools and plentiful cushions scattered around, and a large sort of desk holding more bottles and jars with a huge mirror on the wall behind it.

Griffins didn't have water-bathing facilities; the pool Jessika and the other humans used had been created specifically for them, but it was primitive—although charming and lovingly crafted by Starbright—compared to this. The royal family would have bathed here.

Jessika left, and went on to the next room, turning back towards the entrance. The next door was shut but she tried the handle, and it opened. Her breath caught. It opened on a landing of stairs that went downward. Light filtered up from below as though there were a lantern a little ways down. This was it. It had to be.

Heart pounding, she stood there for a few moments, thinking ahead, wondering what she would do when she found Hawkjoy. The griffin wouldn't be able to fit up these stairs; they were very much people-sized. She would have to find another way out, possibly the way they came in, but didn't someone—maybe Cray—say that Altare would be fortifying those tunnels now that he knew people were poking around down there?

A door opened upstairs and Jessika jumped.

Footsteps sounded, coming down the stairs from above. Jittery with adrenaline, Jessika shut the door as silently as she could and dashed back to the bathing room, her feet hardly making any sound on the thick carpet. Whoever it was, she hoped they weren't coming for a bath.

Jessika slipped into the big room and looked around for a hiding spot. She could hop into one of the tubs, but the angled rack against the wall holding towels and robes had a gap behind it. She ran to it and wiggled in among the hanging cloth. Then she used her hands to try to restore the towels to stillness so they wouldn't sway and betray her presence.

She heard the footsteps reach the bottom of the stairs and go silent on the carpet, just like hers had been. There was no telling where the person was going until some other sound revealed it. That could mean Jessika would be hiding a long time, if she didn't hear anything else.

In the dim room, it would be hard for someone to spot her behind the rack, she hoped, and by adjusting her position slightly she was able to peek out through a crack between two towels and see a narrow slice of the doorway in. A minute passed but it felt like longer, every heartbeat thudding inside her chest.

Then, there was movement. Slowly, methodically, Vor stepped into the doorway and turned her head, almost casually, to look into the bathing room. She was still wearing her gray suit of clothes, or perhaps a different but identically cut gray suit. Her face was blank, almost disinterested, but Jessika had the sudden alarming fear that Vor could sense her because of the magic in her back.

Vor stood there, perfectly still, and Jessika sweated with the thought that Vor knew she was there, and just wanted to scare her, intimidate her, and thereby exert her power over her. Yet, Vor said nothing, and gave no indication that she was anything other than lost in thought for a moment. Seconds stretched out as Jessika tried to keep her breathing silent and calm her pulse.

Finally, Vor continued her slow and steady steps. A moment later Jessika heard a door open, probably the door to the stairs she'd found. The door shut audibly, but Jessika didn't move, afraid that it was a ploy to flush her out, that Vor hadn't actually gone through the door but was waiting just outside the bathing room.

Jessika forced herself to wait, counting a hundred breaths as she recalled what Thornwing had once told her about hunting.

"The patience of predators is greater than the patience of prey."

She was the prey, and she wanted to run.

Then, just as she was nearing her hundredth breath and her muscles were cramping from holding perfectly still, she heard the sound of footsteps going down the staircase behind the door.

Burning adrenaline made Jessika's whole body quiver. Vor had been standing there behind the closed door, waiting—for something. Only once the echo of her steps faded did Jessika extricate herself from the towel rack. She crept to the door of the bathing room and propped herself against the wall.

She was still too scared to look out the hall towards the basement door. Then she had the thought that Vor might finish whatever business she had below and come back up. That would be just as bad.

Fear like glass shards in her skin, Jessika slowly looked around the door jam.

No one was there.

Gasping, she fled as quickly as she could while still keeping her steps silent. The door to the wing would make noise again. She could only hope no one would be near enough to hear it. Jessika tried to open the door slowly and quietly, just enough for her to squeeze through the gap.

After the gloom of the shuttered halls, the bright garden with its colorful blooms came as a relief. She walked down a graveled side path to a bench under a gazebo. Below a profusion of climbing vines thick with dark blue trumpet flowers, she sat, watching tiny, flashing hummingbirds zip about. Her heart was still catching up with her.

In the leafy garden her fear suddenly felt a little silly—but not completely silly.

"Why should I be afraid of Vor?" she hissed under her breath. "Besides that she can make it feel like she's ripping my back skin off while throwing me onto the pavement and into tables? She knows I'm after Hawkjoy. It may be that I'll have to face her, and fight her. Maybe I can't just avoid her?"

She rubbed her face and sat for a while watching a pair of male hummingbirds chase each other around the gazebo, buzzing their squeaky chirps the entire time. It was almost funny enough to lift her mood.

The sun was hardly at noon yet, but her courage was too bruised for her to go back into the private wing for another try, especially now that she knew for certain that Vor was down in the cellars.

"A weapon would be nice," she muttered, "a truncheon, or anything. I wish there were someone to help me."

She looked off in the direction of the gate in the inner wall. Out in the nearby village were Chika and Koki. They would help her if they could; she was sure of it. Was there any way for her to get to them? Could she just walk off the palace ground? But then she'd be putting them in danger, bringing Vor and Altare's attention onto them if she made any mistakes or they got caught.

Jessika shook her head. She couldn't do that.

She sat up, gripping her knees. No, and she couldn't just sit here when Hawkjoy was down there waiting.

"I'll fight her if I must," she growled softly. "She's not keeping me from saving Hawkjoy."

Fueled with anger instead of crimped by fear, Jessika surged to her feet and strode back to the door of the public wing. She pulled it open with no heed to the rumble it made, and marched down the murky carpeted hall. She saw no one, and went straight to the door for the basement. She took hold of the handle, turned, and pulled—and nearly stumbled as she jerked her body.

The door was locked, solidly, irrevocably locked.

She pulled at it, yanked on it, but it didn't even jiggle. It was heavy wood, with thick metal hinges, and she couldn't budge it. Looking at how hefty it was, she didn't think she'd have any luck trying to batter it down either. All that would accomplish was alerting everyone nearby that she was trying to break in.

"Confound it," she snarled.

Again she wished for a set of lock picks.

Jessika ran her hands up into her hair and squeezed, trying not to scream with frustration. She should have gone down immediately, when she'd found it open before. Anger at herself twisted in her chest. Of course Vor would have come down after her and caught her, but, well, she didn't have a solution to that either.

She turned on her heel and charged back out the way she'd come. If she didn't have lock picks, she'd find a way to make some. She'd seen Koki's picks well enough. If she had some stiff wire she could bend it into shape maybe. That would mean she'd have to ask for wire or a thin metal rod, and the means to shape it if it was too tough to do with her own hand strength.

Out through the garden, across the arrival courtyard, and back into the kitchen gardens she walked, trying not to look too agitated when what she wanted to do was run, demand, and maybe kick something.

"Is there a blacksmith?"

Kari looked up from where she'd been picking some green leafy vegetable. "A blacksmith?" she echoed.

"Yes, I'd like to see the palace blacksmith," Jessika repeated. A blacksmith would have metal, probably narrow little sticks of it, even, that might work as lock picks.

Kari still looked stunned, but she seemed to gather her wits. "Of course. Let me just put these down and I'll take you to him."

Jessika waited while Kari trotted to the kitchen, vanished inside, and a few moments later emerged unburdened.

"This way, Princess," she said, striking her apron with her palms to shake bits of dirt and leaf off it. "We shall have to pass through the inner gate. Craft people and the palace animals are kept between the outer and inner walls."

They'd have to pass the guards. Jessika didn't know if they'd been given any instruction about her—like forbidding her egress—but she supposed she'd find out soon enough. Kari led the way with brisk steps, and Jessika held up her head, trying to look both as though she weren't engaged in plans to break through locked doors and as though she had the right to go anywhere she pleased.

Kari didn't pause to say anything to the guards, and though one or two shifted uneasily as Jessika passed, they made no move to stop her. The paving became rougher and dirtier, with bits of straw and the occasional chicken feather being tickled around by a breeze. Quickly enough the scents of animal husbandry reached them. Nearest to the gates were fine stables and corrals for horses. Beyond them, stone and wooden fences along the inside of the outer wall held mules, donkeys, goats, pigs, and cows. Chickens wandered freely, it seemed.

Squat buildings along the outside of the inner wall appeared to be workshops. Some had an outer wall open to the main thoroughfare that Jessika and Kari now walked, orbiting the palace at the center. Looking ahead, Jessika could see the buildings thin out, until near where the road curved out of sight, there didn't seem to be any structures at all.

"There's more space here between the walls than the crafters and animals need," Kari explained. "A little ways around the craft people have their homes, with their families, far enough that the smells and sounds of the animals don't bother them. The blacksmith is just over here."

There was no sound of striking metal, but when they came within view, Jessika could confirm that this was the right place. The forge didn't seem to be currently active and the tools of the man's trade were all carefully racked. The blacksmith himself sat on a stool at a table, with a mug of something in one hand and a book in the other. Incongruously delicate spectacles graced his face.

Jessika found herself smiling, as though she were here to meet a friend, not to try to trick a man into giving her lock picks.

"Master Blacksmith," Kari called out.

The man looked up. His skin was weathered brown, black in the creases, and he had quite a number of shiny old burns on his hands and forearms—

much deeper burns than the cook had sported—and what looked like scars from edged weapons, or maybe kitchen knives if it were possible to slip while cutting a carrot and half cut your arm off at the shoulder. His hair had clearly once been all black, but now was threaded through with plentiful gray. Despite his age and old injuries, from the way he moved there was nothing wrong with his steady hands or powerful arms.

He smiled calmly at Kari and then transferred his gaze to Jessika. "Ladies, what may this humble smith do for you today?"

Kari looked uncertainly at Jessika. "Thank you for escorting me here, Kari. I can find my own way back. I know you have a lot of duties to attend to."

She hesitated, clearly torn between getting her chores done and being a good servant to her princess.

"Really, it's fine," Jessika urged. "I sense I am in safe and capable hands, and I can hardly get lost returning."

"As you wish, Your Highness." Kari curtsied and departed.

The blacksmith had cocked an eyebrow. "Your Highness?" he repeated, not mocking, but rather curious.

"I was born here, before the invasion," she explained.

Suddenly, the blacksmith looked alarmed. For a moment he seemed too taken aback to speak, but then he came to a conclusion. "You're Jessika? Princess Jessika?"

"I am," she confirmed. Perhaps her initial sense of safe and capable—or at least safe—had been in error.

"You survived? How?" he pressed, and then seemed to catch himself. More loudly he said, "Won't you come in? Have a seat. My services are at your disposal."

He produced a second stool from behind the forge, brushed off the top with his hand, then perhaps decided it wasn't clean enough, and fetched a folded towel from a shelf, which he placed across the seat. Jessika sat on it, and he sat back down, too. He glanced around, shiftily, just his eyes darting this way and that. He grimaced and then reached out to snag a scrap of smudged paper from a basket on another shelf, and a charcoal writing stick from beside it.

"You've come to the right place," he said aloud. "Any service you need, if it involves metal, I can do for you. The finest shovels, hoes, and axes; weapons to protect our grand kingdom; and no horse or mule too feisty for me to shoe."

While he spoke, he scratched out on the paper: "I knew you when you were little. I was here at the invasion."

"Most excellent," Jessika said, but already her mouth had gone dry. "I'm glad to know you're here to serve your kingdom."

She took the charcoal stick with trembling fingers.

"What is your name, good blacksmith?" she asked, almost shrilly.

"I am Rikan, my lady, son of Riko."

Jessika thought her heart might stop. She almost dropped the writing stick. Shaking with fear and joy, she wrote, "I escaped with Rikah. He's alive."

The blacksmith stared at the words for a couple breaths, as if refusing to believe. He glanced up at Jessika, who gave a tiny nod. He looked back down at the words, eyes flicking as he read them over and over. Then she saw his chest pulse, like his breath had caught. He looked up and down, up and down, between the words and Jessika's face. She bit her cheeks to keep from beaming, but she couldn't stop the tightening of her eyes and forehead. She nodded again.

"Any service you need!" Rikan the blacksmith crowed, throwing up his arms.

Tears streamed down his face, filling up his creases and wrinkles.

Jessika forced herself not to show any glee at all, and Rikan got himself back under control remarkably fast, although his face seemed perpetually on the verge of weeping or laughing now. With a casual gesture he crumpled up the paper and tossed it into the quietly glowing forge fire. There was a matching glow of life to his face that hadn't been there before, and it made Jessika giddy inside that she'd been able to give him this news.

"So what can I do for you today, Your Highness?" he asked sincerely.

"I need a special tool, or two," she began as lightly as she could. "A short bit of metal, much thinner than my finger, with a little kink in it."

She picked up the writing stick and Rikan provided another old scrap of paper. She drew a line with the shape she wanted for the lock pick. Rikan's blissful glow shifted a little, and he gave her a quick look that said he knew excatly what she was drawing, and was both intrigued and without reluctance to make her such a thing.

"Ah, I see, you're looking for some fine metal hair pins," he declared. "You are in luck, my lady. Not many blacksmiths are so skilled as to be able to create such artistry as befits a princess. I can create for you exactly what you need. I don't, however, have anything ready right this moment. Will you be able to return tomorrow?"

"That is easily done," she agreed. "Is there any particular time that my order will be ready?"

"If you would come after lunch, around this time, it would be best. I take my midday break when the sun is hottest. This evening and tomorrow morning I will complete your order."

"Very good," Jessika nodded.

Not feeling safe to stay any longer, as it could draw undue interest, Jessika departed after Rikan had given her a deep bow.

It was only as she was walking back to her rooms that she realized she didn't know how Rikah had fared after the battle with Vor and the soldiers, at Cray's cottage. He'd been badly injured. She hoped it hadn't been so serious that he'd died. To give Rikan word that his son was alive only to discover he was dead, would be to Rikan as though he'd died twice, and he would mourn his son all over again.

Jessika went back to the kitchen to ask if she could make some lunch for herself, only to have Marklin the cook flatly refuse and insist on making it all with his own hands. She was allowed to wait and watch, while the other servants cleared and cleaned a spot for her at the kitchen table. Then she sat down to another delicious repast and was sure to impress on Marklin how much she enjoyed it.

As she climbed the stairs up to her floor, she realized that she could enjoy living here, if it weren't for Vor and Altare and the Skire—and who knew what her father was up to. If the griffins could be restored to the Feathyr barracks, if the mystery of the invasion could be solved and made known, if, if, if a dozen things could be changed, she'd be willing to spend most of her life here. Regular trips back to South-scree to see all her friends and her griffin family would of course be a given.

Jessika went to the library and found a stack of paper in a drawer with wells of ink and spare quills. Afraid that Vor or Altare might be somehow watching her room, she snuck into a different, unoccupied room and crafted a letter to Blacksmith Rikan.

"Burn this immediately after reading," she wrote in big letters at the top.

She proceeded to recount—without revealing too many details—how Rikah had survived, where he'd grown up, and what sort of a man he'd grown into. She included the simplified path of her journey since she'd left South-scree, how it had ended when she'd last seen Rikah—being totally honest about her lack of knowledge of his current situation—and what her objective was now.

She folded the letter up and tucked it deep inside her clothes, next to her skin. After that, she retired to her room and tried to read while her thoughts and emotions joined hands and spun around together really fast the way little kids do until they go flying apart, land, get bruised, get up laughing, and do it again.

Dinner arrived at her room with no contact from Vor and she ate in solitude. Not even Amlee came to see her. She asked Kari to help her re-bandage her back, which was feeling better but not yet totally healed. If the young woman was shocked or appalled at the injuries, she made no comment, although she did look a little white around the eyes after. The whole time, Jessika kept her letter for Rikan either on her person or in direct sight. When she went to bed she tucked it under the top layer of her bandages.

Chapter 21
Blacksmith, King, Mage

The lock picks wouldn't be ready until the afternoon, so in the morning, Jessika went directly back to the private wing of the palace to continue her exploration. The door down to the stairs was still locked, so she explored the rest of the first floor. She discovered a small library, but it seemed to be missing more than half its books, judging by the number of empty shelves.

She lingered there anyway, pulling down a few of the remaining books and glancing into them. Most of them were natural history treatises, records of exploration trips into the nearby wilderness, or logbooks relating to household activities. She didn't see a single mention of the name "Northnest," nor anything to do with magic, or griffins or drakes. It was as if every book she'd encountered so far was determined to pretend that the invasion hadn't happened, although people she'd met at the palace had not been reluctant to mention it.

Beside the library was a large room that looked unused. The outside wall was nothing but windows, all shuttered, with layers of curtains closed over them. The furniture consisted of a varied collection of items that Jessika wasn't familiar with. Although a few seemed to be high desks with tall stools, others looked more specialized. A few were covered with sheets to keep off the dust, but even still their shapes looked strange.

Jessika went to the nearest perplexing construction and reached for the fabric covering it—and she jumped when she heard the main door to the private wing groan open. Someone was coming.

Her first instinct was to hide or run, but she mastered the impulse and set her feet firmly against the wood floor. She couldn't hear the footsteps of the approaching whoever-it-was, so she had to stand, waiting, heart pounding. She straightened her back, staring defiantly towards the open doorway. If Vor came in and started—

Amlee stepped surely through the door and startled, hands going reflexively to her throat.

"Princess," she gasped. "I had no idea you were in here."

Jessika let go her breath, relaxing.

"I see I have surprised you as well," she went on.

Jessika hesitated a moment, then said honestly, "I thought you might be Vor."

"Oh, ah, as you see, I am not she." Amlee gave a weak smile. "I am actually here hoping to accomplish something for you, Princess, and you are already right where I was heading."

The housekeeper went to the mysterious structure Jessika had been about to reveal and did the same, folding back the sheet that covered it.

"What is it?" Jessika asked.

"It's a loom for weaving tapestries," Amlee explained. "After some research I've learned that the tapestries decorating the palace have long been the work of the royal women of Northborn. You asked if there were some way you might employ yourself. As currently our only royal woman, I thought you might take up the traditional hobby of your position."

"I don't know how," Jessika said, reaching out to gingerly touch the machine.

"I'm afraid I am not familiar with the skill, either, but I've located a few books, and I expect we can figure it out together."

As soon as Jessika got her lock picks and found a way to get Hawkjoy out, she wouldn't be around to weave tapestries, but Amlee didn't know that.

"This was the room where the royals most often passed the time, when they weren't engaged in ruling or other duties," Amlee went on. "They came here to read or sew, write, weave, or make music—either the playing of it or the composing of it. That's what the rest of this furniture is for. I expect that, in time, you'll want it all aired, cleaned, and possibly refurbished."

"Naturally," Jessika said, trying to sound enthusiastic when she wasn't very.

"Whenever you like. There is no rush, of course." Amlee paused to observe her. "Kari tells me you've been exploring, trying to bring back memories. I can imagine that may be painful. The recent history of this country has indeed been unfortunate. I hope we can look forward to a bright future now that you're here, Princess. I hope you won't dwell on the shadows of the past."

She sounded sincere and concerned, but Jessika couldn't predict how anything would work out, and even if she could have, she didn't think telling secrets to Amlee would help the woman's position. Doing that could only bring the housekeeper more to Vor or Altare's attention, and that couldn't be good.

"Maybe you can send one of the books about weaving to my room, and I will study it as I am able," Jessika fumbled out.

Amlee brightened, "certainly, Your Highness."

She continued removing the sheet from the loom, and Jessika tried to help her.

"I don't expect anything will be broken, but if it is, I'll have it repaired."

Amlee went on, talking about the state of the loom and all her resources in keeping things in the castle in working order. Jessika let her talk, idly walking around the room and peaking under other sheets, but her mind was on Hawkjoy and her noontime appointment with Rikan. She wished Amlee would bid her farewell and leave her, so Jessika could go again to the door to the stairs and try the handle—because maybe something had changed and it was suddenly unlocked now, and she couldn't think of anything other than getting down there.

That was when an idea struck her.

"Amlee," she interrupted, "do you have a key for the door over in the corner of the hallway, between this room and the bathing room?"

The housekeeper fished in a pocket. "I should. That's the door into the basement. Skire Germaine has her storage rooms down there, and she doesn't like anyone messing about in them, so the servants don't go down there. I expect it's filthy without anyone giving it regular cleaning. You might want to tell her you're going down there, Princess. Not that you can't go wherever you wish, but, she is particular about it."

Amlee extracted a key ring with just a few keys on it.

"This should be it. Let's give it a try," she said. "I suppose the Skire must have locked it, but I thought it was usually open."

Jessika followed her with eager steps, trying not to run her over in her urgency. When they reached the door, Amlee fitted the key into the keyhole and tired to turn it, but it was immediately apparent that something was wrong.

"No, must not be this key," Amlee sighed. "I might have left it on its hook. I so rarely need it."

"It's not one of the others?" Jessika pressed.

"I'll try them, but I don't think so."

Jessika waited, trying not to bounce with frustration, as the castellan tried one key after another, but at last Amlee shook her head. "I'm sorry, Princess, I don't seem to have it with me."

Jessika gritted her teeth. Perhaps Amlee did have the right key, but whatever Vor had done to lock the door was magical in nature, and the key wouldn't open it anymore. If that were the case, Rikan's lock picks wouldn't work either.

"Thank you for trying," Jessika unclenched her jaw to say.

"I'll check for the key and see if I can unlock it for you later."

"That would be kind of you," Jessika agreed.

Apparently having noticed none of Jessika's agitation, Amlee turned and went back to the room with the looms. Jessika stood and stared at the door. A door: that was all that was keeping her away from Hawkjoy.

An axe might be the only way—or was that reckless? It would be so noisy someone would notice. She knew very well that Vor could subdue and restrain her magically. Altare would be too much of a match for her, too, unless his burns had left him an invalid magically and physically. If neither of them were around, she didn't think Skire Germaine would stand any chance, but the woman had summoned Altare just by screaming his name. Nothing would stop her doing that again unless Jessika could surprise her and incapacitate her right away.

She might stand up to a guard or even two, but any more than that would overwhelm her easily, especially if she were unarmed. And still—what would she do when she got to Hawkjoy? What if the griffin were drugged or injured? Although part of her was screaming to just get to her, the logical part of her knew she had to plan the escape also.

"Princess Jessika?"

She jumped, but it was just Amlee.

"Shall I fetch the key right now? You really want to explore the basement?" Then her eyes widened a little and her voice faltered. "Is, is it something to do with the invasion? Or, is there something else," she paused and dropped her voice to the smallest whisper, "wrong?"

Amlee was too kind. Jesika refused to get her involved and let her get hurt.

"No," she said, but she knew it was unconvincing, and Amlee's expression reflected it.

"I will go now," the housekeeper said hesitantly.

"Yes, thank you."

She curtsied and exited down the hallway.

Jessika figured it might be close to noon. After trying the door handle again—no luck, no surprise—she followed in Amlee's footsteps, heading for Rikan's forge.

Jessika found Rikan sitting at his table with damp hair as though he'd just washed up, uncovering a plate of thick bread coated with something that smelled and looked like salty meat sauce. As Jessika approached, he looked up, smiled and covered the food back up, stepping forward to meet her with a bow.

"Please, eat your food good smithy," Jessika said. "I insist. You've worked hard on my account."

His expression was slightly dubious, but he sat back down. The same stool Jessika had used the previous day was still in place, and she took it. As Rikan uncovered his food again he reached into a pocket and pulled out a small skinny bundle. He passed it across the tabletop on the side far from the street.

Jessika reached out to take it, hiding in her hand the letter she'd written. Hidden from view by the plate of bread, she deposited the letter and took the bundle. Without a twitch Rikan took the folded letter into his own palm and it vanished like it had never been.

"Thank you for your time and skill, Master Rikan," she told him. "How can I repay your efforts?"

"You have, never fear," he said sincerely. "It was a pleasure, Your Highness. Thank you for your patronage. Is there is any other way I may be of assistance?"

The subtle inflection in his voice conveyed his meaning—that if she were in trouble, he'd be willing to help. She widened her eyes to convey that she understood and nodded, but she had no intention of putting Rikan in danger any more than Amlee.

"I will contact you should I have something I'd like your help with," she said. "Please, have your lunch. I should go."

As she stood, so did he, giving her another deep bow. "Thank you, truly," he breathed. "Stay safe, Your Highness."

Rikan

Jessika managed a wobbly curtsy, but she had the urge to reach up and scratch his head in imitation of griffins affectionately preening each other, as she and Rikah and Karo and Kassandra did with each other. She didn't, because she knew enough to realize that would be a weird thing to see and people might comment on it—not to mention that Rikan would probably find it strange.

"I'll try," she whispered back. "And you," she eyed the pocket he'd slipped the letter into, and Rikan nodded seriously.

Jessika left, trying to walk with decorum back to the palace, and not reveal her urgency. The bundle of lock picks was heavy in her pocket, bouncing against her leg. Rikan's bread and meat had smelled delicious, but she decided to skip lunch and go straight back to the locked door. It was only when she stood in front of it that she faced the thought again of how she'd get a great big possibly injured, possibly drugged griffin out and away safely.

Perhaps she could just scout out the situation, but how could she go down, see Hawkjoy, and not take her and escape immediately? How could she turn and leave her there, go back to her comfortable room, and wonder what the Skire might do to her in her absence?

No, she had to see her. She'd figure it out later.

Jessika knelt in front of the door and took out the two picks Rikan had made for her. Trying to keep her breathing steady and her hands from shaking, she inserted the two picks and started feeling for the tumblers.

A few minutes later she pulled out the picks and swore silently. She hadn't picked many locks, so maybe she just didn't have enough experience, but nothing in there would move. She couldn't seem to get purchase on anything.

She gave herself a little while to rest, and then tried again, and again, and again, to the point that she started to worry she might be damaging the picks, she was pushing and fiddling so hard.

No one disturbed her and she had a nice long spell to keep trying, but soon her knees were aching on the floor and her fingers were sore, and she'd made not the slightest progress. The faint shadows from the sun had moved across the carpet and Jessika's stomach was squeezing with emptiness. She rested her palms and forehead against the stubborn door and wondered what to do.

Her head hurt and she felt like crying, but knew that wouldn't help anything.

Jessika pushed to her feet, almost stumbling as her knees protested. She limped back to the public wing and headed into the kitchen. The servants and Marklin the cook seemed particularly attuned to noticing signs of hunger, and within seconds of her sitting down at a clean spot a bowl was set before her, filled with a stew from a big pot that was suspended over a low flame, staying hot. A couple slices of bread just as thick as the ones Rikan had had appeared by her left hand, followed by a big glass full of water and slices of lemon.

She ate, frustrated almost beyond the ability to think. Perhaps there was another way down? She could ask someone, but the more she asked, the more likely reports of her activities would get back to Vor or Altare. Maybe Amlee would get a key that worked, but now Jessika was suspecting more than ever that Vor had locked the door with magic.

The stew disappeared down her throat and the bowl was replaced with a slice of pie overflowing with blueberries, drowned in cream, the top crust sparkling with sugar. That managed to distract her enough that she looked up into Marklin's smiling face.

"Our princess strives for her objectives, but she must not forget to eat," he said.

"Thank you," she told him, trying to smile and failing.

"Would you prefer strawberry?"

"No, no, I mean, no, I mean, strawberry would be great also, but blueberry is wonderful, I like them both," she stuttered. "I'm sure any pie you make would be fantastic."

"Ah, for the pie, you must thank our mistress of sweets, Berthana," he gestured.

She looked and a tall, lanky woman grinned at her from over where she was washing dishes.

"Thank you Berthana," she said, dredging up a smile. "This is exactly what I needed."

"Pie solves all problems," the woman caroled back, "at least those of the spirit."

Jessika focused on savoring the pie while she tried to calm her mind. Finally she settled on a course of action. She would try to find another way down. When she'd been exploring under the castle before Hawkjoy got caught, she'd encountered the dungeons. She hoped there might be a way down to there. Then, if she went through them and out the way that had been locked before—maybe Vor hadn't magic-locked that one and she could pick it, or open it freely from within—she could come around at the Skire's room from the same direction she and Hawkjoy had initially.

Cray had thought Altare would trap the passages under the castle, but she'd have to find a way through. It was her best option, she thought. As she finished the pie and cleaned the bowl with her finger, she was resolved. After thanking the kitchen staff again, she went back out the way she came, back to the private wing.

She'd explored the first floor. Perhaps there was some kind of back stair she could find from the second floor down. She didn't know what else to do; she was out of options. She took the stairs up, finding a hallway that circled the open stairwell, with doors along it.

Jessika went to the first. She figured this was probably where Vor, Altare, Skire Germaine, and her father—and maybe other people she hadn't met— had rooms. She might encounter any of them. The thought made her heart pound. She strained her ears, listening for any hint of other humans. As silently as possible, she set her hand on the first door handle and twisted.

It turned smoothly, and she inched the door open just a crack. Peering through she saw no one, and pushed it open a bit further. Still no one, she opened it wide enough to enter and stepped through, shutting it behind her.

The room had a sense of being unused. The curtains were drawn and she saw no personal possessions, only furniture. On quiet feet she explored the suite, but found no sign of anyone, or any kind of stairway down. There could be some kind of hidden passageway, but she didn't know how she'd find one— they weren't called hidden for nothing.

With that room searched, she again moved cautiously into the hallway and went for the next door. With the same careful process she peeked in and entered. Seeing no danger, she crept inside and looked around.

Down the hall a door opened and shut. Jessika looked up, alarmed, but she'd shut the door to this suite behind her and there should be no hint of her presence. Nevertheless, she hurried into the bedroom and stepped into the empty wardrobe, shutting the door all but a crack.

There she waited, but as before couldn't hear footsteps on the thickly carpeted hallway floor. After a few minutes, faint and distant, she thought she heard the main door of the wing groan open and close. She waited a while longer anyway, listened and looked carefully out into the hallway before she left the suite.

Her feet took her to the next door: one larger and more ornate than the others had been. She tried the handle and found it unlocked, as well. As before, she eased it open just a crack, and then a bit more, and then enough to step through.

As she had expected, it was another suite of rooms. The curtains were only partly open, and there was no fire in the sitting room's fireplace, nor any lights currently lit. The air felt a bit fresher here, as well as scented with flowers and soap. She spied a cut-flower bouquet in a vase on the table under the windows, and suddenly feared these rooms might be in use.

She moved deeper, skin prickling. To one side she saw a bedroom, with the bed made up and tidy. She looked to the other side where there was another doorway.

And saw a man sitting in a chair looking out the window, his face in profile.

Jessika went still like a frightened rabbit, afraid that moving might attract his attention. At any moment he might look over and notice her. When after a few breaths he still hadn't looked away from his view out the window, she slowly stepped backwards, until she couldn't see him anymore.

Feeling safe for the moment, she took a breath and gathered herself. It wasn't Altare at least. This man was much older, with a tidy beard that was completely gray, and a wrinkled, somber face.

Jessika crept over to the wall next to the door. She leaned over just enough to see him, now at an angle slightly behind him. He wore a fine cloak with a hood that covered his head except for his face. His gnarled hands rested limply on the arms of his chair. Now that she was able to look longer, she observed that he was staring out the window without expression, eyes fixed, and only rarely blinking, as though he were lost in thought and not really seeing.

Jessika's heart was pounding. This wasn't Altare and certainly wasn't Vor or Germaine. Who else would be living up in the private wing? Could it be another advisor of some kind, or was this her father?

She had to know.

Jessika straightened her back and prepared to step into the room.

"He won't recognize you."

She almost screamed with fright, and jumped, stumbling and turning about, retreating until her back hit the wall beside the sitting room window.

"I didn't want you to see me like this."

It was Altare, although he wasn't wearing a fancy suit like before. He wore an enveloping robe that covered him from head to foot except for his hands and face, and he wore gloves over his hands. His face, however, was red and scarred.

"I haven't finished healing the burns your griffin friend inflicted on me," he went on, his voice oddly devoid of menace.

Jessika gulped, swallowing air, fighting the impulse to run.

"Vor tells me your back has healed well, however, thanks to her minstrations. I do regret the scarring that must remain, but perhaps someday you will allow me to remove that for you as well."

"You can remove the magic Vor left in my skin, that lets her jerk me around," Jessika gulped out, although the actual thought of Altare doing anything magical to her was worse than having Vor's magic in her back.

"I would be happy to," Altare said, sounding sincere.

He took a short step, starting to lift a hand, and Jessika thumped herself against the wall again in instinctive retreat.

"Ah, I didn't think you meant that," he smiled, making his scars twist.

He relented, keeping himself still, as though to help her stay calm. Perhaps it worked, for Jessika was able to put her weight back on her own feet and lift her chin.

"Release me and Hawkjoy," she ordered.

"I won't be doing that."

"At least release Hawkjoy. Let her go, and I'll stay."

He spread a hand. "The griffin belongs to Skire Germaine. You'll have to ask her."

"The griffin belongs to no one," Jessika argued back. "Nobody can be owned by someone else. Moreover, she's hurting her."

"Skire Germaine is a valuable commodity. She is important to me. I want her to be happy. Doing research makes her happy."

"And you think that's more important than Hawkjoy?"

"Yes," he said simply. "The griffin will not be released."

"Then I'm taking her and leaving."

This seemed to amuse him. "How?"

Jessika panted, angry, and unable to answer.

"Little girl, you cannot 'save' anyone." He took a few steps closer and Jessika bristled with mingled terror and disgust. "Not even yourself, not even your father."

Frightened into immobility, she couldn't resist as Altare reached out and put an arm around her shoulders, propelling her upright and towards the study where the old man sat. He hadn't moved through all the shouting, and remained still as Altare pushed Jessika relentlessly into the room, his gloved hand flat on her back between her shoulder blades. He let her stop beside the chair, and lowered his hand. His voice hummed into her ear.

"Your father is also useful to me."

"What's wrong with him?" Jessika asked tremulously, afraid of the answer.

"He's had a difficult life. The death of his entire family struck him hard, not to mention the conquering of his kingdom. He was offered a chance to work together with the new rulers, to play a role. He chose instead to try to escape, and when that failed, to take his own life, but you understand we couldn't let him do that. He was so much more useful alive."

The whole time Altare had been talking, that Jessika had been standing there, within touching range of her father, the old man hadn't moved, hadn't made any sign that he knew they were there.

"He doesn't suffer," Altare murmured, "but if he wouldn't comply of his own free will, steps had to be taken to acquire his compliance. Unfortunately, no members of his family remained to be used as a hostage against good behavior. The other wizards—and myself, although I was just an apprentice then—spent months making a solution to the problem."

Jessika sensed him step away. Altare circled around to stand behind the seated old man. Lightly, he touched the hood he wore, and pulled it down so it fell onto his shoulders.

Jessika gasped and stepped back, hands going to her chest.

The old man wore a sort of cap that covered the entire top and back of his head, where his hair should be. It was made of a silvery metal, swirled and inscribed with patterns and symbols, with gems of many colors set into it. At its edges the old man's skin abutted it, thick and bumpy.

"We devised this crown for him," Altare explained. "Of course he didn't want it at first, but there was really no choice." He stroked the metal. "It keeps him calm. I think it gives him more peace than he could have had any other way, what with everything he'd been through."

"That's not right," Jessika gritted out, appalled. "Take it off."

"Oh, no. I'm afraid any attempt to remove it would just result in his death. It is not merely skin deep, you see."

Jessika thought she might be sick.

Altare laid a hand on the man's shoulder. The king immediately looked over at him, and smiled.

"Altare, my friend," the king said in a scratchy, dry voice. "All is well?"

"Very well, Your Majesty," Altare replied firmly.

"Is it time to see the people again?"

"Not yet, in a few days. The people will have cause to rejoice."

"That is wonderful to hear."

"You see, your daughter has returned to us. She is here. Do you see her?"

Altare put his other hand on Jessika's shoulder, and pulled her closer. Now she thought she might cry.

"Ah, yes," the king said. "Very lovely."

"We have to tell the people that the princess is here with us again," Altare instructed.

"Yes, we must," the king agreed, still with the same pleasant smile. His eyes didn't seem to focus on Jessika, although she tried to meet his gaze. Tears slid down her cheeks.

"I will come to get you when it's time to see the people," Altare assured him

"Yes, yes, please do."

Altare took his hands off the king and Jessika. The king's face went slack, and he slowly turned to look out the window again. Altare delicately replaced his hood, hiding the gruesome ornament on the back of his head.

Jessika fell to her knees beside the chair and clasped her father's flaccid hand.

"He didn't really see me," she protested. "He didn't know me."

"No, but it's for the best."

"How can you say that?" she hissed.

"Easily. Do not distress yourself, Princess. Now that you are here, things can be different."

"Different?" she echoed, still looking up at her father's empty eyes. His hands were cold.

"You are the heir. It's your kingdom to rule now."

"What?" This was all so confusing. If only her father would look at her, smile, and greet her with joy and tears.

"Allow me to present a token of my respect and admiration."

Jessika didn't respond, didn't care. Altare moved closer again but she hardly noticed as he reached down around her neck. Then a pendant, a diamond the size of her thumb set in gold, dropped down against her clavicles, and some of the pain faded.

"I miss him," she murmured.

"Of course you do, but you are not alone," Altare soothed.

He was right. She wasn't.

"I wish to invite you to rule with me. Together we can care for this country."

That was what she'd come here to do, right?

"You don't have to answer now. Think about it for a while. See how you feel."

"Thank you. That's kind of you," she replied.

"I only wish to be a kind and just ruler."

She nodded.

"Let me walk you out. Take your ease in the gardens. It's peaceful there. I'll send a servant to fetch you for dinner."

Altare took her arm, and Jessika stood when he urged her.

"Your father will be fine here. A specially selected servant sees to all his needs," Altare assured her.

He led her out of the suite and to the stairs, but then Jessika jerked to a halt.

"There was something I was going to do up here," she told him.

"Perhaps it will come to you after a good night's sleep. Surely it was nothing so urgent or you would remember."

That made sense. Before she could think about it further, Altare was guiding her down the steps. He took her as far as the main door.

"Here I must leave you, Princess," he said, bowing. "Until I can fully heal my face, I prefer to keep to myself, to avoid frightening anyone."

"Your face?" she repeated. "What happened?"

He seemed oddly pleased at the question. "Just an accident. I will be back to my normal self again soon. Don't worry yourself on my behalf."

"Alright," she concurred.

Altare opened the door for her. "I will see you again soon, as soon as I am healed. Then we will have your coronation."

Somehow, he'd taken her hand, and before she could exit he lifted it and bowed over it. His lips brushed the back of it, and Jessika jumped like she'd been shocked. It felt like that, like a spike of intense sensation—pain, cold, heat, pressure all at once—shooting up her arm to her elbow, shoulder, and into her chest.

"May you have a pleasant evening," he said.

"And you as well," she said automatically.

Jessika stepped out the door, and Altare shut it behind her.

As soon as the door groaned closed, Jessika took a gasping breath. She rubbed her face. She'd seen her father, and Altare was taking care of him, because he was ill and infirm, but now she was going to take over ruling the country.

She walked into the garden and found a spot to sit down. The afternoon was waning towards sunset but—that's right, Altare would send a servant to bring her in for dinner. He really was very kind. With his help, surely she could put right anything that was disarrayed. All would be well.

Not Kari, but a different servant, a boy approaching his teens, came to call Jessika for dinner just as the sky turned red with sunset. She followed him back to the public wing where a meal had been laid for her in one of the small dining rooms. Other servants came in to attend her, and at one point Amlee stuck her head in to check on everything.

As soon as she saw Jessika, she straightened up, and curtsied deeply. As she turned to go, Jessika thought she might have gotten something in her eye. Kari took her to her room after dinner and helped her bathe and dress for bed. She went to sleep and enjoyed the best rest she'd had in what seemed like a long time.

The next day, Amlee taught her how to use the loom, and she started work on a simple, small tapestry with just a basic pattern. In the afternoon she read in the library. After another week had passed, she completed her tapestry, and Amlee helped her hang it in her bedroom. She began making plans for a bigger one with some kind of image on it. She decided on flowers after sitting and taking her ease in the garden one day.

A few days later, after she'd started her tapestry, she had a visitor in what she'd come to call the "loom room."

"Lord Altare," she exclaimed, looking up at a gentle knock.

"I didn't want to startle you," he said, stepping in.

He was dressed in a dark blue suit now, with a half cape. His hair was black and fluffy and he wore a neat beard. He smiled widely.

"You're healed," Jessika observed, standing to go to him.

"I am. It just took me a little time."

He took her hand and she smiled at him.

"I am hoping you might wish to plan your coronation now," he said. "I know your father the king is very excited about it. He almost can't sit still. Do you still wish to rule here?"

What a silly question. "Of course. I wish for nothing more than that, to take care of my people."

He smiled even wider. He really was quite handsome. "Most excellent. Then I would like to schedule it for later this week. We will need time for your gown to be made, of course, and to prepare the festivities."

"What else can I do to help?"

"I will send Mistress Vor to assist you. She will have a list of duties. It is, of course, her job to see them attended to, but there will be some you can help with."

"I look forward to it."

"As do I."

He bowed over her hand and kissed the back of it again, but longer, more slowly this time, and he looked up at her through long black eyelashes. Jessika felt her cheeks flush and she put her free hand to her throat, brushing against the diamond pendant that hung there. She hadn't taken it off since he'd put it on her, and had forgotten it was there.

Altare straightened and took a step towards her, but suddenly she went cold, chilled, and her head hurt for a moment. She thought she might vomit and the room spun. Dread like a frozen rock dropped into her belly and she had the thought that everything was wrong, and that she was in awful danger. Altare put his free hand on her shoulder, and she had the piercing instinct to slap it away—but then it faded. She took a breath, and found Altare gazing at her with concern.

"Are you alright? You seemed about to faint."

"I, yes, I think so," she stumbled.

"Perhaps you should lie down and rest. I can help you to your room."

An echo of the cold came back and she pulled away from him. "No, thank you, kind sir. I'm fine now."

"As you wish. I will send Vor to you this afternoon, Princess," he said. "Be well."

"And you," she murmured.

He dropped her hand and strode from the room.

Vor greeted her politely when she came with a trio of seamstresses to begin measuring Jessika for her coronation gown. She stood and let the women debate and design, while Vor gave them direction. The firmest requirement seemed to be that it left Jessika's back bare. Once they departed, Vor told her about the preparations that would be made for the celebration, and invited her to give feedback or suggestions, but everything Vor said sounded so proper and necessary that Jessika really couldn't say much.

After that, she ended up in the kitchen watching Marklin and Berthana orchestrate the servant army, sending them to fetch this and that, beginning to marinate meats and vegetables, and arguing over which dishes to serve. Every now and then they turned to Jessika, asking for an executive decision. Not knowing really what most of the food was, she tended to alternate her siding between them, so neither had all their ideas rejected.

The next day was much the same, except the seamstresses brought things for her to try on and Vor denied or approved each option. The third day they brought a nearly finished dress, and some of the food was completed, going into the cellar to chill overnight. The fourth day was the coronation itself.

Jessika awoke excited and nervous. She ate lightly and mid-morning Vor brought the seamstresses and the finished dress to her. It was pale blue and white, with ruffles and more ruffles and a long train that two girls carried as she walked. Vor filled her in on the coronation, which would take place on a balcony overlooking the main courtyard. There wasn't much required of Jessika besides standing and smiling.

They reached the balcony by a hallway from the second floor of the private wing, which led to a staircase up. She heard Altare speaking as they approached and a thrill of excitement went through her. There was the sound of cheering. Vor caught her arm to keep her from walking out too early. Altare was saying something else now, but Jessika's pulse was pounding in her ears and she didn't hear it.

Vor gave her a prod at the right moment. Someone drew back the curtains shielding the balcony, and Jessika stepped out. The crowd stirred and exclaimed. Vor and Altare took her elbows and turned her around, showing the marred golden wing tattoo on her back to the people jamming up the courtyard below.

The crowd roared, but again Jessika felt she might be sick.

Altare was saying something more. Jessika saw her father seated to one side, smiling vacantly. Altare lifted a silver crown up above her head, and lowered it down to rest lightly on her coiffed hair.

The crowd roared louder.

Suddenly, the sun seemed so bright. Altare was smiling at her through the brilliant glow, and she smiled back, her nausea fading. He took her hand, urging her to turn and face her people. Without being bidden she raised her free hand, waving to them, and saw them wave back. They all looked so happy.

Happiness rose in Jessika's chest to mirror theirs. Everything was so right. Altare squeezed her hand and she glanced at him. He looked so proud of her. She was smiling so widely she thought her face might split open.

At last, he led her back through the curtains and they fell shut, cutting off the sunlight, yet still somehow leaving a pearly glow everywhere. Altare took her arm, linking her elbow with his and stepping closer.

"Your crown suits you, Princess," he said, still speaking over the noise of the crowd.

He walked her to the stairs and steadied her as they descended.

"We shall have to have your things moved into the private wing," he said with a slight frown. "That should have been done long ago, but everyone has been so busy. Once the celebration is concluded and cleaned up, I'll detail some servants to see to it."

"That would be lovely," she said. "Can I have the rooms next to my father?"

"That's exactly what I was thinking. You'll also be included in all the governing functions now, although it may take some time before you feel competent and comfortable with them. We all must patiently learn new things."

"Of course," she agreed.

They reached the bottom of the stairs and moved through the dim hallway.

"This is such an exciting time for Northborn," Altare sighed. "Your reign will bring the people much joy."

Jessika's feet faltered. "Joy?" she echoed.

Altare turned towards her, close in the darkness. She startled when his free hand brushed her face.

"Don't worry," he murmured. "All will be well."

"All will be well," she agreed.

For a moment she watched his eyes glimmer, heart thudding and a strange upsetting ache in her head. He leaned in closer, then a pair of servants helped her father down the stairs.

"Wonderful, wonderful," the king was repeating: a smile fixed on his face.

"Indeed, Sire," Altare said at once, moving to take his hand.

They walked out into the second floor hallway, Vor trailing behind. Altare took the king off to one side, along with his attendants. The two girls who had previously carried Jessika's train joined the group and took up their task again.

"Vor, see the princess to her rooms," Altare ordered.

"Yes, Master," Vor said.

Jessika allowed herself to be led away. Her head was hurting and somehow she couldn't keep her thoughts straight. Again the feeling of dread was trickling into her, but overlaying that was the memory of Altare's hand on her face, and she found herself wondering what would have happened if they'd had a few more moments alone in the hallway. Whenever her imagination provided the answer, the dread would surge up.

Vor didn't take her through the courtyard to the public wing—for obvious reasons. Instead, they went through a door on the first floor. To one side stairs led down, probably to a basement, but Vor turned and took her to another hallway around a corner, which led back through some other building, and through a door Jessika had never noticed into the first floor of the public wing.

Servants appeared to help Jessika out of her gown and into a simpler one. They left her with food and a book in her sitting room. She stared out the window, listening to the distant celebrating of the crowd, and wondered if she should try to sort out her thoughts.

Chapter 22
At Midnight

That night she had disturbing dreams of Altare. She seemed to see him in a red suit, and a dark green one, angry, fighting. She saw flames engulfing him. Dark beasts that seemed to be made of shadow stalked around him. Then she felt his touch, felt burning hands all over her, felt a primal hunger that reached out to consume her. Even as the burning invaded her, she tried to wrench herself away.

The sound of the bedroom door latch opening made Jessika's eyes spring wide open. It had hardly made a sound; someone had been trying to be silent. Still, the dreams had brought her close to consciousness; it hadn't taken much to awaken her. A slice of errant light spilled in through the door as it drifted open only a foot or two. Into that light stepped a silhouetted figure.

Jessika's subconscious was working faster than her tired mind. Within a heartbeat she'd tossed back her bed covers. The shape, the stance, and the stride: something in her recognized them and moved her without her sluggish brain's consent. Her bare feet touched the chill stone floor without a flinch, and she met the intruder in the middle of the room, at the center of the intricately woven circle rug, where she swept the dark figure into a sharp embrace.

She heard a brief gasp of surprise—and then strong, lean arms wrapped and gripped her back. She felt his disobedient curls flattened against her neck, and wondered if the pounding heart she felt against her ribs was his or her own: maybe both.

Finally, some fragment of her brain caught up.

"Koki?" she whispered.

A tremor went through the one she held.

"Yes."

His voice against her ear lit up her skin, every tiny hair standing on end, and sent a jolt through her—but a pleasant jolt, nothing like her nightmares. The faun pushed her back, gently and not too far; she could still feel the warmth of his body through her silk nightdress. His hand, holding a handkerchief, fumbled at her throat. He gripped something there, the cloth between his hand and whatever it was, and ripped it away.

Jessika felt a quick flash of pain on her neck as the necklace chain broke, and a rushing sound filled her head. She swayed but Koki held her up. Her thoughts felt all messed up, as though someone had stirred everything up inside her. Only one thing could she really be sure of.

She gripped his arms. "Koki?" she repeated.

"Yes, it's me."

Jessika's breath caught as he stroked her face and neck with wondering, reverent fingers. It felt good. Somehow it helped clear her mind. She tightened her hands in his shirt, trying to pull him close again.

"I'm here," he breathed.

He seemed to obey her pull, leaning into her. His breath rushed across her lips, and then suddenly his mouth, once, twice, pressed urgently to hers.

Jessika was so shocked she couldn't respond until she again saw his eyes glinting from several inches away. She licked her lips, belatedly tasting him, body thrilling.

"I shouldn't have done that," he whispered in the close darkness, "but I won't apologize."

Jessika swallowed, trying to kick her voice into working. "Good," she stated at last. "Don't—apologize, that is."

He froze for an instant like a startled animal, and then seized her, an arm shooting around her waist and a hand grasping at the nape of her neck. She met him this time as he swooped in, and had just started experimenting with how to return the kiss as good as she was getting, when he broke it.

"More later," he mumbled, voice husky. "We have to go. We came to get you out. Here, put these on. Leave that nightdress; it'll have Altare's mark on it. Put this necklace on, too. Starbright made it. Altare surely has some of your hair by now. This will stop him from scrying you by it. Took her a week to make it."

Lips still tingling—along with the rest of her—from Koki's kisses, Jessika numbly accepted the bundle of clothes he picked up from where he'd dropped it. One word penetrated her jumbled mind.

"Starbright?"

"Yes. I know you're confused. That pendant was manipulating you. I'll tell you everything later, but we need to go now," he repeated, "before we're caught. Get changed."

Still befuddled, Jessika began unlacing the front of her nightdress. Koki made a strangled sound and turned away.

"What?" she asked.

"I can't look at you right now. Just get dressed."

It seemed like a dream; it couldn't be real. Koki in her bedroom, telling her he was there to help her escape, and holding her, kissing her? It was very pleasant though, so she saw no reason to resist. She pulled on the sturdy tunic and trousers and laced and tied them.

"Hurry up," someone hissed from the main room of the suite.

"Hawkdare is out there," Koki explained. "He's watching the door to your rooms. Are you dressed?"

"Yes," she answered, and he turned back around.

"Here," the faun grunted, taking the necklace from her and stepping behind her to tie it.

The brush of his warm fingers on her neck made her skin goosepimple. As he tied the knot, however, she felt a strange obscuring veil lift from her. She grabbed his hand and turned to look at him. His outline was sharper, the contrast of light and shadow on his face more dramatic. He was suddenly real, and the situation was real.

"You're really here," she remarked. "Really?"

"Do you feel better?" Koki asked intently.

"Yes, somehow." She put her fingers to the crude stone, wood, and shell necklace. "He did something to me, was doing something to me, was going to do something to me." Panic rose in her. "He had me. I couldn't think. I forgot everything. Koki—"

The faun put his hands over hers, stepping close again so his forehead touched hers. "I know. Easy, it's all right now. We saw you at the coronation. Chika recognized what was going on. We'd been planning to get you soon, but realized it had to be now, or it might be too late."

Jessika nodded a little, trying to calm herself.

"Starbright said even if we get the pendant off you, you might be under some compulsions or obfuscations, and if you were, that her necklace would break them."

Jessika furrowed her brow. "She was right, both of them were: Chika and Starbright. Everything's different now, and you," she trailed off, touching her own lips, just lightly, and looking at his, before looking up at his eyes.

A flood of warmth surged through her body, and she wanted—nay, needed—to be back in his arms, against him, as tight as possible. Something of that must have shown on her face; Koki's eyes crinkled with delight, but his words were sober.

"We need to focus now," he insisted. "To get out of here you'll need to be paying attention."

Jessika bit her lip, nodded, but Koki stepped in, relenting enough to smile as he brushed at her mouth with his fingers.

"Hey, don't bite that," he teased.

It was only with her every shred of will that she didn't manhandle him down onto the bed behind her and wrap herself around him.

"I know," he whispered. "Later. Focus now."

She nodded again, and he dropped his fingers from her lips, stepping away.

"I shouldn't have done that," he repeated, "wrong timing."

A spark of indignation flared in Jessika's belly. "Hey, I started it," she argued.

He grinned back at her. "Yes, you did."

"I just need to grab one thing, and we'll go."

Rikah was waiting in the sitting room. When Koki led her out, he practically leapt at her, wrapping her in his arms while she was still stuffing Rikan's lock picks into her pocket. Since the magic pendant, she'd forgotten she had them, but luckily no one had noticed or taken them.

"You're safe," he whispered. "We were all so scared."

"Me, too," she whispered back. "And you're alright? You were hurt. Is everyone else alive? Oh, and I met your dad. He's alive."

"My father?" Rikah gasped.

"Later," Koki hushed. "We have to get out of here now."

"You're the one who took a whole ten minutes to get her," Rikah nearly growled. "What were you doing?"

Jessika blushed, but the darkness hid it.

"Let's go," Koki grunted.

They hurried as silently as they could down the hall towards the stairs, although Rikah shuffled along with a bit of a limp. Jessika went to descend the stairs but Rikah and Koki pulled her further on. She complied and they stepped into the lift. Koki and Jessika crowded towards the back and Rikah closed the door and grate.

"We can't go out the front door," Koki breathed in her ear. "It's guarded."

His breath made her skin shiver delightfully. He nuzzled her neck and she almost made a whimper of pleasure. Before she could reciprocate somehow, the lift shuddered and began moving.

"Who is operating the lift?" Jessika asked softly.

"Edgard," Rikah answered.

"He and Amlee are helping us," Koki explained.

"Tell me about my father," Rikah prompted.

"He's still a blacksmith. He has a shop between the inner and outer walls," Jessika whispered. "I gave him a note about you. He was really happy. He cried."

"Thank you," Rikah said, and from the thickness of his voice, Jessika thought he might be crying a bit, too. "I want to go see him. I will go see him, once it's safe."

The lift kept dropping and dropping. In the near complete darkness, Jessika found Koki's hand and held it. He put his other arm around her waist.

"We're going down into the wine cellar," Rikah said.

A few moments later the lift halted and the door and grate opened. Rikah stepped out into a candlelit room. Jessika and Koki followed. She saw wine barrels arrayed around all the walls. The tall dark shape waiting for them was Edgard.

"This way," he whispered, leading them down the room to stairs that led up into the pantry.

The four of them ascended and stepped out into the kitchen. Amlee was standing there beside another candle. As soon as she saw Jessika she strode forward and embraced her.

"Princess, I was so worried," the castellan whispered. "Altare took my daughter, with a pendant like that, years ago. I never saw her again. I was so scared it would happen to you, too."

Jessika shook her head. "It won't. It's all right. I'm leaving now. Will you be safe? You won't get in trouble? Do you want to come with us?"

"We must stay," Edgard said. "But you will return, Princess. You will remove the corruption from this castle. We will await that day."

"This way," Amlee said, releasing Jessika and pulling her towards the door into the garden. "Walk, don't run, and tiredly, like servants who have had a long day, just in case someone sees us."

Edgard stayed behind. Amlee walked with Jessika and the two men followed. A crescent moon lit the sky, giving little light, but Amlee moved with practiced grace through the rows of vegetables. Jessika feared at any moment a guard might confront them, or Altare himself would appear and destroy them all with magic.

A sudden thought struck Jessika, and she clenched Amlee's hand and turned back to Rikah.

"No, we can't leave," she hissed. "We have to get Hawkjoy. She's here, in Skire Germaine's dungeon. We can't leave without her."

"We have to," Rikah whispered. "We'll come back. We're going to need help to free her."

"She's still alive," Amlee murmured, urging Jessika to keep walking. "There are still loads of raw meat going down to the Skire's lab."

"I can't leave her again," Jessika protested quietly.

"If you stay, you know what he will do to you," Amlee said as they reached the entrance to the servant's quarters. "You are free from his influence now; you must realize what his plans were concerning you."

Jessika swallowed painfully.

Amlee didn't flinch. "He would have seduced you, wed you, declared himself king and done away with your father, then sired children on you to cement his blood into the royal line and ensure right of ruling. You would have become as mindless and slavish as he's made your father."

The thought of it made Jessika want to punch something. As Kari appeared with a lantern, Jessika caught a glimpse of Koki's face, and it looked like he felt the same.

"Hurry, this way," Kari whispered.

"Will he know I'm gone?" Jessika asked the group at large as they followed Kari down a narrow hallway.

"Not with that handkerchief around the pendant," Koki answered. "Thornfire enchanted it to hide that it's no longer on you, but it'll wear off by morning."

"Thornfire's alright?" Jessika rejoiced—as silently as she could.

"When I woke up, Thornfire had dragged everybody away from the house, including Cray. It was burning and I guess he didn't have the power to put it out," Rikah explained as they turned and headed up some steep stairs.

"So is everyone alive?" she pressed. "It looked like Waterleap, Thornwing, and Thornspike were really hurt."

"They were," Rikah confirmed. "If that sleeping powder hadn't worn off as fast as it did, I think all three of them would have died. Waterleap certainly would have bled out. Thornfire and Starbright managed to save everyone. Karo helped, too, but mostly he helped keep me alive. Kassandra showed up pretty quickly, too, and she helped as well."

Jessika sighed with relief, feeling one fear at least lifting from her.

"Because we were all on the verge of dying, we couldn't go after you. Most of us couldn't walk, much less fly, and if Starbright or Thornfire had gone, someone would have died for sure," Rikah insisted.

Koki poked him hard in the back.

"I'm sorry," Rikah blurted, too loudly, earning shushes from Kari and Amlee. "We all wanted to go after you. We wanted to go save you," he continued more quietly. "There just wasn't any way we could. No one was fit for it, and Kassandra looks too weird now. We all agreed she wouldn't be able to pass safely."

"I'm sure that's what Vor intended," Jessika soothed. "I forgive you." At least, she thought she did. There might have been some small part of her that didn't fully.

They reached the top of the staircase and turned out into a large hallway. There were some old benches along it, and a thick coat of dirt and debris coated them and the floor. It was wide enough to walk abreast and Koki came up beside Jessika and timidly took her hand. She squeezed his and walked a bit closer to him.

"But everyone will be alright now?" Jessika went on. "They're all going to heal up?"

"Thornwing and Thornspike can't fly for a while," Rikah murmured. "Thornspike especially took some deep wounds. Thornfire said some of her internal organs were damaged, but he did his best to help her body heal them.

Thornwing just took so many wounds to his pectorals that he's going to take a long time to heal."

"Waterleap's throat wound?" she prompted.

"It missed his larynx. He can still talk," Rikah provided, "but the biggest problem is that it hurt his throat pretty badly. Karo stitched it inside and out, but he won't be able to eat normally for a few more days yet. They're feeding him like a chick, tiny tidbits. Starbright said he'd also lost so much blood that he was unconscious when she got to him. She had to use magic to shock his heart into beating again, and it was hard to get the blood flowers into him, what with his throat torn up, he couldn't swallow. That was tricky business."

They reached the end of the hall where a heavy door stood ajar. It looked like it had been only recently opened. There was a clear, smeared area where the bottom of the door had slid along the filthy floor, and a ridge of dirt had built up where it stopped.

"Where does this lead?" Jessika asked as they paused before it.

"To the Feathyr barracks," Amlee answered. "Your winged friends are waiting at the top."

The housekeeper gave Jessika another hug.

"Don't worry about us," she said, smiling encouragingly. "We will await your return, Princess. Stay safe, and rescue Hawkjoy. I will silently revel in the mayhem it causes."

"Go now, hurry," Kari urged them.

They didn't take a light, but Rikah and Koki seemed to know the way. Jessika figured a trio of griffins must have dropped them off and they had come this way into the palace grounds. It made sense if the wall gates were always guarded.

Jessika tried not to stumble up the stairs and through the rooms they traversed. Rikah limped along, cursing under his breath as he tripped and stubbed his feet. Koki seemed surefooted and agile, leading them both on with hardly a pause.

She was panting as they climbed ever up and up. At last she felt a breath of cold air and saw a square of lighter night sky above them. They ascended up a ladder and through a trap door, emerging on a steeply raked rooftop covered with broken slate tiles.

"Watch your footing," Koki cautioned. "The griffins are on the other side, over the crest, so they can't be seen from the palace."

The trio began climbing up the slope, trying not to send loose slate sliding down. They'd nearly reached the top when a voice called out behind them.

"Princess Jessika, stop where you are."

They halted, all startled, and Rikah slipped a bit, knocking a broken tile into a tumble down the incline. In the darkness they couldn't see her face, but Jessika recognized the voice. Vor had appeared below them from the trapdoor. She was breathing hard, having apparently been running.

"You may have discarded the pendant and put on that charm to stop scrying, but my magic is still in your back," the young mage declared. "I can tell wherever you are, and when I sensed you leave your rooms, I knew something had happened."

"But you didn't wake your master to pursue me," Jessika challenged. "Why not?"

"Why bother? You aren't going anywhere. My master will reward me for my recapture of you, along with your strange companions."

"What does she mean her magic in your back?" Koki asked, raising his voice as though afraid.

"She removed the taint of shadow magic in my wounds, allowing them to heal," Jessika explained. "What she didn't tell me was that she was leaving a new taint behind: her power. She can hurt me and throw me around with it."

Vor reached out a hand and made a grasping motion. Jessika's feet lost traction as Vor yanked on her, pulling her down towards the trapdoor.

Koki was quickest, setting his hooves and grabbing Jessika's flailing hand as she went down on her side. Rikah was only a little slower, fastening his hands around Jessika's wrist just below Koki's hands. Vor tightened her fist and the pain flared. Jessika gritted her teeth against it and snarled.

Then Vor jerked her hand to one side, and Jessika's whole body jerked, too. It didn't send her tumbling over the edge of the roof, but it made Koki and Rikah stagger and nearly yanked Jessika's arm out of her shoulder socket. Before the men could fully recover, Vor jerked Jessika the other way.

Rikah went down on one knee, but Koki's cloven hooves were sure and steady. With the next jerk, though, back the other way, Rikah lost his grip before he could stand up, and Koki hopped and skidded across the roof. He withstood the next jerk, while Rikah was trying to recover, but had barely set his feet down when Vor yanked on Jessika again, the hardest yet.

Jessika shouted with pain, rolling across the roof and bruising herself on the sharp, broken slate—but she felt Koki's grip break, and the faun lost his stance, falling and skidding down the roof among loose pieces of slate tile. His fall accelerated as he neared the edge, unable to catch himself.

"No!" Jessika screamed.

Koki went bouncing off the roof with several shards of slate, falling into the open space, a dozen floors above the courtyard below.

Rikah regained his grip on Jessika, but she was fruitlessly scrambling towards the edge, and he held her back. There was no chance of her being able to catch him. Koki was already gone.

Then she heard the swift slice of wings through the air. She followed the sound with her gaze. Far down towards the other end of the roof, a griffin swept upward out of a dive, carrying something in its arms. It circled over and Koki waved, safe.

Its path led Jessika to look up towards the crest of the roof. There stood two more griffins silhouetted against the sky in full threat display: every feather lifted, fur fluffed out like angry cats, and wings spread open to touch tip to tip overhead like sunbursts.

The pain faded from Jessika's back.

"I see you, mage of Light," Vor growled.

"Retreat," a low griffin voice ordered, "and you live."

Rikah pulled on Jessika and she struggled to her feet, and followed him up the incline again.

"She is mine," Vor challenged. "I caught her for my master."

There was no other warning. Vor flung her hand out and a darker darkness in the night stabbed out like thrown knives. One griffin reacted as though there had been warning, rearing up and sweeping both wings forward in a mighty flap. The inky thrown shards sparked like flint on steel and vanished.

The wind from that single magical flap roared like a storm and slapped into Vor, lifting her off her feet. As she had done to Koki, she went tumbling, scrabbling among the loose slate, and dropped over the edge of the roof, but there was no griffin swooping down to catch her.

Jessika, aghast, looked up at the griffin mage, and by size and shape identified Starbright. "You killed her," she accused.

Lightly, Starbright leapt up and took a short glide to the edge of the roof. She looked over. "No," she said after a moment. "Her talent has landed her safely. We should go before she makes another attempt or summons her master. He would not be so easily taken by surprise."

Koki and the third griffin appeared at the crest. "Yes, let's go," he urged.

"But one thing, first," Starbright said. "Hawkwings, come here."

The griffin scrambled over to her, before Jessika could actually get up and come to her. Starbright set a hand on Jessika's back.

"She has put magic into you," she confirmed. "Hold on while I remove it. This will tingle a bit."

A bit was an understatement. A prickling sensation like pins and needles when sleeping the wrong way made a limb fall asleep spread from Starbright's hand out to Jessika's shoulders and down to her buttocks, even tickling a little out into her arms and legs.

"I think that's enough for now," the mage murmured after a few moments, "but you need a thorough examination; you've had so much magic put on you in the past month."

"Later, now get on," the griffin up at the peak whispered.

Koki mounted the giffin who'd caught him and Starbright hopped up the roof to nudge Rikah, who found a grip on her harness and slung himself up. Jessika hiked herself up to the griffin who'd remained at the peak, the one who'd just spoken, and found the harness in the dark, still not sure who it was.

The three griffins powered into the air and flew off into the night.

By the time they started to circle down for a landing, Jessika was chilled bone deep by the frigid sky air and shivering so hard she could barely hold on. She couldn't see a campfire, and they clearly hadn't gone far enough to reach South-scree, but the griffins were moving in concert and seemed to know where they were going. All Jessika could see were the tops of trees—and indeed they seemed to be running right into them.

Small branches and leaves lashed at her as her mount struck the tree tops, but only for a few moments. Then they were descending among the trunks, the griffins doing quick fluttering flaps to slow their fall until they touched down.

Only then did Jessika detect a faint glow in the near complete darkness under the forest canopy. It showed an edge too even to be made by nature, and as she slid off her mount's back and her eyes started to adjust, she realized she was looking at a large ruined structure made of stone blocks. Trees crowded it on all sides and other greenery wreathed it, but there was a square opening through which came the trace of light.

The griffin who'd carried her gave her a nudge and she headed towards the doorway, being careful to take secure steps on the uneven paving. The opening was just big enough for a large griffin to squeeze through. Beyond it was a small room with three doorways leading from it. The light, stronger now, came from the right hand one and Jessika took it, pulling back a tanned leather hide that covered the opening and blocked most of the light.

"Wings!" Karo exclaimed from his meditative seat by a pile of glowing stones.

The slender young man pushed up to standing without needing the help of the crutch lying along the floor behind him, so Jessika could embrace him. There was a handful more griffins in the room, too—Thornfire, Thornwing, Waterleap, and Thornspike—which was large enough it could have held a dozen comfortably.

Jessika moved over to the side so everyone else could come in. Rikah came in next, followed by Starbright, Thornsoft, then Koki, and last came—

"Hawkmother," Jessika exclaimed.

So that was who her mount had been. Her first instinct was to run up to her, throw her arms around her, and hang on tight, but she paused halfway there, stopped by the griffin's expression.

"No, little Hawkchild, the Hawkmother is not here," she rumbled.

"Hawkwind," Jessika corrected in a tiny voice. "I'm sorry. I'm so sorry."

"Do you realize what you've done?"

"Hawkwind," Thornfire spoke up. His voice sounded a bit slower than it used to, as though he were measuring his words more carefully—or having to focus hard to produce them. "I was the one in charge of this quest. I allowed it. The blame should be on me."

Something impacted Jessika from behind and she staggered. Little claws hooked into her shirt as the bat-cat pulled itself up.

"Ugly girl saved my life," Breeka declared from where it now clung to Jessika's shoulder.

"Cray is here?" Jessika asked.

Wherever Cray was there Breeka would be.

"Did you think I'd allow him brought to South-scree?" Hawkwind nearly snarled.

"He's here," Thornwing said, "in the back of the room, back there, but he's still unconscious."

Koki came over and took Breeka off of Jessika. The bat-cat made no comment as it transferred its grip to the faun. Hawkwind glared at Jessika for another few breaths, and she began to feel like a lame deer facing a mountain cat. She didn't think the griffin would actually hurt her, and she couldn't blame Hawkwind for being upset; Jessika was furious with herself, too. If Hawkjoy was not rescued soon and in good health, she didn't think she'd ever forgive herself. Hawkwind, Hawkswift, and the rest of the Hawk Line would probably never forgive her either.

At last, Hawkwind's crest lowered.

"It is done. Blame and anger will not help the Hawkmother," she conceded.

"What are we going to do?" Jessika asked in a small voice.

Hawkwind's crest flared back up to its full height. "We are going to take her back."

"Altare will call in drakes," Jessika was saying. "I'm sure of it, once he knows there are griffins involved."

"We won't give him time," Hawkwind declared.

The former Hawkmother hadn't sat down, but paced across one end of the room, occasionally flipping her wings and growling.

"We're going after Hawkmother at dawn, or just before, a few hours from now," Hawkwind explained. "They won't expect us to return this night, and just before dawn is when humans sleep the deepest."

"But how?" Jessika asked. "I couldn't imagine how to free her."

"Nor did we, until Koki joined us," Rikah said.

"I was there," the faun said quietly. "They lowered griffin captives in through the roof."

"The roof of the Skire's laboratory?" Jessika clarified, baffled. "And what do you mean you were there?"

"Later, children," Hawkwind cut her off. "I've scouted the grounds from above and confirmed what I remember from my youth living there. There is a private courtyard inside the palace, beyond the ones by the entrances to the main wings. It's small, but big enough for us to land in. The ballroom has double doors that open onto it."

"And the floor of the ballroom opens up," Koki contributed. "Right below it is the laboratory."

"If we open it, we can carry the Hawkmother up and out."

"We made a harness," Thornwing contributed, "because we doubt she'll be capable of flying."

"And I made another charm," Starbright said, "like the one we gave you, Hawkwings, to keep anyone from tracking her."

"It will take four of us to carry her," Hawkwind resumed. "Myself, Starbright, Thornsoft, and Waterleap."

Jessika looked over at the injured male griffin.

"My throat hurts, but my wings work fine," he said softly.

"Waterleap is healing well," Thornfire concurred. "He hasn't been able to eat as much food as I'd like, but I think he'll be strong enough. I wish I could come, but I'm too weak yet."

"I can open the floor," Starbright said firmly.

"Once you get it started, Thornsoft and I will lend muscle to the task," Hawkwind nodded. "As soon as the gap is big enough, Waterleap—the smallest—will leap down and neutralize any enemies. The rest of us will follow once the doors are all the way open. We'll get Hawkmother into the sling, haul her out, and take off. It will be a difficult takeoff but Starbright has said she can give us a magical boost."

"I want to come," Jessika announced.

Hawkwind paused to frown at her.

"I got Joy into this mess," she insisted.

"No one can be spared to carry you," Hawkwind sighed.

"You might need a human," Karo spoke up.

"I wish we all could come," Rikah grumped.

"I'd happily carry you, but I'm not healed enough," Thornwing apologized. "I'd just rip open my wounds trying."

Jessika suspected Thornspike was regretting missing out on this, too, but she was sleeping in the back of the room, so didn't say so.

"We could carry you in, but not out," Hawkwind said.

"Someone could fly us out over the walls, one at a time," Rikah suggested. "Then we could run off into the woods and get back here."

Thornsoft stepped up into their view and gestured, "I'll do it."

"We don't have time to wait for anyone to make four trips over the walls and back," Hawkwind argued. "I am anticipating that we're probably going to be seen or heard, and there will likely be conflict. We need to get in and out as fast as we possibly can."

"Just me, then," Jessika insisted. She looked at Koki and Rikah. "Sorry."

Koki raised his hands. "I wasn't planning on coming, and I don't think you should go, either. What if he recaptures you?"

"We could escape through the tunnels under the palace," Jessika realized. "Rikah and I both mapped them. We've gone through them before."

"The tunnels we think Altare probably put traps in to keep you out?" Thornfire rumbled, sounding more like his usual self.

"To keep us out," Rikah echoed triumphantly, "not to keep us in. I bet we could get through them, coming from the inside."

The griffins exchanged dubious glances.

"I can see how having a human along might be useful," Koki commented. "You might need smaller hands to manipulate keys, if Hawkmother is locked up, but it shouldn't be Hawkwings."

"I know how to pick locks," Jessika argued, "and you said you're not going."

"I know how, also," Rikah said. "Koki taught me, too."

"Well, I think you'll need another mage," Karo spoke up. "Thornfire isn't coming to help, and Starbright is going to exhaust herself."

"I'm fine," the griffin mage said.

Thornfire made a face that expressed his doubt, but didn't say anything.

"I'm an adult," Jessika declared. "I'm going."

Hawkwind scowled at her. "I let that argument sway me into allowing this whole quest to happen in the first place. Swift is an adult, an adult far older than you. She wanted to come. I said no. She stayed."

Jessika flinched a little. "Well, someone had to watch the chicks, right? With Thornsoft and Thornwing both here, it must be hard by herself, but of course someone had to stay."

"She has help, but that's not the point."

"Who's helping her?" Jessika wondered, genuinely curious.

"The sires of Dusk, Sun, and Noon," Hawkwind grumbled.

Jessika raised her eyebrows. She'd never heard Hawkwind mention who had sired her chicks, although it was rather obvious that Thornsoft and Thornwing were the sires of a few. She'd never met those other sires, either.

"They'll make sure the chicks don't starve, should the Hawkmother and I not return," Hawkwind explained. "If that happens, Swift will be steward of the Line until Day awakes."

That brought the angry mood to a halt. If things went terribly wrong, they could indeed be caught or killed trying to free Joy. Everyone was risking their lives—and by extension, the lives of Hawkwind's chicks and the future of the Hawk Line.

"I'm sorry, Hawkwind," Jessika said again. "I really am. She's my sister. Thinking about what might be happening to her makes me sick. I want to save her. Please let me help."

Hawkwind squeezed her eyes shut, her crest and raised ruff flattening completely.

"Jessika, don't you see that I don't want to lose you, too?" she pled.

"I know." Now she went to Hawkwind and wrapped her arms around the griffin's neck. "But you can't protect me forever. I have to make my own choices and my own mistakes. My mistake led Joy to getting hurt. How can I let someone else risk themselves to fix what I did, while I stay safe at home?"

Hawkwind encircled her with an arm and a wing, holding her close, and Jessika ran her fingers up under the griffin's neck feathers, against her hot skin.

"You can come, then," Hawkwind agreed, head bowing in defeat as she preened a bit of Jessika's hair. "You should try to get some sleep. I'll wake you in a couple hours."

Chapter 23
Just Before Dawn

Sleep wasn't what Jessika wanted, but as Rikah and Karo began arguing that they should be able to come, too, Koki picked up a blanket from a pile and caught her eye. She nodded, and took his wrist as he headed for the door. Hawkwind turned her head from the argument long enough to chuckle as they went past. Jessika blushed but didn't drop her gaze.

"Oh, go on," Hawkwind grinned, making a shooing gesture. "I'm just glad you didn't try to pick a griffin as your mate."

That made Jessika blush even hotter, but Koki smiled.

"Over here," he whispered once they'd let the leather door fall shut behind them.

The entry room had a bit of stone wreckage that might once have been furniture or statues, but behind some of it in one corner was a dense layer of accumulated leaves and moss that had formed over years and cushioned the hard floor. Since summer was well enough underway for the days to get hot, it was dry enough to sit on. Koki threw the blanket around them both and they huddled in the corner, propped against the walls, arms around each other and heads resting together.

"This is a safe place," Koki said. "The unicorns are guarding it. Hawkdare told me Hawksky convinced them. I didn't know you knew a nymph, and she has a griffin name like you. You'll have to tell me the story sometime."

He nuzzled her neck and Jessika's breath caught, her heart pounding. It was distraction enough that she couldn't articulate the question of why he called Kassie a nymph. But then Koki sighed and pulled back a little.

"I didn't bring you out here for sex," he murmured.

Jessika was swimming in too many sensations to reply.

"Much as I'd like to," he grunted, "but I can't just carry you off to a dark corner and forget everything else, not right now."

She tried to focus, to gather her scattered wits. "I know," she managed to reply, "but how can you be so calm?"

His eyes glinted at her in the darkness. "I've had a lot of practice. I'll tell you about it once you get back and we're safe." He sighed, as if steeling himself, "we should talk about other things, too."

She thought she knew what he was referring to, but she didn't want to think about it. Finally, Jessika contributed, "I guess we should."

"It's just," he said, "are you sure? I'm," he hesitated, "not human. I know I look it from the waist up, and sound like it, and spent more years living with humans than I did with my own kind, but I'm not."

"And I'm not a faun," Jessika countered. "I'm a human raised by griffins. It's not like I'm normal, either."

For several breaths they sat in silence, and Koki leaned back in to rest his forehead against hers again.

"We can't have kids together," he murmured. "It's been tried. Humans and fauns can't make babies. I like you, I'm attracted to you," he swallowed, "a lot, but ultimately we might not be happy together, years from now."

"I don't care about years from now," she whispered back. "If we stop being happy together, we can stop being together, any time, but we're happy together now."

He held her tighter. "Alright. Just, remind yourself."

Koki pulled away again and dragged up the legs of his pantaloons. Then he found one of Jessika's hands and placed it on his knee.

"You're comfortable with this?" he confirmed in a small voice.

She stroked down his leg, slowly, past his hock, until she reached his cloven hoof. It was as wide as her palm, smooth, and a little warm, not cold like stone. His fur was thicker and softer than deer fur, more like griffin fur, with more undercoat and fewer guard hairs.

"I'm comfortable with this," she assured him.

"I have a tail, too," he confessed, "but it's short, like a deer's."

"You can show me later."

From his reaction she thought she'd made him blush, which was a nice reversal of usual events. While he was still off balance, she reached up and touched his cap, which he'd managed to retain somehow, even through his fall off the roof. That made him flinch, and she paused.

"Is it alright?" Jessika asked.

He didn't answer for a moment, and she worried she'd gone too far, but then he reached up and pulled the hat back and off, releasing more curls that fell around his face. The light was dim, but she could see faintly his two horns, emerging just at his hairline, slightly wider apart than his eyes. They were only a couple inches long, arching slightly backward, just sharp points.

"May I touch?" she breathed, mouth gone dry.

"They're not like antlers," he murmured. "Antlers are dead. Mine are alive. They'll grow longer my whole life. If I live to be very old they'll even curve back and around so the points are even with my jaw. They have sensation. I can feel when they're touched."

Jessika hesitated. "I won't, if you prefer."

He swallowed. "No. I mean, yes. You can. Go ahead."

Sensing she'd been granted trust he'd not given to anyone else, Jessika first touched just his cheek, and he leaned his head into her hand. Gradually, she worked up to his forehead, and then so gently brushed her thumb along one horn. Koki shivered.

"Only lovers touch each other's horns," he confessed. "Not even parents and children. It's intimate."

"I'm sorry I don't have any," Jessika whispered back, the truth of it like an ache inside.

Koki stroked her face and hair in turn. "It's alright."

She moved her hand away, and held him. For a while they stayed that way, dozing a bit, until the intense emotions faded. Feeling more comfortable, questions were beginning to surface.

Jessika asked, "So female fauns have horns, too?"

"Yes, but they tend to be more slender, without the big bumps and ridges that some males have," Koki answered easily.

"Do you fight with them?"

She thought he might be grinning. "Like bucks during the rut? No, we fight like humans, with bows, knives, or our fists—and our feet."

"You said you were there, in the Skire's laboratory."

Whatever momentary mirth he might have had chilled at once.

"My family was captured," he said. "Me, my older sister, my mother, and my father: the new mages at Northborn were out in the forest, hunting or exploring, and they caught us all."

"And they killed your family?" Jessika whispered. "That's why you said, when Dare and I went into the tunnel, that your whole family died in there."

Koki didn't answer for long moments. "I'm not going to describe everything they did to them." His voice was like winter ice at midnight. "I was young, seven summers old. The Skire said she wanted to keep me to observe my development, my growth from child to adult. One of the mages would come, once or twice a month, and paralyze me with a spell. They'd take me out of the cage and she'd examine me. Then they'd put me back in and the spell wore off. She never cut me, but I was always afraid she would."

His arms tightened around Jessika.

"I saw everything that went on in there. They had griffins. One by one she cut them all apart. They did things to humans, too, mainly testing magic and drugs on them. It always smelled of blood and offal. I was always afraid I'd be next."

Koki buried his face against her neck and shoulder.

"I've never told anyone about it," he mumbled.

She squeezed him and rubbed his back.

"The worst," Koki choked out. "That man, that man in there you're calling Cray, he brought in a unicorn foal."

Jessika jerked alert. Was this what the unicorns hated Cray for?

"The mages couldn't knock it unconscious, because it was too magical. Their spells just bounced off," Koki went on. "They tied it down. It screamed. It screamed all while the Skire was cutting on it. When it finally stopped," he had to pause to try to make his words more intelligible. "I didn't know if I should be happy or sad."

Jessika found herself leaking tears along with him, rocking him in her arms.

"I hear it," he wept. "I hear it screaming in my dreams."

She held him harder, wishing there were something she could do. She couldn't change the past. Were there any words that could help? Jessika opened her eyes again when she detected the room getting lighter. Was it dawn? Already? The rescue—then a sense of soothing balm seeped in around her. The light was coming from the square door into the ruin. Even Koki lifted his head to look.

Something bright, so bright, was coming inside. The light was golden like honey and dandelions and smelled of summer. Through the glow, Jessika could see the shape of four legs, mane, tail, and horned head on a slender neck. The unicorn stepped methodically closer, the debris in the room somehow providing no obstacle.

The light almost blinded her, but it didn't hurt, as the unicorn stopped close enough to touch.

"Child of the forest," it said, and Jessika thought by its voice that it was a mare. "You were never meant to bear such a burden."

The unicorn lowered her head, slowly, like a tree bent by the wind. Jessika thought she would touch Koki with her horn, but instead she placed a velvety soft kiss on his forehead, right between his own horns.

"Be free of it," she said, "and sleep without hearing my child's cries. Let that be my punishment alone."

Koki slumped in Jessika's arms, as though he'd fallen suddenly asleep. The unicorn's head turned slightly, and Jessika felt its attention shift to her. She tried not to quail beneath it.

"You go to strike a blow against those who tormented my child and slew my mate," she said, her voice making Jessika's head ring like silver bells. "Take a gift, to help restore the balance."

This time, she tipped her head to touch Jessika with her horn. It was like warm water washing over her and made her every muscle relax. She sighed with relief.

"Only until the sun reaches its peak," the unicorn murmured.

Without another word, the unicorn turned. She passed out of the room, and the brilliant light went with her, leaving them in darkness.

"Koki, are you alright?" Jessika asked.

He muttered something she couldn't understand, and shortly was blinking his eyes open again. She brushed his hair away from his face.

"I'm alright," he slurred. "That was a unicorn."

"The mother of the one you saw killed, it seems," Jessika whispered. "Did she help you?"

He sat up under his own power and rubbed his face. "I feel different. Those memories, I remember them, but it's not," he stared at his hands, "it's like, they still don't feel good, but it doesn't feel like I'm getting stabbed every time they cross my mind now. I know they killed that foal, I know it screamed, but," he sighed and dropped his hands. "I can't really remember what the screaming sounded like anymore."

"It doesn't help you to keep reliving that event," Jessika surmised. "You know better than to kill things like that, and you always have. You didn't do anything wrong. It's not a lesson you need to learn."

"That man in there needs to learn it," Koki growled.

"I think he's learning," Jessika nodded. "The unicorns are punishing him."

"Are they? Good."

He settled back against the wall and rubbed his face again.

"She gave me something, too. A gift, she said."

"A gift?" he echoed.

"She touched me with her horn." Jessika put her hand on her forehead. "I felt warm. What did she mean?"

She looked intently at Koki, hoping he might have some answers as a quasi-mythical beast himself. But then she noticed that she could see the contours of his face, individual strands of his hair, and the precise set of his eyebrows. Before, she'd been lucky to make out the silhouette of his face and the reflection in his eyes.

"I can see you," she said.

He cocked an eyebrow, "as opposed to?"

"Humans have poor night vision. I couldn't see much before. Now, I still can't see colors, but I can see everything around me. It's just a little dim, murky, but I can see where everything is."

"You think the unicorn did that?"

"I think she must have. Can unicorns do that sort of thing?"

He shrugged. "I don't know. That was only the second unicorn I've seen in my life."

"I wonder if she did anything else to me?" she mused.

"Like?"

"Like making me stronger, or faster, or giving me better hearing."

"Maybe you should be careful," Koki suggested. "If you're stronger and don't realize it, you could hurt someone."

"I'll be careful," she agreed.

They sat back, and after a little time to reflect, Jessika resumed the line of questioning she'd started.

"So how did you escape the laboratory?" she said.

Koki didn't seem bothered that she'd asked. "Chika freed me, and took me out with her. We escaped through the tunnels."

"She was a prisoner, too?"

Koki scowled. "She was Altare's," he whispered the name, "pet. One in a long line, it seemed, or maybe just one of many. Chika might be able tell you which. He got a child on her, as he did to them all. They were all brought to the lab for the birth, including Chika. When it didn't come out the way he wanted, he set fire to them both."

"That's where her burns came from," Jessika said.

"That's right. He left them to burn after the birth. He said he'd come back to dispose of the remains. I don't know why he didn't stay to watch; that's usually more his way. As soon as he left, I picked up the pail of water in my cell and threw it at them. The pail bounced off the bars, but the water went right through: that put out most of the fire. Chika had been tied down, but between the fire and water, she was able to break one of the ropes and free herself. Then she went through the Skire's things until she found the key to my cell. She let me out and I carried the baby, since Chika had just given birth and gotten burned. I sort of half-carried her, too. We escaped out the tunnels."

"The baby wasn't hurt?"

Koki smiled something that wasn't a smile. "The baby was Verika. The fire didn't hurt her because of her scales, just scared her a bit."

"And Altare didn't track her and find her?"

Now Koki chuckled grimly. "Fire cleanses. He thought it would kill her, and it certainly hurt her, but fire also clears spells and enchantments. It wiped out any tracking spell he had on her. Obviously, we couldn't use that on you, so Starbright made the necklace instead."

She nodded thoughtfully. "What do you mean Verika didn't come out the way he wanted?"

"Chika could tell you more about it, but from what I could tell, he was trying to breed a," he groped after the words, "like, a demon, some kind of creature with human thought but a strong, animal-like body, with claws and all kinds of things that would make it the ultimate warrior. He did things to his pet girls, to try to make that happen—spells and potions and ceremonies. I didn't see most of them, but from what Chika has said, it was pretty awful."

Indeed, Jessika's stomach was turning.

"Can we go back to talking about sex?" Koki suggested. "That was much more fun."

She grinned widely, finding herself wishing with a thrill of apprehension that they had time to try some sex. Instead, she put her arms back around him, snuggling close, and there was no talking but murmurs for the next space of time, until Hawkwind came into the entry room and announced it was time to leave.

Striding out to hop on Hawkwind, Jessika found she covered the ground with astounding ease. Even heaving herself up onto the griffin's back required not even a grunt of effort.

"So the unicorn did give me more than night sight," she remarked.

"What? What unicorn?" Hawkwind questioned.

Koki had walked out with her. "The unicorn that came and visited us."

"Visited you while you were—?" Hawkwind trailed off, looked back at Jessika, down at Koki. "I won't ask," she said.

Koki snorted with humor, but sobered quickly. "Be careful, all of you," he said. "Come back safe."

Four griffin heads nodded, and Jessika reached down to hold Koki's hand for a moment.

"Wait, wait, take this," Rikah called out, running as well as he could out of the ruin to them.

He held up two sticks towards Jessika.

"I made you new truncheons," he said. "You might need them."

Jessika took the weapons. They were hard and rigid, smoothed down except for the grips, which were ridged so they wouldn't be as likely to slip out of a sweaty palm.

"Thanks, Dare," she said.

"I knew we'd get you back," he replied, stepping away from the crouching griffins. "Be safe, and bring back Joy."

Starbright took off first, carrying the bulk of the harness and fighting her way up among the trees. The males went next, each burdened with ropes that would hook onto the harness, and then Hawkwind leapt up after them.

Jessika tucked herself down against Hawkwind's back, finding that holding on was no struggle even against the jerking, flinging movement of the griffin's altitude-grabbing flight. The four emerged above the treetops into the night. It was even colder than a few hours ago when they'd landed. The unicorn's gift apparently did not extend to increasing natural body heat and Jessika was soon fighting her shivers.

In the distance the capital city was dark but for a few faint pricks of candlelight. After some minutes the palace loomed up black against the sky. Jessika could neither see nor hear any activity. A couple lanterns glowed along the inner and outer walls. The griffins banked around to approach from the side opposite the main gates, staying as low to the trees as they could.

The courtyard they aimed for turned out to be tiny indeed, but it was possible for all the griffins to land in it one at a time, although Waterleap nearly fouled a wing on a tree. With her heightened night sight, Jessika located the big double doors into the ballroom and went up the three wide steps to stand before them. She pulled on the handles but they wouldn't budge.

"Let me," Starbright whispered, nudging Jessika aside.

The griffin put a hand on the door and bowed her head for a moment of concentration.

"I don't sense any wards," she breathed. "Either he took them down or never bothered with these doors."

After another moment, Jessika heard the little thunk as something hit the floor just inside. Now she and Starbright each took a handle and pulled the doors wide open. On the floor was a bit of melted metal. Starbright had just heated up the locking latch until it got soft enough to lose its shape and fall off due to gravity.

Waterleap made a controlled leap across the ballroom floor to land by the door into the hallway. He silently wedged a doorstop under it to hopefully prevent it from being opened while the rescue attempt was underway. Starbright was examining the floor, finding the seams of the big trapdoors and checking for magical traps.

Hawkwind gestured for Jessika to come to her, and she obeyed. The griffin spoke with hand speech instead of voice.

"You're the smallest," she said. "As soon as you can fit, squeeze through the gap and drop into the room. If there are any threats, go after them. Waterleap will follow as soon as the gap is big enough for him."

"Thank you, Hawkwind, I will," she gestured back.

Her heart was starting to speed up. It would be a bit of a fall into the room, but she hoped her unicorn gift would help her land safely. She hoped even more that Skire Germaine was not inside—and hoped even more than that that Altare and Vor were not inside.

Starbright flipped her wings to get everyone's attention.

"I'm ready," she signed. "Hawkwind, there, and Thornsoft, there. Waterleap come here beside me, and Hawkwings here in front. Be ready. I'll cast a spell of silence first, since this is likely to be noisy."

Jessika took her position and tried not to frown. Starbright was going to exhaust herself, especially if she had to do any more magic after they got the doors open. Jessika felt the faintest tingle go over her skin, and then she could no longer hear the pounding of her own heart or the subtle sounds of her breath.

She was crouched right at the outside juncture of the two trapdoors. Starbright extended a hand down, past Jessika's head, pointed towards the seam. She saw the griffin's hand start to tremble. From what she knew of magic—which wasn't all that much—magic didn't move objects with ease. Starbright and Thornfire were great at producing heat or cold or light, or wind, or projectiles of energy, but she'd never seen them pick up or throw objects with their powers. She couldn't imagine how Starbright was going to lift up two massive doors. Hawkwind and Thornsoft stood by, ready to stick their hands into the gap as soon as it appeared, but Starbright would still have to lift the doors a good few inches with magic alone.

Starbright's hand and arm were trembling and the doors weren't moving at all. Then suddenly the griffin mage made a fist, snapping her fingers in. The doors bounced up as if they'd been struck from below. Hawkwind was ready, shooting out her own hands and catching the door on her side, but Thornsoft missed his, and it flopped back down, still silent.

"Help Hawkwind," Jessika gestured before his dismayed face, and the male griffin leapt over to join the big female, grabbing on with her and pulling up the door.

Light spilled upward through the crack and Jessika grimaced in dread. Unless the Skire had left a candle burning, there was somebody down there. Hawkwind and Thornsoft worked quickly together, and once the gap was a foot or so wide, Jessika hurried into it feet first, not knowing what she would land on. Scraping herself on the edges of the door, she pushed through, and dropped into the Skire's laboratory.

Jessika didn't fall very far, landing on a table without the slightest stumble. She swept her gaze rapidly around the room and fixed on a figure standing two tables over, bending over what seemed to be a large mound of bloody gray fur and feathers.

The Skire's back wasn't completely towards her, but the woman was so absorbed in her work that she hadn't yet noticed the silenced ceiling doors opening, or the young woman who had dropped in to save her sister. She had lanterns placed only beside her, which would be making it difficult to see into the darkness in the rest of the room.

Jessika took her new truncheons firmly in each hand. There would be no hesitation this time. She had to incapacitate her quickly, or the Skire would scream for Altare like she had before, and then there'd be real trouble.

Barely enough time for one breath had passed when Jessika leapt off the table and hit the damp floor running. The Skire must have seen her movement out of the corner of her eye; she looked up just as Jessika landed a smashing blow to her skull.

The woman went down with only the smallest cry, and Jessika followed her to the floor, pinning her body down with her knees on the woman's shoulders, and pressing down with a truncheon across her throat to keep her silent, but the Skire seemed to be unconscious from the head blow. Still, Jessika took no chances.

She was torn between jumping up and down on the Skire's throat until she died, and jumping to her feet to see to Hawkjoy. There was nothing else that the mound of bloody gray fur and feathers could be, but Hawkjoy was behind her now, and she dared not take her eyes off of the Skire. If Altare and Vor were somehow summoned, the four griffins and Jessika couldn't hope to stand up to them, not without at least Thornfire and Karo to help.

Gradually, the Skire started to twitch and her eyelids flickered; she was waking up. The spell of silence must have started to wear off, for Jessika began to hear the scrape of claws and fluffy impacts as griffins dropped down through the trapdoors. Then someone shoved her aside, knocking her to the floor and off of the Skire. She recovered to see Hawkwind, every feather bristling with rage, standing over the Skire's body, one clawed hand around her throat. Her wings shook and her bill gaped.

Under the sharp grip, the Skire flinched, wiggled a little, and then jerked violently. The woman's hands went to Hawkwind's wrist and she struggled, mouth opening into a panicked dark circle. Her hands and arms were coated with Hawkjoy's blood; it left stains on Hawkwind's amber fur. Jessika got to her knees and crawled closer.

"She can't breathe," Jessika whispered.

"If she can't breathe, she can't call for help," Hawkwind growled. "Look. Go look at what she did to Hawkmother."

Jessika got to her feet, terrified to see. First, all she saw was Starbright, glimmering golden in the light and casting Hawkjoy's body into shadow. Jessika moved closer, saw, and put her knuckles in her mouth.

Hawkjoy was strapped down to the table, on her back, all limbs spread. The feathers on her wings and tail had been cut completely back so only stubs remained. Her head was encased in a leather hood, also strapped down. Waterleap was working on the hood, trying to remove it, while Thornsoft was untangling the carry harness.

Jessika stared at Hawkjoy's unmoving body, afraid she was dead, until she detected the achingly slow movement of her chest: breathing. She stepped up beside Starbright, where the Skire had been standing.

Hawkjoy's underside had been shaved, and her lower belly opened up with a long incision. Beside it were two other similar incisions that were stitched shut with horsehair: both healing but still red and swollen. One looked older than the other. There were long metal hooks that came up from the edges of the table, holding the cut open. Inside were Hawkjoy's glistening internal organs, coated with blood. Blood ran out of the opening and pooled on the table. Starbright was preparing to remove the hooks so the edges of the cut could come back together.

Jessika had to look away, trying not to be sick.

"Can you help her?" she choked out.

"I can only cauterize," Starbright whispered back. "And I don't think that's how this kind of cut should heal. It's all the way through her body wall, through her muscles, through everything. Master might know what to do."

Starbright's voice caught.

"Stay calm," Jessika urged, even though she herself felt the farthest thing from calm. "Just stay calm and do your best."

Jessika strode back over to where Hawkwind was strangling Skire Germaine and the woman's face was starting to turn purple. Jessika knelt down and held up her truncheon.

"If you scream I'll knock your teeth out," she threatened. "Now tell me how to heal Hawkjoy."

Hawkwind's talons relaxed a tiny fraction and the Skire sucked at a little air.

"You don't understand," the woman gasped out. "Early embryonic development is an exciting new field. It can answer so many questions. That creature is my chance—"

Hawkwind squeezed and the Skire gaped and flailed.

"I asked you a question," Jessika snarled. "Answer it."

Hawkwind relaxed her hand again.

"I'll pay you for her," the Skire begged. "She's too valuable of a specimen. However much you want, I'll pay."

"So you can keep cutting her open, over and over?" Hawkwind demanded.

"Shh," Jessika cautioned.

Hawkwind crouched down lower, talons tightening. "So you like looking at the insides of people, while they're still alive?"

The griffin braced her wings against the floor so she could lift her other hand and show the Skire her claws.

"Would you like to see your own insides?" Hawkwind hissed. "How about I show them to you, one organ at a time?"

Jessika's mouth dropped open. Surely Hawkwind wasn't serious? But she sounded serious. Jessika had never heard her use such a tone.

"You think we griffins are just animals," she went on. "We have the courtesy to kill our prey before we eat it, but what do you do?"

"It's science," the Skire croaked. "It's important."

"Can you do it without your fingers?" Hawkwind asked. "What if I bite off each of your fingers, until you tell us how to close up that hole you cut in my Linedaughter's belly?"

The griffin captured one of the Skire's flailing hands and brought it up to her bill. The Skire writhed like a worm under a raven's foot.

"You have to irrigate it, and stitch it," she managed to gasp, "with two different threads, inside and out. Then wrap it."

Hawkwind eyed Jessika, who shook her head. "I don't know how to do that. I could try and see."

"If you agree to leave her with me, I'll return her once she gives birth," the Skire said, "if she gives birth."

Any feather on Hawkwind's body that might have started to relax bristled again. Her grip on the Skire's throat tightened. "If?" she demanded. "If she gives birth?"

"When studying," the Skire coughed, "embryonic development, there's a high chance of damaging the fetus, causing miscarriage, but it's a risk worth taking."

Hawkwind mantled, body shaking, and Jessika could see her restraining her need to scream in fury. The Skire jerked and bucked as Hawkwind's hand crushed her throat. Jessika leapt up and grabbed her griffin-mother's arm.

"You're killing her, you're killing her," she exclaimed. "Let go."

"Not yet," Hawkwind snarled. "I'll spill her guts before her own eyes before I kill her."

Hawkwind slashed down the Skire's front, shredding her clothing and ripping whatever didn't shred easily. The Skire arched and twisted, eyes popping and mouth stretched in fear and pain. Lines of red ran down her skin where Hawkwind's claws had scored her, but she hadn't cut so deeply as to do serious damage. Jessika was forcibly reminded of the shadow-beast clawing up her own back much the same way.

"No, you can't!" Jessika begged. "Hawkwind, you've never hurt a human. You swore to defend the people of Northnest. You're my Feathyr. I forbid it!"

Hawkwind's enraged gaze turned onto Jessika.

"This mad beast has been torturing your sister. She tortured Koki and his family. She tortured other griffins and people here in this room. She might have killed Hawkcall or Eagleye, or my mother and sire, and you beg mercy for her?"

"No," Jessika shook her head, on the verge of tears. "No, not mercy for her," she emphasized. "What she's done is terrible, but—," she put her hands on Hawkwind's cheeks. "You mustn't become a torturer because of her. You mustn't give her that power over you. Don't let her make you into what she is."

Hawkwind's furious expression flickered for a moment.

"We can't let her keep doing her evil," Jessika said, "but if you become evil because of her, you will have to live with what you did forever."

This time a hint of true doubt crept into Hawkwind's face.

"Look at her," Jessika ordered. "She's weaker than you. She can't stop you. She can't fight back."

The Skire was nearly blue with air deprivation. Her struggling was subsiding.

"Hawkwind," Jessika pled. She put her arms as far around the griffin as she could. "Don't become a monster. Be my Feathyr. Save Hawkjoy. Don't torture other creatures. You said it yourself. Griffins kill their prey before they eat it."

Hawkwind released the Skire and stepped back. She turned her head, eyes squeezed shut, shaking with reaction. Skire Germaine seemed hardly conscious again, but Jessika got down and pinned her with her knees, keeping a cautious truncheon across her bruised throat. With her free hand she put as much of the woman's clothes back in order as she could. Skire Germaine was sick and twisted, but it hurt to see her suffer even still.

Hawkwind stepped away. Jessika didn't watch what they were doing with Hawkjoy. Several minutes later, Waterleap stepped up beside Jessika.

"We're ready to leave," he said softly. "I've asked to be the one," he gestured towards the Skire, "to finish it, quickly."

"You're going to kill her?" Jessika whispered. "Did Hawkwind tell you to?"

He made a helpless gesture. "If we leave her, she'll call those mages, and whether they catch us or not, once she's recovered she'll go right back to cutting people up."

Jessika stared down at the semi-conscious woman: bruised, battered, and clawed.

"We have her at our mercy," she bemoaned. "If we kill her, if I stand by and let someone else kill her, even with all she's done—I can't do that."

"If you don't," it was Hawkwind, come back to see what the hold up was, probably, "you allow her to kill others, aided by mages: helpless, innocent others, children, oldsters, males and females, anyone and everyone she can get her hands on."

Jessika quivered with indecision. What Hawkwind said was true, but surely there must be another way.

"She would have let my chick die," Waterleap said, "mine and Hawkjoy's.

Then she would have cut it up. If it had been born alive she'd probably have cut it up, too, and then gone back to cut some more on Hawkjoy, and others, as she's done numerous times before."

Waterleap leaned in, raising his crest and hackles. "I'm finishing this," he said, slowly, deliberately. "You can't stop me, Hawkwings. I'm not your Feathyr. Step away."

Jessika was tempted to stand her ground, even though she recalled clearly the charnal chamber not far from the laboratory, with the pit full of remains. So many had died in this room, unable to fight back, unwilling to be the Skire's research subjects.

Hawkwind put a hand on her shoulder. "Come, Princess," the griffin murmured. "The woman is mad, like a sickened bear. She will not suffer any-more, like her victims. Come with me."

Jessika stood, started to turn and let Hawkwind lead her away, but then the Skire moaned and opened her eyes. Her gaze fixed on Jessika and her face twisted with some emotion—rage or fear or revulsion. She took a deep breath and snarled, "Alta—!"

Waterleap moved with the swift strike of a predator, ripping out her soft throat in a spray of blood.

There was hardly any sound to it. The body twitched and jerked, gurgled on its own blood, and went still. A few seconds later, Waterleap walked away. Skire Germaine lay motionless on the floor in a spreading pool of red so dark it looked black, except where it gleamed scarlet in the lantern light.

Jessika started crying and couldn't stop.

Chapter 24
The Return

Nearly blinded by her own tears, Jessika went to the door into the tunnels and fumbled for her new lock picks, ready to try to get through, but Thornsoft came and nudged her. She jumped and looked up at him, for a moment hardly recognizing him.

"We think we have time," he gestured. "I'll fly you over the walls, to the forest. The tunnels will be too dangerous."

"Are you sure?" she managed.

He nodded. "If we go now. They're getting Hawkmother ready."

They walked to below the big open trapdoors. The darkness outside was already lightening. Thornsoft gave her a boost up and followed, then knelt in the courtyard for her to mount. He was wearing the harness that would help him carry Hawkjoy, but there were still plenty of places to grab on.

With Jessika's unicorn-amplified strength, she had no trouble keeping her grip for the quick flight over the edge of the palace. Thornsoft set her down in the first spot big enough for him to land in. He pointed.

"The ruin is that way," he added by hand. "If you get lost, I expect a unicorn might come find you."

"I'll be fine," she assured him. "Hurry, and get Joy back safe."

Thornsoft nodded and leapt away. Jessika turned without another glance and dashed into the forest. Between her temporary night sight, extra strength, and extra speed, bounding through the forest like a doe was no problem.

Her tears dried on her face, leaving her cheeks feeling stiff and crusty. The image of Skire Germaine's body seemed burned inside her eyelids. So, too, was the vision of Hawkjoy, cut open and bleeding out. How would that awful gash ever be healed?

Jessika's thoughts and worries gradually faded, pushed to the back of her mind by the run through the forest, launching herself off fallen logs, leaping over streams and ravines, and arrowing through the gaps between trees. It was exhilarating, especially since she didn't exhaust herself. Her heart pounded fast and steady, and her breath burned, but she was able to keep going, trying to head ever in the direction Thornsoft had pointed.

The sun was up by the time she thought she might be getting close. If the griffins had been able to leave without interference, they were surely already back at the ruin. Jessika began looking around for signs of the ruin or unicorns.

"This way," a cheery voice called, and Jessika looked towards it.

Kassandra was dashing through the underbrush some yards away, waving at her and wearing nothing but a few strategically grown leaves and some bark. Her mass of curly black hair bounced against her shoulders, woven through with little vines.

Jessika altered her path, making her way towards her Linesister. As she got close, Kassandra slowed and smiled.

"You run fast," she commented.

Jessika came to a walk. "Just for now," she panted, "a unicorn gave me a gift."

"Witch Hazel," Kassandra nodded. "I know."

"Witch Hazel?"

"That's the unicorn's name. Glacier once told me something bad had happened to her in the past, but not what. Now I know."

Jessika nodded and caught her breath as they walked. She'd heard Kassandra mention Glacier before, and knew it was the name of the unicorn who had saved them from a drake shortly after their escape from Northnest, so many years ago.

"Koki said you're a nymph," Jessika said bluntly.

"He's right."

"You never told me that," she accused.

Kassandra shrugged. "You didn't need to know, and you wouldn't understand."

"What's a nymph?"

"See?" she said, but gently and without condescension.

"It means you can grow plants wherever you want, including on your own body."

"That's part of it," the nymph nodded.

"How did you become a nymph?"

"It's sort of a secret."

Jessika snorted.

"The unicorns: they helped change me. That's all I'll tell you."

"Alright," Jessika subsided. "I won't tell anyone."

"I'm still me," Kassandra said after a moment.

"I know you are," Jessika agreed. "In fact, you might be more you than you've ever been."

Kassandra looked over at her and smiled so sweetly she nearly glowed like a unicorn.

They came upon the ruin after only a few more minutes of walking. There were no unicorns in sight, but Jessika thought she sensed them near, observing everything. In the little clearing in front of the ruin was the carry harness. A trail of blood led into the ruin through the square doorway.

Kassandra stopped at the edge of the trees, while Jessika ran inside at a trot, almost colliding with Koki and Rikah, who were standing at the doorway to the left, opposite the one where they'd all been living. Koki grabbed her in a hard hug immediately, but from everyone's expression it was not a happy moment.

"She's dying," Rikah whispered. "They can't get the bleeding to stop. Even Thornfire can't close that cut."

Jessika wanted to scream. They'd finally gotten Hawkjoy out and it was too late, and it was all her fault. It was her fault for getting Hawkjoy into trouble in the first place, and her fault for coming on the wrong night. If only they'd chosen a different night, the Skire might not have been cutting on her, and they could have gotten her out whole.

The room they had her in was a twin to the one on the right. Someone had pulled up a paving stone in one corner, exposing dirt, and Kassandra had made another blood flower plant grow there. It looked like several of the flowers had been stripped off. The center of the room had been cleared of rubble and a thick mattress of boughs and grasses covered with hides had been prepared. Hawkjoy lay on it, partly on one side, but mostly on her back. The mages were sitting together by her belly, concentrating, while other griffins tried to hold the incision shut. There were layers of bandages wrapped around her, except for a portion where everyone had their hands, trying to do something.

The bandages were stained deep crimson; the floor was sticky with blood.

Hawkjoy was moaning slightly, but it didn't seem like she was fully awake yet. Jessika slipped past all the observers and made her way around to kneel by Hawkjoy's head. The big leather hood was off, and Jessika could see sores where it had rubbed away both feather and skin due to improper fit. She petted Hawkjoy's crown and cheeks, murmuring to her love and reassurance.

"Her heart's failing," Starbright whispered.

Fresh tears poured down Jessika's face.

"Not enough blood left in her," Thornfire confirmed.

"And the chick is too young to survive," Starbright sighed.

"Master, we can't give up," Karo pled.

"What would you have us do?" Thornfire asked weakly. "What spell do you know that we don't?"

Then a breathless hush fell over the room.

Jessika looked up. A unicorn stood in the doorway, the same one that had come to her and Koki in the night: Witch Hazel. Everyone around the door had stepped away. Once she had everyone's attention, the golden unicorn moved into the room, shining like a sun.

"Leave us," the unicorn ordered. "Let me be alone with her, mother to mother."

Most of the griffins departed at once, not quite tripping over each other. Thornfire bowed deeply and departed after them. Starbright and Karo lingered.

"I can help you," Starbright offered.

"You cannot help with this," Witch Hazel replied kindly. "You will have a chance to help your own children soon."

Starbright looked both startled and puzzled, but got up and left as if half hypnotized.

"Go with her," the unicorn said to Karo.

He gulped, staggered to his feet, and followed Starbright out. The unicorn turned its blazing gaze onto Jessika.

"This is the last time you will see a unicorn so easily," Witch Hazel said. "I will tend to your sister. Go to your faun."

Jessika tried to resist, but no mortal could withstand such an order from such a creature. She petted Hawkjoy's head as she stood and made her way out of the room. Koki was waiting with open arms for her and she hid her face against his neck.

"Hawkjoy has the best care there can be now," he murmured to her. "We can only wait."

They all sat together in the opposite room and Thornsoft told in gestures about the rescue of Hawkjoy. Somehow, it was easier to absorb the telling when it was not done by someone's voice. She felt Koki's arms around
her tense and then relax as the killing of Skire Germaine was recounted. His
breath released into her hair.

After that, a couple griffins went to clean up the carry harness and the
blood. Most everyone else lay down and went to sleep, or tried to sleep. After
a few quiet minutes of sitting among all the sleepers, Koki gave Jessika a little
nudge and pointed with his chin towards the door.

She got up and he followed her out into the little entry room. Someone
had hung another hide over the door where Hawkjoy—and presumably the
unicorn—lay. Jessika wondered what was going on in there, but she resisted
the urge to go look. She doubted there was anything she could do anyway.

"I made us a place," Koki murmured. "This way."

He went into the other interior doorway, the one across from the main
entrance. It was partly collapsed, but there was enough room for something
human-sized to squeeze through. Jessika followed, into a huge shadowy hall
with the broken remains of wooden benches and other bits of rubble. A dozen
or so pillars held the ceiling up. A few had fallen, but the ceiling had stayed
intact. Narrow windows along each wall had buckled slightly. Branches and
vines grew in through them and obstructed the light.

At the far end behind a raised platform was a set of stairs leading up.
Jessika followed Koki up them. They ended on a small landing with three
doorways. One showed a collapsed room beyond. Another was only partly
ruined, and the third was still in good shape. It was into this third one that
Koki stepped.

"I started making a spot for myself when I came here," he explained. "The
griffins had already established that main room for themselves, and I sort
of felt like a stranger. Of course, I was a stranger; only Hawkdare knew me.
Sometimes I felt like being alone, so I found this spot."

The room wasn't very big. Jessika couldn't touch the opposite walls if she
put her arms out, but they weren't more than a foot away on either side. Koki
had put down leafy boughs and bundles of grasses, with a couple blankets on
top and what were likely borrowed pillows. It made a tolerable nest. A back-

Hawkjoy
and
Witch Hazel

K A Smith 8/87

pack in one corner probably contained all his wordly possessions. There was an unglazed window in one wall that was almost totally undamaged. From it Jessika could look right out into the canopy of the trees and glimpse a little sky between their flickering leaves.

"It's a nice spot," Jessika told him. "Sometimes I prefer being alone, too. I probably would have made a place much like this."

"I don't mind sharing it with you," he offered.

She smiled. "I'd like that."

Koki touched her hand with a couple fingers, and she took his in reply. They stepped closer, facing each other, and leaned in to kiss, unhurried this time. Jessika knew what was going to happen, and it made her nervous, but also excited.

"I don't know what to do," she whispered. "I grew up with griffins and didn't have much chance to ask other, uh, people more like me."

Koki seemed mildly surprised. "I thought maybe you and Hawkdare?"

Jessika was even more surprised. "Rikah? I mean—oh, his real name is Rikah—no. He's my brother."

"He's not your real brother, not by blood," Koki pointed out. "And there's Hawkrain, too. He's not your real brother, either."

"But they're," she fumbled after words, brain befuddled by Koki standing so intimately close to her, and kissing her. "Yes, we could have, but we never wanted to."

Koki chuckled. "You never wanted to," he clarified. "I can assure you that they both wanted to."

"They told you that?" she asked, stunned.

"No," he admitted, "but if young human males coming into adulthood are anything like young faun males coming into adulthood, they are torment-ed by sexual desire on a regular basis, if not constantly. I guess female humans aren't the same?"

"Well," Jessika prevaricated, rubbing at a seam on Koki's vest. "Some, but I never wanted Rikah or Karo."

Koki made a sound of acknowledgement and moved a bit closer to her. He tucked his head against her neck and shoulder, resting it there, and Jessika realized he must be exhausted. She at least had slept a little before he'd come to rescue her.

"That's why I've had a lot of practice staying in control," he muttered.

"Do you want to lie down?" Jessika asked.

"If I lie down, I'll probably fall asleep."

"That's alright. I can be patient, too."

He snorted with amusement. Jessika urged him down into his nest and lay down with him. Koki groaned and tried to pull her close, tangling his legs with hers.

"When I started to mature, it was difficult for me," Koki went on. "I sort of lost my head. I couldn't focus on anything because I was so distracted." He sighed. "It got really bad. Luckily, Verika was too much younger than me for me to be interested in her, but the other young women around were a problem for me."

He hid his face back against Jessika's shoulder. "I lost control one day and tried to," he swallowed, "I sort of went after one of the neighbor girls. She was nice to me. She smiled at me and talked to me. I thought maybe she'd like to do, um, things, with me."

Koki made a sound of distress. "I realized pretty quick that she didn't. I didn't even get to kissing her, just tried to hug her, sort of, and she got upset and yelled at me. I ran away. I was so ashamed. Her father came and talked to Chika. I apologized over and over. Chika confined me to the house and set me all kinds of chores, and I had to tell her about everything that was happening to me, and—over several days—she sat with me and told me about women and sex and all kinds of stuff."

Jessika stroked his back and just let him talk.

"So I had to learn," he concluded. "I didn't want to be like that. I had to learn to control myself. I don't know if human males are like that. When fauns start to mature, we just start having sex for fun, whoever wants to, until we eventually pick one permanent mate for the rest of our lives. I guess humans don't do that?"

"I don't really know," Jessika confessed. "I think some people say we're supposed to wait until marriage for sex, but I don't think many people actually do that. I know we're supposed to only have kids when married, not before."

"What about griffins?"

She chuckled. "They're totally different. It's probably best if you ask one of them to explain it. They will, happily."

Koki's arms tightened around her. "And what about you?"

She hugged him back and it was her turn to hide her face against his curly head, being careful of his horns.

"After what Altare was trying to do to me, I just want something honest," she said. "I don't know if I want to get married or have kids. I don't know what to do about Northnest now. I don't know what my future is going to be."

She ran her fingers through his hair.

"I think I'd like to stay with you," she whispered, "but I don't want to stop you if you want to go be with other fauns, and pick a mate, and have a family."

"I don't know if they'd take me back," he said with a catch in his voice.

"They might. Do you want to try to find them?"

"Then I'd know, and it might be the wrong answer."

"Which is the wrong answer? They accept you? Or they don't?"

"That's the problem," he sighed. "I don't know."

They lay together for a while, as the sun reached its apex and Jessika felt the unicorn's gift of senses, strength, and speed melt off her. She drowsed a little and thought Koki was sleeping, too.

Jessika woke fully when the sun had moved to glitter through the trees and the light was dancing over their bodies and the nest. Koki was sleepily petting her cheek. She blinked at him. His eyes were warm, the pupils large and dark.

A flutter went through Jessika's belly and she felt blood rushing to her skin. One arm was still around Koki's waist and she pulled on him. He responded without a hint of hesitation, levering himself over her and slowly settling his weight down onto her as she rolled to her back.

After a series of slow kisses she asked, "So you don't know what you're doing either?"

He made half a shrug. "Not really, but I'm not worried. Chika told me we should try to take our time."

"Sounds good," she gasped as he transferred his mouth to her neck.

"She also said," he mumbled, "there's a chance it could hurt you, if you've never done it before."

Jessika shook her head. "Don't worry about that either. That's not always the case, I heard," she managed. "It's more common if there's reluctance or fear, and there's none of that here."

Koki pulled back and propped himself up to take some weight off her. "Good," he murmured.

Smiling, with his curly hair falling into his eyes and the light playing across his face, he looked more handsome and charming than ever, but also a little nervous; Jessika was glad it wasn't just her. She reached up to tuck her thumbs under the collar of his vest.

"So, shall we?" she whispered.

He nodded. "Yes."

The afternoon vanished. After the first exploratory joining, they rested, napped, and a few hours later woke and made a second venture, with modifications based on the experience of the first. They lay, stretched out together, adrift in a much more satisfying aftermath.

"That was already a big improvement," Jessika sighed. "I think we'll get really good at it with practice. That's what Hawkjoy said to do: practice."

"Lots of practice," Koki grunted.

She laughed. "Yeah." Thinking of the time needed for lots of practice led to: "I wonder where I'm going to live now. I can't bring you back to South-scree."

"You can't?"

"Hawkwind promised she wouldn't add to the population of the non-griffins living with the Hawk Line."

"Ah. Well, we'll figure something out. We could even stay here for a while," he suggested. "The griffins will be staying, most of them, while the hurt ones recover."

"I wonder how Hawkjoy is."

"I was thinking of her, too."

Koki traced Jessika's scarred wing tattoos with his fingertips as sweat dried on her skin. "I was really angry, when he bared your back to the crowd."

"At the coronation? You were there?"

"I was there."

Jessika frowned. "I can remember, but not clearly."

"He had you enchanted. I could tell by how you moved. Doing that, displaying you all scarred from what his shadow-beast did to you, it made me want to," he hesitated, "to do something very violent to him."

"He's still out there," Jessika mentioned. "You might get your chance."

"He won't find us while the unicorns are protecting this place, but yeah, I don't think we can stop worrying about him. Somehow, sometime, we're going to have to face him again. I mean, unless someone else gets him first."

"Wouldn't that be nice," Jessika remarked dryly.

They lay there a while longer, Koki following the lines of tattoo and scars with his fingers. Jessika watched him, thinking how much she liked him and replaying their lovemaking in her mind. Her body still ached and tingled from it, and she already looked forward to the next time.

"What are you smiling at?" Koki grinned.

"You, I guess," she shrugged. "I," she breathed, "really like you."

"Yeah. I really like you, too."

They stared at each other for a while.

"Do you want to go down?" Koki asked. "I'm hungry."

"Sure, let's go. I want to check on Hawkjoy now."

They got their clothes back on and tried to restore some order to mussed hair before they went back through the ruin to the room everyone else was using. All the griffins were asleep in furry, feathery piles. Karo was stretched out, snoring beside Cray's unmoving body, with Breeka curled up in a grey ball nearby.

Only Rikah was awake, and he practically glared at them as they came in.

"I cooked some meat, if you want it," he said, gesturing to a covered pan by the glowstones.

"Yes, please," Jessika said.

"Thanks," Koki added.

"Is the unicorn still there?" she asked as she lifted the lid. Koki fetched a couple sharpened sticks to spear the meat with and they each took a piece.

Rikah nodded. "It was still there a little while ago. I peeked in. They're both just lying there, not moving, but Joy was still breathing, and all the blood on the floor was dry, like she'd stopped bleeding."

"That's good," Jessika said with a sigh of relief. "Maybe she's going to be alright. I mean, physically at least. We don't know how she'll be in her heart and head. Maybe it's best if I don't go back to South-scree."

"Joy loves you," Rikah said softly. "You grew up together like sisters."

"That makes the betrayal all the worse."

"I'm not going to argue with you about it," Rikah grumped. "You'll have to work it out with her, when she wakes up."

Jessika subsided, chewing the slightly tough meat. Then she heard the distinctive sound of hooves on stone. She tossed the uneaten part of her meat back in the pan and lunged to her feet. When she flung open the leather door she had to shield her face. The unicorn was so piercing bright she couldn't look at it.

"I told you," Witch Hazel murmured. "You'll not look on us so easily anymore."

The unicorn's light faded, and Jessika snuck a look between her fingers. She was stepping out of the entry room, into the courtyard beyond.

"Your sister is healed," Witch Hazel said clearly over her shoulder. "I failed to save my mate and child, but I could save this griffin and hers. My debt is slightly eased. Farewell."

Rikah stepped around Jessika, stumbling to the exit. "We thank you," he called. "Thank you so very much."

If the unicorn made a reply, Jessika didn't hear it.

"Hawkwind," she shouted. "Hawkwind wake up. The unicorn's gone. She said she healed Joy."

Griffins roused with chirps and hisses, but Jessika didn't wait for them. She almost tripped and slammed her face into a wall as she jumped for the doorway to Joy's room. Rikah and Koki tumbled through right behind her.

Hawkjoy was curled in a ball now, her lacerated belly hidden. Her wings and tail hadn't magically regrown, but she'd get new feathers when she molted, or if she wanted to pull out the dead stubs of the old ones. Her sides rose and fell smoothly and naturally. Her bandages were stained, but the blood had dried and they hung loose.

Jessika went to her knees by Joy's head. Cautiously, she petted her crown. An injured griffin surprised out of sleep could react with alarm, and nip or claw without realizing what was happening, but Jessika figured she deserved it if that happened.

Hawkwind shouldered her way through the door and went to lie down against Joy. She opened a wing and extended it over her, like a mother brooding a chick. She preened her neck feathers, and Joy made a little chirp—and then, a grunt.

Jessika and Hawkwind's gazes snapped onto each other.

"Joy can't make noises like that," Jessika whispered.

Hawkwind nibbled her feathers some more, trying to urge her awake.

"Joy, wake up," Jessika murmured. "You're safe now, and healed."

Waterleap, Thornsoft, Starbright, with the rest of the griffins—even Thornspike was on her feet—appeared at the door, but none of them tried to come in except Waterleap. The slender male took a patient seat in a corner, watching with apprehension. Hawkjoy twitched and winced, tightening her limbs. She moaned: an odd unmodulated sound full of hitches.

"She can't do that," Hawkwind hissed.

"The unicorn healed her throat," Jessika whimpered. "She healed everything about her, even where the talis hurt her throat as a chick." She stroked Joy's cheek. "She's going to talk. She can learn to talk now, with her voice."

She darted a look over at Thornsoft, suddenly painfully aware that he had received no such healing, but he smiled a little, shook his head, and gestured, "it's alright. I'm fine as I am."

Jessika wondered if that were really true, but there was nothing to be done about it either way. She knew she couldn't go begging unicorns to heal all the griffins who had come from Snow-in-lee and couldn't speak. Even if she had been able to bear looking at them, the unicorns would have refused.

"My chicks can speak," Thornsoft continued. "That's more than enough for me, to hear their voices, even when they're shrieking loud enough to knock stones off the mountain."

Hawkjoy was rousing further. Hawkwind trilled to her, like a mother to a scared chick, and Hawkjoy relaxed again. After a few more minutes of petting and preening, she at last opened her eyes. Her gaze fixed on Jessika and she lifted a hand.

"You're alive," Joy signed. "I thought he killed you."

The griffin extended her arm so she could touch Jessika's face.

"I'm so glad," she went on. "I was so afraid you were dead."

Jessika collapsed on Hawkjoy in sobs. "I'm so s-sorry. I took you down, down there, and they caught you, and that woman—"

Hawkjoy hissed at her and pushed her gently away. "I knew, if you were alive, you'd come get me, or someone else would."

"She did," Hawkwind rumbled. "She insisted on coming with us, even though that mage had caught her and imprisoned her and enchanted her. I'm told his magical beastial constructs clawed her back to bits when she tried to protect another innocent before that. Then she stopped me from becoming just as bad as him, when I wanted to slowly kill the one who tortured you, Hawkmother."

Joy shivered. "Is she dead?" she gestured.

"She's dead," Waterleap proclaimed.

Hawkjoy seemed to notice him for the first time. Her crest fluffed a little, and Waterleap stepped over to nibble her feathers.

"Thank you," Joy signed. "Thank you all."

"There is no thanks needed," Hawkwind affirmed. "Rest, recover, and bring the next Hawkchick safely into this world."

"A unicorn healed you," Jessika explained. "She said she saved you and your chick."

"I remember," Joy confirmed, "a little, golden light like music."

Then everyone else crowded forward, taking turns to hug or pet or preen Hawkjoy, smiling or crying over her. Waterleap brought her food and tenderly fed her.

Jessika stood back and watched, with Koki's arms around her, so relieved that at last, everyone could go home safe.

Epilogue

In the deepest, darkest winter, Hawkjoy successfully brought her chick into the world. Jessika had made the journey to South-scree for it. A fully recovered Thornwing—except for some scars that were so large no fur would ever cover them—had come to announce the imminent birth. He'd carried her from the home she and Koki had made with Kassandra's help, where she and Koki and Karo still tended to Cray's sleeping body.

Hawkjoy had insisted that Jessika be present. Hawkwind and Hawkswift were there, too, with Starbright to help just in case—except now, Starbright was being called Starmother. Not long after her return to South-scree, the former Starmother had birthed her final chick and her body had gone back to sleep. Starbright had awakened then, and was a few months pregnant with her first chick, when Joy had hers.

Jessika had feared that despite the assurances of Witch Hazel, Skire Germaine had somehow managed to hurt Joy's chick beyond repair, but the remainder of the pregnancy had been smooth, and the birth had been—according to Starbright—no worse than any mother's first birth.

Now the new chick, eyes still shut but chirping, was huddled in the warmth of Joy's breast feathers. It was rather ugly, as all newborn griffin chicks were, but Joy couldn't have looked happier. It had no feathers yet, but its slick, short baby fur was mostly black.

"A female," Hawkwind announced. "Did you have a name in mind, Hawkmother?"

Joy nodded, snuggling her bill down next to the tiny bill of her daughter. She said aloud, "Hawkstar."

Deep below the palace of Northnest, two dozen griffins and dozens more mules and donkeys dug, loaded, hauled, and unloaded minecarts of rock. The work was slow, and the stone their masters sought was becoming scarce. The mules and donkeys thought of nothing but their lightless daily suffering.

The griffins, however, suspected what would happen to them when there was no more of that slick, silvery-gray stone to be found. The masters with the whips and clubs would need them no longer. Griffins were stronger and had better vision in the dark than humans did, although there were human slaves, too, sorting through the rubble, cracking open small chuncks, looking for the nodules of silver stone.

The griffins knew their time was limited. They knew they'd be given to the Skire when the veins were exhausted. But then one day came a rumor, whispered from mouth to ear, among all the slaves who had language to speak or listen with.

"The Skire is dead."

Falconsong, the youngest of the griffin slaves, who had been born in the Skire's laboratory and somehow—she'd never known exactly how—been spared the cutting to be sent instead to be a mine slave, lifted her head just a feather's width from her work, to listen.

"They say a griffin killed her."

Dormant hope burst like a cracking log in a fire, sending up sparks and flares that burned into her heart.

"There are still griffins," she breathed, "Out There?"

Out There: Falconsong had never seen the sky, only heard of it. She'd been told about trees and clouds and the wind, about mountains and rivers and snow and sun. She didn't know what any of them really looked like. All she knew were the mines. She had only the vaguest memories of the Skire's laboratory. She had never flown.

Her chains clanked but she hardly heard it as she resumed her work. The manacles had long ago worn sore after sore into her wrists and ankles. Now there was thick, calloused, warped skin below them, and she didn't feel them anymore. Nor did she hear the clamor of the metal, ever shifting as she moved, every day of her life.

"We won't get cut up," someone else whispered, relieved.

"We'll still be killed," another said.

Falconsong didn't say anything else. Speaking was a guaranteed way to get beaten, if the overseers noticed. She thought, however. Thinking was the only thing that offered any relief in the mines. Her thoughts were not chained.

And so, she thought: no. We'll not be killed. This is only the beginning. The Feathyrs are coming; we will be liberated. And if they don't come, well then, I will have to see to it, myself.

Jessika lay exhausted in Koki's arms after the most vigorous lovemaking they'd enjoyed in some time. Spring was come, and they were both feeling the stir of nature. They'd managed to knock all the pillows and most of the blankets off the bed they shared, and at some point someone had kicked over the bedside table. Luckily, it was one of Rikah's sturdy constructions and it hadn't had anything breakable on it at the time.

"Better with practice," Koki panted.

Jessika laughed. "Just like Hawkjoy told me, about this time last year, when she was with Waterleap."

They shared their little home among the trees with Karo, who had devoted himself to tending Cray's nearly lifeless body, but he was up in South-scree visiting Thornfire and Starmother for lessons, now that the snow had melted enough to allow the hike up. Jessika and Koki tried not to disturb Karo with their snuggling, but in his absence they saw no reason to hold back. Breeka didn't seem to care; it would insult them no matter what they did.

Rikah didn't live with them. He'd announced he was going to see his family—now that he knew they were alive—and left for the capital the previous summer, once it had been clear that Hawkjoy was recovering well. At first, Jessika had been afraid for him, but he'd returned after a month or so in cheerful spirits, thrilled to have been able to see his father, mother, and a couple new siblings. After that, Jessika hadn't worried as much, and now Rikah was living with his family far more than at South-scree.

"I'm glad you liked it," Jessika told Koki. "Maybe we can do it again tonight."

Someone cleared their throat, and both Jessika and Koki startled violently, grabbing for sheets or clothing to cover up with, spinning about to face the emaciated, half-crippled old man who stood in the open doorway to their room. Jessika had snatched up a truncheon in case it was an intruder—although what intruder bent on mayhem would have called their attention so courteously?

"I'm terribly sorry to interrupt," the old man wheezed. "I heard a loud noise. Some assistance, perhaps?"

Jessika's mouth dropped open.

"Cray," she exclaimed.

She pulled her nightshirt back over her head and went to support the wizard where he was almost collapsing to the floor. His whole body shook with the effort to stand. Breeka crept out from behind him, eyes stretched wide as though it couldn't believe he was alive.

"How did you even make it this far?" she asked.

"Determination," Cray croaked.

Their kitchen was right next door, and Jessika managed to get him to a seat at the table, but even there it looked like Cray might topple right out of the chair. Jessika poured him a glass of water and put more water on for tea.

"Drink slowly," she cautioned.

He waved a hand weakly. "I know. I can't imagine how you kept my body alive all this time."

Jessika stared at him once the teapot was on the stove heating. He took a slow sip of the water, and then another.

"You look like you've seen a ghost," he coughed, almost grinning.

"I stopped thinking you'd wake up," she admitted. "I thought eventually you'd just die one day."

"I thought I might, too. Where my former apprentice sent me, it took a long time returning."

"Do you want food?"

"Not just yet. Let me see how I handle some water and tea. I owe you a great debt, for taking care of a nasty old man for—how long has it been?"

"Nearly a year, not quite. Maybe nine or eleven months," Jessika told him. "It was mostly Hawkrain caring for you."

Cray lifted his head and looked her over. "It seems the hawk has fledged," he remarked. "I saw the wings on your back. So, a Northnest royal, and with a faun lover?"

Jessika blushed, but didn't drop her chin.

"The one you let the Skire torment for years," Koki said from the doorway.

A flinch of pain went across Cray's wasted face.

Koki had only put a pair of shorts on, making no effort to hide his legs. His arms were crossed over his bare chest where he leaned against the door-jamb. His head was slightly lowered, like a ram contemplating a charge. He

hadn't hidden his horns with a hat either.

"She's dead now, the Skire," Jessika said.

"Is that so?" Cray said. "It is a shame she could not be saved. Somewhere in her, I thought there might be a kind woman."

No one responded to that.

"I am sorry for what happened to you," Cray said. He sighed. "With every cut the Skire made, she made an identical one in her soul, but she numbed herself, like she numbed her victims, not to feel it."

The tea water boiled. Jessika went to get it, but Koki stepped forward instead.

"I'll do it. Go get dressed," he offered.

Jessika started to go when Cray asked, "my former apprentice. Is he still in power?"

She paused. "Yes."

Cray sighed and turned to look between Koki and Jessika, his expression dark. "We shall have to do something about that."

To be continued...

Thank you for reading!

Did you enjoy the journey?

Please leave a rating or review on Goodreads, Amazon, or wherever you talk about books. Reviews help books get to readers who might enjoy them.

You can find more information about me and my books, and updates on future books, at my website or on my Facebook page or Goodreads page.

www.elucidationimages.com
Kasmith Art & Books